For the Rest *of* My Life

Also by Harry Kraus, M.D.

Could I Have This Dance?

For the Rest of My Life

HARRY KRAUS, M.D.

ZONDERVAN™

GRAND RAPIDS, MICHIGAN 49530 USA

Christian Medical Association
Resources

ZONDERVAN™

For the Rest of My Life
Copyright © 2003 by Harry L. Kraus

Requests for information should be addressed to:
Zondervan, *Grand Rapids, Michigan 49530*

Library of Congress Cataloging-in-Publication Data

Kraus, Harry Lee, 1960-
    For the rest of my life / Harry Kraus.
      p. cm.
    ISBN 0-310-24978-3
      1. Women physicians—Fiction.   2. Huntington's chorea—Fiction.
   3. Fathers and daughters—Fiction.   4. Virginia—Fiction.   I. Title.
PS3561.R2875F67 2003
813'.54—dc22

                                                        2003017377

Interior design by Nancy Wilson

Printed in the United States of America

---

04 05 06 07 08 09 /❖ DC/ 10 9 8 7 6 5 4

*For all my fellow laborers
serving with Africa Inland Mission.
May love be your highest aim,
Christ your heart's constant treasure,
and God's glory the result.*

Acknowledgments

As always, I have so many to thank. Special thanks to:

Carmen Leal (writerspeaker.com) for her review of the manuscript for an accurate description of Huntington's Disease. Any errors are mine, not hers.

Larry Whitten, M.D., a friend and OB/GYN physician who provided medical advice.

Roy Ferguson, friend and attorney (yes, really, M.D.'s have attorney friends) who provided advice on legal matters.

Bobbie Forkovitch, R.N., who provided information about the S.A.N.E. (Sexual Assault Nurse Exam) program.

Gene Rudd, M.D., from Christian Medical Association for his assistance in making this project possible.

Dave Lambert, who provided much needed editorial advice.

Sue Brower, Sherry Guzy, Joyce Ondersma, and the whole Zondervan team who make projects like this successful.

My wife, Kris, for patience, love, and for being my first-reader.

My loving heavenly Father. *Soli Deo Gloria!* Ultimately, all the credit and glory belong to him.

Grace!

Harry Kraus

For the Rest *of* My Life

Chapter One

It was well past closing time at Stoney Creek Family Medical Center when Claire McCall, M.D., saw her through the front window. Bruised, her blond hair caked with sticky blood, and her bare arms draped around the neck of the man who carried her, the young woman's face reflected sheer terror.

Claire leaned against the front door of the clinic and sighed. She had her hand on the lock she was ready to twist, bringing a ceremonial end to another day in the clinic. It was a private ritual, a small celebration of survival in the rural clinic where she was as likely to see a life-threatening cardiac arrest or a chain-saw accident as she was a benign case of the common cold. She desperately wanted to secure the bolt, to hear the click as it slid into place, signaling the end of office hours and the promise of a quiet night ahead. Or even better, a chance to spend some time with John Cerelli, the man who graced her life with laughter, friendship, and the hope of a lost love rekindled.

She glanced again through the front window. She knew she would open the door. She was the only physician in the town. Turning the patient away would mean, for the young woman, a long trip to the hospital in Carlisle, a trip that many of the locals would forsake for a patch-up on the kitchen table. "Set up a laceration tray, Lucy. And keep the light on in the X-ray room."

"What? Not another one." The gray-haired nurse shook her head. "Lee and I were going to the Ruritan Hall for a pancake supper."

Claire opened the door. "Tell him you'll meet him in an hour."

Her patient clutched the neck of a muscular man wearing a white T-shirt soiled with the day's work. Black grease and dirt mixed with a bib of sweat below an unshaven face and dark, curly chest hair. He entered as

11

Claire held the door, his back to her, stepping around the empty chairs, looking toward the empty reception desk.

"Is the doctor here?"

"Yes. You can take her in there," Claire answered, pointing to a hallway leading to the back. "The first room on the left. The nurse will help you."

Claire followed the couple, catching the unmistakable scent of stale sweat and whiskey, an odor she knew only too well from her father, Wally.

"She fell down the stairs," the man offered, setting the patient down on the old examining table covered with white paper.

Lucy didn't bat an eye. "Leave her with me," she said softly. "I need you to give some information to the receptionist."

He shook his head. "She wants me to stay with her. She's afraid."

The woman, appearing no older than a teenager, had her right eye wide open, darting between the nurse and the man who towered over her. Her left eye was closed, swollen shut by a lid the color of grape jelly. A jagged laceration crossed her eyebrow, gaping open, split by the force of whatever had contacted her face, pinching the skin against her supra-orbital ridge, the boney rim of skull above her eye.

Claire watched as she made eye contact with the man, who appeared older, perhaps thirty-five. "I'm so clumsy," the girl said. "I should have been more careful."

The man nodded. "It's okay, baby. We'll get a doctor to help."

Claire put on a sterile glove and stepped in front of the man. "Excuse me." She touched the patient's fair face, gently feeling the cheeks and forehead for step-off deformities or crepitance, signs of a facial fracture. She looked at Lucy. "She'll need an X ray." Then, to the girl, she asked, "How long's it been since you had a tetanus shot?"

The patient shrugged. "Don't know. I think I had one last year."

"You got one when you wrecked your bike, honey," the man said. "You split your lip on the handlebar trying to carry in the mail."

Claire nodded silently. "We can close the wound here. If she has a fracture, I'll need to call a maxillo-facial surgeon in Carlisle."

"I want the doctor to see her. She needs a doctor."

Claire offered a plastic smile.

"Where's old Doc Jenkins?"

"He retired. I'm his replacement. Doctor Claire McCall," she added, without extending her hand.

The man shook his head. "You're a real doctor?"

It was a reaction Claire had come to expect. Overcoming gender bias was a daily part of life in Stoney Creek, the town that women's liberation forgot.

The girl reached over her short cut-off jeans, which were purple with blood. "I twisted my ankle."

Claire checked the patient's right ankle, which was swelled with fluid, obscuring the normal bony landmarks. "We'll X-ray this, too." Claire examined her legs, dotted with bruises. She touched the girl's thigh. "You fall often?"

The girl shrugged and looked at her escort. "I'm so clumsy."

The standard answer. Claire had heard it before. She touched the girl's chin. "What's your name?"

"Lena."

"Smile for me, Lena."

She did, parting her fattened upper lip to reveal a chipped front incisor.

"Are you hurt anywhere else?" She slid her fingers along the girl's neck. "Any tenderness here?"

The girl shook her head silently.

Claire studied the man for a moment. He stood by the girl's side, too close for Claire's comfort. "You'll need to fill out some paperwork. We need her insurance information. If you'll follow Lucy here, I'll make sure Lena gets taken care of."

He stepped even closer to Claire. "I want to stay with her. Bring the papers to me. I'll fill them out."

Claire didn't want to challenge the man. If her suspicions were right, he wasn't a man to tangle with after he'd been drinking. "Bring me a wheelchair. Let's get her X rays."

They transferred Lena to a wheelchair and rolled her across the hall to the X-ray unit.

"You'll have to wait out in the hall, sir," Claire insisted. "We're going to be x-raying. It's not safe."

"I'm stayin' with her. I'm not afraid."

Lucy took a deep breath and grasped the man by the arm, attempting to face him toward the door. "Come on. A big strong man like you don't want children lookin' like aliens, do you?"

Obviously, the warning about genetics was over his head. "Wh–what?"

"We don't want to radiate your manhood, sir. Stand out in the hall."

The man jerked his arm free from Lucy's grasp. "I'm going nowhere. I know what you're trying to do."

Claire forced a smile. *An alien child would be an improvement over their father.* "You were warned."

"Trouble here, Dr. McCall?"

Claire turned to see Cyrus, her office maintenance man, standing right behind the other man. Cyrus, a young man whose stature matched the other man's, had been an answer to prayer, appearing two weeks before on a warm summer's evening as Claire was locking up the office. She'd walked to the parking lot to find a man loading a lawnmower into his pickup. She hadn't remembered asking anyone to mow.

"Ma'am?" He wiped his large hands on a towel and extended his right hand to her. "Cyrus Hensley. I understand the clinic is lookin' for a maintenance man?"

She studied the immaculate job. He'd edged the sidewalk and trimmed the unruly bushes. "Uh, well, yes." She hesitated. "You did all this?"

The man beamed. "I can do plumbing and electrical work, basic carpentry if something's broke."

"Did you fill out an application?"

He lifted his hand and gestured to the freshly cut grass. "This is my application."

Claire shook her head. She had prayed for help. Until Cyrus showed up, she had bugged her boyfriend to help her with the maintenance items she couldn't handle. Two weeks before, she'd mowed the grass herself. "Okay," she responded, marveling at the ease of doing business in small-town America. "You're hired."

The man nodded. "Thank you, ma'am."

For a moment, they looked at each other without speaking, doctor and maintenance man sizing each other up. The grin on Cyrus's face never broke. Claire pulled her gaze away and stepped toward her car. She found her voice again after she heard him slam the tailgate on his truck. "We still need the paper application for our records," she called, then shook her head. The man was already pulling out of the lot.

Now, Cyrus proved his knack for showing up at the right time yet again. He repeated his question. "Trouble? Anything I can do?"

Claire smiled. "Stand with this gentleman in the hall while we do an X ray on his, uh . . ."

"Lena's my wife," he said. "I need to stay with her."

"Not in there, you don't," Cyrus said.

The man sized Cyrus up and down. Even with his alcoholic bravado, he had enough sense not to challenge the sober maintenance man.

"Any chance you're pregnant?" Claire asked the patient softly.

"I wish." She looked away. "We haven't been successful yet."

"Just the same, let me shield your ovaries." Claire put a lead apron over the girl's lower abdomen and positioned her ankle for the first shot. She looked up to see Cyrus closing the door. She leaned close to her patient's face and whispered, "He's been hitting you, hasn't he?"

The girl pulled her fingers through her tangled bangs. Her eyes were wide, brimming with tears.

"You can trust me. I can take you to a safe place."

"Billy Ray loves me. I'm just clumsy is all."

"Lena, listen to me," she whispered with quiet fervor. "What's to stop him from killing you next time? Men like him need help. But till he gets it, you need to get away."

"He wouldn't hurt me."

"He already has. I can't help you unless you let me. He needs help, Lena. But the next time could be the last. Men like this can kill."

"I fell down the steps."

Claire sighed and scribbled her number on a piece of paper. She folded it and shoved it into the front pocket of the girl's shorts. "This is my phone number. Think about this, Lena. I can take you to a safe place anytime you change your mind."

This time the girl did not speak, but only wiped her eyes with the back of her hand and sniffed. Then, for a moment, her eyes met Claire's. And she nodded.

They took the X rays. They were negative. No ankle fracture. No supraorbital fracture. But on the facial X rays, Claire could see another telltale sign of abuse: an old, healed fracture of the patient's mandible, or jaw.

It took thirty minutes to clean and suture up Lena's eyebrow, leaving a fine row of suture, evenly spaced and symmetric. While Claire sewed, Billy Ray stood close by, stroking his wife's arm, calling her "baby" and "sweet thing."

Claire had just about finished when Billy Ray presented his own theory. "Ever heard of the Stoney Creek curse, Doc? For generations people been stumbling around this town. Think that's what Lena's got? She's always fallin' down."

The doctor's head snapped upright. "Don't even start in on that with me."

Claire was the doctor who had solved the Stoney Creek curse mystery last year, uncovering an undiagnosed pocket of Huntington's disease patients in and around the Apple Valley. Unfortunately, the illness is genetic, with those carrying the HD gene coming down with symptoms during midlife. The symptoms consist of progressive mental deterioration and a loss of control of voluntary muscles until the victim is tormented by constant flailing motion of the arms and legs, and is eventually unable to swallow or eat. Even more bittersweet than the notoriety of making a great diagnosis was the fact that Claire herself stood directly in line to inherit the disorder. It was that fact, along with her desire to help her mother with the care of her father, who had HD, that drove her to leave her surgical residency training in spite of her lifelong dream of being a surgeon. HD had changed everything for Claire McCall. Her greatest diagnostic triumph in solving the Stoney Creek curse became her greatest fear, looming over her life like a dark cloud pregnant with rain.

"Come on, you must have heard of—"

"I said, don't go there!" Claire took a deep breath. This jerk not only wanted to cover up his inexcusable abuse, now he wanted to do it with ignorance. She looked at Lucy. "After you've wrapped Lena's ankle and fitted her with crutches, could you give Billy Ray here a copy of the article I published in *Contemporary Neurology?*" She looked at Billy Ray without flinching. "Read the article about Huntington's disease in the Apple Valley. I think it will sufficiently deal with your fears about your wife's curse."

Claire pivoted and walked out. It had been a long day, capped by a malodorous wife-abuser with an attitude about women doctors. She'd had enough.

She passed Cyrus in the hall where he stood on a ladder changing a fluorescent light. "Thanks for your help, Cyrus. You saved the day again."

He seemed preoccupied and replied with a silent nod.

She cleaned off her desk, shoving two medicine periodicals into her canvas briefcase. As she closed it, Betsy Jackson burst in without a knock. Betsy cleaned the office in the evenings, and on most of them, found Claire sitting in her desk with her head in a book. Betsy was fifty, and knew more about most of Claire's patients than Claire did. Of course it was all the stuff the doctor didn't ask: who was dating whom, who was engaged, who was divorced, who was cheating, and who had problems with their boss. It wasn't that she was a busybody. She just had such a big heart that everyone ended up telling her their problems.

She grabbed Claire's left hand. "Well? Let me see it!" She dropped her jaw. "What's wrong? Don't want to wear that rock at work? I don't blame you. I don't wear my solitaire around this joint either. You never know when—"

"Betsy! Slow down. I didn't get it."

"He didn't give you a ring?" She dropped Claire's hand and leaned over to pull a trash can from beneath the desk to empty it into the large black plastic bag she carried. "I don't get it. Did he give you something else? I heard of a man that gave a woman a car for an engagement present once. But it's not like you can wear a convertible or anything. I—"

"He didn't ask me."

This news stopped Betsy's pressured speech. "I, uh . . . well."

"We had a nice quiet evening in Brighton. We ate by candlelight at DeAngelo's. Then we saw a movie. That was it. No ring." She shrugged and looked away. She didn't want Betsy to see her tears. She quickly dabbed her eyes.

"You said he wanted it to be a special night."

"It was, I guess."

"Maybe Italian food is special to a man," she said. "But a woman needs jewelry to make a night special."

Claire lifted her briefcase. "It's been a long day, Betsy."

"What is that boy waiting for? It's not every day that a beautiful, smart young lady like you comes along."

Claire had expected an engagement ring. The night was going to be special, John had said. *The* night. That's what he'd been hinting at, hadn't he?

But he hadn't come through, and now, at this moment, with all the other pressures, Claire just felt like having a good cry.

"He must be crazy to let a woman like you get away," Betsy continued.

Not as crazy as you might think, Betsy. John knows all about me, all about the baggage I'm carrying around.

"Look at you. You're a doctor, pretty as any model I've ever seen. That boy must not be too—"

Claire brushed past her, avoiding her gaze. "Thanks, Betsy."

Claire walked up the hall, past Cyrus, who seemed to be hanging out near the exam room where Lucy knelt wrapping Lena's ankle. She hurried by, choking down a sob as memories of her broken engagement to John Cerelli came tumbling back.

I missed my chances with John. Now he knows me too well. Any relationship with me could spell a life of disaster.

He knows all about the cloud I live under. And he's afraid to make it his. He knows all about the curse.

Chapter Two

laire pulled into the long driveway leading to her parents' home and wiped her tears with the palm of her hand. She hadn't wanted to move home. Now, with her medical degree behind her, she was supposed to be moving onward and upward, not backward. She hadn't lived with her parents since age sixteen, when she'd left to escape an intolerable situation with her father and his short fuse. But that was long before they'd come to know that her father's problems were deeper than the alcohol he used to drown his trouble, long before she'd even heard of Huntington's disease. Now she spilled tears because of her father's misery, because of the disruption to her plans his illness had forced upon her, and because every day she knew of her own risk to inherit the HD gene that had unraveled her father's life.

She switched off the ignition to her new Volkswagen Beetle, a gift from her grandmother, Elizabeth McCall. She spent a moment collecting herself. It was time for strength. Her mother would need encouragement, not another burden to carry. She took a deep breath and exited the car, pausing briefly to polish away a water spot on the shiny blue fender.

Della, her mother, met her at the doorway. Della was Claire twenty years in the future. Both were strawberry blond, medium height, with a pretty smile and a voice that fell pleasant upon a listener's ear, soprano and strong, not piercing but soft, touched by the South in an accent perfect for comforting a child with a skinned knee or melting a man's soul.

Della smiled and held Claire at arm's length. "You didn't call me."

Claire shrugged. "I didn't have news."

Della frowned.

"Mom, he didn't ask."

"But you said—"

"I said I thought he was going to pop the question," she said, collapsing on an old flowered couch. "It turns out that just being out for a quiet romantic dinner with me is enough."

Her mom sat across from her and leaned forward. "Give him some time. He'll come around to realize the gem he gave up."

As their conversation lulled, Claire picked up the sounds of her father's arms and legs whistling across the sheets of his bed and thudding into the padded railing with erratic, senseless rhythm. Although he was down the hall in the master bedroom, the noise reverberated around the tiny ranch home as a constant reminder that illness lived there too.

She stared straight ahead, talking to her mother, but looking past her through the front window to the green yard and the forest beyond. "John's afraid of the curse. He—"

"Don't call it that. You hate it when other people use that term."

Claire sighed. Her mother was right. But Huntington's disease *felt* like a curse. Unfortunately, no one knows just what child of an HD parent is going to be affected. Huntington's disease is a genetic illness passed from parent to child at the frequency of a coin flip, one half cursed, one half free. The HD gene lies dormant for decades, unleashing its disastrous and eventually fatal effects in midlife just as work, life, and love are supposed to be generously sampled and enjoyed. The HD gene is dominant. If it is present, the person carrying the gene will develop the illness, unless they die first from another disease or trauma, an event which for most would be a tragedy, but for the person carrying an HD gene, could be a blessed Rapture before the Tribulation. And so, at the peak of life, the person with Huntington's disease begins a slide, maybe slow, maybe rapid, through mental dullness into a noncommunicative apathy. Life's goals are crushed. Relationships are shattered. Even simple jobs become monumental obstacles. And there is no cure.

Claire looked at Della. "John doesn't want to have to care for me if—"

"He never said that."

"He doesn't have to."

"He does so well with Wally, though."

"Mom, I see it in his eyes, the way he looks at me."

"That's called love, Claire."

"No, he's trying to see inside me, Mom! He looks at me as if he could stare past my mind into my cells, right into my genes."

"Don't you go lettin' that boy look in your jeans!"

"Mom!"

Della grinned, then restrained her lips into a proper, more demure smile, more subtle, then pushed her lips forward in a silent kiss to accompany a wink with her left eye.

Her mom could be so silly. But silliness was part of what made living with her mother such a joy. In the midst of the mess of changing her husband's diaper, Della would diffuse the stress by calling out, "Code brown, ward three," as if she were an army general.

She coped. They laughed. But everything was not always happy. She'd seen her mother on bad days. On days when she yelled back at the disease after Wally had cursed her again. "Give me back my husband! Give me back my Wally!" Della took his face in her hands and slowed the bobbing that made eye contact impossible. "I know you're in there," she said, tears streaking her mascara. "And I know you still love me, Wally McCall."

Claire allowed the corners of her mouth to turn up. "You know what I'm talking about!"

Her mother shook her index finger at her daughter. "You're talking about letting a boy see inside your jeans, and I won't have it! Not while you're under my roof!"

Claire snickered. Her mother couldn't say it with a straight face.

Eventually, their smiles faded, and Claire listened again to the thumping noise coming from the other room. "John will propose to me if I test negative for the HD gene."

Della shook her head. "He'll ask you whether you're negative or positive."

Claire couldn't dismiss a nagging doubt. "Maybe, but he's the one who pushed so hard to get me through the testing process."

"He just wants you to know, Claire. He wants to know so he can move on with life, knowing what he's facing, not the unknown."

"Knowing what he's facing?" Claire raised her voice. "What about me? I'm the one who could end up like Wally."

"There are times when I'd change places with Wally in a second."

"You're crazy!"

21

Della's hand came down on Claire's arm, which she squeezed to attract Claire's attention. "And what about your spouse? Don't you think I've suffered? I'm the one saddled with taking care of everything. I do the cleaning, the cooking, the feeding, the bathing, the diapering. Then there's the finances that HD has stolen, the work that never ends on an old house that needs a major makeover, and I never get to have my husband hold me. Even a kiss with Wally is a bruise waiting to happen."

"But you have your dignity. Wally's lost everything."

"Self-pity isn't an attractive option for you, child."

Claire took a deep breath and relaxed back against the couch again. "I know, Momma. I know you've suffered."

"Don't blame John for wanting to know. I think he should know what he's getting into."

"Or not getting into, as the case may be."

"You really think he'd run away now? You think he'd leave if he knew you would get Huntington's?"

"He did before. He broke our engagement."

"The circumstances were different, Claire. Do I need to remind you how you strayed away while you were in Boston?"

"It gave him an opportunity to get out and still save face."

"I can't believe you said that. That man is a diamond. I can't blame him if he takes it slower this time. He doesn't want to have his heart shattered twice."

"Mom, he should be sure I love him. Last year in Boston was different. I've grown."

"And you should be convinced he loves you. He moved down from Brighton to be close to you, didn't he?"

"Maybe he wants to keep an eye on me this time."

"Should he?"

"Mom!"

"John has spent many hours in this house, many of them just with Wally and me, while you slaved away up in Boston. He watched how I dealt with the Huntington's, asking me questions about how I cope and where my strength comes from. He knows what he's getting into, and I'd be surprised if he turns his back on you if you are carrying an HD gene." She stood up and walked to the kitchen. "I think he just wants to know so he can meet the future straight on, and not be blindsided by the unknown."

Claire nodded. She hoped her mother was right. John had called it quits during their former engagement, but Della was correct in reminding Claire that it was only after Claire had foolishly entered another relationship. This was different. John needed space, more time.

Della interrupted Claire's thoughts. "Wally choked again this morning. Turned blue and everything. I thought I was going to have to call the ambulance."

"Did you give him coffee? You know we can't give him that."

"Of course not," Della said. "I was feeding him oatmeal. Dr. V told me to avoid liquids without a thickener. Thin liquids go down so fast he can't swallow without choking."

Claire nodded. Dr. Visvalingum, or simply Dr. V, was Wally's neurologist over at Brighton University. He'd come by the house numerous times, in spite of the hour drive. He'd handed out practical information by the gallon. He wasn't lost in esoteric tangents, as happens with so many professors.

"Do you think we did the right thing with refusing the feeding tube?"

Claire nodded emphatically. How many times did she have to assure her mother that it was okay? "Daddy said he didn't want it. He told me that months ago, and I know he understood what he was deciding. When he's finally lost his ability to swallow, he wants to die. We have to let him go when the time comes. It's his way, Mom."

"I hate to see him choke." She put her hand to her lips. "It scares me."

"I know. But the day is coming—"

"Don't say it, Claire. I know it's coming. He's going to die. And some days, believe me, I'm tempted to push him over the edge." She lifted the curtain to the window over the kitchen sink. The sky was just beginning to color. "But then there are other days that, just for a moment, I catch a glimpse of the old Wally. And I know I can go ahead for another day."

"Grandma offered to pay for a nursing home. You don't need to do this, you know."

"It's my job, Claire."

"Why? Penance for past behavior?" The words were out before Claire could stop them. She'd always suspected her mom was motivated by guilt over her unfaithfulness, yet somehow always appeared to be the loving wife to everyone else.

Della didn't flinch. "There was a time that I stayed with him only because I felt guilty. But that was long before HD." She paused and locked eyes with her daughter. "Love isn't about what my spouse can do for me."

"I'm sorry, Momma. I don't know why I said that."

Her mom walked forward and tussled Claire's blond hair. "Because you inherited my keen sense of intuition, I guess."

Claire turned and looked down the hall toward her father's room, the room her parents used to share. Della slept in the guest room now. Sleeping with all Wally's noise was only possible for those with total deafness. "I hope you're right . . . about John, I mean."

"I guess we'll find out soon. You will keep your appointment for the results, won't you?"

"John is picking me up at eight."

Della nodded. "God is sovereign."

Claire knew what her mother meant. God's control over our lives cannot exert itself outside his loving character; that is, she needed to trust that even the bad things in life are to be received from God knowing that he is working in love, working everything for eventual good.

God is sovereign. She'd heard it a million times. But to Claire God's sovereignty sounded like an excuse to cover up for God's mean streak.

"I know," she responded numbly. "Tomorrow I'll know. The threat of uncertainty will be gone."

She plodded down the hall toward Wally's room.

Tomorrow I'll see if John really loves me. The cloud will be gone. It will either be sunshine for life, or time to prepare the lifeboat. Heavy rain is comin'.

Chapter Three

he next morning, Claire opened her eyes to complete darkness, except for an eerie green glow coming from her clock radio that said 4:00. Next door, Wally rustled the sheets and rattled the rails. He was quieter at night, not calling out or grunting, but even during sleep, he tossed his limbs around as if he were a marionette and HD a cruel puppeteer with insomnia. Claire rolled over and back, left and right, and finally rose to make coffee. *Today's the day.* She'd habitually referred to it as "D day" for "DNA day," the day when she found out the results of her genetic testing for Huntington's disease.

She counted five scoops of coffee as she filled the filter, then shrugged and added a sixth, figuring she would need the extra jolt to overcome the hour. With the coffee brewing, she anticipated, for the millionth time, her reaction to the test results. Would she laugh or cry or merely show no reaction at all? Could a loss be so deep or a relief so comprehensive, that she would be paralyzed from expressing emotion at all?

Perhaps she would faint, or dissolve into retching sobs, or jump up yelling, "Yes! Yes! Yes!" She'd imagined her responses so many times that she feared whatever response she might show would seem practiced.

But how can someone know what her response will be, when given a magic glimpse into the future? Maybe God never intended for her to know. Maybe he designed HD to strike in midlife, so people at risk for HD would live normal lives, work and bear children, and unknowingly pass the genes along. *No, that didn't make sense.* God had given some researcher somewhere the smarts to figure out the gene and formulate a test, so he must have intended for her to know.

Claire shook her head. That made little sense either. Somewhere, somehow, God had given someone else the smarts to make an atomic weapon, so that means we're supposed to use it? Her reasoning was circular, and the thoughts wore a deep groove in her mind from going over and over the same territory.

How would John react? Predicting his response was easier for Claire. Positive or negative, John would put his strong arms around her shoulders . . . to give support, or commemorate the new freedom. His hug would be a brace, or a celebration, but a John-hug, nonetheless. That thought brought a smile.

She inhaled the rich aroma of the coffee and sat at the kitchen table alone, thinking about John. John, the great hugger. She liked that about John Cerelli. She'd known other guys who didn't know the art of a great hug. They either hugged stiffly like she was their little sister and their mom made them do it, or saw a hug as some kind of passion avenue to get farther down the road. But not John. He hugged gently when she needed support, passionately when she needed love, and with added zest when the Atlanta Braves performed well in post-season.

She drank two cups of coffee, read the underlined portions of the Pauline epistles from her mother's leather Bible, then changed into her running shorts and a T-shirt just as the sun was coming up. She slipped out into the morning air and jogged three miles, trying not to think about the test results. It was a hopeless endeavor, as anyone who has tried not to think of a white elephant has discovered. Pretty soon it became an imaginary game of fate in the balance. Every truck that passed her was a positive test; every car was a negative. She grumbled under her breath as she slowed to a walk up the lane. She should have never grown up in the country. There were too many stupid trucks.

She returned to find her mother busy with Wally's first diaper change. She helped her dress him in a pair of jeans, which hung baggy over his bones. They slipped on a buttonless knit shirt. Buttons and Wally were a near-impossible combination. Claire shook her head. Her father's chest looked like pale skin stretched over a birdcage. *He's in the final stages. He can't consume enough calories to keep up with his constant motion.*

She touched a reddened area over his ankle. They tried to keep socks on him, but he often worked them off against the sheets. She carefully cleaned the skin with alcohol, let it air dry, and applied a protective porous adhesive bandage to protect the boney prominence. She looked at her mother, whose attention was elsewhere. "Release death grip, Della Force," she snapped with authority.

Her mother smiled and uncurled her white knuckles from Wally's shin where she gripped him to prevent his movement during the dressing application. "Oh, goodness, I've just about strangled your poor foot, Wall."

Wall. That's what she'd started calling him since they first knocked heads trying to kiss. She'd complained that kissing him was like banging her head against a wall. What made it funnier was that her father was the one that made the joke. "No, your banging your head against a Wall . . . ee!"

Claire pushed a button to raise the head of the bed, while Della retrieved a quart container of lemonade she kept by the bed. They'd used water for a while, but now she used any opportunity she could to add calories to his skeleton. She emptied a packet of a powdered thickening agent into a plastic cup and stirred vigorously before snapping on a lid. From the top of the container extended a long, expandable straw fitted with an enlarged bulbous end that Wally could close his mouth around. Claire put her hand gently on his forehead while her mother pushed the sphere into Wally's mouth. He slurped happily, coughed, then sucked some more, apparently delighted at the simple pleasure of cool liquid against his parched throat. *Daddy still finds pleasure in the simple things, like sucking lemonade through a straw.* "When life gives you lemons, make lemonade." She smiled at the remembrance of the goofy saying. *What will I do if lemons sour my future? Will I be content? Angry? Apathetic like Wally?*

Her mother waved her hand in front of her face. "Della Force to Claire Force One, come in."

"Sorry," she said, releasing her father's forehead, seeing her restraint was no longer needed.

Claire walked to the bathroom, trying not to think about the test results. She read the side of the shampoo bottle and wondered if anyone ever really rinsed and repeated like they were instructed. She read the side of the toothpaste tube, and smiled at the near-perfect row of white teeth in the mirror. *Fluoride must really work.* She laid out three different outfits, contemplating what would be the most appropriate attire for attending a prophecy about her future. *Black? No, the test might be negative.* She looked at a chic dress she'd purchased in Boston. *Too partylike if the test is positive.* She finally selected a grey suit, the one she'd worn for a malpractice deposition during her internship. Professional. Cool. Conservative, ready to receive news good or bad without falling apart. Besides, she had to be back to work at the clinic in Stoney Creek by one. *That should be enough time. Results at ten, then fall apart or celebrate for three hours, then back to work, just like any other day.*

She dressed, then walked into the kitchen to see her mom with her Bible open on the table. Della lifted her cup. "Coffee?"

"Already had my quota for the morning."

Her mom looked at the clock. "John should be here any minute."

Claire nodded and chewed the inside of her cheek. She didn't feel like making small talk.

Della chatted on. "Today's the day."

Another nod.

"Are you sure you don't want me with you? I could ask Margo to come to sit with the Wall."

"Mom, we've been over this a thousand times. I'll be okay. John is going to be there. I'll call you from Brighton as soon as I find out."

Della sighed. "I wish you'd taken the day off."

"I don't have to work until one."

"Are you sure you'll be back in time? All the way to Brighton and back and all that time in the—"

"Mom, I'll have plenty of time."

"You'd better have John drop you by the office, just the same. If time is tight, you don't want to come all the way out here to get your car. I can come in and get you after work."

Claire held up her hands. "I'll have time."

Della put her hands on her hips. "I don't think you should be driving today."

She didn't feel like arguing. Claire pivoted and headed for the front door. "Fine."

"Where are you going?"

"Out to my car to get my stethoscope." Claire clenched her teeth. "I won't be coming back for it."

She let the screen door slam behind her. *She doesn't think I can handle the news. She must have a gut feeling about this. A bad feeling.*

Claire sat in her blue Beetle and closed her eyes. "Oh, Father," she whispered, "Make it be negative."

She sniffed. *This is crazy. I've carried the same DNA since I was conceived. A prayer doesn't change that.* "But just the same, God, make it be negative." *He can do anything, even change my DNA. So if I'm negative, was I negative all along, or did God change my DNA in response to my prayers?*

She adjusted the rearview mirror and studied her reflection. *That's it. I'm losing it.* She wiped at her eyes with her hand. Mascara on a crying day is never a good idea. She squelched the urge to sob. *This is crazy. I've been dealing with HD risk for months, and I finally get to the place where I am comfortable with leaving it in God's hands and trusting him, only to fall apart when I think Mom suspects I'm a carrier of the HD gene.*

She used to pride herself on being strong. She'd come so far on her own: the first woman from Stoney Creek to attend and finish medical school. She'd matched at one of the most prestigious surgery programs in Boston.

"I thought I'd learned to trust you, God," she whispered. "Haven't I been through enough to teach me that I can't do it alone?" She ticked off a mental list from her internship. *Enduring a barrage of sexist males who think women have no place in surgery. A broken engagement. A malpractice suit. Losing my twin brother. Threats from a jealous surgery resident. I almost drowned in the ocean trying to escape from that psychopath.*

She heard gravel crunching in the lane behind her. *John's coming.* She tried to quickly conclude her prayer with a confidence she didn't feel. "I know you love me, God. So whether I'm HD negative or positive, I'll know it's in your plan."

She pushed the rearview mirror back in place. John hadn't noticed her in the Beetle; he was already bounding up the sidewalk toward the house. It was better that way. He wouldn't see her tears. She grabbed her stethoscope off the passenger seat beside her. It was time for confidence. If she didn't feel it, at least she could look it.

Claire sighed. "Amen," she whispered.

She walked around John's red Mustang and opened the passenger door, dropping her stethoscope in between the front seats. She straightened, smoothed the lapels of her jacket, and was about to close the door when a small black object next to the driver's seat caught her eye. She leaned into the car, placing her hand on the small felt box partially wedged beside the seat. Her heart quickened. She knew exactly what it was. She had held that very box in her hand before. She glanced behind her. The front door was shut. John was inside. She swiftly opened the box to see the diamond he'd chosen for her. The same one she'd returned a year ago at his request. She closed the lid. She'd been right. He *was* planning to ask her again. But why not the night before last during their romantic dinner?

He's waiting for the test results. He won't ask me until he knows I'm negative.

She shoved the box back between the driver's seat and the center console. She wasn't sure whether to be thrilled, or feel betrayed. John's timetable was certainly understandable. She backed out of his car, instinctively picking up her stethoscope. It wouldn't do for John to know she'd been in the car yet. She tried to close the door without a slam, then skipped up the steps feeling a bit of mischief.

She entered the front room and looked at her mom, still sitting at the kitchen table. "Where's John?"

"Talking to Wally. He's trying to collect on a bet they made on the Braves game last night."

Leave it to John to carry on with Wally just like he was normal. Claire smiled. She liked that.

She heard him coming up the hall saying something about double or nothing. He was dressed in a tie.

"Whoa."

"What?"

"Since when do you wear ties?"

"Hello to you too," he said, kissing her cheek. "I always used to wear ties at the office."

Claire shrugged.

He mimicked her action. "It's a special day."

She forced a smile. "*Special* is one word for it."

"We'd better get going."

She nodded and yelled, "Bye, Daddy." Her mom approached with her arms open. Claire accepted her hug and whispered, "Sorry for being so touchy."

Her mom patted Claire's back. "I think you're a saint."

Claire pinched her eyelids. Now was the time to stay strong. "We'd better get going."

She turned and grabbed John's hand.

It's now or never.

Chapter Four

ena Chisholm cringed at the sound of Billy Ray stirring on the double bed they shared. Her right eye had been open for two hours. She was fully alert, unable to sleep, predicting her husband's next move with the accuracy of Isaiah the prophet.

If I lay real still, he'll think I'm sleepin' and maybe he won't bother me.

She concentrated on holding her mouth open so her front teeth would show and kept her breathing deep and regular. She remembered when Billy Ray told her how cute she looked when she slept, with her lips parted just so. She had blushed then, unable to believe that William Raymond Chisholm really cared enough about her to pay that much attention.

That's how she always dreamed of him, as William Raymond. It sounded so dignified, not like every other Tommy Joe or Jimmy Lee redneck name so common in the shadow of the Blue Ridge. She used to whisper it in his ear when they slow-danced, listening to Garth Brooks. He was so romantic then. He'd put his boom box on the open tailgate of his pickup, turn up the music, and take her in his arms. But the only time he'd agreed to be William Raymond in public was on their wedding day when Pastor Pritchard asked, "William Raymond Chisholm, do you take Lena ..." Everyone snickered and thought he was trying to be uppity, so he wouldn't let her say it anymore.

Billy Ray moved again, this time scooting a little closer to Lena and stopping with his hand resting on her thigh. Her pretend sleep wasn't going to work. Once Billy Ray started, he would get what he wanted. The scenario was trademark Billy Ray: drink himself into oblivion, beat Lena, pass out, then wake up in the morning promising never to hit her again, blame the alcohol, and turn on his best charm while he begged for forgiveness. Forgiveness, of course, needed to be demonstrated in an appropriate way. And Lena was afraid to say no.

She kept her back to him, facing the wall, silently praying that he'd leave her alone. But now he was gently massaging her thigh, a sure bet that Billy Ray wanted forgiveness again. Lena squeezed her eyes shut. *It's William. William Raymond. I live in a mansion overlooking the valley and William Raymond is here . . .*

"Baby, I'm awful sorry about yesterday. Lester wanted to stop for a drink at Dixon's after work."

She could feel his breath on her neck, smell its sour scent. She slid her leg forward an inch, away from her husband. Pain awoke in her right ankle. She grimaced, but did not cry out.

"I won't hurt you again. Please forgive me, baby."

Lena tried not to recoil from the scratchy kisses on her neck. *It's not Billy Ray. It's William Raymond. We spend hours just looking in each other's eyes.*

"Come on, Lena. I was just down about work. I drank too much. How could I have taken it out on you?" His voice was soft, filled with the tenderness that had once filled her heart with passion. "I love you, baby. I won't hurt you again."

She continued to shut the real world out. *William Raymond has come to comfort me after my fall down the stairs. He loves me. He touches me so tenderly.* She sensed a stirring within her, an inkling of desire rising in response to her fantasy.

Now, Billy Ray's hands encouraged her to cooperate. Lena was in the real world, biting her lip. "Promise me, Billy Ray," she whispered. "Promise me."

"I promise you, baby. I'll never hurt you again."

Lena turned her head away from Billy Ray, wandering off into the arms of William Raymond. Her ankle was on fire with pain. Their little bedroom seemed smaller with her left eye swollen shut. She kept her good eye open, staring at the wall, wondering what kind of flowers William Raymond would bring home after work.

She felt nauseated.

But at least Billy Ray would feel forgiven again.

Claire opened the door to John's red Mustang and climbed in just before John. She busied herself with her seat belt and pretended not to see him casually push the ring box out of sight between his seat and the center console.

John pulled the car onto the road and headed toward Fisher's Retreat, the first town beyond Stoney Creek on the way toward North Mountain and Brighton beyond. "Want to eat at Fisher's Cafe on our way back?" John tapped his fingers on the steering wheel.

Claire shrugged and looked out her side window away from John. The honeysuckle grew so thick in the summer in the Apple Valley that if she let her eyes blur, she could imagine it to be a continuous green wall. She didn't feel much like talking. "I might not be hungry," she mumbled.

"We could get Mr. Knitter to make us chocolate malts."

She spoke quietly, but her reply felt awkward, as if she was being polite to an acquaintance, but not a close friend. "That would be nice."

John's right hand slid down beside his seat again. He was touching the side of the secret box and Claire knew it. What was he up to? Claire watched him. He was looking at the road, one hand on the steering wheel, one hand on her engagement ring. He glanced her way, then back at the road. John's right hand stayed put, his fingers tapping occasionally with feigned nonchalance. She raised her eyebrows and continued to watch.

He glanced her way again. "What?"

She slowly batted her eyelids and looked away, clenching her teeth to keep from smiling. "I didn't say anything."

"But you were looking at me."

"It's a free country." She looked away from him and edged her hand over to his, stroking the back of his hand with her fingers. Now the only thing between her fingers and the ring box was his hand. She wondered what he would do if she tried to hold his hand by insinuating her fingers beneath his hands. She edged her fingers around between his thumb and index fingers.

John quickly pinched her fingers, halting their progress.

She intentionally kept looking away from him, so if he glanced at her, he would see she was not looking at her hand. This was fun. What would he do if she just slipped her hand down beside his seat?

33

She strained her fingers to free them from his grip, wiggling them down toward the ring. She watched as John jerked her hand in the air, glanced at Claire, then suddenly pulled her hand to his mouth, landing a noisy kiss on the back of her hand.

She smiled. She was sure John thought it was because of his kiss. And that made her smile even more. It was a lousy cover-move, but John had no idea Claire was on to him.

Claire wondered again why John hadn't given it to her during their special dinner out. *He's probably waiting to know the results, wanting to ask me only if he knows I'm not going to end up like Daddy. Maybe he's bringing the ring along today so he can give it to me if my test result is negative.*

If John had her engagement ring beside him, was he planning to give it to her as soon as she got her results? Suddenly, another thought struck her. Wouldn't it be romantic if right before she opened the envelope showing her results, John restrained her hand and gave her the ring, pledging his love forever whatever the future might hold, telling her he loved her so much, it wouldn't matter if she had HD, he had to be with her?

This new thought put things in a different perspective for Claire. Maybe the reason John didn't ask her during their special night out was because he was planning this all along. He was going to ask her to marry him right before she got her test results. She looked at him through the corner of her eyes. *John Cerelli, you hopeless romantic!*

"You haven't said anything about the test results," John said.

Claire sighed. "What else is there to say? I've been talking about this for months. I'm just ready for it to be over."

"I've been thinking about something. If you end up being a carrier, I think it shouldn't stop you from following your dream. I still think you should become a surgeon."

She exhaled sharply. "I've thought about it, believe me. I'd have a minimum of four years more to train before I'd ever get into practice. And HD usually has its onset in midlife, but there are no guarantees. If I've got the gene, I could start losing control anytime." She shook her head slowly, her excitement over her anticipated engagement quickly waning as her attention returned to the cloud. "And honestly, I doubt I could even purchase malpractice insurance. No one would even think of insuring a surgeon who might put a patient at risk by a sudden jerk of a scalpel."

"But it might be years before you show any symptoms at all. You've told me yourself that some people don't get symptoms until age fifty. By then you could have practiced nearly twenty years. It would be genetic discrimination for an insurance company to refuse to cover you."

"It's moot anyway. What hospital would give privileges to a surgeon they thought was unsafe? They'd be setting themselves up for a suit." She looked away toward the side of the road. They were meeting too many trucks, a reminder to Claire of her stupid mental game played during her morning jog.

"But what about your experience in Lafayette? Your chairman in surgery didn't seem to mind knowing you were at risk for HD. He wanted you to continue in the program, didn't he?"

"Sure, but being at risk for carrying the HD gene and actually carrying it are two different things."

John didn't reply. He squeezed her hand that he held in his, resting it safely on his knee away from the little ring box.

She closed her eyes and lay back against the headrest. The night before had been one of fitful slumber, tossing and rolling in anticipation of receiving the test results. The morning couldn't pass soon enough for her. And now that she was on to John's little engagement surprise, she was even more anxious to get on with it. She leaned over and snuggled her head against his shoulder. "What's in the future?"

"The future?"

She hugged his right arm. "For us."

John downshifted his Mustang to begin the climb up North Mountain and kept his eyes straight ahead. "How would I know?"

"Come on, John. If you were in control, what would it be like?"

He glanced at her, lingered, then quickly put his eyes back on the curvy road. "I wouldn't let you suffer. I'd make you free of the HD gene, and free to pursue your career in surgery." He smiled. "Of course, I'd want to be in the picture, maybe living in a doctor house in the country with a few horses, a dog, and a passel of kids." When he said "doctor house" he lifted her hand with his to make a quotation-mark gesture with his fingers.

"You want to be in the picture? A doctor's husband?"

He shrugged. She studied his face, delighted to see the edges of his mouth turning up.

She pulled her fingers free from his hand and stroked the side of his face with her index finger. "What's that, a marriage proposal?"

"I didn't say anything about marriage."

"You said you wanted to live in a doctor house. I presumed I'm the one who bought it. And if I bought it, and you're living in it, we'll have to be married, so if that's what you want for the future . . ." She softened her voice and leaned close to his ear, ". . . then it sounds like a proposal to me."

John laughed. "I think you'll know it if I'm proposing."

She straightened, leaning back in her chair. "You're no fun."

"Maybe you should be the one proposing. I had to do it last time."

Claire nodded and remembered what a disaster that had been. Right at a time she'd felt her heart attracted to another man, John had surprised her by coming to Boston and giving her a ring. So when she was supposed to be overjoyed, she'd run to the restaurant bathroom, locked herself in the stall, and cried. She shook her head and closed her eyes. She didn't want to think about the last time.

She tried to watch him from the corner of her eye. He'd fallen silent, and she wasn't about to just pop the big question herself. John turned right, left, and right again as the road wound along the edge of North Mountain. He wasn't about to be rushed into proposing, even with an engagement ring so close at hand.

The rest of the trip, Claire closed her eyes, wanting to surrender to sleep, but wondering instead just what John had up his sleeve.

Forty-five minutes later, they arrived in Brighton. The day was already beginning to heat up, and John stopped for gas and bought a Diet Pepsi. The whole time, Claire stayed silent, occasionally checking her watch, and only once while John was getting gas did she sneak another feel of the little felt box.

When they pulled into the parking lot in front of the Brighton University Medical Center, Claire stalled, wanting to stay in the car to see how and if John would retrieve the ring. He looked at her, waiting for her to get out. "Well," he said with a sigh. "This is it. Are you ready?"

"I feel a bit like a Peeping Tom."

"What? How's that?"

"Like I'm about to look into something, something maybe I shouldn't, but I can't quite resist doing it."

John nodded.

Claire found her mind running from being a Peeping Tom to what her mother had said the evening before about not letting John look into her jeans. She put her hand on the door handle and hesitated. John was not budging. Finally, she surrendered, opened her door, and got out, but snuck a quick look back to watch him discreetly slide his hand beside his seat and close his fist around the ring box. He jumped from the car, his hand disappearing from view. He reappeared around the front of the car, his hands empty and in plain sight. But a subtle lump over the left front pocket of his pleated khaki pants provided the telltale clue. Now Claire was more convinced than ever. John was about to propose before she opened the letter revealing the test results. No wonder he had passed up his opportunity during their romantic evening. This would be even better. Why else would he bring the ring into the genetic clinic? If he were only going to ask her if she didn't carry the HD gene, he could do it at a better time than after she got a negative result.

She pretended to look straight ahead, but snuck frequent peeks at John from the corner of her eye. *Most people drop their middle name when they marry, but since I've always gone by Claire, I think I'll just drop McCall. Elizabeth Claire Cerelli.* She smiled. *That has a nice ring to it.*

They were early for Claire's appointment with the counselor, so after registering at the window, she sat down and fidgeted through three women's magazines in five minutes. The words passed without comprehension, the pictures a blur. She couldn't have cared less about the contents which swung like a pendulum between elaborate recipes and articles about dieting secrets.

She lowered the magazine and looked at John and mouthed, "D day."

"Elizabeth McCall." The receptionist's voice was distinctly nasal. Only people who didn't know her personally called her Elizabeth.

She stood with John and took his hand. They walked together through a lime-green door into the clinic beyond. Virginia Byrd stood in the second doorway on the right. She brightened when she saw Claire and reached up to give Claire a hug. "Final session," she said, leading them into the room.

Virginia, a genetics counselor, had spent hours talking with Claire over the past few months and had spent considerable time with Claire's sister Margo last spring just after Claire had solved the mystery of the Stoney Creek curse. Margo wholeheartedly recommended Virginia as her choice for the sessions leading up to a genetics test for the HD gene.

Virginia's friends all called her Ginny. She sat on a padded wooden chair and folded her hands in the lap of her denim skirt. She was just shy of five feet tall, and her gray-streaked blond hair was pulled back in a long single braid which nearly reached her waist. Claire estimated her to be about fifty-five years old, and thought she would look quite natural at an anti-Vietnam-war protest. Ginny's office was neatly decorated with African art, small wooden carvings of elephants, Cape buffalo, and giraffe dotting the hanging shelves behind an old oak desk.

Claire sat next to John on a green flowered loveseat across from Ginny. She took a deep breath. *This is it.* She leaned forward and knotted both hands with John's.

Ginny's smile revealed a double row of full braces, a luxury she'd allowed herself when her youngest son graduated from college. A fine spray of wrinkles extended from the corners of her eyes when she smiled, the only evidence other than her streaky blond hair that she had lived before John Kennedy's assassination. "Well," she said, laying her hand on top of the couple's, "we've been down a long road together." She paused and looked at Claire, her blue eyes soft and searching. "How are you doing?"

Claire managed a little shrug. "A little scared, I guess." She looked over at John. "And a little excited."

John nodded his agreement.

"Both quite normal emotions at this time, I assure you." She released their hands. "And you, John?"

"I'm okay. I'm ready for whatever you tell us." John squeezed Claire's hands a little tighter.

Claire looked at the bulge over his left front pocket, then at her boyfriend, and forced a smile. *You are ready for anything, aren't you?*

Ginny leaned back and reached over to her desk and picked up a file on her desk. It was labeled with Claire's full name. "We have the test results. We have been over the implications of a negative and a positive test in some detail during our past sessions. Any last thoughts?"

Claire shook her head and looked at John. His thick curly brown hair had spilled over his collar since he moved away from his normal hair salon in Brighton. It framed his handsome face and offset his chiseled features with tenderness. *You can give me the ring now. She's going to hand me the envelope at any moment.*

John shrugged. "God's in control. It's in his hands. Our place is to trust."

Claire nodded. That was a conclusion she'd come to months ago, before making a decision to leave her surgery residency in Boston and return home to Stoney Creek to help with her father. At that point, she'd lost her twin brother, as well as a close guy-friend in residency. She was nearing the end of her ability to cope with being at risk for HD when she realized she didn't need to be in control. It was a revelation accompanied by the gentle rain of God's peace. She'd finally found the trust born from the knowledge that God loved her more than she could ever understand.

But over the months since that time, while Claire accepted the revelation in her head, she struggled to apply it in her life. She knew God loved her. She wanted to believe he was working everything in her life for the good, but every few weeks, she entertained a nagging doubt that God had been looking the other way when the devil scrambled up her ancestors' genes. How could a loving God ever allow such indiscriminate suffering?

Claire cleared her throat and vainly tried to find a comfortable position nestled between that paradox of faith and doubt that provided her constant companionship. She was on the verge of knowing whether she had the gene for Huntington's disease, and terror nipped at the corner of her mind. She looked at John, and her chin quivered as she spoke. "I want to trust." She halted. "So why do I feel afraid?"

"It's all normal," Ginny responded. "And I want you to know that whatever the result, positive or negative, this office is at your disposal for counseling. Some of our most difficult cases have not been with those coping with a positive result. Some who are negative feel a horrible load of survivor's guilt because they got off so easy." She twirled the tip of her long braid. "Either way, we're here for you."

Claire nodded, aware that she was clenching her teeth.

Ginny opened Claire's file and withdrew a white envelope. "Ready?"

Another nod from Claire, but this time she was studying her boyfriend. She released his hands and received the envelope Ginny was extending.

John's left hand immediately felt for the ring box in his pocket. Claire watched him with anticipation. She was sure he'd brought the ring for this very moment. He was going to tell her he wanted her to be his wife regardless of her HD gene status.

She turned the envelope over in her hand and ran her index finger along the top. She'd waited so long for this moment. A revelation of her future was in her hand. She was about to peer into the crystal ball. She looked at John, studying him for a moment. *Well? You can ask me to marry you now.*

She slipped her finger under the lip of the envelope, popping it free. She glanced again at John's left hand. It was draped casually over his thigh, covering the engagement surprise. He was drawing this out unbearably. She couldn't open an envelope much slower. *Ask me now, John. In a moment, I'll have this paper open and you'll have passed up the most romantic proposal opportunity.*

She pulled the folded paper out of the envelope. She looked at John, desperately wanting him to drop to his knee. She squinted. "Do you have anything to say before I look at this?"

He shook his head.

Nothing? What about the ring in your pocket? What about confessing your undying love for me?

She watched as John dropped his head and closed his eyes. The realization crashed in: He was waiting for the result before asking. His head was bobbing slightly as if he were straining. He looked like he was waiting for the inevitable bad news.

Claire watched as the paper in her hand began to shake. As she began to unfold the paper, her eyes flooded with tears. Insecurity assaulted her full force. She'd asked John along, as her closest friend, for the support and love he'd provide regardless of the result. Since they'd gotten back together in Stoney Creek, John hadn't hesitated to confess that he'd never stopped loving her. So what was holding him back from a real commitment?

She couldn't focus. In her hand was the answer to the mystery, but if John wasn't going to propose without knowing the result, what kind of love was that? Claire knew the answer. Love bears all things. Love that couldn't make the commitment of "in sickness and in health" wasn't real love at all.

"Honey?" John's voice was soft. He waited a moment longer before squeezing her shoulder gently. "Claire?"

She was staring at the open paper in front of her, but couldn't read anything. And even if the tears would have allowed her to see, she'd lost the desire to know. If John wasn't going to propose, she wasn't sure she had the will to know the future. The penultimate question of whether she carried the Huntington's disease gene needed to be answered if Claire wanted to plan her future, but without the assurance that John Cerelli was part of her life, she wasn't sure she wanted to know.

"I can't do this," she stammered. "Not now." She pushed the paper back in Ginny's hands and stood up. "I don't know what's wrong with me." She held her forehead with both hands and released a sob. "I'm just not ready to know." She wiped her moist cheek with her palm and sniffed, before turning her back on John and striding to the door.

She ran down the hall and through the crowded waiting room. Once she was outside, she kept her mouth covered until she was safely alone in John's car. There, she dissolved into a fit of sobs, laying her forehead down upon the dashboard. She clinched her hands into tight fists and cried.

She had counted on love to get her through D day, only to doubt that the love John pledged was really love at all.

Chapter Five

John glanced at Claire without speaking before turning on a CD of classic Italian opera. It was an infatuation that Claire didn't share. For John, it was a reconnection with his heritage, and an excuse to practice the Italian language he'd studied during college. Claire gave him "the look," which in this case meant, "not now." He snapped off the CD and took a deep breath. Claire didn't speak on the way back to Stoney Creek, except when John slowed in front of Fisher's Cafe in the small town of Fisher's Retreat, and she mumbled, "I'm not hungry." At that, John let out an audible sigh and drove on.

They stopped at the Stoney Creek Family Medicine clinic an hour early for Claire's afternoon clinic. John leaned toward her, and she passively accepted his good-bye kiss on her cheek. Then she let herself out, slipped in the back door of the clinic and into her office, and closed the door.

She had to get her mind off John, her disappointment over her expectations, and her HD test. The best way was to immerse herself in patients and the challenges they presented. Here in her office, her desk groaned with the load of work demanding Claire's attention. She smiled. Here there was work to do, people with problems bigger than her own. She sat at the desk and leaned forward. If she filled her life with solving other's problems, she wouldn't have to deal with her own.

Claire looked at a stack of charts in her in-box with labs and X-ray reports to review, and her dictated notes of previous office visits to review and sign. She lifted the first chart, a fifty-two-year-old diabetic woman who refused to watch her diet. Her glucose control was horrible, and she had come in with a pressure ulcer on the bottom of her foot at the base of her great toe. The entire digit was bright red with streaks extending up to her ankle. Claire had urged immediate admission to the closest hospital in

Carlisle for IV antibiotics and possible toe amputation. The patient, Mabel Henderson, was a lifelong resident of Stoney Creek. She refused admission, stating she'd never been to the hospital and wasn't going to start now. After a twenty-minute discussion, Clair relented, warned the patient of the life- and limb-threatening consequences of her decision, and wrote her a prescription for oral antibiotics. "Don't you have any samples? Dr. Jenkins always gave me samples. The pharmacy is all the way over in Fisher's Retreat," Mabel whined. Claire raided the sample closet and returned with a five-day supply of Cipro. She was afraid to give her more for fear she wouldn't come back soon for follow up. Claire signed her note and prayed that Mabel would cooperate.

The next chart was Buzzy Alderson's. Buzzy had a hernia the size of a cabbage, and hadn't sought care until it started affecting the fit of his baggy bib overalls. Just looking at Buzzy's hernia made Claire long to be in surgery again. She referred him to Greg Branum, a general surgeon who'd escaped a big-city practice and come to work in Carlisle a year ago. She smiled at her nurse's notation of Buzzy's chief complaint. "I've got a rupture." Claire signed her office note and forged ahead.

The next chart belonged to Lena Chisholm. Claire couldn't forget the girl whose one good eye danced with fear. Claire felt her stomach tighten, knowing that this patient also had ignored her advice. She wondered how many punches it would take until Lena would consider leaving. Claire knew it was only too hard for many abused women to leave, and for some, the result of staying was fatal. She shook her head and checked the face sheet. "Lena Chisholm. 82 Briary Branch Road." She kept reading. "Spouse: Billy Ray Chisholm." What a jerk. Why would Lena stay with a guy like that? *Maybe he's a real saint when he's not drunk.* She answered her own thought with a sarcastic whisper, "Yeah, right!"

She thought of her own childhood, and how crazy Wally got when he'd been drinking. And now, looking back, she didn't know how much was the moonshine and how much was the early manifestations of HD.

Claire leafed through the old record on Lena, something she hadn't had a chance to do when she'd treated her the first time. She'd been treated two times before, once for a lip laceration, and once for fractured ribs. Each time, Billy Ray came with her. Each time there was a story of a fall or accident. The pattern was similar, both occurring on Mondays. Probably Billy

Ray got paid on Friday. He gets a little cash, then spends some on booze on the way home. But yesterday was Thursday. Billy must have been doing a little celebrating before the weekend.

She shivered, thinking about what tonight might bring for Lena. She signed her dictated note and thought about calling Lena. *She won't listen to me anyway.*

Claire busied herself in desk work, eating only a few packaged cheese crackers for lunch. She'd perfected eating on the run during her surgical internship, following the advice of her chief resident, affectionately called the O-man: "Eat when you can. Sleep when you can." But now, she ate on the run only because she didn't want to stop and eat anything that would prevent her from her work, because right now, work was the only thing stopping Claire from thinking about John and the morning fiasco at the genetics clinic.

The door opened after a soft rapping. "Knock, knock." Her nurse Lucy always said that after she knocked. Lucy was close to retirement and knew everyone in Stoney Creek on a first-name basis. The room wherever Lucy was always smelled of roses, from the hand lotion she applied after every handwashing. "You're being pretty quiet back here." She leaned forward, her hand on the desk. "Does that mean you got bad news?"

Claire had told only one person at the clinic that she was getting tested for the HD gene. That one person was Lucy. Claire knew her nurse had kept a thousand patient confidences, and Claire knew her secret was safe. She looked up at Lucy's large brown eyes and shook her head. "I chickened out at the last minute. I just couldn't go through with it."

Lucy patted Claire's hand, leaving a floral scent and cool moisture behind. "Don't be too hard on yourself, Claire. Not many of us would be ready for a glimpse into our own futures."

Claire stayed quiet and turned her eyes to the work on her desk.

"How's John? Upset?"

"Not that he'd admit, but we barely talked on the way home." She shrugged. "Not that I felt like talking."

"I didn't mean to pry."

"No, I know that. It's not like I go around sharing this load with too many people." Claire pushed the charts away and drummed her fingers on the desk. "I just didn't feel like talking to John about it."

Lucy raised her eyebrows in an unspoken question.

"If I know John, he'll go away for a few hours and think it through, then come back to me with a rational argument with six points on why I should read my test results."

"It's a man thing, honey. Half the time I spill my guts about some problem to Lee, he immediately suggests three ways to fix it, when all I really wanted was someone to listen. They do it because they want to help." She reached for Claire's hand again. "John really seems to love you. I think he's as interested in your future as you are."

"It's my future."

"And his as well. You can't blame him for wanting to know what he's up against."

Claire couldn't voice her fears about John's motives. John had easily popped the question last year before he knew about HD, but now he seemed to be dragging his heels. She smiled politely at Lucy. "Maybe."

Lucy's eyes narrowed.

"John has been the best friend I could ever want. And ever since he came to Stoney Creek to be near me, I was sure we had a future together, but . . ."

"But?"

"I don't know. I guess I'm sensing some reluctance on his part." Claire looked away. "I don't think he can stand to think of living with me if I end up like Wally."

Lucy stood up straight. Her response was quiet. "Oh, my."

"John's picking me up after work. He'll probably be upset."

"Or maybe just a little disappointed."

Before Claire could process Lucy's response, Lucy changed the subject. "I hope it wasn't a mistake to schedule patients this afternoon."

"I'll be fine. I need to stay busy."

"That shouldn't be a problem," she said, pointing at a list of scheduled appointments. She took one step back, then added, "But problems don't just disappear if you ignore them. If you want me to have the receptionist reschedule, everyone would understand. We could—"

Claire silenced her with an uplifted hand and a raised voice. "I said I'll be fine."

Lucy retreated with a shrug and a tight smile. "Okay, then, let's get started," she responded. "Brittany Lewis is in 'A.' Bellyache after the Ruritan dinner last night."

Claire pushed back from the desk, thankful for a reason to stop talking about John. "I'm on it." She walked down the hall and picked up the chart from the rack. Other than for routine childhood checkups, Brittany had been in good health. Now, at nineteen, this would be her first appointment with Claire. Claire pushed open the door and addressed the patient by her first name, something she did routinely with patients under twenty. "Brittany," she said, holding out her hand, "I'm Dr. McCall. Lucy tells me you've got a stomachache."

The patient nodded. "About an hour after eating sausage and pancakes. Right here," she said, pointing to her right upper abdomen.

Claire finished taking a complete history and decided that gallbladder disease headed the short list of diagnostic possibilities. She was just finishing the physical examination when a rap on the door, followed by "knock, knock," signaled Lucy's arrival. She pushed open the door to reveal the old ultrasound machine in the hall. "Thought you might want this."

Claire nodded. Sometimes she felt like a puppet. Lucy had done this for so long, she knew all the workups. "Good thinking." She squirted some ultrasonic gel on Brittany's abdomen and picked up the probe. Dr. Jenkins had bought the hospital's used machine when they replaced it with one with more bells and whistles. He used it on his patients, half of whom wouldn't follow through and go to Carlisle for an ultrasound if he ordered it. Claire had learned to use ultrasound to evaluate trauma patients up in Boston during her internship.

She placed the probe on Brittany's firm abdominal wall, pressing gently to get a good look at the liver and gallbladder. "There," she said, "see that? There's your gallbladder." She adjusted the probe. "The wall is thickened."

Brittany winced. "Ow."

"And here is a cluster of gallstones. Are you sure you've never gotten sick with this before?"

The patient denied it. And when Claire recommended referring her on for surgery, Brittany balked. "Isn't there anything else? Can't you give me a pill? My grandmother took some pills for her gallbladder and she didn't need surgery."

"Surgery is really the best way. The procedure can be done up in Carlisle as an outpatient."

"With that laser thing?"

Claire didn't feel like explaining it. Removing the gallbladder wasn't commonly done with a laser, but it made no difference to the patient. Claire understood that Brittany was referring to removal of the gallbladder using a laparoscope. She nodded. "Right. You probably won't even need to spend the night."

"I don't have insurance. I can't afford it."

She felt her patience wane. She didn't have time to argue with patients who came seeking her advice, and then didn't want to do what she'd ask. "I'll send you to Dr. Branum. I'm sure he will work out a deal."

"I really am feeling better than last night."

"Fine!" Claire snapped. "You be the doctor, then! Do what you want to do. But remember, I warned you—" She stopped short as the door opened and her eyes met Lucy's. Her nurse's gaze interrupted Claire's outburst, but not her building emotional stress. She looked at her index finger which was still wagging toward Brittany's wide eyes. Claire slowly folded her fingers into a fist and pulled them to her chest. She dropped her gaze to the floor and proceeded with her voice monotone and soft. She warned her patient of delaying too long, sighting the possible complications of her disease if left unchecked.

The patient looked down and played with the silver stud piercing the skin above her umbilicus.

Claire sighed and attempted to get her young patient to refocus. "Brittany."

The patient looked up, meeting her doctor's eyes for a fleeting moment.

"This could be serious."

"I took some Tums last night. I feel better now. I'm not even sure why I came," she added, slipping down from the examining table. "I can't miss work right now. Alice McMillan lost her job when she had to have surgery."

"If you have surgery, at most you'll need to avoid heavy lifting for a week or two. Most people can do light work a few days after having the gallbladder removed. If you keep having attacks, you'll end up missing more work."

In spite of Claire's best arguments, the patient stood her ground.

Claire wanted to scream, but the patient wasn't going to take her advice, so she saved her breath. She handed the patient the billing sheet and recommended that she avoid eating fried or greasy foods. *You'll be back.*

She pushed past her nurse and into the hall. She had only taken one step toward her office when she felt a hand on her shoulder. She knew the gentle touch to be Lucy's before she turned, determined not to let the older nurse make her feel any worse about her actions than she already did. She didn't want a motherly reminder to see things from the patient's perspective. To avoid the lecture, she launched into a tirade. "Fat, fertile, forty, fair, and flatulent!"

Lucy's face reflected her shock. She lifted her hand. "What?"

"The five F's of gallstone patients. Certainly you've heard of them," Claire added with a wave of her hand. "But why should I even bring up typical characteristics that the medical texts teach?" She raised her voice and kept her eyes locked on her nurse's. "Because no one in Stoney Creek is anything close to typical! And none of them want to take my advice anyway! All they want is some white-haired *man* with a white coat to give them some antiquated advice." She twirled and left Lucy with her mouth open.

She stomped down the hall to her office and plopped into her desk chair. She opened Brittany's chart and prepared to dictate an office note. *Why can't I have just one patient who will take my advice? And why can't anyone present like I was taught during my internship?*

She looked up and gasped as Cyrus Hensley rose up from the other side of her desk.

Cyrus winced, an action which dimpled his reddening cheeks. "Sorry, Dr. McCall."

She nodded and studied him a moment, observing his hasty retreat to a standing position against the wall. He was young, midtwenties, she guessed, and he would have been a real hunk if it wasn't for his need for a haircut. His hair was dark and curly, hanging to the bottom of his collar. He flipped his bangs away from his eyes with the back of his hand.

He looked down. "I, uh, need a haircut. I just haven't had a chance to get up to Carlisle to get it done."

He had read her mind exactly. "Don't worry about it. What were you doing on the floor?"

"Lucy asked me to hang an X-ray viewbox on this wall. I was just looking for the closest electrical outlet."

Claire sighed and tried to quiet her runaway heart. "Oh."

Cyrus shuffled his feet. "What were you talking about?"

She squinted and leaned forward. "When?"

"You said something about fat."

"I was talking about gallstones." His expression told her he wasn't getting it so she continued. "People with gallstones are supposed to be fat. Fat, fair, forty, fertile, and flatulent."

He nodded, but didn't move on. "My mom was sixty when she had her gallbladder out."

"Well, she must have been from Stoney Creek."

"Why?"

"Because every patient here seems destined to be different from the way they are supposed to be."

He nodded again silently.

Claire continued to vent. She knew her maintenance man couldn't care less, but he just happened to have the only other set of ears in the room. "The patients in Stoney Creek never seem to typify the patients in my textbooks." She picked up the chart. "Take this young woman. She has only one characteristic which typifies gallstones."

"She's fat?"

Claire smiled, amused that Cyrus had actually listened. "No. Not fat at all. She's fair. Very fair, beautiful in fact, but she's not fat, not fertile, and nowhere close to forty. She's only nineteen. I wanted to refer her for surgery, but she has every excuse in the book." She paused. "What is it with these folks? No one wants to do what I tell them."

"Hey, don't look at me, Dr. McCall. You're the one from Stoney Creek, not me."

"I've been gone too long. I've forgotten how self-sufficient these people are." She glanced at her maintenance man. "Where are you from?"

"All over. My father was military. His last assignment was just over the mountain in Sugar Grove. I loved it there." He shrugged. "Coming to

Stoney Creek felt as much like coming home as anywhere." He stepped toward the doorway. "Don't let these folks get to you, Dr. McCall."

She sighed. "Thanks."

He nodded and turned to go.

"Uh, Cyrus, where do you get your hair cut?"

He shrugged. "Haven't really found a place I liked."

"I'll do it for you."

"You?"

"Sure. I used to cut my brother's hair all the time."

Cyrus wrinkled his nose.

"Don't worry. I think I'm qualified. I can do it after work."

She turned back to Brittany's chart, not waiting for Cyrus to answer. She read Lucy's handwritten note, something she hadn't bothered to do before entering the room because she liked taking the history herself. "Patient's father died after gallbladder surgery. Patient is very afraid of surgery."

The words cut like a fresh scalpel. She had taken her frustrations about her own problems out on her patient and her nurse, and hadn't even realized what Lucy already knew: the patient would likely avoid surgery at every cost, not because of lack of insurance, or losing her job; she was afraid, and Claire had been too preoccupied to notice.

Claire shook her head. *God help me.*

Lucy's voice interrupted her prayer. "Knock, knock," she said as she tapped the doorframe.

Claire looked up at Lucy, half expecting an I-told-you-so, but knowing her nurse was above rubbing her nose in her problems. And also smart enough to know when to give Claire space when she was creeping close to the edge. Lucy didn't smile. At least she wasn't the type to be plastic. If Lucy didn't feel like smiling, she didn't. "Marge Nichols has her son in room B."

"Another earache?"

"You got it." Lucy straightened. "And don't even mention the word *surgery*. Her mother just entered Crestview Adult Home, and Marge and Dan are giving every spare dime they can scrape up just to make the payments."

"And just what if the right answer is ear tubes?"

"Sometimes we have to modify the book answers to fit the real world." She shook her head. "And you're not going to believe what I've got for you in room C."

"Try me."

Lucy shook her head. "Have a look for yourself. Better go there before you see the Nichols boy."

Claire smiled. "An emergency?"

"Yep," Lucy said, as she led the way back down the hall. "What is it with you surgery types? You like emergencies?"

Claire shrugged, knowing Lucy couldn't see her. *I used to love emergencies. But that was before I was out here on the front line on my own.* She kept up the surgical bravado. "It's the adrenaline that keeps me coming back for more."

Lucy gestured toward the exam room and stood aside. "Be my guest. Your emergency beckons, Doctor."

Claire's pulse quickened as she reached for the doorknob. Why would Lucy stand aside? What would she see inside? Blood? Active labor? Acute abdominal pain? She paused and listened to the muffled sounds coming from behind the door. Someone was in distress. And the noises sounded like those of someone with a severe hearing or speech impediment.

She pushed open the door to see a grade-school boy sitting on the exam table holding a glass bottle up to his mouth. The boy's eyes were wide open, and darted quickly between an elderly woman standing at his side and Claire, whose first thought was that it couldn't be a very big emergency if the patient was sitting here enjoying a beverage. But that was before she heard him speak.

The patient mumbled indistinct gibberish without sharp consonant sounds, clicking his teeth against the glass bottle neck. He gripped at the old woman's arm and ducked his head, never lowering the bottle. He began to shake his head and lifted his hand up to halt Claire's progress, at the same time releasing the bottle and pinching it between his teeth. He turned away from Claire and lowered his hands around the bottle. It was still half full of what appeared to be chocolate milk.

The woman wore a blue flowered dress with a grease stain over her ample stomach. She lifted her hand toward Claire, revealing a scar midway up her arm above the wrist. "I'm Edna Shaffer, Stevie's grandmother. Can you help him?"

Claire accepted the firm handshake. "I'm Dr. McCall." She leaned toward the boy.

Edna pried her grandson's fingers from her arm and pulled his other hand away from the bottle. "You're going to have to show her if you want any dinner tonight."

The boy shifted enough for Claire to see something dripping from the bottom of the bottle, which was hanging on the end of his tongue. "Eeth sthuh!"

Edna translated. "It's stuck." She nudged the boy's shoulder. "Let the doctor see."

Claire reached forward and touched the boy's hand. "Stevie? I won't hurt you. Let me see." She snapped on a pair of disposable examining gloves and touched the bottle which glistened with saliva. Through the green glass, she could see the boy's tongue, which was dark purple, and swollen beyond a slight narrowing at the neck of the bottle. Left without treatment, the swelling would continue until the blood flow to the tongue ceased altogether, causing the superficial layers to die and slough. She gently pulled the bottle away from the boy's mouth.

His head came forward with the bottle. "Aaaaah!"

It appeared that the vacuum had sucked the tongue deeply into the bottle.

"We need to break the vacuum in the bottle." Claire sat on a rolling stool. "Do we have anything here to cut the glass?"

Lucy rubbed her chin. "I can ask Cyrus. I know he's got a hammer. Maybe we can break it." She disappeared through the doorway calling for the maintenance man.

The boy's eye's widened. "Ahhh!"

Edna shook her head. "It could cut him."

Cyrus appeared, looming large in the doorway and holding a toolbox. He shook his head. "My drill is in the truck." He hesitated. "There's a glass cutter up in Carlisle."

"Thirty minutes away," Lucy responded.

Edna imposed herself between the exam table and Cyrus. "Is he a doctor?"

"Me?" Cyrus smiled. "I mow the grass."

The boy screamed again and scooted to the far side of the exam table. Claire could see that the situation could quickly deteriorate into hysteria.

"Nine wah wah."

Edna shook her head. "This doctor will help you." She looked at Claire, her eyes pleading. "He wants me to call nine one one. You can help him, can't you?"

Claire looked at Lucy. "Bring me the emergency drug box. We'll need an IV for sedation."

Lucy's hand went to her mouth.

Claire motioned her to follow her into the hall, where she whispered, "We've got to do something here. The poor guy's tongue is going to die if we wait for an ambulance to take him to Carlisle." She looked at Cyrus. "Get your drill."

Lucy wrinkled her forehead. "What are you going to do?"

Claire wasn't sure. She was plunging ahead in uncharted waters. But she was Stoney Creek's front line for medical care, and that meant she had to do something. She put up a steeled expression of confidence, knowing Lucy could read her true feelings like a book. "Just get the emergency drugs. I'll do the rest."

Back in the room, Claire faced the slobbering ten year old who had backed against the wall. He bared his front teeth like a trapped animal. The boy may have been in grade school, but he was already at least a hundred pounds. She wouldn't be able to handle him alone. Suddenly, she found herself wishing for an equipped O.R. and an anesthesiologist to control the child's airway. All of those things would have been available up in Boston where Claire did her surgical internship last year. But that was then, and Stoney Creek was a long way from Boston. And although she knew that a hospital was a thirty-minute ambulance ride away, she knew the best chance to get the bottle off without surgery would be now before too much swelling compromised any chances of removing the bottle without surgery.

Claire looked at Grandmother. She was large, but feeble, and her eyes were squinted in concern. The situation was deteriorating. The patient was on the verge of hysteria and Edna was losing trust in Claire. "You like baking, I see," Claire began, hoping to inspire Grandma with a little confidence.

Edna looked down at her dress. "Oh, yes, but, uh, how did—"

"You have baker's burns," Claire responded, reaching out and gently touching the older woman's forearms. "I noticed when you shook my hand. These are commonly seen in bakers. When they are loading the bottom rack of an oven, the forearms often contact the rack above," she said, depressing the scars. "Right here."

The older woman nodded. "That's right, Doctor. Exactly right."

Claire captured the woman's eyes and spoke calmly. "I'm going to help your grandson, Edna, and I may need your help. We need to try to remove the bottle here before the swelling gets any worse and causes more problems." Claire stayed intentionally vague and lowered her voice to a whisper, while leaning toward Edna's face. She didn't want the not-so-little Stevie hearing about his tongue dying. She wasn't sure that if he made a break for it, she could do much to slow him down.

Grandma eyed Stevie pensively. "The doctor here needs to take a look, Stevie."

"Can you climb back up on the exam table?"

The boy pushed tighter against the wall and shook his head. "Ooo!"

"I won't hurt you, son. I'm going to help you. I'll give you some medicine to make you real sleepy."

Grandma Edna tried coaxing of a different type. "If you let the doctor help you, I'll give you some of those caramel brownies you love."

Claire took a half-step forward and lifted her hand. The chubby youngster let out a muffled squeal and shook his head. To Claire he certainly didn't look like he needed any more brownies. In fact, the thought of brownies in Stevie's stomach brought a sudden chill to Claire's spine. If this kid was halfway through his chocolate milk, what else might be lurking in the depths of his belly that he might need to vomit if he worked himself into a lather? And if she sedated him, could he protect his airway if he started to vomit? She knew there was an endotracheal tube in the office's emergency box, but putting a tube into a child's windpipe can be a treacherous procedure under the best of circumstances; it could be next to impossible with a bottle of chocolate milk in the way. *What I wouldn't give for an anesthesiologist right now.*

She clenched her teeth. She needed to work quickly, to dispel the worries which challenged expedient thought. *Help me, God.* "Stevie, I need you to get up on the exam table. I won't hurt you. If you want me to help you, you'll have to trust me."

Stevie's eyes were wide open, wild with fear, and wet with fresh tears. His grandma nodded. "Come on, Stevie."

Lucy returned with the emergency box and pulled out the IV supplies.

Stevie took one look at the IV and made a break for the door. His grandmother lunged and missed. Claire managed a fleeting grasp of the boy's shoulder, and watched as he shoved Lucy forward and came face to face with Cyrus. For a second, the little tyrant stared down the maintenance man before attempting to dive between his legs. In a blink of an eye, Cyrus spun, lifted the boy by the waist of his jeans, and pulled the twisting flail of limbs to his own body. In another second, Cyrus had entrapped Stevie's arms, while holding him from behind in a firm hold. He pried open Stevie's right arm, forcing his elbow straight. He looked at Lucy. "Think you can hit this vein?"

Claire looked on with amazement and concern. She wasn't thrilled at the use of force to restrain him, but she didn't see much choice. She traded glances with Lucy and whispered, "Go ahead."

The boy screamed and tried to kick at Lucy, who was holding an IV catheter.

Cyrus responded by jumping back up on the exam table, carrying the youngster with him, pulling him onto his lap where he could wrap his own legs around the writhing patient. "There," he said, showing a thin smile. "Better hurry. He's slippery."

Claire took a deep breath. In spite of Cyrus's words, it didn't look like the boy could go anywhere. She quickly painted the inside of Stevie's elbow and punctured the vein with the IV catheter. Stevie strained against Cyrus's hold as Lucy taped down the IV and Cyrus spoke softly in the boy's ear. "Come on, Stevie. I'll loosen up if you cooperate."

Stevie yelled as Claire quickly stabbed the IV port with a needle and pushed in the Versed, a rapidly acting sedative. After two agonizing minutes, Stevie's eyelids drooped and Cyrus loosened his grip. Claire injected two milligrams of morphine and waited until Cyrus placed the quieted patient on the exam table. "Don't leave us," Claire cautioned. "He may wake up if he feels pain." She lifted the bottle to make her first close exam of Stevie's tongue. The tip was deep purple and tense like a grape. She looked at Cyrus's toolbox. "Do you have anything to cut the glass?"

Edna paled. "His tongue is so swollen. You'll hurt him."

Claire avoided eye contact with the grandmother. "We need to release the vacuum in the bottle. We have to break the bottle somehow."

Edna tugged the lapel of Claire's white coat. "You do it. You're the doctor."

Claire shook her head. She had to fight the rising panic within her. Her patient was quiet, ready for her to do something, but she wasn't sure what that something should be. She tried to twist the bottle but the tongue moved with it. She tugged it forward but quickly met resistance as the tongue was already protruding as far as Stevie could let it.

Cyrus clanked through his tool box, lifting first a hammer, then a pair of pliers and a screwdriver.

"I don't have a drill bit that will work for glass. Maybe you could break it with this," he said, weighing the hammer in his hand.

Claire shook her head and tapped the bottle with her knuckles. "The tongue could be lacerated if the glass shattered."

"Perhaps I could just tap the edge of the bottle," Cyrus offered.

"No." She couldn't very well let Cyrus take over responsibility for the patient. She had to do something. *Not that I have a clue. I've never seen anyone with their tongue stuck in a bottle before. How can I introduce air into the bottle without breaking it?*

"Wait. I've got an idea." She motioned to Lucy. "Bring me a spinal needle."

Lucy shrugged and left the room, returning in a moment with a small box.

"Give me the twenty-two gauge."

Claire snapped on a pair of sterile gloves and bent the needle into a sharp angle after removing the stylet. She drew up a local anesthetic into a syringe and attached it to the bent needle. She pulled the bottle aside. "Hold it here, Lucy, so I can see the base of his tongue."

Claire pushed the needle into the exposed flesh at the base of Stevie's tongue and injected a cc of the numbing medicine. She watched Stevie's eyes, which opened briefly during the injection. Then, Claire twisted the needle so she could manipulate it through the muscle of the tongue and out through the swollen tip and into the bottle. Immediately the plunger of the syringe slid forward as the clear anesthetic fluid was pulled into the bottle, mixing with the brown contents. Claire pulled the syringe free from the needle, allowing a hiss of air to suck into the bottle through the spinal needle.

Claire pulled back the plunger to fill the syringe with air, then reattached it to the needle and forced additional air into the bottle before sliding the needle out. She twisted the bottle again, noticing a slight movement. She gently pulled the bottle away from Stevie's face. Slowly, she added force, lifting her patient's head from the table. Then, she laid her opposite hand on Stevie's forehead and trapped it against the padded exam table before giving the bottle a forceful clockwise torque.

Stevie screamed as the bottle broke free in a spray of milk. Claire looked for the gush of blood. She was sure she'd sheared off the boy's tongue.

Edna and Lucy gasped.

Stevie's head landed against the table with a thud. In the silent moment that followed, Claire examined his tongue. It was swollen and purple, and had a rim indentation from the bottle neck. She took a deep breath. The tongue oozed blood from the needle stick, but was otherwise intact.

Relief and exhilaration flooded Claire's veins as her lungs exploded in a laugh that broke the silence. She turned and slapped Cyrus on the shoulder. "We did it!"

He smiled and backed up to let Claire pass.

She handed a white gauze to Lucy. "Pinch his tongue to stop the bleeding. Then get him an appointment to see me in two days." She looked at Edna and smiled. "Keep him sitting up most of the day once he's awake. And give him some ice or a popsicle. It will help with the swelling."

Claire was pumped, thrilled with the success of her innovative treatment. For her, this was the immediate gratification that fueled her surgical personality: see a problem; fix a problem; go on to the next problem.

She watched as Cyrus dropped his hammer into his toolbox and walked down the hall toward the back door and the parking lot beyond. She hadn't liked having to get him involved, especially to physically control a patient, but she had to admit, without his help, they'd have never been able to restrain "little" Stevie. She dismissed her anxiety about the use of force, and reminded herself of what an answer to prayer Cyrus had been.

Claire reassured Edna, then hurried from the room, excited to face the challenges the next patient would offer. Best of all, she mused, when she was busy with a difficult patient, she couldn't think about the cloud. *I can do this. I don't have to know the future. I have enough to keep my thoughts busy just concentrating on the here and now.*

She nodded, opened the chart of her next patient, and began to read.

Chapter Six

Lena Chisholm listened as the back screen door slapped against its frame. Billy Ray was home early. She looked at herself in the mirror and pushed a blond strand of hair behind her ear. It was a reflex. Billy always wanted her to look her best when he arrived. But today, he'd have to put up with things just as they were. She didn't feel well enough to make the effort. She'd slept until ten, a fitful slumber interrupted by pain and her husband's restless trips to the bathroom to empty his bladder of yesterday's beer enthusiasm.

When she'd awakened that morning, her left eyebrow had been stuck fast to her pillowcase, the blood and fluid that oozed from the freshly sutured laceration forming a natural bond that had brought tears to her eyes as she'd torn her face away from the linens. Now, studying her reflection, she could just get her left eye open above the raised purple flesh of her cheek. She hopped to the TV, shutting off Oprah and collapsing onto a well-worn couch.

"Lena?"

"In here." She listened to his footfalls and the squeak of the hall closet.

"Did you wash my bowling shirt?"

She leaned back to accept his kiss. He paused as their eyes met, before looking away and setting his bowling bag on the couch beside her.

"You're home early."

"Mr. Bowman left early. He likes to spend weekends at his cabin."

"When the boss is away, the mice will play."

"Yeah, yeah. What he doesn't know won't hurt him. What about you?"

"I called in sick. Couldn't exactly work like this."

He wouldn't look up. "It won't happen again."

She didn't reply. She'd heard it before.

He lifted his hand and gently touched her cheek. "Can I get you some aspirin or something?"

She shook her head. "I'm okay."

He lifted a blue couch pillow and slid it under her foot. "You should keep this elevated." He stroked the bottom of her bare feet and glanced over just in time to see her wipe her eyes.

He could be so sweet.

And so violent.

"Why don't you have your ankle wrapped?"

"I took the bandage off so I could wash my feet." She pointed toward their little bathroom. "It's on the counter by the medicine cabinet."

Billy Ray retrieved the ace wrap and rerolled it with slow precision, making sure the edges were even. "There," he said. "Can you hold up your foot?"

She obeyed and studied his face as he focused on wrapping her foot and ankle. "You should have been a doctor."

A smile broke his mask of concentration. "I used to dream of being a surgeon."

She giggled. "You?"

"Shut up! My biology teacher in high school said I'd be good." He clipped the ace wrap in place with a little more vigor.

Pain shot through Lena's ankle. "Ow! I was only kidding." She paused. "I'm the one who said you should have been a doctor." She paused and studied her husband for a moment. Billy Ray had a vulnerable side, like a little boy, insecure and searching, afraid to challenge the world. He lifted his chin and nodded quickly to himself, perhaps reassuring himself of the properness of his job. His brown eyes gave his hardened face a hint of tenderness.

His eyes met hers. "What are you staring at?"

"What happened, Billy Ray? Why'd you give up a dream?"

He shrugged. "I blew out my knee playing football. It was my only ticket to college." He pulled his hand through his dark hair and shuffled his feet.

Lena knew he felt inadequate, but didn't know why. He was strong and good-looking. "So, you're a car surgeon now. I'll bet that Dr. McCall can't even change her own oil."

He smirked and picked at the grease beneath his thumbnail. "She probably doesn't even pump her own gas." He picked up his bowling bag. "We're bowling up in Carlisle. Eddie's gonna drive."

So you can drink. "Don't go, Billy. Stay home with me. You could rent a video. We'll eat popcorn."

"The guys are counting on me."

"Okay, I'll come along. I can root for the gang."

He shook his head. "Don't start, Lena. You can't show up like that."

"I'll tell them I fell down."

"No!" He slammed his bag down on the kitchen table.

Lena winced.

Billy Ray dropped his head and took a deep breath. Then, with his voice softer, but on the frayed edge of control, he continued, "I mean, no, baby. You need your rest. You don't like Lester and Eddie much anyway."

That was an understatement. Lester drank too much and didn't like to drink alone. Eddie knew only three adjectives, and she would only repeat one.

"Stay with me, Billy Ray. We'll listen to Garth Brooks."

He clinched his jaw. "Don't nag me, Lena." He walked away into the kitchen where she heard the refrigerator open. He returned holding a can of cheap beer and chewing cold cheese pizza with his mouth open. He dropped into the chair across from the couch. "Want some pizza?"

She shook her head and changed her tactic. "We're in a rut."

He grunted.

She chose her words carefully, tiptoeing around his abuse so as not to anger him again. "We always make love in the morning."

He raised his eyebrows and stopped chewing. He leaned forward as Lena formulated her next sentence.

She listened to him swallow. Why did beer drinking always have to be so noisy? "You go out with the guys. You party. We fight and go to bed mad." She bobbed her head. "Then in the morning, you feel bad, beg my forgiveness, and we make up." She smiled to herself, glad to have avoided the word *drunk* and the straight-ahead accusation of his violent temper. She had said "we" and not "you." With Billy Ray, she couldn't be too careful.

Billy smiled back. He thought she was smiling at him. "So just what are you suggesting?"

"Why don't you skip the first part, and let's get right to the makin' up part?"

He crushed the aluminum can in his fist and pulled off his shirt. He stood and closed the distance between them in one step. "You're crazy, baby," he whispered, leaning over to kiss her forehead. "My kind of crazy."

She gave him her best stiff-arm to his bare chest. "Not so fast."

His eyes squinted.

"Not here." She smiled. "I'm not ready." She pointed toward the bathroom. "I want you to draw me a warm bath and wash my hair." Billy Ray loved washing her thick blond hair. And she loved how distracted he became every time he tried. "I need you to help me so I won't get my stitches wet."

Billy Ray grimaced. "We shouldn't do that. The wound could get some infection or something." He kissed her neck. "Besides, we don't have time."

She pushed him away again. "Help me, honey. I still have blood caked in my hair. I feel gross." She lifted her hand. "Help me up. Watch out for my ankle."

He assisted her to her feet, then quickly lifted her into his arms. She clutched her arms around his neck. He was strong. The years may not have been kind to his knees, but he still had the upper body of an athlete.

He carried her from the couch, but instead of turning left into the bathroom, he turned right into the bedroom.

"Not here, silly. You can't wash my hair in here."

He nuzzled her hair. "It's fine, baby. You don't need to worry. I like it."

He laid her on the bed.

"No, Billy Ray."

He pouted. "Some things can't wait."

She lifted her hair from her collar and flung it from side to side. "Some things are worth waiting for." She teased him with a kiss on the nose before drawing back again. "Bring me my crutches so I don't have to hop to the bathroom."

He leaned forward, ignoring her request. "You're so beautiful. I just—"

A horn blared, stopping Billy in midsentence. He cursed and slapped the bedspread beside Lena. It was Eddie. The tinny sound of his car horn was unmistakable.

Anger flared in his eyes. "I told you we didn't have time!"

She started unbuttoning her blouse. "Tell him you got a better offer. Tell him to go without you."

He huffed. "I can't." He stood up. "Where's my bowlin' shirt?"

"Don't go, Billy."

"Shut up!" He grabbed his shirt from the closet floor and stomped from the room.

Lena hopped after him, pain shooting through her ankle with every bounce. "Don't drink, honey. You promised you wouldn't do this again."

He took a step toward her and she shielded her face with her arms.

He softened his voice and touched the back of her arm with his hand. "Don't you believe me? How about a little faith in your husband?"

Lena began to cry. She tried to hold back, but once the tears started flowing, she just couldn't stop. She dropped her hands and pressed her closed fist against her mouth and stared at the man she used to love. She shook her head in disgust at her own gullibility. Why didn't she see him like this before? *I'm not the first woman he's hit.* The thought erupted like a sailfish breaking the surface of the ocean, free in the air before it realizes it has left the safety of the water. Her question came out in rhythmic sobs. "Wh–why did R–Rachel leave?"

His face blanched.

"D–did you hi–hit her too?"

She shielded her face again, expecting a slap which never came.

She backed up and looked between her hands. *One beer must not be enough to make you break a promise.*

The gravel in the driveway began to crunch. Eddie must be in a hurry. It sounded like he was turning his Ford around.

Billy Ray raised his index finger and stabbed it in the air toward Lena. "Don't you leave, baby. I'll find you."

She hopped back another step to the wall and sank to the kitchen floor. "I'm not leavin', Billy Ray. You are."

"Don't ever mention that woman's name again."

Lena looked down as Eddie beeped his horn again and the screen door slammed behind Billy Ray. The engine revved, gravel danced against the metal garbage cans, and Eddie screamed his favorite adjective as they headed out.

"William Raymond," she whispered, "don't forget my flowers."

⤜❦⤛

John Cerelli sat quietly in the corner booth at Fisher's Cafe, sipping a chocolate malt alone. This was *their* booth, the one he always shared with Claire. Today, he was supposed to be here with her, staring into her eyes, watching her as she shared the joy of her diamond ring with the other regulars in Fisher's Retreat. It was funny how he'd dreamed of this day a thousand times—dreamed of listening to Claire as she told the story of his proposal to Abby the waitress, of sharing quick kisses with her as she leaned across the table to squeeze his hand or to accept a gentle swipe of his hand as he brushed away her fresh tears. She would giggle as Abby would scoot in the booth beside her and compare the diamond she wore to Claire's.

Instead, John sat staring at the backwards writing on the front window, the writing that proclaimed the name of the little eatery to those passing on the street: "efaC s'rehsiF." His life seemed mixed up and a little backwards now. Like the life which he'd imagined for so long was suddenly revealed as the silly dream it really was.

John spun the little ring box on the table in front of him and sipped the malt. Mr. Knitter had made it just the way he always did. Extra malt, laced with a ribbon of fudge syrup, and topped with a swirl of whipped cream and dotted with shavings of imported Swiss chocolate. But even his favorite beverage seemed flat without good company. He looked around at the regulars. Mike and Larry Martin were sitting at the bar talking about some Little League catastrophe. Mike's team had been robbed again by a nearsighted umpire. The mayor was sitting at a table reading the paper. Old Doc Jenkins was looking at a girl's throat and telling a mother not to worry. It seemed that even though he'd tried to retire and give the business to Claire, the Apple Valley locals couldn't leave him alone.

He sighed. If Claire was here, their booth would have been alive with visitors. Everyone was so proud of the first female to break out of the Valley doldrums and go to Boston as a new doctor. There were always women dragging their daughters up to meet her, asking Claire to tell them to study their math and science. Men would come by and slap John on the shoulder and wink. The old ones would smile at him. The young ones wouldn't meet his eyes. The body language was clear. John had stolen their strawberry-blond prize. The brightest, most beautiful woman in the world walked in on his arm, and every man paused to take inventory of his thoughts: jealousy or joy, but not much in between.

But there was none of that now. Without Claire, they left John alone. Even Abby, who was normally talkative and friendly, had barely left a greeting beyond, "What'll it be?" And so he sat in silence and contemplated his next move. He had planned for today for weeks. He had prayed, sought advice, and prayed some more. He hoped his plan had originated in heaven. He wanted to spend the rest of his life with Claire McCall, but because of the rocky way their first engagement ended, John sensed at a deep level that he'd only have one more chance to get it right.

And so he prayed. And planned. Today was to be the day. D day for Claire was to be engagement day for John. But Claire, beautiful and spontaneous Claire, proved herself to be true to form and acted in a totally unpredictable way.

John sighed at the memory of Claire's flight from the genetics clinic. It's not as if getting a revelation of the future wouldn't freak out most normal people. But Claire was far from normal. She was a rock, the doctor who'd brought light to the Apple Valley, dispelling the myth of the Stoney Creek curse and standing strong when she'd learned she was at risk to inherit its madness. She was resting confidently in God's loving sovereignty, ready for the future, come what may. And John wanted to be there with her.

But somewhere, something hadn't gone like he'd planned. And now he wasn't sure if Claire would ever return to the clinic for her test results. But John needed to know. More accurately, he needed Claire to know. She needed to know so he could give her a ring with a promise she could trust. Without it, John feared the foundation of their engagement would soon fatigue and crack.

"Girl troubles?"

He looked up to see Abby McAllister. She was a young woman, a curly brunette with Mediterranean blood and a sharp tongue. She was a fixture at the café. Everyone around knew her story. She worked to support her husband, an ex-policeman who'd been crippled by a gunshot wound to his neck.

He tapped the felt box on the table and smiled at himself. "I guess it's pretty obvious, huh?"

"I know a little about women." She peeled off his bill from the pad in her hand and let it float to the table.

When he didn't respond, she slid into the booth opposite him. "That's your second chocolate malt. If I did that, I'd hit two hundred in record time."

"Grampa Cerelli says men will be happy if they have plenty of pasta, red wine, and a full-figured woman."

Abby laughed. "So what's up, Cerelli? You in here to drown your sorrows in chocolate?"

"It's the Italian way."

"Get serious." She put her hand over his and squeezed the ring box through his fingers. "Claire troubles?"

He nodded. He wasn't sure what to say. The thoughts made his heart ache and his voice thicken. "Claire's a real gift, the Valley's little gem." He looked away. "She's so unpredictable, Abby." He hesitated. "I'm afraid my prize is getting away."

Abby released his hand. "Can I give you advice?"

"Could I stop you?"

"I've got Italian blood too, you know. Momma's advice comes with every meal."

John smiled and kept quiet.

"I used to think Nathan was my prize. But I didn't know what real love was until I learned that marriage isn't about getting things smoothed out for us. Marriage is an invitation to come and die."

"Oh, that's rich. It sounds like everyone's heart's desire."

"Don't be sarcastic, John. What I mean is that love is all about putting someone else's wants and needs above your own. It's about dying to yourself." She paused before continuing with her voice just loud enough for him to hear above the background chatter. "Maybe you should worry less about her being your prize and try being hers."

He checked his watch and nodded. "You're handing out more than just good malts today." He slid out of the booth and shoved the ring box in his pocket. "I've got to run. I promised Claire I'd pick her up after work."

He turned to leave and felt a hand on his shoulder.

"I'm a small-town waitress, Bub. The advice comes free, but the malts are three bucks apiece."

He felt his cheeks flush. Claire was distracting his thoughts again. He pulled a ten from his wallet and handed it to Abby.

"I'll be right back."

"Keep the change. The malts were fine as usual," he said. He touched her arm. "But the advice is worth . . ." He paused and smiled before continuing. "Well, maybe twice that."

Abby smiled and swatted his back with her hand.

He turned and walked away, still feeling the sting on his shoulder a minute later when he buckled the shoulder harness of his Mustang.

Dr. McCall enjoyed a steady pace of patient problems through the afternoon. There was nothing else so memorable as little Stevie's purple tongue or as hectic as the schedule of her predecessor, Dr. Jenkins, but continuous enough for Claire to lose herself in her work and forget about the cloud for a few hours. And fortunately, her focus on the problems kept her from snapping at Lucy or another patient after young Brittany had ignored Claire's treatment recommendations.

Claire's head sagged as she recalled the patient encounter with a twinge of remorse. *I shouldn't have let my problems make me jump on my patients or dear Lucy.* She retrieved Brittany's chart from the stack on her desk and copied down her address and phone number, before scribbling an apology to her nurse for her eruption.

She checked her watch and sighed. Everyone in the clinic was long gone. Closing time was an honored ritual, and unless you showed up after four-thirty unconscious or bleeding, you were likely to be greeted by a recommendation to reschedule or head to the E.R. in Carlisle. And even so, it often took Claire until five-thirty or six to see the poor working souls who trudged in under the four-thirty wire.

Today, she was finished by five, and the staff had disappeared at light speed, enjoying a rare opportunity to spend a Friday night eating with their families. But this was Claire's quiet time, the time she spent reflecting on the day's problems and hitting the books to review the latest treatments. The certificate on the wall over her desk stated the fact: She was licensed to practice medicine and surgery in the Commonwealth of Virginia. Licensed to practice, but not board certified in anything. If she was to ever get admitting privileges to a reputable hospital, or be hired by a large clinic to practice outpatient medicine, she would need to be boarded. But that required more years of residency. Two more years if she wanted to sit for the Family Practice boards, and at least four more to sit for the American Board of Surgery exam.

Her level of experience was barely adequate to serve in the clinic, but Dr. Jenkins had searched high and low for an adequate replacement. Board-certified family practitioners were taking higher-paying city jobs, taking monetary rewards far above what a town like Stoney Creek could afford. But Claire had agreed to come, mostly to fill in until a permanent replacement could be found. Her roots from the small town gave her an inside understanding of the patients' rural mindset. But mostly, Claire had agreed to set aside her residency dreams for a time in order to reconnect with her father, and help her mother fight the illness that would soon demand his life. She'd come home to heal, to restore the relationship with the same man whose erratic temper and enthusiasm for the bottle had driven her from home.

As a result, Claire had learned to stand on her own feet the hard way. She was toughened by life, unlikely to bend under the rigors of rocky situations or surgical training demands. Yes, Wally's behavior had sent her away, but the result was a better woman, fiercely independent with the discipline to delay gratification of long educational goals. But this return to Stoney Creek was also about learning to lay aside her own independence of self, to trust in someone beyond her own strength, to find solace in a loving God, and to put her family in front of her own life. On most days, her sacrifice felt right. On others, she fought the temptation to run back to Boston with the grit of a foot soldier.

Claire looked at a note on the desk. A call from Ginny, her genetics counselor. She probably wanted to follow up with Claire, see if she wanted

70

another counseling session. Claire frowned, crumpled the paper, and tossed it in the can beneath her desk.

She had just opened her medicine text to read about hypercalcemia when her cell phone chirped. Her phone was pink, hinting at the feminine side she sought to keep in the often manly world of medicine.

"Hello, Dr. McCall." She waited. "Hello?"

Claire looked at the digital readout of the incoming call. The number was local, one she didn't recognize.

The line went dead, leaving Claire staring at the phone, her mystery caller upset or in trouble. Or perhaps it was just a prank. She scribbled the number on a prescription pad. She didn't give her number to many people. Mostly she used it to stay in touch with John. Often they'd talk three or four times a day just to stay in touch.

There was a knock coming from the back door. It would be John, pounding to break her concentration from her studies.

"Coming!"

She opened the door to see John holding a bouquet of red roses.

"Cerelli!" She accepted the flowers and planted a kiss on his mouth.

She searched for a vase, while telling John of her mysterious phone call, and finally settled on a near-empty Tupperware tea jug in the refrigerator in the staff lounge.

"Why don't you call the number?"

It was the obvious solution. "But what'll I say? Hello, I'm just calling to find out who you are."

"You'll know what to say. You always do."

She shrugged. "Cursed with the gift of gab, I guess."

Claire picked up the phone and dialed the number and listened. "Nobody's home."

John rubbed his hands together. "Or they're dead."

"That's not funny!" She held up her hand suddenly. Someone was picking up.

It was a man's voice. "You've reached the Chisholms'. Leave us a message after the beep."

John held up his hands. "Well?"

Claire pressed a red button to terminate the call. "It was an answering machine. A man's voice. Definitely local. Very country." She imitated it. "'You've reached the Chisholms'.'"

"So, who are they?"

She thought for a moment before the answer clicked. "Lena Chisholm. I gave her my cell-phone number yesterday."

"Who's she?"

"She's a young woman I treated. Her husband hits her. Busted her eyebrow wide open and gave her a nasty sprained ankle when he shoved her down the stairs."

"She told you this?"

"Didn't have to. I could tell." She hesitated. "We need to go out there."

"What? Uninvited?"

"She could be in trouble. I told her to call if she wanted help."

"You don't know she's in trouble, Claire. How long ago did she call?"

"Right before you knocked."

"Okay, she probably couldn't get to the phone or something. You said yourself, she has a sprained ankle. Call and leave a message."

Claire thought about arriving unexpected at Billy Ray's door. It might not be pretty. She picked up the phone and keyed in the number again. After listening through the message, she begin to speak slowly, praying that Billy wouldn't answer the phone. "Lena, this is Dr. McCall. I'm just calling to follow up your clinic visit to make sure everything was working out—"

"Hello."

Relief. It was Lena's voice. "Lena! Are you okay?" She made herself slow down and lowered her voice, as though she was in the room with her. "Is your husband home?"

"No. I'm alone."

Claire looked at John and passed along the message by shaking her head. "I was concerned about you. Are you okay?"

She sniffed. "I'm okay."

"You called me. Has Billy Ray been hitting you?"

"William Raymond would never do that. He loves me."

"Is he out with his friends?"

Lena sighed, then answered, "Yes."

72

"Were you afraid, Lena? Is that why you called?"

"I got my stitches wet washing my hair. I wanted to know what I should do." She paused. "But I thought it was stupid to bother you, so I hung up."

She listened to Lena's answer, knowing it wasn't really why she had called. Then: "Listen, Lena, I know what it's like to be with a man with a violent temper. My father was a different man when he was drinking."

"William's not like that. He only drinks a beer or two. He says it helps him bowl better 'cause he can relax."

Billy had smelled like more than beer yesterday. Claire understood Lena was covering for him. She just couldn't understand why. Maybe Lena was just too terrified to tell. "I want you to keep your appointment for next week. I need to look at your ankle and remove the sutures."

"Okay." *Sniff.*

Claire took a deep breath. "Listen, Lena. I keep this phone on all the time. You have my permission to use it anytime. Call me if you're afraid."

The line went dead again.

Claire turned to John and shook her head. "She's in denial. Or just covering for him. She keeps saying he loves her, and he wouldn't hit her. Anyway, I think we can relax for now. She said she's alone."

"So she's okay until this Billy Ray gets home."

The thought hit her in the gut. "From what I saw in the chart, she seems to come into the clinic after a weekend."

John nodded and Claire sat down at her desk and sighed. "I've still got paperwork to finish."

"I can wait." He walked around and sat in a second chair next to her bookshelf. "This was going to be a big day for us, Claire."

She shook her head. She had hoped he wouldn't bring it up. "D day."

"D day," he repeated.

"I really don't want to talk about it, John. I just want to get my paperwork finished and go home for a nice long bath."

"You can't just ignore it, Claire."

"Watch me."

"Claire."

"Can't you leave it? I just want a normal life. Work, family, friends. I don't want to spend my whole life thinking about ending up like Wally."

"Claire, you said you wanted to know. *We* wanted to know, so we could plan the future, remember?"

"Maybe I've changed my mind. Getting some test result isn't going to change the future. My DNA has been set ever since that fateful joining of Wally's—"

"I know the biology, Claire. But we've been through this. A thousand times. We talked to Ginny at the center. We've talked to your mom. We prayed. The test won't change anything, but at least we'll be able to plan."

And you can avoid a life of misery like Della. Lovely Della McCall, once the queen of the Apple Blossom Parade, now the nursemaid to a slobbering invalid.

The abruptness of her thought made her drop her head into her hands. Della seemed able to see the old Wally she loved through the HD. Sometimes all Claire saw was the drunk that drove her away. After a few long seconds, she held up her hands. "I know all this, John. And I above all people know the value of being able to plan for the future. But I'm just not ready, I guess. I know I've got to trust God regardless of the answer, but maybe I'm just not as strong as I need to be."

"You're strong, Claire. The strongest."

"But maybe I'm afraid, okay? I'm afraid I won't be ready to face what comes next if I know some ugly disease is just around the corner ready to pounce."

"I'll be there with you."

"Maybe once you know what's coming, you'll feel different."

"Claire, that's unfair, you know I'm here—"

"Look, John, I don't want to go into this. It's been a rough day. I lost it in the genetics clinic, I blew up at a patient, I snapped at my nurse, and now you want to pressure me into finding out the future. Well, maybe I just don't want to know!" she yelled. "Maybe I just want a normal life." She pushed away a stack of charts. "There are enough problems here for me to fill my time. I just want to help these people." She started to cry. "I just want to have one day where I don't worry about ending up like my daddy."

John's mouth hung open, unspeaking. He walked forward and put his arms around Claire.

With some reluctance, she surrendered to his coaxing.

"I'm sorry."

"Me too." She wiped her eyes.

"Help me, Claire," he whispered. "I don't know what to do to help."

She pushed free from his embrace. "Don't try to find a solution, John. Just let me be. I don't need a knight to rescue me." She picked up a chart and opened it to the face sheet of intake information. "If you want to rescue someone, why don't you rescue lovely Lena when her husband shows up drunk enough to kill her."

"Claire, I'm—"

She held up her hand. "Listen, I've still got charts. Why don't you go on? I'll just call Mom to pick me up when I'm done."

His upper lip stiffened like it always did when he was trying not to show his disappointment. He studied the chart in his hand for a moment, then handed it back to Claire. "Fair enough." He nodded and walked slowly from the office. She heard the back door open, and then John's voice. "Your maintenance man is sitting in his truck. He was there when I came in, too."

Suddenly Claire remembered her promise to cut Cyrus's hair. Was he just sitting out there waiting for her? "Oh dear," she said, running out after John, "I forgot all about him."

She made eye contact with John, who whispered, "Should I stay?"

She waved him on, and said Cyrus wouldn't be any problem. She walked to the door of the truck where Cyrus sat in the heat without the AC. At least his window was down. "I'm sorry, Cyrus. Were you waiting for me?"

He nodded and lifted his dark curls from his collar.

"Come on back in. I didn't realize you were waiting."

"It don't matter. I knew you were busy."

She walked into an exam room and selected her tools, a sharp pair of scissors, and a number-twenty scalpel blade to shave his neck. Cyrus watched with interest until she snapped the blade onto a knife-handle. His eyes widened from lazy slits.

"You're not going to use that to—"

"Relax, Cyrus. It's only to finish up. I'm going to use the scissors."

She looked at his hair for a moment and decided that cutting it after a day's work in and around the office had produced an oily challenge. She picked a little twig from his bangs. "You must have been trimming the shrubs."

"The boxwoods are growing great."

She looked at the little wash-up sink. "Scoot your chair over here and wet down your hair. I think I have some shampoo in my Nike bag. I keep it here in case I want to go up to the fitness center in Carlisle after work."

"You work out?"

She smiled and admitted, "Well, I did once." She shrugged. "But I'm ready in case the urge hits."

She found the shampoo and turned on the faucet. "Tilt your head back. There." She began massaging the lather into his curls. Cyrus seemed nervous, shifting first left then right in his seat.

"I thought you were just going to cut it."

"You can't expect me to cut it before it's clean." She continued to massage his scalp into a thick lather. The action brought memories of cutting her twin's hair, something he'd let only her do until she left for Boston. It was always a moment of bonding for the twins. Clay and Claire McCall, so alike, and so very different.

Suddenly she didn't feel like talking. And fortunately, Cyrus was too inhibited, or too put back by the treatment of having his hair washed. She cut it to fall above his ears, pausing only once to ask him if he approved of the length. Then she soaped and shaved his neck with the scalpel with light short strokes. She balanced the blade in her hand when she was done, enjoying the feel of the cool steel handle against her fingers.

"I'll clean this mess up," he said.

"And I'll work on my charts."

She watched as he studied himself in the mirror above the sink. He seemed okay with her job. He wasn't smiling, but at least he didn't faint.

A few minutes later, he stopped at her desk. "I'd better get going."

"Not so fast. Now I need a return favor."

"I need to be going."

"Me too. Can you give me a lift? I'll come in on Saturday and finish my paperwork."

He agreed. At his truck he moved a toolbox and a collection of paper and foil fast-food wrappers from the passenger seat to make room.

"You were quite impressive helping me out with little Stevie like you did."

"It was nothing."

"Oh, yes, it was. I could have never controlled him to get the IV without you." She studied his nonresponse. "And if the truth be known, you gave me the idea to relieve the vacuum in the bottle like I did."

She watched as the corner of his mouth turned up. He didn't look half bad with his new haircut. Her sister Margo would have called him "hot." But somehow Claire hadn't gotten used to calling handsome men "hot." "Buff" maybe, or even "hunk," but not "hot." She smiled at him, knowing his concentration was on the road. *Yes, Cyrus, I think I'll go with Margo's choice of words here. You are hot, aren't you?*

She looked back at the road, and the lane coming up on the right. She lifted her hand to point. "Turn here."

Surprise was evident in his response. "Here?"

"I live with my parents. My dad is ill. I help take care of him."

Cyrus stayed quiet and drove up the lane, pulling to a crunchy stop in the gravel lane in front of the house. She let herself out. "Thanks."

He pulled away as she paused on the porch for inventory. She hadn't talked to her mother since the test, so she needed to be ready for the reaction.

She went straight through the living room to the kitchen, where she found her mother slicing potatoes to mash. It was one of the few dishes that Wally enjoyed and didn't choke on or spit out. Della put her hand to her mouth. "I've been so worried—"

Claire held up her hand. "I chickened out. I didn't get my test results. I've already been through this with John and I don't want to talk about it."

Della tried to protest, but Claire cut her off. "Why don't you let me finish up? I'll feed Wally. Go to a movie in Carlisle. You need a break."

"I—well, I could use the time to get groceries."

"Go," Claire said, picking up a pan and putting it on the stove.

Della put her hands on her hips. Claire could feel her stare drilling into her soul. "Look, Mom, I'll talk when I'm ready. I'm just not ready."

Her mother nodded and pulled off her apron, the one she wore when she fed Wally. The one with a hundred stains from feeding fiascos, the result of trying to stuff a meaningful amount of food into a moving target.

Claire cooked, fed Wally, put on his extra-large nighttime diaper, and finally found solace in a wonderland of bath bubbles. She dried her hair, kissed her hand, which she transplanted to her father's forehead, and retreated to her room.

There, long after Della returned from a rare moment without Wally, Claire lay staring at the ceiling listening to her father's noises. Gentle thumping of his arms and legs against the padded rails, whistling sounds as his feet slid across the sheets. Grunting gurgling preceeded the coughing spasms that inveritably pulled Claire back from the brink of slumber time and time again.

"Oh, God," she whispered in the darkness. "I wish I wasn't Wally's girl."

Chapter Seven

'amore é svanito.
Íl mio cuore non canterá mai piú.

John turned down the opera so he could concentrate and slowed down for another curve in the aptly named road. He doubted you could find a straight stretch of any significant length on a briar. He squinted at a mailbox as the light from his Mustang's headlamps illuminated it. "Forty-four Briary Branch Road."

I've still got a ways to go. Lena's chart said eighty-two.

The hills leading toward the Allegheny Mountains south of Stoney Creek were sparsely populated with poultry farms with their long barns, which stayed lit long after sundown. But here, where the road began to wind up toward Blue Knob, the forest was too thick for agriculture, and the only clue that anyone populated the trees beyond the narrow roadbed were the uniform mailboxes that stuck out from the tangle of sweet honeysuckle and briars.

He passed another mailbox and then another a quarter mile up the road before he needed to downshift to a lower gear. With the grade getting steeper, the houses were even less frequent and John's music more out of place.

He wasn't sure what he should do once he got there. Or why he had convinced himself to try to find her on a lonely Friday night. But maybe that was just it, he thought. He was lonely, and he found solace in his music and in his convertible, driving in the country with the wind tangling his curls. At first his drive had been random, turning first right, then left, then heading toward the mountains, perhaps hoping to escape his wounded heart. He'd sat watching the sun go down from an overlook which gave him a view into West Virginia. There, he sang along with his music, and thought about Claire and the past that they'd shared.

After soothing his aching soul, John descended from the mountain-top and saw the lane that sparked the thought that he would at least drive by to see where Claire's patient had endured such torture. There was nothing else to do. His Friday night plans for a celebration with his fiancée were trashed. Perhaps he should do as Claire had suggested—rescue Lena when her drunken husband returned home. The idea seemed almost ludicrous to him now, as he slowed his car to a stop a few hundred feet beyond a mailbox that said "82 Briary Branch Road." There, it appeared that a logging road exited, a turn-off not much wider than his car. It disappeared into the thick woods just beyond his headlights. He pulled off the road onto the dirt logging trail and switched off the ignition. Then, listening to the night sounds, he trained his ear toward a faint light deep within the woods. He imagined it to be the house he was seeking, but the trees were too thick to be sure. The wailing, rhythmic braying of a hunting dog responded to the silence as the engine died.

Maybe this is a bad idea. Just what am I to do now? Sneak up on this house by the moonlight, and wait for some giant redneck to beat up his wife? And what if he does show up? Then how do I explain what I'm doing?

But John was unafraid of the dark, and intrigued by the thought of collecting some helpful social background for Claire. If nothing else, perhaps he could reassure her that he snuck a peek at a happily married couple playing Scrabble at the dining room table. Claire always felt more responsibility for others' actions than she needed to. Perhaps this was just another example of her oversensitive conscience, a remnant left over from a life where she learned too young that fathers and husbands can be cruel. After all, hadn't Lena denied it all?

The thought prompted him to slip out of the car, over his door, not through it, as he didn't want to slam it shut and stir up whatever monster hound was waiting to sing again. He backtracked up the road, wishing he hadn't left his keys in the ignition, but telling himself that no one would steal a car from the middle of nowhere. The moon was out enough to create dim shadows, so he stayed on the grass beside the road where the light was poor, but he was less likely to be seen by the hungry dogs. Besides, walking here was quieter than the gravel. He paused at the mailbox and squinted toward the light, which he could now see was on the apex of a detached garage. A steep bank fell off beginning three feet from the road's edge, descending into a thicket of scratchy torture. If he wanted to get a better look at the house, he'd have to use the narrow yard on the other side of the lane. He dashed from tree to tree, pausing at each one to catch his breath and question his sanity. There were two vehicles in a gravel driveway, a Toyota sedan, circa 1992, and a fairly new red Dodge Ram pickup. It appeared Billy Ray must be home already and he drove a much nicer vehicle than his wife. The house was dark except for a single light in the front window. He studied the front yard and, hearing no monster dog, crept to a vantage point just beyond a large bush in front of the house. His heart pounded as he ventured a peek around the bush. He could see a young woman sitting alone on a couch with her foot propped up on a pillow. He quickly looked behind him, suddenly afraid because of the absence of the woman's husband. If he wasn't with her, then would he be coming home soon? He studied the garage, which was dark except for the single light at the apex of the roof. The house itself was a small ranch, perhaps two bedrooms, with pale aluminum siding that looked blue-gray in the moonlight. The only noise, beyond John's own breathing, was a chorus of cicadas and frogs.

He stood just enough to see over the bush again. Lena was stretched out on the couch reading a dimestore romance with a couple clutched in a tangle of desire on the cover. From his vantage point, he could almost make out the title. She wore only a short summer nightie and had her hair up in a thick, blue towel. He squinted at her flimsy top which was buttoned only partway above her slender waist.

John ducked down again, his heart racing, his conscience screaming. Whatever stupid curiosity had brought him this far had to be controlled. He couldn't just knock on the door and ask her how she was doing. And the more he looked at the size of the truck in the driveway, the more he could imagine the gorilla that must drive it. Claire hadn't really mentioned what he was like, but no one would be happy to see a man peeking through the window at his wife. No, he needed to retreat to a safe spot to watch until he returned, or just get out of there to the safety of his car so he could get back to Stoney Creek. Life was too short to be pulverized for being a Peeping Tom.

He dashed back across the yard in full retreat, not bothering to avoid the sticks which snapped under his feet and set off the braying of the hounds.

He prayed they were chained or behind a fence somewhere out of reach. He slowed only when he'd reached the mailbox again, covering the one hundred meters faster than he'd run since college. *This is insane!* He chided himself. *The love of that woman has finally driven me to the brink and beyond.*

He sped up again to jump the driver's door. He landed in his convertible with his foot squarely on the ring box on the center console.

He slid into his seat and picked up the felt box whose lid was now twisted at an odd angle and flattened by the impact. He felt like cursing. This was supposed to be a night for celebrating. Instead, he'd spent the night alone, fantasizing about what might have been, fighting off voyeuristic urges, and smashing Claire's ring box. It snapped open at an odd angle. In the dim light, the setting appeared unscathed.

He wanted to laugh, even cry, but at the moment, he just felt a little stupid. He took a deep breath and switched his ignition far enough to run his CD player. There, in the stillness of the little logging road, he answered the symphony of insects with the quiet music of the opera.

He tilted his head back to still his racing heart and lost himself in the anguish of the song.

L'amore é svanito. Love is gone.

Il mio cuore non canterá mai piú. My heart will never sing again.

Non tenere stretto l'amore. Don't hold tight to love.

Se lo lasci libero, tornerá da te. It will return if you only set it free.

John took a deep breath and let the music transform him, letting the emotion of the music nudge his soul to the edges of human emotion, from anguish to love and back again.

He listened with his eyes closed, aware of only the song. As he listened, he shut the little box in his hand and gripped it as he began to sing.

Lascia libero l'amore. Let love go.

Cosí prenderá le ali e tornerá. Give it wings so it will return.

Lasciolo in libertá. Give it freedom.

Dagli il volo. Give it flight.

John's heart thrilled. His grip tightened on the little box, as tears could not be held back behind his eyelids. Emotion was leading.

He started the car, still clutching the box, and slowly backed onto Briary Branch Road, intending to leave. Then he paused, accepting the message of the music.

He'd wanted to reclaim Claire as his own. Love had driven him to spend countless hours helping with Wally, to move to a small town, which meant spending more of his work week on the road. He loved her. He wanted her. But he'd lost her. She wasn't going anywhere close to that genetics clinic anytime soon. And as far as John was concerned, that meant the ring wouldn't be hers until she did.

Claire was like a beautiful dream. But the dream was fading with the reality of the approaching dawn. The music swelled. His emotions rose with each gripping phrase, until he was experiencing each note, his soul buoyed and crashing with every rise and fall of the melody. The words were not just those of the wail of a man's lost love. They were John's words, the song speaking to him, a song played on the strings of his own life, a song of tragedy and sorrow.

L'amata mia é andata via. My lover is gone.

Lascia libero l'amore. Cosí prenderá le ali e tornerá. Lasciolo in libertá. Dagli il volo. Let love go. Give it wings so it will return. Give it freedom. Give it flight.

John mouthed each word as his hand weighed the little ring box. He glanced at the crimped box, a metaphor of his ruined relationship with Claire. The felt was soiled from mud, the top unhinged and dented. This ring was for Claire McCall, intended for no one else. "Let love go," he sang.

Then, with the swiftness of a dove flushed from its roost, he launched the box from his hand into the dark thicket. He watched it fly in a high graceful arc, then lost it in the trees. He would not be bound by love. He would let Claire go.

John depressed the accelerator, and let the music guide him home.

Lena turned her attention away from the novel in her hand to listen to old Jeb, Billy Ray's best bear bagger. She didn't even know what kind of dog he was. She only knew if Billy Ray cared for her half as much as he did that dog, then everything would be all right. Old Jeb treed six bears for Billy Ray last fall, three times what he was allowed to take, but he'd gone right on hunting, leaving long before sunup with his new pickup and his little satellite dish tracker and heading up the logging road somewhere below Blue

Knob. There, he'd fix up old Jeb with a transmitter on his collar and let him go with the rest of the nameless hounds. Then, Billy Ray would sit in his truck and drink his favorite beverage until the dogs stopped moving. Lena heard that even old three-adjective Eddie had killed one last year. And if he could do it, there couldn't be much in the way of brain cells required.

Old Jeb brayed again and made the fine hairs stand up on the back of her neck. She didn't like it out in the country so far, alone at night. Every time old Jeb would bark, she imagined some large animal on the prowl, or worse. She knew it wasn't rational to worry so. But she'd seen enough of the big bad world on *Oprah* to know that she wasn't the only woman in the world with justified fears of men.

And so she retreated back into her fantasy life after Jeb settled down, whatever rabbit or possum smell he'd remarked about having drifted on by. She looked at her nightgown. She'd worn the short one, planning for a little romance once William Raymond returned from the office. Once she'd even let it slip, telling Billy Ray how he was finally home from his hospital rounds and where would she put all the flowers he was constantly bringing her? He'd looked at her funny and said he wanted to play doctor all right. She'd giggled and taken him in her arms.

But she'd seen less and less of Billy Ray lately. And more and more of William Raymond. It seemed so much nicer when Billy was gone. Oh, he was perfectly fine when he was sober—a perfect ... well as perfect a gentleman as any man living in the shadow of Blue Knob could be. But when Billy Ray was drinking, he was a different cowboy.

And so tonight, she turned her attention from Jeb's barking to the novel in her hand, and played the game that made her life tolerable. She'd played it so well lately, and so often, she was having a little trouble separating the two. She looked down at the novel in her hand. *I'm sure all the doctors' wives will be raving over this at the next book club. But I suppose William won't let me go. He's always insisting on taking me off to the country club for dinner.*

She fluffed the pillow beneath her swollen ankle. *If I had just stuck to my guns and refused to go to the Alps skiing, I wouldn't have to be sitting here alone while my friends are at the club.*

Lena read until eleven, and then started dreading Billy Ray's return. The later he came in, the more time he'd have had to drink.

She brushed out the tangles in her hair, then hopped to their squeaky double bed and collapsed into a fitful sleep.

In the early hours of the morning, she heard thumping on the front door. It was a playful rhythm. "Knock, knock-knock, knock-knock . . . knock-knock."

Billy Ray must have lost his keys again. Well, he's out of his mind if he thinks I'm going to hop out there in front of Eddie dressed like this. He'll just have to figure out I've left the back door unlocked for him as usual.

The thumping stopped, and she listened for a while, drifting back to the edge of wakefulness and slumber. *Billy Ray must have gone to the back door. At least he's trying to be quiet.* She closed her eyes and took a deep breath, willing herself to rest, concentrating on her fantasy world where life was easy. Sleep rescued her as she dreamed of William coming home . . .

Sharp neck pain compelled her back into consciousness, suddenly aware of the weight of someone smashing her head into her pillow. She tried to scream. *I can't breathe!* Facedown, she gasped for air as her head was snapped back by a hand in her hair. That's when she took in her first scent of him, the stale stench of whiskey, an unmistakable Billy-Ray trademark. She screamed, "I'm sorry I didn't come to the door. I didn't want Eddie to see me like—" Her head slammed forward again, this time knocking the headboard.

For the next moments, Lena fled into a world where little girls are never mistreated by their fathers, where flowers grow, and rain, when it comes, is always gentle and soft. It was the imaginary world where William Raymond protected her from harm and caressed her cheek when she cried.

Her own scream jolted her back to reality. The weight lifted. And he was off, finished with his need for control. She glanced at the full-length mirror by the bed. The only image she had was a reflection of him dressing to leave. He looked back at her, illuminated only by the moonlight through the window. He was wearing a mask! Not like a bandit, but more like the ones she'd seen doctors wear on TV or at her dentist's office. She dropped her head back on the pillow and began to sob. Was this some kind of a sick game for him, a drunken version of his idea of playing doctor?

Was he just seeking revenge because she'd refused him his quick fix before he left for the bowling alley?

She listened as he stumbled away, leaving her alone and confused. Billy Ray was back. And she was done with William Raymond. This was too bad to even pretend away. There, in the quietness, she vowed her revenge. Billy Ray had crossed the line. He'd never forced himself on her before; the marriage act had always been his selfish way of making things right. But now he'd ruined that.

So now, she vowed to make him pay.

And that's when the heaving anguish in her soul began to fuel a plan for freedom.

What he'd done exactly didn't scare him until he'd turned off the music and his head began to clear. *Oh, God,* he prayed, *what have I done?*

He'd been lost in the emotion of the opera, lost in the moment. The hour was late. The time had vanished in his search to soothe his loss. He began a frantic search for clues that it was all a nightmare. *Claire's ring. I've got to find the ring.* John's hands searched the crevices beside his seat where he'd hidden it earlier. "Let this be a dream. Let me wake up," he mumbled.

But it was no dream. He'd thrown away the ring in a fit of despair, driven by the music and his disappointment of the day. He shook his head and tried to formulate a plan.

He had no choice. He'd have to go back and get it. He slammed his hand against the steering wheel. He was already back in Stoney Creek. He shook his head and reminded himself of the advice he'd heard from his father a hundred times. *"Wait long enough past each mistake to laugh, and then you'll have the perspective to act without reacting."*

I'll bet my father never threw a three-thousand-dollar engagement ring into the woods. He turned left into the small parking lot in front of his duplex. He could imagine the howls at the next Cerelli family gathering when he told them about this. He wished his mother had never dragged him off to the opera as a child. Maybe then he would have kept his head. Maybe if he called his father, he'd feel bad enough about passing along his impulsive Italian personality to help him out, maybe even float him a loan for another ring.

He limped from his car, more from pain in his heart than any pain in his feet. He entered the front door wondering if those stupid metal detectors he'd seen back at Leonard's Hardware could ever help him find the ring. *As if I wouldn't get attacked by that monster dog if I went out there anyway.*

He trudged to the refrigerator where he stared at the meager offerings. The last thing—in fact the *only* thing—he'd had since a bowl of Captain Crunch cereal yesterday morning was two double malt specials at Fisher's Cafe. He needed a justification for his rash behavior. If he couldn't blame his Italian heritage, maybe he could opt for caloric deficiency. It wasn't working. He looked at the clock. It was too late to eat, and too late to call his parents for advice. He wasn't sure he wanted to hear his father laugh at him tonight anyway.

He let the refrigerator door drift shut, then pushed it tight to seal it. He ran his fingers through his hair and sighed. *How could I have thrown away the ring?* Now even if things would change with Claire, and even if he knew the time was right for a second proposal, she would never believe he was sincere if he didn't have a ring.

He thought back to comments Claire had made over the prior weeks since his move to Stoney Creek. She'd talked in playful jest, but often enough to make it clear. She wanted that ring. It seemed to John she needed that specific ring, as if by having the same ring, she could erase all the horror that had intervened since he'd given it to her the first time.

He'd just have to figure out a way to get it back. Monster dog or no monster dog. He'd just have to get a flashlight and look. Or wait for daylight and risk meeting the gorilla with the red truck face to face. He prepared for sleep and hoped for a revelation.

Maybe things would seem better in the morning. He was too tired to face returning to Briary Branch Road before then anyway. He set his alarm to sound with the arrival of the sun and then collapsed, praying for a solution, some light that would offer some hope for a reasonable conclusion to his misery.

Lena lay staring at the mirror beside the bed, studying her dim reflection looking back at her. When she finally slept, there were no dreams of bliss and beauty to embrace her. Her dreams were alive with pain, sensations of suffocation, and deep tearing angst that offered no respite from reality.

She opened her eyes at sometime past sunrise, suddenly aware and amazed that she'd been able to sleep at all. Methodically, she rehearsed her plan, hoping it wouldn't be too late to follow through. She extended her hand behind her, slowly sliding it in Billy Ray's direction. She met only cool sheets. He hadn't dared to return to their bed. She held still and concentrated on the noise coming from the other room. Billy Ray was snoring peacefully. She moved slowly so as not to awake the pain in her ankle, and not to awaken Billy Ray.

She winced at the squeaking of the bed, and slowly turned her head from side to side, accessing a new agony at the base of her skull. She glanced back at the bed to see the scarlet stain she'd left behind, then touched herself to discover the source of yet another ache. She slipped on a pair of jeans, holding her breath as she pulled them across her still-swollen ankle. Then, she held first the bedposts, then the dresser, and then the door frame to assist her to the den where her husband had passed out, fully clothed, on the couch. She lifted her crutches from the floor and worked her way to the kitchen to retrieve the keys to the large oak gun cabinet in the den. With trembling hands, and a resolve to be free, she unlocked the cabinet and selected the only weapon she'd ever fired, a Remington semi-automatic twelve-gauge shotgun. Running away would have been a whole lot cleaner, but she knew he'd come for her. And after last night, she knew there was only one answer. His warning echoed in her mind: *Don't you leave, baby. I'll find you.*

And so she hoisted the weapon into her arms, and realizing she couldn't hold the shotgun and the crutches together, she quietly laid the crutches aside and limped back to the couch using the gun for a cane. Then she steadied the gun against her shoulder and shoved the other end up under Billy Ray's chin. As she did, the rage within her bubbled up again and she paused for a moment to jab the barrel deeper into his neck.

His Adam's apple bobbed up against the cold steel shaft, and he began to awaken with a gurgled snort.

"Good-bye, Billy Ray," she whispered.

Her index finger flexed. He opened his eyes to meet hers just as she depressed the trigger. The look of terror made it all worthwhile.

Chapter Eight

~~~~~~~~~~~~~~~~~~~~~~

Claire stood silently watching her mother at the kitchen table reading her Bible. Even with the relaxed look of contentment on her face, Della looked older than Claire had remembered. The years with Wally were taking a toll. The early years of alcohol had been tough, the later years with Huntington's even tougher.

Claire hesitated to speak. She knew the importance of this time alone for her mother. If anyone modeled the need for silence and solitude within a frenzied life, it was she. But when Della looked up, she nodded for her daughter to join her.

She didn't speak, only returned to the passage in front of her, a passage yellowed with a highlighter and punctuated with notes in the margin. Claire poured a cup of coffee and sat across the linoleum-topped table from her mother.

Summer Saturday mornings were made for an extra cup of coffee enjoyed with the morning paper, a chance to wash the car, mow the lawn, or read a favorite mystery. Other grandmothers were out early to watch the children play soccer on a dew-laden field or off to Ruritan Park to watch a grandson in a Little League tournament. But that was not the life meted out to Della McCall. Every day for her was much the same. Wally came first.

"Do you ever feel like killing him?"

The initial startle on Della's face melted when her eyes met Claire's. She softened, hesitated, then nodded her response with a sigh. She closed her Bible and pulled her coffee mug up to her chest with both hands. "Almost every day."

"Last night, I lay awake until morning, listening to him move, and I thought of how difficult life is for him . . . and us. And I found myself fantasizing about ending his torment, just a little morphine and he'd—"

She put her hand to her mouth. The thoughts had made her feel guilty. Speaking them was even worse.

"Relax, Claire. Everyone dealing with a chronic illness like HD has thought like that. The fact that it scared you is what means you're going to be okay."

She nodded at her mother. Della could see through her soul like a sister. "Thanks."

A moment later, Claire continued to vent. "When I lived in Boston, the threat of HD hung like a cloud over my head, but I seemed able to work and forget. A fifty-fifty chance seemed like a mathematical probability, somehow remote, something for Margo and Clay to deal with. I was away, and busy. I was able to cope."

Her mother nodded.

"Here, as much as I knew it was right to return and help, the fifty-fifty threat seems to have grown." She looked down. "I can't get away. Every evening it's the same. Feed him, talk to him, and wonder what's behind his silent, darting eyes."

"He's still in there, Claire. As bad a father as he was, this HD has given him a frame of reference, some glimmer of understanding of what has been going on for years."

"How do you do it? How do you keep going?"

"Some days I don't. Some days I don't think I can change one more diaper for a man who won't speak to me for days, and then only curses." She took a sip of coffee and wiped her eyes with the back of her hand. "And then God will let me see a glimmer of my old Wall. And that's all it takes to help me go another day."

"I'm not sure he knew who I was last night."

"Oh, he knows all right. When you were away, he talked of you every day. Losing Clay was tough, don't misunderstand me. But Wally and Clay were always at odds, much like Wally and his father were." Della reached over and squeezed Claire's hand. "He feels like he is responsible for one good thing on this earth. It's the only thing he feels good about."

Claire wasn't getting it. "One thing?"

"You, dear. Your father is proud of you."

Claire dropped her head and stared at the mug of coffee in her hand. The irony was not lost on her. The very thing he was proudest of, the fact that his seed had brought her into being, was the very thing she hated the most. "I'm not sure I can keep this up." She kept her eyes on the table. She liked order, predictability. She liked her coffee the same way every morning: straight up with two tablespoons of French vanilla creamer. Nothing about life with HD offered predictability. "Why don't we put him in a nursing home? What would be wrong with that? You need a life." She set down the mug. "If it's the money, Grandma Elizabeth will come through. I've heard her say as much."

"The time's coming, Claire. I know that. But months ago I made a promise to keep him here as long as I could."

"So how can you make it? Who pays the bills since you've stopped work?"

"I get his disability check." She stood to refresh her coffee. "And your uncle Leon adds a little each month. I couldn't eat without that."

That her uncle Leon would pitch his brother a bone surprised Claire. He had always been Grandpa McCall's golden boy, the one who towed the line and joined the family business of McCall Shoes. And he looked with scorn on his brother who ran off to the Navy, off to Vietnam, then returned to a small town that had expectations of McCall boys. It was an expectation that Wally couldn't meet, and one he lost in an enthusiasm for moonshine and beer.

The wonder must have registered on Claire's face, because her mother explained. "Oh, you know Leon. He has his McCall pride. But I did work in that blasted shoe factory for close to twenty years, so he calls it my 'pension.' It's not enough for steak, but I can do hamburger once in a while. I think down inside even Leon has a good heart. He won't let us starve."

"Wally chokes on steak anyway."

Della smiled. "You see, everything works out." She sat back down. "He's not going to last forever, Claire. You should make plans to restart your training. Go back to Boston. Take that prissy Beatrice Hayes' spot. You could operate circles around that girl."

"Mom!"

"That's what you told me. That backstabber won't be half the surgeon you will."

"I can't go back to surgery." She held up her hand and tried to hold it still, but the pressure to demonstrate her rock stability made her nervous.

She closed her wiggling fingers into a fist. "What if I began to twitch? I'll cut someone's aorta or something."

"So get your test result so you can know. Then go to back to your love of cutting with a clear conscience."

"You think I'm negative."

"It doesn't matter what I think."

"Fifty-fifty," she moaned. "Did John tell you about my clinic visit?" Della shook her head.

"He wants me to get the result."

"I know."

The phone rang. Della rose to get it. "Ugh," she said, "the day begins." She picked up a wireless phone from the kitchen counter. "Hello."

Claire listened to the one-sided conversation.

Della brightened, then shook her head. "No, but Claire's right here." She hesitated, then covered the mouthpiece and lowered her voice. "It's John's father. He wants to speak to you."

John's father, Tony Jr., was a pudgy man full of heart and smiles. In her years at Brighton, he had treated her like a daughter.

Claire enjoyed going to the Cerelli house as much to see John's parents as to spend time with their oldest son. Tony was constantly saying corny things about the old country even though he'd only spent his first six years there and his Italian was limited to a few folk songs he'd learned as a boy. She wasn't even sure that "Mama mia!" was authentic Italian, or just authentic Tony putting on the Italian show that he played with such passion.

But a call from Tony was unexpected. Perhaps he knew of D day, and she'd have to explain yet again why she didn't know. She took a deep breath and prepared to justify her flight from the genetics clinic. "Hi, Pops."

"Morning, Claire." He chuckled and quickly went on. "I'm lookin' for John. He doesn't happen to be with you, does he?"

The tension in his voice wasn't camouflaged by his laughter. "No. What's up?"

"Oh, you know John. It's probably nothing. Some manufactured crisis."

She felt her throat tighten.

"He called early this morning while Mary and I were out in the garden. His message indicated he was in some sort of a jam. He'd been up half the night. I couldn't really make sense of what he was sayin', to tell you the truth."

"A jam? I haven't seen him since yesterday around six. Just what did he say?" *And why didn't he call me if he was in trouble?*

"Nothing too important, I'm sure. He said something about needing advice. He'd done something stupid and sounded sorry for it, that was all. I figured it had something to do with you, maybe a lover's spat or something. I was sure he'd be there by now, roses in hand, begging your forgiveness." He laughed again.

The roses! I left them at the office in the lounge. "I don't get it. What did he say he'd done?"

"Okay, okay, I forget you medical types need all the details. Let's see, what did he say? I shouldn't have erased the darn message so I could remember exactly. Hmmm." He paused and imitated John. "'Uh, Pops, pick up the phone, will you? I hate this machine. I need some advice about a little jam I'm in. Aw shucks, pick up the phone, will you?'" He hesitated. "I think that's about it. So I tried calling him back, but all I get is *his* stupid answering machine."

"This is bad." Claire pushed her blond bangs back from her forehead. "Something's bad."

"Oh, don't jump to conclusions. I didn't call to worry you. I've known this boy longer than you have, remember? He's left messages like this before. Once when he thought he was failing an accounting class in college, another time when his Mustang let him down before spring break." A chuckle interrupted his message again. "You know Italians. Everything's a crisis. He probably left his Visa card at the bakery or something."

"I hope you're right."

"You be good, Mama. Come to see me soon, okay? You can bring the boy if you have to." He laughed.

She lowered her voice, not wanting to parade the relationship she had with John's parents in front of Della. She repeated the words which were a common part of the Cerelli family language. "You know I love you, Pops."

"I love you."

She heard the click signaling the end of the conversation, before looking up to meet Della's gaze. "John's in trouble of some kind. Tony doesn't know much, only that John called and said he was in a little jam." She clicked her tongue against the roof of her mouth while she pondered what to do. "Can I take some time away this morning? I've got a few house-calls to make, and maybe I'll swing by John's apartment to see what's up."

Della threw up her hands. "Hey, take all the time you need. I had my two-hour date with Tom Cruise last night."

"Mom!"

"Hey, I've still got hormones. I may be aging, but I've still got eyes."

Claire shook her head and left to get ready to go. Behind her, she could still hear her mother mumbling about Tom Cruise like he had really wowed her again.

But Claire's thoughts quickly turned away from Tom Cruise and onto John Cerelli. Something was up. Something bad. She knew him well enough to be afraid, not so much of the call he'd placed to his father, but because of the one he hadn't placed to her. If he was in trouble, and he hadn't called her, it had to be something he didn't want her to know.

And that's what made her determined to find out what had happened.

❧

Another briar pulled at the flesh of John's shoulder, making him wish for the hundredth time that he'd worn a jacket for protection. He was beyond regret at his impulsive behavior. Now, with every new scratch on his arms, he was tempted to curse his actions. It wasn't just the money. He could work hard and make up for that. It was the fact that Claire seemed so fixated on this ring as "hers." He sighed at the memory of a recent conversation.

They had stood facing each other, holding hands, on her parents' front stoop. "Do you know diamonds are like snowflakes, John? Each one is different." She leaned closer to kiss him, then pulled away at the last moment and whispered, "When the time is right for us, don't feel like you need to get me a new ring."

"Isn't it your turn? I bought the last one."

She squeezed his hand. "Be serious. The last one is perfect. Please don't trade it in."

94

He wasn't sure he understood. "Why does it matter, Claire?"

She shrugged as if it didn't, but her eyes betrayed her. "I guess I just want the original, the one intended for me. A new one would remind me of things I'd rather forget."

Now, the memories served only to mock his impulsivity. He had to continue. He dropped a handful of leafy soil mixture to the ground in front of him before glancing back up the bank toward the road. He tried to calculate just how far the mangled ring box could have flown. *It shouldn't be too far from the edge of the road. The trees are so thick it couldn't have traveled—*

A shot rang out, snapping John's thought train and calling his attention to the house beyond the trees. It was a gunshot, he was sure, an unsettling sharp contrast to the buzz of the background forest noise. The report of gunfire seemed to echo around through the thicket, as though it too was trapped, unable to escape the hollow without effort.

He strained his eyes toward the sound. The house was over that way, but invisible to him from this distance through the trees. After a moment, the gunfire was replaced by the bellowing of the dogs. This time John counted at lease three differing barks that seemed to be excited by the shot.

He looked back at the little area he'd managed to cover, a small path from the road's edge down the bank and straight into a thorny patch that only Brer Rabbit would appreciate. He searched on his hands and knees, filtering each decaying leaf through his fingers, praying that if he did find the smashed little box, Claire's precious ring would still be inside. After the single shot, there was no more gunfire mixed in with the baying hounds. He knew it wasn't hunting season, a fact that made traveling in these woods a safer venture, but in light of that, the gunfire unsettled him even more.

He focused his attention on the small area of ground in front of him, carefully mapping out a fixed pattern he would follow to be sure each inch of ground would be covered. But after twenty minutes, he had inched along only two feet, and he had more scratches than a Schnauzer in a cat fight. Disgusted at his progress, he squinted at the treetops, where the canopy of leaves filtered out the morning sun, leaving him wishing briefly for winter when the trees would be bare, but then remembering that all those leaves would be on the ground covering his little treasure below a blanket of color.

That's when he heard the unmistakable voice of the monster dog, the hound that had reported his trespass only hours before. But this time, the rhythmic lament from the hound continued, intensifying in volume and frequency. Initially, he thought the noise had trailed off to his left, likely following the scent of a frightened rodent, but as the barking grew louder, he began to hear the snap of twigs just beyond the thicket where he cowered. After a moment, he began to hear the panting breath of the beast between each wail, and he knew the dog must be closing in. John reached for a low branch of the nearest tree and pulled himself up, grabbing first one limb and then another until he flattened himself in a bearhug around the trunk, standing on a branch that sat mere inches above the snapping jaws of the biggest spotted hound he'd ever seen.

John stayed, trembling in a tight embrace with a gum tree, figuring he would either die of starvation or become a feast for the monster below. Finally the dog stopped jumping and just sat down and stared at John like he'd never seen a man up a tree before. "Nice doggy," John said quietly.

If he got out of this alive, his father was going to howl.

⁓⁕⁓

Leon McCall always called his attorney "Harvard." It was part of the informal banter between them that seemed to lessen the seriousness of the business of looking out for number one, a business where lesser-do-wells would be squashed with a frequency matched only by the Stoney Creek possum population. In fact, that's what Leon always called it: "roadkill," an unfortunate consequence of paving the way for newer and better technology.

Alfred D. Pittington never smiled when Leon called him Harvard. He preferred to forget the days he'd spent burning the midnight oil in the law library of his alma mater. But Alfred D. Pittington never smiled unless he was on the winning side of a seven-figure judgment.

"What'll it be this morning, Harvard? Oatmeal as usual for me," Leon added, winking at the waitress standing at his elbow. "And put some raisins and a banana on the side, and bring the brown sugar in a separate dish."

She wrote as he talked. He wasn't sure why. She'd taken the same order from him every Saturday for forever.

Harvard ordered more black coffee and lox and bagels. Leon knew it was because he had told Harvard that just the thought of cold, moist fish made him sick.

Leon leaned forward. "She sure is cute, but dumb as a post."

Harvard nodded. "Too young."

"You're no fun."

"So what is all the urgency? I know you didn't get me up on a Saturday morning to admire a full-figured waitress in a small-town cafe."

"You did notice."

The lawyer squinted. "Bald men have more testosterone. I read it in a magazine."

Leon grunted, then leaned forward and lowered his voice. "McCall Shoes has just endured the worst quarter ever. We're down another six percent over the same time last year and until now, that was our record low."

"What about the Eddie Bauer deal?"

"We can't make the boots fast enough for them. And that was great until they found a foreign company to make up the difference."

"What's wrong with that?"

"Now they've switched to the foreigners alone. They get twice the volume we can pump out at a cheaper price. Nobody cares if it's made in the U.S. anymore. All they care about is price."

"So what about the buyout? Is Sugimoto going to bite?"

"We're down to final negotiations. I'll bring a proposal to the board by midsummer."

"So what's the problem? The largest athletic shoe company in the world wants to rework your factory to make the shoes right here. What could be better? McCall stock is going to skyrocket."

"Exactly."

Harvard sniffed. "I don't get it. It's perfect. You have a downsloping business. This is the solution that will put you on a sailboat to retirement."

"The stock's only half mine," Leon huffed. "Or it will be."

Harvard's head started bobbing. "So this is what it's all about. You're still hung up about the will."

"And you're not? If I prosper, you prosper, that's how it works, remember?"

"Don't be greedy, Leon. You're going to be worth millions."

"It's not just the money. It's the disgrace of my father's name. Did you know Wally McCall isn't even a blood McCall at all? His father raped Elizabeth. Why, he—"

The attorney held up his hand. "You've told me the story before. But that doesn't change the fact that his name is in the will, and he gets half the estate when your mother dies."

"Did you know my mother has offered to pay for a nursing home for Wally? Do you understand how much money that's going to eat up?"

"So why is Wally at home?"

"Because I feed Della just enough to keep him there." He held up his cup and motioned for the waitress. "And I've convinced her it's best for Wally." He chuckled. "And a whole lot cheaper for Grandma Elizabeth."

The waitress came back and refilled their coffee mugs. "Creamer?" she asked, looking at Harvard.

"Just black, thanks."

She disappeared as the attorney added, "Short memory."

Leon nodded. "But the food is great, I promise. Abby should work Saturday mornings. She's great. A real looker. And smart." He hesitated. "Are you sure the will can't be contested on the basis that John Wallace McCall only left Wally a fortune because he thought he was blood?"

"I don't think it will wash." He tapped the side of his cup. "But there is another way to keep more of the cash in real McCall hands."

Leon waited and watched Harvard sip his coffee, obviously enjoying the control he had over his client. "So?"

"Keep the size of the estate down."

"I'm listening."

"If the estate is devalued, what she has to divide up will be devalued."

"I'd be shooting myself in the foot."

"Shut up and listen. You've said Elizabeth is tiring of the business. But she still has a controlling interest of stock. Tell her the bad news about the business, how McCall Shoes is going down, the worst quarter ever. The future really looks bleak, you know."

"But—"

Leon's protest was silenced by Harvard's interruption. "Offer to buy her out. From the goodness of your heart, of course. Do it now before the company goes south. She's old, after all. She shouldn't have to be the one

98

at the helm when McCall, Incorporated flops for the entire valley to see. She has other things to pay attention to, like Wally, for goodness' sake. Offer her enough so Wally will be taken care of and—"

"Buy all her stock?"

"Yes, all of it. She'll have to forfeit her position on the board, of course." He paused, making a little flare with his hand, flopping around a limp wrist. "But do it soon, before you present Sugimoto's offer. Then, once you have Elizabeth contented that she's done the best she could for her unfortunate Wally . . ."

"Sell to Sugimoto," Leon interrupted, folding his hands across his waist. "My stock value quadruples, and Elizabeth's estate stays flat. Harvard," he said, raising his coffee mug, "you're brilliant."

Claire circled the parking lot in front of John's duplex and sighed. His Mustang wasn't in his spot, and the shades were still drawn, something John the natural-light enthusiast would never permit if he were home. *Perhaps he left before dawn? Or maybe he never came home?*

She scolded herself for her runaway fears about John's crisis and concentrated on what Pops had told her. *It's nothing too important, I'm sure.*

Next she drove her blue VW bug to the office and filled her old college backpack with supplies. In went antibiotic samples, dressing supplies, saline, hydrogen peroxide, iodine solution, a glucometer, a blood-pressure cuff, and a small wrapped package of sterile instruments. In the front pocket she loaded needles, syringes, a bottle of local anesthetic, cotton-tipped applicators, and a half-dozen packaged sterile gloves, size six. She held out her fingers to convince herself of her steady hands and smiled. She'd spent last night staring at the ceiling listening to Wally when she came to a private revelation. She'd spent six weeks banging her head against the wall trying to practice Boston medicine in Stoney Creek. Here, her patients were used to medicine of a different kind. They'd hung on every word Dr. Jenkins provided, but why didn't they listen to her?

It wasn't just a gender issue. Dr. Jenkins listened, really listened, and let the patients participate in their own healing. He didn't try to force a foreign concept too quickly into what they thought was best. He adapted his treatment to their framework, and when they made a bad choice, he did the best he could to steer them in a better way.

It was no secret, of course. Dr. Jenkins had explained that she'd have some adapting to do, that the white towers of academic medicine needed to be filtered with some practicality before they'd work in Stoney Creek. And a test couldn't be ordered simply because the physician needed to cover her backside to prevent a frivolous lawsuit. Lawsuits may be a way of life for Boston, but in Stoney Creek, a test had better make a difference in a medical decision if the patient was going to pay. In Boston, medical insurance was the norm. In the areas around Stoney Creek, where Old-Order Mennonite farms were the norm, medical insurance was a worldly concession they wouldn't permit.

So she'd decided to try a new approach. She was going to listen more, and start warning her patients of their stupidity less. She'd adapt where she could, and she was going to start by making a few housecall amends.

Once her packing was complete, she headed for the first house, a brick ranch in the center of the next town of Fisher's Retreat. When Claire rapped on the front door, Mabel Henderson called, "It's open."

Claire entered the dim house which smelled of old laundry and mold. "Ms. Henderson?"

"Back here."

She followed the voice to find Mabel sitting at the kitchen table staring into an electric fan. Her bad foot was propped up on the chair beside her, not exactly above her heart as Claire had urged, but at least off the floor.

"Dr. McCall?"

Claire smiled sheepishly. "I wanted to check on your progress," she said, opening her backpack. "I brought you some more antibiotics so you wouldn't have to come back to the clinic so soon. I want you to stay off the foot, you know."

"That's why this place is a wreck. It's hard cleaning up with your foot above your heart."

You were listening. Claire nodded and put on a pair of exam gloves before unwrapping the day-old bandage. "I've been thinking about your foot. Are you willing to go to the hospital? A surgeon may need to help this drain."

She shook her head. "I'm doing just fine right here."

"Well, perhaps we need to do the best we can with what we've got to work with right here." Claire probed the area around an ulcer on the bottom of Mabel's foot near the great toe. "You see that drainage? I think you've got a trapped infection behind this eschar, uh, scab."

"I can't see it, Doc. But this diabetes is tearing up my vision."

"I want to lift off this callous here. I have some local anesthetic."

"Honey, I can't feel anything you're doing down there. You could cut my toe off right here and I doubt I'd cry one bit."

The image made Claire wrinkle her nose. Meticulously, she painted Mabel's foot with antiseptic, then taking a scalpel and forceps, she began to trim the thickened skin and the dying flesh at the base of the ulcer. She was rewarded with an ooze of tan cream. She collected some pus for a culture and cleaned the wound before placing a new dressing.

"I'll send this up to the lab in Carlisle." Claire checked her watch. "What time did you eat breakfast?"

"Around eight."

"Okay, hold out your finger." Mabel obeyed as Claire held her middle finger against the glucometer and pushed a trigger to release a small lancet. Then, she collected the drop of blood on the test paper and waited for the result. "Two eighteen," she said, scribbling a note on a piece of paper. "I want you to increase your morning regular insulin by three units."

Claire looked around the kitchen with dishes overflowing the sink. "I want you to rest on the couch. Prop your feet up on a pillow."

"It's too hot in there. The cord on the fan is too short to reach to the table in front of the couch."

Claire sighed. "I'll bring an extension cord by on Monday. I know I have one packed up somewhere."

Mabel protested, but Claire wouldn't hear of it. "It does me no good packed away. You can give it back in the winter." Then Claire attacked the dishes, shushing Mabel's protests again. "Somebody's got to do this or you'll soon have a houseful of ants." She pointed at her patient. "And you need to stay off that foot."

After the dishes, she called the cafe and talked to Mr. Knitter, who agreed to have someone deliver supper three times a week. "Make it broiled chicken or fish, maybe some rice and a salad," Claire instructed. "And no dessert. She's a diabetic."

She hung up the phone to see Mabel's eyes brimming with tears. Claire gave her a hug.

"I can't pay you today," she said.

"You already have." Claire sniffed and broke the choke hold Mabel had on her neck. She scribbled her cell phone number on the front of a yellow phone book on the table. "Use this number if you need me. Call if you start having fever, chills, or redness running up that foot."

Claire gathered her supplies and got back in her Beetle. In twenty minutes, she was sitting in front of an old white clapboard house with green shutters. She knocked on the door and waited. She heard children squealing inside and a radio. This didn't seem right. Brittany Lewis was supposed to be single.

A young mother with a baby on her hip pointed Claire around back. "She lives in the apartment downstairs. She might not be home. She works weekends sometimes."

Claire followed a decaying sidewalk around the side of the house to the back door. She knocked loudly.

"Coming!"

Brittany yanked the door open, wearing only a pair of shorts and a top to expose her middle. The look of surprise on her face told Claire she'd been expecting someone else. Her jaw slackened. "Dr. McCall?"

"In the flesh." She hesitated. "May I come in?"

"Sure, I guess. What do you want? I told that lady I'd bring my payment on Friday."

"It has nothing to do with your bill, Brittany. I came to apologize."

For the second time, Brittany opened her mouth without speaking. She pointed to a green couch. "Uh, have a seat."

Claire studied the little apartment. The furnishings were meager, but the rug was swept and the few items on the bookshelf next to the couch were evenly spaced and dusted. She squinted to read the name of a book she recognized. It was authored by Max Lucado. Claire sat and pointed to the book. "Are you a Christian, Brittany?"

She nodded.

"Good, then you'll understand why I'm here. I wanted to tell you how sorry I was not to pay attention to your real problem with having surgery for your gallstones."

Brittany shifted in her seat across from Claire. "I'm really okay now," she said, rubbing her right side.

"I heard about your father. Would you like to tell me what happened?"

She looked away. "I really don't remember much. I was only eleven. He had diabetes and went to the hospital real sick. The surgeon operated and took out his gallstones, but he died a few days later. My mom told me that gallbladder surgery is one of the most dangerous areas to operate on. It's near the liver and all." She shrugged. "That's what she said the surgeon told her."

"Listen, Brittany, a lot has changed since your father's surgery. It's much safer for you if you go in while you're not sick. And you're not diabetic like your father. It doesn't have to be such a big deal anymore." She hesitated and asked if she would call her if she had more trouble. "I'd be glad to schedule an appointment with a surgeon if you call."

"I'll think about it, okay?"

"My mother had gallbladder surgery a few years ago. She'd be glad to tell you how it was." Claire leaned forward. "You can't even see her scars. She's way over fifty and she still lays out in a two-piece."

Brittany smiled. It was a good sign, a point of contact.

Claire shook her hand and turned to go, but stopped just short of the door. She took a deep breath. She'd heard of doctors that incorporated their faith with their medicine, but she had never tried. She cleared her throat. "Would it be okay if I prayed for you? I mean, right now?"

Brittany shrugged. "I guess."

Claire spoke a simple prayer for guidance and wisdom, for release of Brittany's fears, and for a complete healing in whatever way God would see fit. With that, she winked at Brittany, taking note that for the second time that day, she'd left a patient with eyelids holding back the tears.

The third stop on her list actually turned out not to be a stop at all. Besides, she only wanted to see the patient's status to satisfy her own curiosity. When she pulled up in front of little Stevie's house, he was sitting on the front steps licking a chocolate ice-cream cone. She slowed and waved.

"Hi, Dr. McCall!" he yelled.

His speech was clear and he was licking ice cream happily. And that was enough follow-up for Claire.

Chapter Nine

By the time John heard the slow, regular crunch of the forest floor signaling the arrival of a man, he was sizing up a tree limb to snap in preparation for fighting off the monster dog. But once he got a good look at his new company, he thought he might be better off facing the dog.

If this was the gorilla, perhaps John's imagination had run away. The man stood about John's own height, although he really wasn't used to judging stature from this vantage point. He had dark curly hair, like John's, and a muscular medium frame. But what made him appear so daunting was the shotgun leveled at John's chest.

The man spit and stared at John for a minute before speaking. "Watcha doin' up there?"

"Is that your dog? Could you call him off, please?"

"I said, watcha doin'?"

John contemplated the relative value of his life, and what it might cost him if he told this stranger he'd lost a three-thousand-dollar diamond ring on his property. John opted for vague. "I'm trying not to be the big doggie's dinner."

The man nodded. "I mean before."

John Cerelli was a stickler for the truth. He knew his conscience would smite him if he lied, even if it was a self-preserving move. "I lost something around here. I was looking for it."

The man squinted and didn't move his gun.

John gestured one hand nonchalantly and tried to maintain balance on the tree limb. "Something small and metal flew out of my car. I thought it may have landed here in the trees somewhere. So I came to look. But your dog found me."

The excuse sounded so lame to John, but maybe it was just lame enough that the gunslinger would believe he didn't make it up. The man smiled. "Old Jeb thought you was a bear. I was out getting him used to the gun again. You have to fire it around them in off season. They might get jittery if they hear it only during bear season."

John felt a little jittery himself. "Do you mind calling Old Jeb off? I'm getting a little tired of this tree-hugging."

The man reached forward and took the dog by the back of the collar. John slid down the tree and looked at the bark imprints in his forearms. "Does it still run?"

"What's that?" John asked.

"Your car. When this little metal thing flew off, did it just quit running?"

"Oh no, it still runs fine. It's just that—"

"Well then, I reckon that part really wasn't that important. You'd probably best conclude your looking."

John looked at the dog, who strained against the man's grip. "Thanks. I owe you one." He backed up a step and turned to go.

The man called after him. "I wouldn't think it'd be too smart to keep snoopin' around here. There are plenty of folks out in the woods sightin' in their hunting rifles. It wouldn't do to be gettin' shot by accident."

Or getting eaten by a slobbering monster named Old Jeb. John didn't look back. He scrambled up the bank, the briars ripping at his arms. When he examined himself on the road, his forearms looked like maps with red roads. He jogged to his car, checking over his shoulder for the gunslinger. He started the Mustang and pulled back out onto the road, slowing by the spot where he'd tossed the ring to think again exactly what its direction was and where it could have fallen. *Maybe I should get a few more ring boxes and toss them out to see where they land.* He nodded. *A reenactment of my insanity. Not a bad idea.*

He checked his rearview mirror to see the man with the shotgun in the road, standing next to Old Jeb. He stomped the accelerator when he saw the man raise his gun.

It's going to be a long time before I laugh about this, Dad.

The blast from the shotgun roared in his ears and died in the trees. Billy Ray Chisholm lowered his shotgun from his shoulder and pulled on Old Jeb's collar. Then, laughing, he said, "Easy boy, just having a little fun. I was just scaring him, that's all." He laughed again and sniffed the smell of burnt tire rubber mixed with the acrid gun smoke. "That city slicker's going to have to change his shorts."

He laughed at his own joke, then pulled a cell phone from his pants pocket. "It's not right to trespass, is it, Jeb? And I wouldn't want to take the law into my own hands now, would I?"

Old Jeb walked off the road and lay down in the shade of the trees, apparently uninterested in the mystery of the intruder. If it wasn't bear, Old Jeb didn't get too excited.

Billy Ray punched a number on his cell phone, all the while still talking to his dog. "I think I'll see what Deputy Jensen has to say about trespassin'."

Claire's phone chirped just as she was pulling into her parents' gravel driveway. *Maybe Brittany has already come to a decision.*

"Hello."

"Claire."

"John, where *are* you? I've been worried."

"No need to worry. I'm in my car."

"Your father called looking for you. He said you were in some kind of trouble. I went by your apartment, and you weren't there, so I—"

"Hey, slow down, would ya? I'm okay. Just some guy-thing I wanted to talk to my father about. It's nothing for you to worry about."

"John, if you were in trouble, you'd call me, wouldn't you?"

"Claire, I'm not in any trouble. I just had a guy problem, that's all."

She huffed. *A guy problem?* "Answer my question, Cerelli. You'd come to me if you were in trouble, right?"

"I get it . . . a hypothetical situation, huh?" He paused, and she could hear the wind blowing against his cell phone. *The top must be down. He loves it that way. I'm going to have to get some leatherguard for his seats so they don't bleach in the sun.* John continued, "Sure, I'd call you. My troubles are your troubles. That's what love is all about."

He does love me, doesn't he? So why do I find myself doubting him? Do I really think our relationship would change if he knew I would get HD? But if his commitment wouldn't change, why didn't he give me the ring when he had the chance?

"Hello."

"I'm still here," she said.

"I thought you may not agree or something. Love is all about taking someone else's problems as your own, right? What was that verse you're always quoting? Greater love hath no man than this . . ."

"Than he would lay down his life for his friends," she responded.

"Uh-oh."

"What?"

"I think I'm being pulled over. Dog it! Uh, wait a second, Claire, I think this cop wants me to pull over."

She waited and listened to the wind noise die away.

"Listen, Claire. I've got a few clients to see this week over in Brighton. I figure I'll leave tonight and stay with my folks and go to our old church. I should be back Wednesday night. I'll give you a call."

She heard a deep voice asking for John's license and registration.

"I gotta go, honey. Love you."

She looked at the phone. *That was strange.*

She walked into the house to find Della in the midst of folding clothes on the kitchen table. Her mother didn't look happy.

Claire grabbed a clump of socks and began sorting. "What's up?"

"Your grandmother just called." She patted the towel she just folded. "The shoe company is having a rough time."

"How rough is rough?"

"She's afraid they may lose everything. They've lost some big contracts to the foreign markets. They just had their worst quarter in over a decade."

"She's been through down times before. She always steers 'em back."

"Leon steers 'em back is more like it." Della dropped a stack of towels into a basket. "She sounded down. She's not as spunky as she once was. She's talking about selling out."

"Selling McCall Shoes? Mom, half of Stoney Creek has worked there at one time or another. They can't just cash it in, can they?"

"No, it's not that simple. But Leon is doing the best he can to keep her from worrying about it. He has offered to buy her out for fair market value, taking into account their latest poor sales. She'll be comfortable."

"And what will Leon do?"

"He may try to keep the company going. If not, he's still young enough to switch gears and do something else."

"Grandma has wanted to travel more."

"Sure she has. She's paid her dues. It's time for her to quit. I'm glad for her, really."

Claire's mind drifted to her immediate family. "What about Daddy?"

"We've still got the disability and Social Security. We'll be okay."

Claire nodded at her mother. She wanted so much more for her than just to get by. "I'm starting to make a decent wage," Claire declared. "I'll buy you a steak now and then."

"You need to worry about yourself. I'll be fine. Besides, what I need around here isn't steak. It's a year's supply of baby food for the Wall."

Claire looked at the stack of groceries that her mother had yet to get off the kitchen counter. "I'd gag if I had to eat that stuff."

"Your father gags if I give him anything else. HD is a real bummer unless you really, really like pudding."

"No, Mom. You're wrong about this one," she said, turning away. "HD is a real bummer even if you really, really like pudding."

❧

John complied with the officer's request and handed him his license and registration. "Was I going too fast, officer?"

"No, sir." He lifted his eyes from the cards in his hand to look square in John's eyes. "I'm just following up on a trespassing complaint." He tilted his head to his right. "Seems a local up the road says a man was trespassin' on his place. Said he acted strange. Thought I should check into it." His eyes ran over the car. "Says he was driving a red Mustang convertible."

John offered a sheepish smile. "What a coincidence, huh?"

"Don't get smart with me."

John held up his hands. "Hey, it was me. But his dog chased me up a tree."

"Just what were you doing?"

John thought for a moment, then opted for vague, hoping he wouldn't be questioned. "I thought something had flown out of my car." He felt his heart quicken. "I was looking on the side of the road when a big dog tried to eat me for lunch."

The officer seemed amused. He chuckled, nodded, then retreated toward his vehicle. "I'll be right back."

John squirmed, wiped his forehead, and checked the rearview mirror for what seemed like an hour, but was actually only a few minutes.

When he returned, the officer was still chuckling. "Old Jeb probably thought he'd treed a bear." When he said it, it came out "bar." He handed John his license and registration. "Have a good day, Mr. Cerelli."

John nodded. *He must have thought my excuse was so stupid I couldn't have made it up. They'll probably laugh it up at the police station tonight.*

Lena sat on the back porch swing with an ice pack on her ankle and a cheap novel in her hand. The last few hours had seen another flip-flop in her willingness to give Billy Ray one more chance.

She had pulled the trigger, all right. But she'd forgotten to load the blasted shell into the firing chamber, so all Billy Ray got was a scare. The pin snapped, and he'd let out a blood-curdling scream and rolled off the couch facedown onto the floor.

At first, she'd thought she had killed him, but why hadn't she heard the gunfire? But Billy Ray hit the floor and rolled to his back, scrambling and clawing his way behind the coffee table where he cursed and threw the table up on its side for protection. The look of terror in his eyes was something she'd enjoy for a long time.

She'd thrown the gun on the couch and spit on the table. "I was just seeing if I could do it, that's all. But that's what you'll get if you ever treat me that way again!"

She'd limped off for a cry in the kitchen and made coffee. And that's when Billy Ray asked her what he'd done to make her so angry. He'd come in late and slept on the couch so as not to bother her, so what was all the fuss about? And in the end, she really wanted to believe that he couldn't remember, that he had suffered an alcoholic blackout. He pled. He begged for forgiveness. And when she showed him the evidence of what he'd done, he didn't even want to make up in the usual way. Instead, he sat down and cried with her, actually cried this time, and told her she was his princess and that he'd get some help before he killed her and ruined another marriage. She was right, he said. Rachel had run because he couldn't control his temper when he drank. "Lena, you've got to believe me, baby. It's going to be different this time."

So she'd given him the phone book and had him calling all over the county to find an AA meeting to attend on a Saturday. And so, shortly after he finished working with Old Jeb, he headed into Carlisle to get back on the wagon of sobriety.

The last thing he did before leaving was to fix her a lemonade and fluff the pillow under her ankle and kiss her so sweetly that she thought he really could change. She wanted to believe. He wasn't a bad man, after all. He was just a man with an alcohol problem, the man who had promised to take her away from the terror and abuse of another man she called Daddy.

Lena flipped the pages of the book, nearing the climax where the hero would re-enter and sweep his fair damsel off to a life of ecstasy. But that's when Old Jeb nuzzled her hand, making her leg jump and the pain in her neck return. "Jeb!"

She scratched the dog behind his ears and watched his eyes droop with contentment. "What's that you got, boy?" She reached for a patch of blue half in and half out of his mouth. It appeared to be felt, and was covered with dirt and Old Jeb slobber. It was a little box, like one she'd seen on the shopping channel that they nestle expensive gems in. She held up the box and shook off the moisture, then looked with kindness upon the hound and said, "Why, thank you, William, you really shouldn't have." She giggled and twisted open the dented lid. She gasped!

It was a beautiful ring, a crystal-clear stone on a shiny gold band. She looked around and clutched it to her breast. A real diamond! She had held her grandmother's, and had seen countless others at the jewelry store in Brighton. Those were so little compared to this!

Her heart began to pound as she slipped it on her finger. It seemed to fit perfectly. This had to be a sign. She'd given her husband one more chance. And then found this ring. William Raymond had returned and given her an anniversary present, the ring she'd admired in Paris on winter holiday. She giggled again and held it up to the sun.

But where had it really come from? Was this to be a gift from Billy Ray? The answer to that was a certainty. The more she knew about the real Billy Ray, the more she knew he wouldn't spend money like that—even if he had it to spend.

But still she couldn't help but think that this had happened for a reason. This ring had special meaning for her. She'd read enough love stories to know the significance of a ring, even one that ends up in the hands of one unintended. She might not know the reason now, but she had a strange feeling that in her present state of turmoil, this ring just might be the anchor to see her through the storm.

She twisted it off and examined it from every angle, polishing it gently against her T-shirt, holding it up to the sun to watch the light dance from every surface. And then she saw what cemented forever the thought that she was following destiny's bidding. The two tiny initials engraved inside the band were her own. She smiled and pulled the ring to her chest again. *M.C. Of course, William Raymond always calls me by my real name: Melinda Chisholm.*

The crunch of approaching truck tires brought her back to reality. She quickly shoved the ring in her pocket and threw the mangled box into the bushes. Whatever this ring was meant to be, she knew it wasn't meant for Billy Ray.

Chapter Ten

ven with John out of town, the week flew by. On Friday afternoon, when Claire was hoping to close the office early, she experienced the swell of the I'd-better-not-wait-out-the-weekend problems. By two, she was seeing her one o'clock patient; by four-thirty, her three o'clock patient was finally in an exam room. The walk-ins were killing her, but what else could she do? She was the only game in town, the first encounter most of these patients would have with a medical system that had grown so complex that navigation without guidance was impossible. So she stayed the course and sat down to talk to every patient.

There were a few joys in the midst of the work-ins. She saw Lena Chisholm back. Lena remained closed to talking about her husband, even when they were pried apart for the collection of a urine sample. Her ankle was healing, and her eyebrow laceration was ready for suture removal, but she had new bruises she couldn't explain on the back of her neck and a urinalysis showing red blood cells. Lena declined further workup and limped out of the office on the arm of her man.

By five, she only had two patients to go, a work-in and a followup with Brittany Lewis. Claire was dictating at her desk when Lucy approached and waited at her elbow. Claire finished her note and hung up the Dictaphone. "What's up?"

"I've been anticipating this problem," Lucy began. "It's a unique challenge running this office with totally female clinical staff."

"Why? We're as capable as men. Where's the problem?"

"We have a male patient who is insistent upon having a chaperone if a female doctor is to examine him."

Claire hadn't really thought about this situation. But she understood. She always wanted a female present when her gynecologist was seeing her. "So you've anticipated it. How should we deal with it?"

"We use our male staff member." Lucy smiled as Cyrus stepped around the corner wearing a white coat. He was still in jeans, but the coat was clean and pressed and his hair was combed for the occasion.

Claire shrugged. "Okay, he can stand in. But if I need assistance, I'll want you too."

Lucy nodded. "Hey, this guy's versatile. I taught him to take blood pressure and pulse rate. I had him put down Brittany's vital signs for me. I retook them just to be sure, but he was right on the money."

Claire looked at Cyrus. He did clean up well. "Okay, let him assist you. But the first time the landscape looks neglected, we're getting a new arrangement."

She watched as Lucy winked at Cyrus, who nodded without speaking. *At least he isn't too chatty. There's nothing worse than an assistant who interrupts to socialize with the patients.*

She looked at Cyrus. "I'll have you step in when I'm ready for the exam." Then, to Lucy, she asked, "What's the problem, anyway?"

"He won't sit down. He's just arrived from Asia. He's been flying for two days and has a bad flare-up of his hemorrhoids."

"Great," she muttered with sarcasm. "I can hardly wait."

She entered the exam room to find an elderly gentleman who identified himself with a quick bow at the waist with his hands together. "Dr. McCall. I am Mr. Sugimoto."

She mimicked his action and responded. "Nice to meet you, Mr. Sugimoto."

"It is I who am honored to meet with someone so well known."

She let the remark pass as a cultural oddity.

He explained his problem with exceptional English. "I always have trouble when I travel. Do you have any idea how long it takes to fly from Tokyo to Stoney Creek?" He laughed and answered himself. "Too long."

Besides appearing a bit washed out and tired, he seemed to be in excellent health for his age of sixty-four. He was on a single common medication for blood pressure and no blood thinners. He had no blood in the stools and no constipation unless he traveled outside of Japan. He smiled when he added, "The U.S. is very constipating to me."

The exam was accomplished with her new office chaperone at her side and revealed a single swollen purple grape at the verge of the anus.

"You have what we call a thrombosed hemorrhoid," she said, glancing at Cyrus, who stood with his hand to his mouth. "If I excise it, you will feel much better tonight."

He complied, and she finished the task using a local anesthetic and the dexterity of a surgeon.

"I feel better already."

She smiled and gave him a list of instructions and a box of fiber packets to use when he traveled.

"What will they cost?" he asked.

"Take them. They are free samples."

He nodded.

She asked him to follow up in a few weeks if he was still in town and to see his local doctor to schedule a screening colonoscopy when he had recovered.

"There is one more favor I wish to ask," he said. "Perhaps when I am dressed you will return?"

"Okay," she said, slipping into the hall. She almost tripped over Cyrus, who sat with his head between his knees and Lucy kneeling at his side.

Lucy frowned. "He'll be fine. It was his first view of hemorrhoid surgery."

Cyrus didn't look up and Claire didn't know him well enough to harass him. She was confident it was his first experience with queasiness. Taking blood pressures was one thing. Assisting with surgery, another.

She walked to the next room and picked up the chart. It seemed that beautiful Brittany had had another gallbladder attack. *Predictable.* She opened the door to see her patient lying on the exam table curled up on her side. "Another episode of pain?"

Brittany nodded and explained her most recent attack. "It's mostly gone again," she said.

Claire repeated her exam and gently pulled down Brittany's lower eyelids to inspect the sclera, which remained glistening and white. "Let me feel your abdomen."

Again, Brittany's tenderness was high up under her rib margin, without signs of right lower abdominal tenderness which might signal appendicitis or ovarian pathology. Claire picked up a spiral notebook filled with color diagrams. She paged through until she found the biliary system so she could explain the problem.

After their discussion, and a phone call to the surgeon, Brittany agreed to meet him the following week in Carlisle. Claire concluded by instructing her patient how to check out, but Brittany seemed hesitant to leave. At the door, she turned. "Could you pray for me again?"

Claire kicked herself for having to be asked, then took Brittany by the hand and prayed for her recovery and peace.

When she returned to Mr. Sugimoto, he was dressed in a grey suit, sitting on the exam table. "I am able to sit." He smiled.

She returned his smile, wondering just what he wanted to discuss.

He handed her a copy of an article from a leading neurological journal. "My son is the chairman of neurological medicine in a university back in Tokyo. When he heard that I was traveling to Stoney Creek, he gave me this article in hopes that I could find you. I could not believe my good fortune when I sought help at this clinic and I found the very doctor that he told me should be in Stoney Creek." He pointed at her name in the midst of the others below the title. "You are this doctor?"

"Yes."

"Would you honor my son by signing this for a souvenir?"

As she did, he continued to explain. "My son dreams of making a discovery like you, something that will make a difference to a community, to his country."

Claire shook her head. "I didn't discover Huntington's disease. I just diagnosed a problem that someone else, probably Mr. Huntington, discovered."

"Oh, I know," he replied. "But the article details how you were able to debunk a myth that stood for generations, this Stoney Creek Curse." He nodded. "That is my son's dream as well: to use science to explain diseases which remain entangled in myth and mystery." He reached out to take her hand. "You are a real hero, Dr. McCall."

"Oh no, not me," she responded. "All I did was figure out that my father jerked even when he wasn't intoxicated."

"You are too modest."

She nodded and stayed silent.

"Are there others in the valley around Stoney Creek who are suffering from Huntington's disease?"

"A few. And others will be discovered, I'm sure."

"So your work has impacted the life of this community. They should be grateful. In my work, I teach my employees that they should make a positive difference in the communities in which they serve. Every factory should have a project to improve not just the employees, but their towns as well."

She studied her patient for a moment. "Why did you come to Stoney Creek? What possible interest is here for you?"

"I've come to buy a shoe factory." He smiled. "It bears your name. Could this also be your family?"

"My grandfather founded McCall Shoes."

"Providence has brought me to you."

"Why would you want to buy a factory here?" *You obviously haven't heard of their declining business.*

"Oh, not me. I represent a large firm in Japan." He handed her a business card with the familiar logo of an athletic company. "We want to manufacture athletic shoes right here."

The news fell like a rock. "What?" She hesitated. "Has this already been decided?"

"Not yet. I've come to investigate the community, to see if an offer is in order."

"How would this affect Stoney Creek? What about all the workers?"

"I'm sure we would need to expand. The basic physical plant is in place, but we will need additional equipment and assembly lines."

"More jobs?"

He nodded.

"Mr. Sugimoto, have you discussed this with the board? Why doesn't the community know?"

"Mr. McCall assured me that the board would be informed once an offer has been made. We've been talking about this for months."

"I see."

He stood to leave. "This has been a wonderful gift for me," he said. "I am honored to meet such a fine American physician."

"Mr. Sugimoto, I hesitate to ask, but, well, we have a code of confidentiality in medicine in our country. I have vowed not to speak of your medical problems without your specific permission."

"Of course. We have a similar code of honor my country."

"But could I ask an additional favor?"

"Anything."

"Please do not mention our meeting to my uncle, Leon McCall. He is the man you have been talking to?"

"Exactly." He paused and winked before placing his palms together and bowing again. "I understand. You wish to surprise him yourself."

Exactly. "Will you return to see me when you are in town again?"

"It will be my pleasure."

She bowed, hoping it was the right thing to do. "I'm sure it will be mine."

That evening, as Claire prepared for an evening out with John, she couldn't help but wonder if tonight would be the night. She wanted so desperately to believe in his undying commitment, a love without conditions, but found herself fighting through a fog of doubt. *Could it be an intuition that's important?*

She crept up the hallway from the bathroom toward the kitchen, listening to John and Della as they gabbed about their weeks. Della had never had a malt at Fisher's Cafe, and John was expounding with Italian exuberance about the double malt special he'd drink if he could choose anything as his last meal before facing death by lethal injection.

Della laughed at something John said just as Claire slid onto a kitchen chair. She loved John as much as Claire did.

Claire slipped off her shoe and rubbed at a scratch in the leather toe. It was a McCall product. Having a shortage of shoes would never be a problem for Claire. "Has Uncle Leon ever mentioned selling the company?" she asked when Della stopped laughing.

Della shook her head. The abrupt change in topics didn't phase her. "No." She squinted. "Why?"

Claire was careful not to betray a patient confidence. "I met a man today, a patient, who said he was in town to talk about a possible deal."

Her mother shrugged. "I'll ask him about it, but I'd be surprised if he would ever sell."

"I'd be surprised if he ever turned down a deal that would make him money."

Della gave Claire a look that said, "Enough!"

John broke in to diffuse the tension. "Have you seen Abby lately at the cafe?" he asked Della. "She looks great."

"I saw her at church. Her daughter is her spittin' image," Della said.

"You know what she told me about marriage? She told me it was an invitation to come and die."

"Die?"

"Sure. She just wanted me to understand about what we are really called to do, to place someone else's needs in front of our own."

Claire heard a rapid tapping sound and glanced over at John. *He's drumming his fingers on the table. He always does that when he's serious.*

He went on, "She called it dying to self."

"She's exactly right. Joy never comes to a marriage when you're only there for what you can get. Okay, scholar," Della snickered. "Complete the phrase. I'll give you a hint. It's from Ephesians."

Claire rolled her eyes. Della loved this game. Especially with someone she could impress with her knowledge of the Bible.

"Husbands love your wives . . ." She halted, waiting for John.

Claire didn't want her boyfriend to be stumped, so she interrupted and finished the verse rapid-fire, complete with a concluding argument. "As Christ loved the church. And how was that? He died for the church. Thus, supporting Abby's theory that marriage is an invitation to come and die." She lifted her hand to John. "Let's go. I'm starved."

Della frowned. "Whoa, why the pressured speech? I was enjoying a nice conversation here, something that's somewhat of a rarity around this place, I might add."

Claire dropped her head. "Sorry. It just sounded so depressing, that's all. Makes everyone want to rush out and get married." She lifted her hands in an invitation. "Come and die."

"Abby was making a point," John responded.

Della pushed back from the table. "And she's right."

Claire shook her head. "And just look at the theory's chief proponents. Abby is married to a quadriplegic, and you're married to a . . . well, to Wally. I'd say that's a pretty balanced look at marriage."

Della stood. "Sarcasm isn't your prettiest quality."

The truth stung. She wished she hadn't said it. But her restraints were low and she was hungry. "I'm sorry."

"Wait a minute," John said. "I'm getting a little revelation here myself. Della's love for Wally and Abby's love for Nathan is a lot better picture of Christ's love for the church than most. Here we are, pitiful and unable to help ourselves, but Christ chooses to love us anyway."

Claire pointed at a Bible on the kitchen counter. "But the verse says *husbands* love your wives as Christ—"

"Okay, okay, the analogy breaks down a little, but you get my drift."

Della slapped his shoulder. "You keep preachin' it, John." She pushed him to the door. "Take care of my daughter."

Claire mouthed a second apology to her mother, who waved it off with her hand. "Have fun," she added. Della was hard to offend.

They drove to Carlisle for a Chinese buffet, which John yawned through, in spite of his love affair with General Tso's chicken.

After dinner, Claire declined a movie, seriously doubting whether John could stay awake for anything other than a guy movie. She didn't feel like watching exploding cars or women falling for guys who needed shaving. In fact, when she insisted on driving John's Mustang home, he tossed her the keys to his baby and curled up for a nap in the passenger's seat. This was definitely not vintage John. *Some date he is tonight. His work must be keeping him up late.*

She woke him in her driveway, offering to drive him home and keep his car.

He opened one eye. "Nice try, McCall. I think I can handle it."

"You're afraid I might scratch your baby?"

He jumped out and pointed. "I'm afraid you just want to get me at my apartment alone. Pops told me about women like you."

She laughed and fell into his arms. His kiss was warm on her mouth. Some nights she wished they could just elope. But she was waiting to be sure of his love. She pushed him away. "Go away," she said with an exaggerated pout.

"I'm leavin', love."

"Can I see you tomorrow? Why don't we climb Blue Knob or something?"

"I need to go to Brighton. Ms. Addison has a contract I need to hand-deliver by Monday."

Why didn't that surprise her? Lately John had been scarce. She nodded. "Say," she added. "Could you pick up an order for the clinic at Brighton Pharmacy? We've got an account with them."

"Is it a lot?"

"Just a couple boxes."

He nodded. "Gotta run."

"Get some sleep, dopey."

He threw her a kiss and drove away. She watched him pause at the end of the lane, and heard a familiar melody began to drift from his stereo.

"L'amore é svanito. Il mio cuore non canterá mai piú. Non tenere stretto l'amore."

John pulled off the road once he was safely out of view. Then he popped the trunk and retrieved a pair of night-vision goggles and a metal detector, which he gently laid on the floor in front of the passenger seat. He'd obtained both through a rental shop in Brighton. He hoped tonight would be a better night than the last few.

So far, pickin's had been slim out at Lena's place, and all he'd netted from his efforts were four beer cans, a dozen bottle caps, and a lug nut. But the treasures he found sifting through the silt on the forest floor weren't the only glimpse into country culture he'd had. Last night, long after he'd grown weary of his search, he'd been drawn by the melodies he'd heard streaming from the house's open window. And so, with some trepidation, he'd dared another quiet approach to *her* house. That's the way he thought of it. It wasn't the gunslinger's or the gorilla's place or even the Chisholms'. In John's mind, any goon that would leave a young bride alone at night didn't rank high enough to have his own place. And so, from his protected position at the edge of the woods, he'd paused and watched as Lena waltzed across the yard in her nightgown with a bag of trash. It was odd, really, the way she seemed to be clutching the overstuffed bag to her slender waist and pirouetting in the moonlight.

But he hadn't found the ring. So he whispered a prayer as he thought ahead to the night's work. Hopefully he wouldn't run into the gunslinger or the monster dog again. He was sure theirs wouldn't be a kindly reception.

But he wouldn't mind seeing Lena.

He shook his head and restarted the Mustang and the CD, and shivered at the insanity his nightlife had become.

He should be with Claire. He should be at home asleep. He took a deep breath and made a U-turn to head toward Briary Branch Road. *I hope Old Jeb is chained.*

Chapter Eleven

E lizabeth McCall always used the airport shuttle when she traveled. It was convenient, they picked her up at her door, and the drivers were quiet, leaving her to her thoughts. The week had been hectic. The pace of business certainly wasn't like it used to be when her husband started McCall Shoes so many years before. She remembered those days fondly now, how she would keep the books, and he would drive that eyesore of a truck over to the train station in Brighton to pick up the thick hides of leather himself. She loved the business, loved the bustling little factory, loved even the smell of the place. Her husband would come home with that rich aroma saturated in his flannel shirts. She would bury her face in his chest and savor the fragrance like some expensive perfume. It was a comfort to her now, and occasionally as she was dressing for an evening out, she would find herself lifting her leather purse to her nose to release the memories locked within.

She was escaping to Martha's Vineyard. These few days had been as stressful as any within recent months. The business was failing. She'd suspected it for a long time, and although she missed her husband, she was glad he wasn't here to see the business fold.

Leon had been gracious. He had offered her a fair buyout. He was young enough to begin again, to take care of the selling off of the hard assets or scaling back to rework another shoe line. And that attorney of his was so funny. She'd never seen a lawyer happy to see his client writing such a large check, but she supposed it was because he was glad for her, knowing he had assisted Leon in doing the right thing. It had happened fast, to be sure, but when dealing with loss, she'd found it best not to drag out the process. She had always been able to make a snap judgment on her feet, a trait which she'd passed down to her granddaughter, a trait which would serve her well in the operating theater and in life.

She was thankful it had been fast. She couldn't have stomached the process if Leon would have insisted, as he often did, for a special appointed committee of the board to study the issue from every angle. And with Mr. Pittington, the decision to move ahead was a polished and easy process.

She'd asked her husband for permission, a habit she'd gotten into as she faced life alone after his death. She supposed it was early senility, but it seemed only right to voice her concerns to his picture before selling the business that defined his life.

But now, the deed was done. She'd sold her shares of the family business to Leon. It was time for the next generation to hold the reins. She needed to move on.

She leaned against the window and watched as the honeysuckle blurred past.

"United?" the driver asked.

She turned her head.

"Are you flying United?"

"Yes. To Martha's Vineyard."

She would be gone a week before waking up with chest pain and the thought that she'd moved too fast.

—⁂—

It was three more weeks before Lena Chisholm took her diamond to a pawn shop in Carlisle. Until then, she had taken it out of its hiding place only three times when William Raymond insisted on spoiling her. The last time, he'd made her wear it to yet another of the highbrow affairs he was constantly dragging her to. She had carefully applied her makeup and put on her prom dress, the one she'd worn only two years before during her junior year at Ashby High. Then, William slipped the ring on her finger and danced with her until midnight, when Billy Ray returned after second shift and she frantically pulled off the dress and hid the ring in her sock drawer again.

Billy Ray thought the makeup was for him and she was smart enough to know she shouldn't tell.

There were two pawn shops in Brighton, but that was a good hour away, and she wasn't sure how often her husband checked the mileage on the Toyota, so to be safe, she took the ring to Carlisle. She'd heard from other girls at the shoe factory that you could pretty much double your money if you took your stuff over to Brighton, but she wasn't selling. She was only looking to find out just how much the ring would bring, because a girl with a man like Billy Ray needed options.

The man at the shop lifted the ring from her hand a little too quickly for Lena's comfort. She'd opened her palm, and he snatched it away so fast that she hardly knew what had happened. She watched the little man with too-black hair as he held up the ring and studied it through a little tube. It was like a magnifying glass, she figured, and his humming and grunting was starting to irritate her when she realized her hand was still open palm up. She felt her face redden and closed her fingers into a fist around her empty hand. She wasn't sure why, but she was suddenly seized with the need to have her ring again, and she fought the urge to grab it back from the man behind the counter.

He made a clicking noise with his tongue against his dentures. They seemed a size too big for his small oval face. "I can give you two hundred dollars."

She knew not to accept the first offer. She forced a laugh and held out her hand. She said the first thing that popped in her mind. "I wasn't born yesterday."

"I might be able to scrape up three hundred."

She left her palm open, waiting for her ring.

"Four?"

She shook her head.

"Look, lady, I got a business to run here. You gotta know that your fiancé is going to find out about this and he's gonna run in here ready to pound my head if I don't cough the ring up. Life is too short to take that kind of grief without adequate compensation."

She hadn't thought about what he might think. "No deal. It's my grandmother's ring and I can promise you my grandfather has been dead for years."

"I'll ask the little woman." He folded his hand around her ring and disappeared behind a curtain before she could think to protest.

"Hey!"

She could only imagine what he was doing back there.

"Hey!"

She started looking for a way around the long counter and had just hoisted her foot onto the counter to start climbing over when he reappeared. He touched the tattoo of a rose on her calf.

"How much'd you pay for that?"

She jerked her leg off the glass counter and stared. "I want my ring!"

"Five hundred dollars. I'll give you five hundred dollars and not a penny more."

That was a thousand dollars in Brighton. She held out her hand. "I want my ring!"

"I always wanted a tattoo, but I'm afraid of needles." He handed her the ring.

She turned it over in her hand, looking for the initials, and took a deep breath. It was hers. "No can do," she said, hoping she'd said it with the right inflection. "I'll just have to keep it."

She walked out exhilarated. A thousand dollars! The thought should have made her smile. But instead, she felt a little queasy, almost like she did after riding the octopus at the county fair. She laid her hand over the little lump in her pocket and walked to her Toyota. There she dropped her head against the steering wheel, still gripping the ring through the front of her shorts. The urge to vomit came suddenly, almost before she could swing the door open to lose her stomach's contents onto the street.

She wiped her mouth with a tissue and tried to spit away the bitter taste on her tongue. She'd always had a weak stomach. She felt every new excitement this way.

She looked at her watch and smiled. Old Jeb had given her a thousand dollars!

She wanted to scream, but the gnawing feeling in her gut reminded her not to get too excited. It was time to go home and fix supper for Billy Ray. She touched her ring one more time and headed for Briary Branch Road.

After supper and feeding and changing Wally, Claire retreated to the front lawn and sat beneath an October-glory maple. She leaned against the trunk, not caring about grass stains or dirt. Instead, she closed her eyes and listened to the chorus of insects.

A few minutes later, Claire opened her eyes to watch the traffic pass at the end of the lane. The day was coming to a close in the Apple Valley. It was time for people to be home, and the swoosh of each passing car seemed to speak an unsettled frenzy.

That's when she let her obsession invade. She watched the traffic and began again the mental game. Each truck meant she would develop Huntington's. Each car meant she was free.

After the third truck in a row, she gripped the sides of her blond bangs. "Uggh!"

"It's easier if you'd just let me trim it for you." The voice was her mother's.

"How long have you been standing there?"

"A few seconds."

Claire squinted and suspected it was longer. She looked back at the road where a car passed west and a truck passed east. "Did you ever have an obsession you couldn't control? You know, a stupid thought that you know can't mean anything, and yet you give it significance?"

"Like avoiding the cracks on the sidewalk so you don't break your mother's back?"

"Kind of like that."

"Whatever you do, *do not* think about a white elephant."

Claire looked at her mother. "Whatever."

"All I'm saying is the best way to beat something like that is not head-on."

Claire understood. "If you try not to think about something, that's exactly what you'll think about."

"Right. Give the obsessions attention, and they'll grow. The more you fight it, the more likely it is that you'll think about it again." She put her hand on Claire's shoulder. "Ignore it, kiddo, and it will go away."

"You aren't a dumb blond, Della."

She lifted her hair from her collar. "I'm a gray-blond."

They sat quietly listening to the night sounds before Claire spoke again. "How do I know John will stick with me if I end up like Daddy?"

"You don't. You'll never have complete assurance when it comes to people." She paused. "Oh, I'd bet on John. He's cut from the right stuff. But if you're going to put all your trust in someone, don't choose a man."

Claire rephrased her concern. "Would you have married Daddy if you knew he would turn out like this?"

The quickness of her mother's reply was disconcerting. "Absolutely not."

Then I shouldn't risk putting John through this hell either.

The shock must have registered on Claire's face, because her mother's tone softened and she patted her daughter's hand. "But that's why God didn't let me do the knowin'. He had a plan, and his plan is good, but his plan always involves pain. No one in their right minds would choose a path of pain."

"You sound like a pessimist."

"I'm a realist, Claire. Pain is a part of life. We all have it, in one form or another. It helps us grow. In some way we don't understand, it works out for good, for God's glory, but no, none of us would choose it."

Claire nodded numbly. It made sense. She just wasn't sure she liked it.

She watched four cars pass in a row, and decided to go to bed while she was ahead.

Chapter Twelve

The day she learned she was pregnant was the happiest day Lena could remember. Of course the day Old Jeb brought her the diamond was a good one, and now that she could look back from where she stood, that day certainly was a predictor of wonderful things to come.

She tried to enumerate them as she stared at the little blue strip on the pregnancy test kit. Billy Ray hadn't had a drop to drink in over three weeks. He was attending AA regularly, and he'd taken her out last week after work. They'd gone into Brighton and talked about old times and ate barbequed ribs at Richardson's. She'd felt queasy that day too, but just told herself she was excited about celebrating with Billy Ray. After dinner, he'd even sprung for a new CD of Garth Brooks and played it in the truck on the way home.

She wanted to be a good mother. She wanted to take good care of this baby. She wanted to call Dr. McCall for an appointment soon, so she could start on all the vitamins like her sister Penny had before Lynn was born. Oh, how she wished Penny was close by to share the news. But they rarely talked anymore. Her husband had moved them to California, and Penny didn't like Billy Ray. She never could get past his rough exterior to see that the core of him was gold.

Oh, she wasn't as naive as Penny said. She knew Billy Ray wasn't perfect. But a good man admits his faults and does something about them. And ever since she'd put that shotgun up under his chin, Billy was a changed man. He'd confessed everything, even that he'd beaten his first wife. She knew what a big step that was. Billy Ray was the type of man to keep things inside. But she was committed to him. She could help him through the rough times. She could help him change.

She'd wanted a baby for months, but Billy said they couldn't afford it, or that she was too young, or that they'd have plenty of time for that after they'd had some fun. But six months ago, he'd told her to stop those old pills, and even threw them in the kitchen trash can himself in a fit of celebration. She thought he was joking, and was sure he'd pull them out again, but he promptly tied a knot in the top of the bag and sent her out with the trash.

He was naked when she came back from the garbage cans. That's when he said they'd better get on with the task of procreating. She figured that having children wasn't really Billy Ray's goal. It was hers. What Billy Ray wanted was lots of practice trying to get the whole baby thing started. But she giggled and went along with it. He could be so sweet when he wanted something.

Six months of trying. It felt like an eternity to Lena, but she was only nineteen. She wouldn't be like some modern mothers: too old to play baseball with their sons and too tired to sit up late until their baby girl returned from the prom.

Billy Ray would be home in an hour. That would give her enough time to prepare something special to celebrate the news. She washed her face and put on just the essentials, a lip gloss and eyeliner, then put in four matching earrings, the set of little sterling hearts that Billy Ray had given her on their first-month anniversary.

She wished she had some steaks, his favorite, but money didn't allow for too many luxuries like that. She settled on grilled chicken, with a soy sauce, garlic, and parmesan cheese marinade. She made a tossed salad and put on some rice. She wanted to make biscuits, but Billy Ray would eat white bread and wouldn't care.

The chicken was on the grill when he arrived, and her appearance seemed to lighten his mood a little. She'd counted on him being moody, this being a bowling night and all. He'd gone only once since he'd stopped drinking, and said it nearly drove him nuts. And for once, since he was sober, three-adjective Eddie started getting on his nerves. But tonight, she had news that would make him forget all about ten pins. Billy Ray was going to be a daddy.

She kissed him at the door and pushed him away so she could finish dinner. "There's time for that later."

They ate and made small talk. Billy Ray never liked getting too touchy-feely as he called it.

"Larry quit."

"What?"

"Handed in his resignation today." He folded a piece of white bread around a blob of strawberry jam. "He said Mason's machine shop over in Brighton is looking for supervisors for second shift and he gets time and a half for every weekend."

"So who's left?"

"Just Allen, Len, Gene, and me on day shift. But one of us will have to cover Larry's spot and watch the rookies on second."

"How's the meat?"

His full mouth was all the answer she really needed. He gave one anyway. "Are you going to kiss me if I smell like garlic?"

"Do we have to kiss?"

It wasn't the anwer he wanted. "What's the occasion? Why the fancy dinner?"

"We're celebrating."

He raised his eyebrows in a question.

"You've been sober over three weeks. That's a milestone."

"I told the guys at work that you scared me straight."

"Billy Ray!"

"Hey, it's true. I thought you were going to blow my head off!"

She didn't like his attitude. "Whatever works, I guess."

"Baby, you know that's not why." He dropped his head. "I wasn't treatin' you right." He shook his head and polished off his strawberry jam sandwich. "But what do you expect me to tell the guys? I wanted to stop beatin' my wife?"

"Billy, stop." She scooted her chair closer to his along the side of the table. "Let's not talk about it. That's behind us. We're good together . . ." She paused, then added, ". . . if you're not drinking."

She leaned forward and stroked his hand. They were rough, strong, used to work. "I've got news." She thought about telling him about the diamond, but thought she'd tell him about the baby first, so if he worried about money, she could always show him that second.

"What's for dessert?"

"Be serious, Billy Ray." She sat up straight. "You're going to be a daddy."

You would have thought someone had punched him in the stomach. His hand went to his mouth and he nearly choked on the final piece of chicken he was chewing. "What?"

"I'm not kidding. Remember how queasy I've been feeling?" She touched her lower abdomen. "I'm pregnant! We're going to have a baby!"

His face grew sober. He wasn't smiling like she'd imagined. He didn't grab her in his arms and spin her around the room smothering her with kisses the way William Raymond would. "Don't get your hopes up, Lena. Have you had a blood test?"

"No. I bought one of those tests at the pharmacy."

"Oh, Lena," he said softly. "That's just a moneymaker. Those things don't half work."

"They do work!" She scooted her chair away from the table. "Why aren't you happy? I knew something was different inside. I could tell. The test isn't wrong, Billy Ray. You're full of it!"

"Slow down, girl." He held up his hands. "I just don't want you to be disappointed, that's all."

She marched to the bathroom and retrieved the test strip from the trash can. Then, she came out waving it under his nose. "What color is this, Daddy? Read it yourself!"

She sniffed. This special celebration wasn't turning out so well.

She started reading the side of the box, rattling off percentages of pregnancies detected in the first six weeks, before stopping to look in her husband's eyes. What did she see there? Fear? Maybe she'd misjudged his reaction. His denial was just a cover for his fear.

She let the cardboard box fall to the floor and put her arms around his neck. "Don't be afraid, Billy Ray. You'll be a great dad. You can teach our boy to hunt and—"

"Are you sure about this?"

She planted a kiss on his lips, but he straightened and stared beyond her as if he was processing this latest bit of information.

"Billy Ray, some things a woman just knows. I only got the test kit because my period was so late."

He shoved her away, sending her hurling over a kitchen chair onto the table. A water glass shattered on the floor as he screamed, "You slut!"

Lena didn't understand. She struggled to her feet just as he landed another blow to the side of her face, sending her to the floor.

"You spend your days lost in those silly books. Who's the father?"

"Billy Ray," she gasped, scrambling from the floor to a point of protection on the other side of the table. "Are you crazy? What's gotten—"

He took the table and flung it against the wall. Lena screamed and jumped out of the way. "Billy, stop!"

She picked up the base of the broken glass at her feet. Before she could stand up, he had a handful of her hair, yanking her back upright. She used the momentum of his lift as the initial acceleration to shove the ragged glass deep into his left arm. Billy howled and released her hair to grip his arm. Blood quickly oozed from between his fingers.

Free from his grasp, Lena fell to the floor, gasping for breath. But she knew better than to stop. Billy Ray had a wild look in his eyes. It wasn't fear. It was madness. And if she wanted to survive, she knew she had to move.

She rolled across the floor which was littered with broken tablewear and food. She picked up a fork and sent it airborne in his direction before scrambling to her feet to get to the utensil drawer.

Billy Ray cursed her and started forward, but by some miracle, slipped to one knee on the wet floor. That one second was all she needed. She pulled out a twelve-inch carving knife and waved it in his direction. He lunged forward to stand as she sliced at the front of his shirt.

"What's wrong with you?" she screamed.

He stood up panting, but moving slowly for the first time since his anger exploded. Perhaps the uncapped rage was over. But what madness had overtaken him?

Lena wouldn't release the knife. Her knuckles were white around the wooden handle. She jabbed it forward again, directly toward his neck.

He backed away, tugging at a long tear in his shirt, and dripping blood on the linoleum floor.

"Get out!" she yelled. "Get out!"

"This is my house, Lena," he said through clenched teeth. He backed through the kitchen as she gave him wide berth. "No woman disgraces me. I'll kill you and your boyfriend!"

He slammed the door, leaving her clenching the knife long after she heard the rumble of his truck fade to silence somewhere in the distance down Briary Branch Road. Then, she sank to the kitchen floor and cried.

There were days when Wally didn't speak at all and days when for a time, he seemed to make sensible and recognizable speech. He slurred words and drooled, but there were times when he strained hard to communicate. But just what switch in his brain was responsible remained a mystery.

But that didn't stop his family from talking to him. John did especially well, and would have Wally laughing at his jokes and self-effacing humor. Claire was just coming back down the hall when she heard John finishing up a story. He had pulled a chair up next to Wally's bed and was leaning forward, talking in a low voice through the bedrails. The scene evoked images of someone making a deep confession to a priest, unseen on the other side of the screen. Wally's head was jerking back and forth and his face contorted into one big open smile. It was a laugh without sound, a tear-jerking spasm that happens only when you can't get another breath to vocalize your laughter.

John concluded quietly, unaware of Claire's presence. "And talk about needin' a clean pair of shorts! After that monster dog, I thought I was a goner, but when that redneck unloaded his twelve gauge, I had to check my pulse. I—" He turned and let his mouth stay open for a moment without words. "Oh, hey, baby."

"Just what kind of story are you telling back here? I thought you were feeding him supper."

"Oh, we're done with supper, aren't we, Wall?" He stood and stretched his hands over his head. "We were just talkin' guy stuff. Nothing interesting."

Wally grunted.

Claire shook her head. "Men."

"What?"

"Nothing. If you're done, let's take a walk. I ate too much pie to sit around."

He shook his head and slapped Wally on his shoulder. "See you, Wall-man."

"Why don't guys ever use real names? You're constantly calling him Wall, the Wall-man, or Wal-Mart. Why not just Wally?"

"It's a guy thing." He slapped at her rump. "Don't worry about it, Claire-Bear."

Lena scrambled through the house throwing things into a worn canvas suitcase. She emptied her dresser, then started on her closet, not bothering to remove the hangers as she selected her favorite tops. She lifted her prom dress from the closet bar and threw it into a crumpled heap on the bed. Then she shoved her blow-dryer in between a pair of jogging shoes and her flip-flops, and dragged the suitcase to the bathroom, where she brushed everything on the counter on her side of the sink tumbling over the edge into the bag. She pushed the lid against the contents and managed to get the zipper around to the third corner. Lena lifted the suitcase to see that her curling iron had fallen against the commode. She shoved her it in her pants pocket and glanced around the den. She wanted to take everything: his guns, the dishes, even Old Jeb, but she knew that was a crazy notion. The important thing was that she needed to get away, and soon, before Billy Ray came back to make up.

She pulled the suitcase to her aging Toyota and threw the curling iron through the window onto the floor. She ran back and loaded a grocery bag with a box of cereal and a bag of Snickers, the little ones that her husband could eat in one bite. She didn't know how long she'd be away and she wanted to be ready. She looked around the kitchen, dropped in two apples and a jar of peanuts. She *never* ate peanuts, but Billy Ray loved 'em, and that was reason enough to add them to the bag. She surveyed the carnage on the floor and smiled at the thought of Billy's arrival. He would have to deal with the mess when he got home. *Maybe it will make him real sorry.* She rejected that thought out of hand, and gently slid the twelve-inch knife in beside a box of Wheaties.

When she got to the car, she patted her pocket for the third time, reassuring herself of the location of her diamond. The little lump was there. She slammed the key in the ignition and turned.

Nothing. Not even a click.

"Ugh!" She pounded the steering wheel in frustration. "Help me, God!" She looked up at the evening's last light. "Somebody help!"

She ran around and opened the hood to see that the battery was missing. She slammed the hood and pounded it with both hands. "Billy Ray!"

Obviously he didn't want her getting away. She thought about running on foot, but that seemed ludicrous. He'd find her on the road, and she wasn't about to venture into the woods. She trained her ear to the road. Was he coming?

She tried to quiet her heart. Billy Ray would have gone to get some attention for his arm, and unless he planned on patching it up himself, she should have a good hour. But wouldn't it be just like tough ol' Billy Ray to pour a little iodine on his arm and come right back?

The lady doctor! Dr. McCall said I could call her anytime I wanted to be taken to a safe place. She ran for the house. *Where did I put that number?* She pulled out the desk drawer and dumped the contents to the floor. Then she dropped to her knees and scattered the contents with her fingers. Paperclips, pens, a small Elmer's glue bottle, and Scotch tape were combed aside with a stack of Billy Ray's old checks. She pushed the phone directory away and lifted her grocery receipts, peeling them away by ones and twos until she held only the folded paper that Dr. McCall had given her. She had used it several weeks before when Billy Ray left her crying and alone. That time, in her panic, she asked a stupid question to cover her impulsive call.

She unfolded the paper onto the kitchen counter and punched in the number. "Please be there. Please be there. Oh, please be there."

Claire and John were a half-mile from her home when her cell phone sounded, breaking their stride and eliciting a groan from John. He held up two fingers. "It's your mom or a patient."

"A patient, Mom wouldn't need us this soon."

She lifted the phone to her ear. "Hello, Dr. McCall."

"Dr. McCall! Billy Ray's gone crazy. He's coming back. I know he's coming back and I can't stay here. You said I could call anytime I wanted help. He's broken my car so I can't get away. Please say you'll come and get me."

Claire signaled to John with her finger, and began walking back toward her house. "Slow down." She paused. "Lena?"

"Dr. McCall! Please!"

"I'll help you, Lena. Try to calm down. Where are you? I'll come and get you."

John was at her elbow, nearly at a jog to keep up with Claire's walk. She watched him roll his eyes. "Claire!"

"I live on Briary Branch Road."

Claire repeated it so John could help her remember. "Briary Branch Road. Got it. How do I get there?"

John touched her arm. "I know."

Lena continued her pressured plea. "Just come out of Stoney Creek like you were going to Brighton. Turn left onto Chesterfield Road and cross the railroad tracks. Briary Branch Road heads to the right after the tracks. Up toward Blue Knob."

"Okay, wait. Left on Chesterfield Road—"

John interrupted her again. "I know where the road is."

"Okay." Claire nodded. "Where on Briary Branch Road?"

"Out from town. Maybe six, seven miles from the turn past the tracks. We have a mailbox with our name. It says our number. Eighty-two."

"Okay. Got it. Give me your phone number in case I get lost."

Lena repeated the number twice, and Claire three times out loud so John could memorize it too.

"Please hurry. I don't know how long he'll be away."

The call ended abruptly, leaving Claire wondering if Billy Ray was there already.

Claire sped up to a jog. "It's the patient I told you about . . . the one whose husband knocks her around. We've got to go get her now. She's panicked. Afraid her husband is coming home."

"Let's take my car."

Claire nodded and drew a difficult deep breath. The tension and the sudden increase to a fast jog had her winded already. "I hate running after I eat."

John didn't reply. He ran ahead and brought his car to the end of the lane to meet her. "I hope she has the dog chained."

"The dog?"

John's reply came after he had pulled out onto the road. "Everyone in the country has big dogs."

Claire pulled on her lap belt as John accelerated. They followed the road, making the turn onto Chesterfield Road with a squeal of the tires.

"How did—"

"I heard you say Chesterfield," he snapped. "Now what?"

"Go right after the tracks."

John followed the curves of the road, pushing the Mustang faster. When they approached the blind top of a hill, Claire clutched the door and screamed. "John, slow down!"

They crested the hill without slowing and Claire relaxed only slightly when she saw a short straight section of road that allowed John to anticipate the next turn.

By the time they pulled into the driveway, she was convinced that John had no fear. Either that, or God had assigned them double angel coverage. *As if an angel could keep up with John, the Indy driver.*

They approached the front door on foot, aware of an eerie silence. Claire glanced back at the driveway which contained only an old blue car in front of the Mustang. "I hope that's not Billy Ray's," she whispered. She pounded on the front door. "Lena!"

Inside, she heard a bumping noise, a breathy grunt, and the rattle of a door chain. The dead bolt popped and the door opened. A coffee table and a lounge chair had been shoved away from the door. Lena had a fresh bruise under her left eye and dried blood on her arms. She was clutching a large gun with whitened knuckles.

When Lena's eyes met Claire's, she seemed to relax a little, then looked down at her arm. She laid the gun on the couch. "Let's go."

Claire took Lena's hands in hers. "What's happened?"

Lena looked at the blood on her arms. "It's not mine."

Claire looked around at the clutter and gasped. Lena pulled at her hand. "We need to get out of here."

They followed as Lena ran to the little car in front of John's Mustang. She pulled out a brown suitcase, which John tossed in the backseat. Claire lifted the driver's seat and climbed in the back. John opened the door for Lena. She eyed him pensively.

Claire pushed the suitcase aside. "Lena, meet John Cerelli."

Lena nodded.

They were three miles down Briary Branch Road before John asked where they were going.

"Brighton. There's a shelter that can help us."

Lena didn't speak until they rounded the crest of a hill to see a red pickup in the oncoming lane. "Billy Ray!"

John reached for her head and pulled her toward him. "Get down!"

As the truck passed, Claire could see a shirtless man with a white bandage across his upper arm. His window was down and he stared at them with empty eyes.

Claire watched as his brakes flashed, then stayed on.

Claire flinched. "He's turning around!"

Lena cried, "He must have seen me."

John punched the accelerator. "I don't think so. I think he saw me."

But Billy Ray didn't turn around. Maybe he knew he wouldn't catch the Mustang. Maybe he wanted to get a gun. And maybe he hadn't seen them at all. Claire wasn't sure why he hadn't taken chase, but she breathed a sigh of relief. "Thank you, God."

⸎

The trio rode in silence for most of the way. Claire didn't want to pry, and Lena wasn't bubbling over with details. Claire knew there would be time for that later. So Claire just sat and prayed, watching Lena as she stared straight ahead, quiet except for an occasional sniff.

When John reached over and placed his hand on hers, Lena jerked her head over to see. "It's going to be okay," he said. "It's going to be fine now."

Claire watched as he squeezed her hand before returning his own to the steering wheel.

The tension seemed to melt a bit once they reached Brighton city limits. John switched on his CD player. *"L'amata mia é andata via."*

"Give the girl a break, John. After everything she's been through, she doesn't need that kind of torture."

Her comment broke the strain of the moment. Lena smiled. "It isn't so bad. Not Garth Brooks or anything, but it's okay if he likes it."

139

John snapped it off. Claire could see him rolling his eyes in the rear mirror as he mumbled, "Not Garth Brooks."

"Are you hungry?" Claire asked.

Lena shook her head. "I made a special dinner for Billy Ray."

John smiled. "Burn the roast or something?"

Claire couldn't believe he'd make a joke. "Cerelli!" She touched Lena's arm. "Men!"

Lena joked, "That music probably affected his head."

Claire laughed at that one.

"Very funny." John paused. "Where am I going?"

"Take a left and travel Vine Street up behind McGuire Hall."

"It's on campus?"

"Across the street. It isn't marked."

"Do you have family, Lena? Anyone we should call?"

"No."

"I know the lady who works the shelter. I used to volunteer there as a medical student. You'll be able to stay there until things settle down. Should I call your employer? I don't have to give details. I can just say you're under a physician's care and will be needing some time off. The details are confidential."

"I can't go back to work." She looked out the window, her expression flat. "He would find me there."

"Where did you work?"

"The shoe factory."

Claire nodded. "I'll take care of things there for you. It's my uncle's business."

Lena turned back to her as if she was just putting the names together. She nodded her understanding and spoke softly, "McCall. McCall Shoes. Of course."

"Do you need some money? You shouldn't use a credit card if you don't want Billy Ray to know where you are."

"I have enough," she said slowly. "I can get some money."

"Cathy Rivera runs the shelter. She will expect you to attend some counseling sessions and group discussions. You won't have to pay room and board until you have a job. She has some contacts around Brighton.

The bus line stops a few times on the university campus so you shouldn't need a car."

"You'll like Cathy," John added.

Claire patted John on the shoulder. "She hates opera."

Lena cast a sideways glance at John. "Then I suppose she's okay."

In another five minutes they were standing on a sidewalk in front of a building that looked very much like many others on Greek Row, the area across from Brighton University where fraternity and sorority houses predominated. The only thing conspicuously absent were the universally ugly letters of the Greek alphabet on the front lawn or roof. It was a two-story colonial, all brick with deep green shutters and two-story white columns supporting a roof over the front porch.

Before approaching the building, Lena turned to Claire. "Dr. McCall, I need to ask you something else." She looked at John. "Uh, it's medical."

John nodded and walked on up to the porch as Claire reached for Lena's hand. "Call me Claire, Lena. I'm not really your doctor out here."

Lena kept her eyes on the sidewalk. "There's something else I need from you."

"Sure. Anything."

"I need an abortion."

<hr>

"I've got to hand it to you, Harvard," Leon spoke into the phone, "it's going just like you suggested. Sugimoto faxed me the initial offer tonight."

"Well?"

"I'll have to see what the board thinks." Leon smiled to himself. He knew what they would say. And he knew his attorney was dying to hear the figure. He just liked the feeling of being one step ahead of Alfred D. Pittington.

"When does the board meet?"

Leon pulled hard on a Cuban cigar that his wife only let him smoke on the back deck. "We're having a special called meeting tomorrow. I'm going to present Mr. Sugimoto's offer."

"A sellout takes unanimous vote from every member of the board."

"We've got it. I've polled everyone separately. I've spent more money on steak dinners and champagne than I'd like to think about. Everyone will vote with me."

"What about Elizabeth? She's still active on the board. She'll never go with this."

Leon tapped a thick rim of ash from the tip of his cigar onto the wooden deck, then pushed it between the boards and out of sight with his McCall penny loafer. "I've got her resignation letter on my desk. The first order of business will be to vote to accept her resignation. Then we'll look at Sugimoto's offer."

"He will need legal counsel after the takeover."

"Don't worry, Harvard. You'll have plenty of work with the new firm."

"What's the time line?"

"If we accept the offer, Sugimoto will come back the fifteenth of next month to review the agreement. Then he will hand-carry the contracts back to Tokyo for the CEO to sign. He told me to expect a transition team on site within sixty days of a signed contract."

"Sugimoto certainly spent a lot of time looking at the community. He must have asked me three times what the local concerns were, whether there are current town or community projects that need support."

"It's all part of their company image, Harvard. If it didn't result in more dollars, they wouldn't be doing it."

"What will you do?"

"I'm an automatic co-chairman of the transition committee. My job is safe."

"You won't need a job. Your biggest problem is going to be whether to winter in Aspen, Maui, or the Caribbean."

Leon leaned back on his padded deck-lounger and laughed. He could hear Alfred tapping his fingers on his desk. Leon looked out at the night sky over the Blue Ridge and smiled. Here he was enjoying a pleasant summer night, and his attorney was still at his office. Alfred needed to get out more.

Alfred's tapping sped up. "Okay, McCall. I'm going to see the figures soon anyway. Is there a crime in telling me before the board hears it?"

"It's not a crime."

"Okay, let's review. You bought all Elizabeth's stock for two-hundred-thousand dollars. You're now sitting on ninety percent of the company's shares. You're selling to the most successful athletic shoe maker in the world. Are you happy with the offer?"

"Yes."

"I've got work to do. No more games, McCall. What's the initial offer? Triple? Quadruple?"

"More."

Pittington sneered. "McCall!"

Leon broke into a broad smile. "Twenty million dollars."

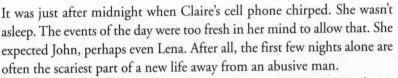

It was just after midnight when Claire's cell phone chirped. She wasn't asleep. The events of the day were too fresh in her mind to allow that. She expected John, perhaps even Lena. After all, the first few nights alone are often the scariest part of a new life away from an abusive man.

Claire jumped from bed and picked up her phone. She answered professionally, in case a patient was calling. "Dr. McCall."

There was silence on the other end of the line for a moment, so she repeated her name. "Dr. McCall, may I help you?"

"Dr. McCall." The voice was male, but not one she could place.

"Who is calling?" She looked at the digital readout of her caller's number. She couldn't place it.

"I should have known this would be your number." Claire strained to characterize the gravelly voice. It was male. Country accent. Slow with some slurring with prolongation of the "sh" sound.

"It's my number all right. Who is calling?"

"What have you done with Lena?"

Billy Ray! How did he get my cell phone number?

"Mr. Chisholm, how did you get this number?"

"Lena left it here by the phone. Nice of her actually." He paused. "I need to know where Lena is."

"She's in a safe place. That's all I can say."

"You can't believe everything she says. She lives in fantasyland. I'm really not a bad guy. What'd she say about me?"

"Nothing. She really didn't feel much like talking."

"You can't believe her."

Claire's patience was growing thin. "Billy Ray, why did you call me? It's after midnight."

"I'm just trying to find Lena. I didn't really know who I was callin', see? 'Cause I found this number by the phone so I just called to see who Lena might have called to help her out. But this all makes sense now, because I saw you and that city slicker comin' down the road. What'd you do? Stuff Lena in the trunk?"

He didn't see her! Why does he call John a city slicker? Must be the car?

"I'm a doctor, Billy Ray. I merely responded to a plea from a patient."

"She's lyin', Doc."

"Billy Ray, I'd advise you to get some help. Learn how to deal with your anger without violence. Goodnight, Mr. Chisholm."

Claire flipped off the phone and lay down on her bed, anticipating a callback that never came. It was after two when she finally conceded to exhaustion and fell asleep.

Chapter Thirteen

wo cases of the flu, three school sports physicals, a forty-eight-year-old contractor with back pain and foot drop, a sixty-one year old with an abnormal mammogram, and a brittle diabetic brought a sense of normalcy to Claire's morning. By noon, she'd put last night's events on the back burner, and the cloud completely out of her mind.

Lisa, her receptionist, paused at the doorway to Claire's office and knocked on the doorframe.

"Hi, Lisa."

"I've got the appointment books open to next summer already. Should I be scheduling visits for you?"

"Next summer already?"

"Annual followups, mammogram checks, school physicals. The patients are starting to ask for you. Old Ms. Denton said she'd never had a lady doctor before, and now she's spoiled. She only wants you."

"Ms. Denton has lived ninety-one years seeing male physicians. I think she'll adapt."

Lisa smiled. "So . . ."

"I agreed to cover until June 30 or until Dr. Jenkins sold his practice."

"So . . ."

"So the short answer is 'no.' I'll be back in residency training somewhere."

Kelly Myers and Amy Stevens, who ran the insurance and billing, walked in behind Lisa. "Do we get to vote?"

Claire was flattered. "You guys just like the new office. How many years did you guys work out of Dr. Jenkins' home?"

"Too long," Amy said.

Kelly set down a stack of disability forms on the desk for Claire's signature. "Why did he build this just when he was retiring?"

Claire groaned at the size of the work she'd been handed. "Two reasons. He wanted some income in his retirement, which he'll get from renting the building. And he realized no one would buy his practice if they had to work out of his home office."

Lucy pushed her way past the clerical staff. "Nurse coming through." She looked at Claire and smiled. "Hate to break up the party. I thought there must be food in here." She dropped Lena Chisholm's chart on the desk. "Cathy Rivera is calling from the women's shelter in Brighton. Shall I have her call back?"

"No. Put her through to the desk."

Lucy didn't budge. "I've got a reminder here to tell you that Brittany Lewis is having gallbladder surgery today. Should be home tonight if you wanted to call."

Claire looked up to get the third item. Efficient Lucy almost always waited to interrupt Claire until she had three things to say. "And?"

"I've got a patient with family history of polycystic kidney disease in A when you're ready."

The quartet disbanded and Claire picked up the phone. "Dr. McCall."

Cathy Rivera laughed. "I'll bet it's fun to say that, isn't it, Claire?"

"Old mentors never give you the respect you deserve." Claire took a deep breath and pulled a stack of charts closer so she could sign office notes while she talked. "What's up with Lena?"

"Look, I know this is the first day. She's going to need some time." She seemed to hesitate.

"But."

"But I think there might be deeper issues here. I may need a psychiatrist referral."

"Psych! She's just scared. What are you seeing?"

"Denial. But that's not what worries me. Not too many women want to admit the magnitude of their problems. She's no different there. She came to group simply because I made her. Then she sat on the floor paying more attention to her shoes than anything else."

"It's the first day."

"When I saw her one on one I had a difficult time sorting things out. She talked about two men. One seems like the ideal man, the other, the prize that beats her around."

"Two men?" Claire started thinking about Billy Ray calling his wife a cheater.

"I get the feeling that she just invented the ideal husband to dream about. That's not too uncommon. But the way she talked, I wondered if she wasn't having some real difficulty knowing the difference between reality and fantasy."

"What are you suspecting? A psychotic break, a personality split?"

"I'm not sure what to think. I'm willing to keep working with her, but I just wanted you to know that I may need some backup here."

Claire sighed. "I really need to come back to Brighton to see her anyway about some other medical needs. You know she's pregnant?"

The tone of Cathy's response made it obvious. "Pregnant!" Then, softer, she added, slipping more heavily into the accent of her native Spanish language, "She's been keeping that one a secret."

"I think Lena has a lot of secrets. I'll come talk to her tonight."

"I've got her intake forms in front of me. Some of the answers she gave look very suspicious for a woman who has had more than just violent anger abuse. I'd bet she's been sexually assaulted as well."

"I can explore that with her tonight."

"Thanks, Claire," Cathy responded. "It sure is nice having you back in the area."

Billy Ray crawled from his bed where he'd collapsed fully clothed the night before, plodded to the medicine cabinet in search of some aspirin, and cursed when he saw only empty shelves. Lena must have taken all the medicine as well. He'd have to opt for strong black coffee instead.

For most of the morning, he tried to restore some order to the clutter, moving randomly from bedroom to den and back, ignoring the kitchen except to clear a path to the coffeemaker.

He picked up the biggest shards of glass and uprighted his kitchen table using his right arm. The pain in his left arm was intense, and the wound was still oozing blood. He swept the floor, wiped up the spots of blood, and took out the trash, pausing to scratch Old Jeb and give him fresh water and food. When he returned to the house, he phoned the machine shop to call in sick before surrendering to the pain in his arm and his hangover and lying down on the couch. He could pull the furniture away from the front entrance when his arm was better.

It was there he saw their wedding picture. It normally sat on the desktop, but must have been thrown aside by Lena before she left. It was on the floor, leaning upside down against the wall, the glass shattered and the frame bent at an odd angle. With his head in his hands, Billy Ray began to cry. Lena had been too good to be true from the very beginning. She was so young and vibrant, filling the void that Rachel had carved in his soul. He'd promised himself that this marriage would be different, that he would stay away from the bottle, and he had, for a while.

Billy Ray cried about the secrets he'd kept. He should have been honest with Lena from the beginning. But it appeared that Lena had been keeping secrets of her own. Her pregnancy proved that. He should have known that he wouldn't be able to keep a woman like Lena satisfied. She had always been the pretty one in high school. She had her pick of the guys her own age. So no one was more surprised than Billy Ray when she agreed to go out with him. But maybe it was because she was so unhappy at home. Her jerk of a father had made one too many mistakes with her, and had driven her straight into Billy Ray's arms. When he thought of their first dates, he remembered how tearful she'd become when she talked about her father. He'd cried with her too. And that's when she'd kissed him and he'd known they could make it together.

He'd been stupid to take her for granted. He'd known that he had to stay dry to be safe. But the pull of alcohol had been strong, and his old friends were no help at all. Lester and Eddie certainly knew how to have a good time. Maybe if Lena would have joined in more, and not bugged him, he wouldn't have turned to his old patterns and they could have partied together. But she didn't like his friends, and his marriage began to stifle him. He still wanted to have some fun with his friends and if she wouldn't come along, it wasn't his fault. He'd go alone. It wasn't wrong to need some space.

But space for Billy provided an irresistible attraction into the world of alcohol. And soon three or four drinks with his pals gave way to binges and blackouts and beatings. But now, with Lena gone, regret surfaced and made him wonder.

He slipped from the couch and picked up the fractured picture. Lena's dress had cost him two weeks' pay, and he hadn't minded at all ... until now. Could it really be the truth? Could Lena really be expecting their baby? Or could she have jumped to conclusions based on a false test? He knew Lena wanted to be pregnant. He had stalled and made one excuse after another, because he didn't want her to know the truth. What had the doctor told him? "Your test results are in. There's no need for birth control anymore, Mr. Chisholm."

But maybe Lena's test was wrong. Maybe he'd exploded for nothing. The thought sickened him. If she really wasn't pregnant, he'd just ruined everything.

He shook his head as he contemplated the other option. That she was pregnant, and that she'd been living a lie, seeking other love when he turned back to his old friends. But who? Billy Ray had moved her to the country, away from her old boyfriends. Could it be someone at work? She always talked as if everyone there was married or a partyer.

A new thought struck him. *What about the city slicker that Old Jeb treed? Why else would he be snoopin' around my property making up lame excuses about something falling off his car?*

He nodded to himself. Things were coming into sharper focus. That explained why he'd seen the red Mustang. *That jerk must have come for her. Maybe Lena planned it this way all along and is just using her doctor friend as a cover. After all, the doctor wasn't driving. It was the man.*

Billy walked to the bedroom to put on a shirt. It was time to go into town. He needed some painkillers. If he could ease the pounding in his head, maybe he'd figure out a way to find the driver of the red Mustang. Anger could be useful if you channeled it in the proper direction. And Billy Ray had done just that.

Lena strolled slowly through the Brighton University commons, where ancient oaks lined brick sidewalks and students sat on wooden-slat benches or lay on the grass with open books. It was summertime at the university, and it lacked the bustle that Lena imagined would be present in the fall. Students were wearing shorts and tank tops, and sandals or flip-flops were the norm. She wished she had brought along a book to carry. Tomorrow she would. She'd seen some textbooks on a shelf back at the shelter. Tomorrow, she'd fit right in.

She was the right age for college. She even dreamed she would go one day. But Billy Ray had changed all that. As soon as they'd married, every time she brought up the idea of attending school, he talked about the money or just changed the subject or tried to kiss her ideas away.

She walked along, enjoying the fantasy of being a university student, walking arm in arm with William Raymond, like the other couples she saw. William pointed out the medical school building where he studied, and showed her his favorite soda shop where she purchased a Dr. Pepper and a Reese's Peanut Butter Cup for them to share. They sat down under a tree to eat and William kissed her tenderly, and then handed her a little box. He wasn't sure how he'd lived so long without her.

Lena pulled the ring from her pant's pocket and slid it onto her finger. The ring sparkled in the summer sun. William Raymond loved her. Life was good.

She crossed the lawn and walked by the library and another brick building with some sort of foreign phrase engraved on a stone above an arching doorway. She thought it must be Latin, but she wasn't sure. She paused by an outside announcement center of some sort, a three-dimensional bulletin board in front of the student center. There, posters advertising local bands, notecards with items for sale, and other papers advertising apartment rentals and class notes were crammed in a cascade of color. She dreamed of having her own place. Maybe once she had a job, she would come back here to look. Two notes held particular interest for her, and she carefully took the phone numbers down, writing them on the palm of her left hand. The Brighton Crisis Pregnancy Center and Brighton Women's Health Center ads were side by side. The health center offered family planning services. Lena knew enough to know what that meant, and she underlined the number on her palm to remind her which to call first. Dr. McCall hadn't been too receptive about offering her an immediate referral, but promised she could bring her some prenatal vitamins and draw her blood for a confirmatory test when she returned.

Her concentration was broken by the tap of an all-too-familiar horn.

"I didn't know when I was cruisin' the campus that I'd run across a goddess." Flirting wasn't Eddie's strong suit.

She looked up to see Billy Ray's bowling buddy leaning from the open window of his Ford pickup. "What do you want, Eddie?"

He shoved his Ford into park and jumped out of the truck. She wanted to run. Was he looking for her? Working for Billy Ray?

He shoved his hands in the front pockets of his jeans. "I didn't expect to see you here."

She tried to be pleasant. But she wanted him to go away. She lifted her chin and looked away. "Me neither."

Eddie shifted from foot to foot and seemed to be concentrating on her shorts. "Say, Lena," he said as he cleared his throat, "Billy Ray told me you'd split. He's pretty broken up about it. He wouldn't even go to work today."

It will be a week till he can move his arm. I doubt he's staying home over me. "Did he send you to look for me?"

"Naw. I just came over to pick up a few plumbing supplies. I always drive through this way. The scenery is better."

And I'm sure the coeds like you and your truck, Eddie. "Oh."

"Is there anything I can do for you? Need a truck for groceries or anything?"

The offer suprised her. She'd always figured Eddie was Billy Ray's friend. She'd never thought he may think of her as a friend too. "Just do me a favor, Eddie. Don't tell Billy Ray that you saw me."

"He doesn't know?"

"Does that surprise you?"

Eddie shrugged his shoulders through his orange tank top. "He just told me you'd left."

"How is he?" She stammered, not really wanting Billy Ray to think she cared. "Uh, I mean, how did he act?"

"How would you expect, Lena? I know you must have your reasons, but I think you'd be a little heartbroken if he'd have done the same thing to you."

His logic was lost on her. She wasn't sure what kind of a slant Billy Ray had put on things.

Eddie lifted his eyes to meet hers, then looked away. She'd never been able to hold his gaze for more than a second or two. She'd heard once that body language for attraction is when a man won't meet your eyes and hold your gaze. "He told me you had a new boyfriend."

She wanted to protest, but just then, he grabbed her hand. "Whoa! Where'd you get this?"

Her hand went immediately to the ring to cover it, but it was too late. Eddie was oohing and oh manning, and was in general almost speechless over the sight of Lena's diamond. "It's just a ring, Eddie."

"Billy Ray gave you this?"

She almost laughed. "No."

He dropped her hand almost like it was hot. "Oh." He started using his favorite adjectives. "Oh man. What is this guy, a doctor or something?" Then he just started shaking his head and cursed again. "Lena, you just left yesterday!"

"Come on, Eddie. I'm not like that. I don't know why Billy Ray thinks that. I'm not cheatin' on him."

"Where'd you get the ring?"

Lena knew he wouldn't believe the truth. Besides, she didn't really care about saving face in front of Eddie. And she was still so hurt and angry at Billy Ray. Her mind went blank. "You just tell him that if you want to, Eddie. Tell him my boyfriend gave it to me."

He stood fidgeting from foot to foot as if he had an itch he couldn't scratch. Then he just shook his head and walked toward his truck, muttering choice words from his limited vocabulary.

He was in his truck and pulling out when she called his name. "Eddie!" she shouted. "Don't tell him where I am!"

She sighed as Eddie slowed momentarily, then nodded and drove away.

She swore under her breath. *Is Eddie likely to keep my secret?* "Right," she answered herself sarcastically, watching his truck disappear. *I'm going to have to leave here soon.*

Claire picked up the chart in the rack outside the exam room door. She had three patients left and she'd already passed the four-thirty mark, so she knew Lisa wouldn't allow another walk-in, short of someone receiving CPR in the parking lot.

The chart was for Stephanie Blackwell, a thirty-year-old woman in for premarital genetics counseling. *Great. Like I'm an expert in this.* Claire carefully reviewed Lucy's handwritten chart entry, which mentioned a personal history of irregular menses and a family history of polycystic kidney disease. Lucy had written, "October wedding planned. Patient wondering about genetics counseling." Claire looked at the patient's blood pressure. It was 126/82 and appeared to have been recorded by Cyrus.

This ought to be interesting. I'm the one who needs genetics counseling. Claire opened the door to see an attractive woman, appearing younger than her stated age. Claire reached out her hand. "I'm Dr. McCall. How can I help you?"

The woman sat with her hands folded over a paper drape and was wearing a disposable examination gown. "I'd like to talk about getting a test to see if I'm going to develop polycystic kidney disease."

Claire looked at the chart. She had been a patient of Dr. Jenkins for years, and although he'd seen her for relatively minor illnesses, when he recommended screening for polycystic kidney disease on numerous previous visits, the patient always declined. "Why now? I see you weren't interested in the past."

"A couple reasons really. Number one, I've met a great guy, and he wants children. He's seen what my father and grandfather have been through with kidney failure and dialysis. He wants to know if our children will be at risk."

"Seems reasonable. I can order an ultrasound of your kidneys. If you don't have any cysts on your kidneys by this age, we can confidently say that you've escaped the disease."

The patient looked down. "I'm an only child. My father has always been active. He retired early just so he could sail and snow ski. I think he's felt some guilt for most of his life for passing on an inherited disease to me."

Claire lifted her pen. "Your father has polycystic kidneys. Is he on dialysis?"

"Just started four months ago. It's killing him. His whole life revolves around his Monday, Wednesday, Friday dialysis schedule. He can't do the things he loves."

"Why does he feel guilt about you? You haven't been tested, correct?"

"I guess he just figures I've got it. His father had it. He was an only child and he got it. Now I'm his only daughter, so I think he just thinks it has to be."

"But polycystic kidney disease is autosomal dominant. That means if your father has it, you have a fifty-percent chance of inheriting it. But it also means you have a fifty-percent chance of being disease-free."

"I've never wanted to know before. I always had the same assumption that my father has." She looked up and met Claire's gaze. "I didn't want to know the news if the news was bad. If I can't change the future, I was afraid to know." She hesitated. "You have no idea what it's like living with those kind of odds. A flip of a coin. Heads, I end up on dialysis. Tails, I don't. That's a mental torture I've lived with ever since I watched my grandfather struggle."

You have no idea how much I understand. Claire looked at her watch. There wasn't time to explain if she was going to be fair to the other patients. "Are you being pressured to get tested by your fiancé?"

"No. I think it's only reasonable for him to want to know. He loves me. It's not like we won't be married or something if I've got it. But children, well, that's something we'll have to decide about if I've got it."

"You can still bear children who can have productive lives even if they develop kidney failure. It's usually not until late in life. You've obviously lived a long time with the threat hanging over your head. How will it change your life if you find out you've got the disease for sure? Will you still have kids?"

"Probably. They could still be negative. It's only fifty-fifty."

"So if getting tested won't change what you do, why get it?" Claire paused. "I'm only challenging you to see if you've thought through all the angles."

Stephanie smiled. She was Harley Davidson-calendar pretty, something that would likely change if her skin aged and bronzed with kidney failure. "If it was only about me, I wouldn't have the test. I've learned to deal with the pressure. And it's not really about my fiancé, although he'd like to know. It's about my father."

"You want to relieve his guilt?"

"No. I want to donate him a kidney."

154

The thought hadn't occurred to Claire. "Oh, of course." It made wonderful sense. A live donor, if an appropriate match, would be the most successful transplant option, and a daughter would have the greatest chance of being a close match. Claire hadn't stopped to focus beyond her patient. She nodded her head with admiration for her young patient. "Then maybe your father could get back to his active life." She paused, then proceeded with an exam, adjusted the patient's blood-pressure medication, and scheduled her for an ultrasound of the kidneys. "If the ultrasound shows no cysts, I'll send you over to the transplant coordinator at Brighton University to see if your tissue type is a match for your father."

Claire walked out of the room struck with the patient's statement. *If it was only about me, I wouldn't have the test.*

But it isn't always just about us, is it, Stephanie?

After work, on the way to Brighton, Claire checked with Dr. Branum for an update on Brittany Lewis. The surgery was described as a "chip shot." "This was an intern gallbladder, Claire," he said, "you'd have loved it."

His comment had hit the mark. She would have loved it. But somehow, her heart warmed knowing she was the one who'd been able to assist Brittany through her fears and get her to do the right thing. Claire smiled and muttered, "I'm sure. Maybe I'll stop by and see her tonight."

"Don't stop tonight. I'm going to keep her in the hospital on observation. The poor girl's only nineteen and she's on her own. I'd send her out if she wouldn't be alone."

"She's nineteen, but she's tough." *This valley seems to grow 'em that way.* "Tell her I'll see her in the office next week."

Branum laughed. "Perfect. I cut 'em. You watch 'em."

Claire said good-bye and laid the phone on the seat beside her. Route Two over North Mountain wasn't exactly a one-hand steering job.

An hour later, she pulled up to the women's shelter. Lena seemed glad to see a familiar face. Cathy Rivera let them use the library room. There was a two-seat couch with two other upholstered chairs, and shelves lined with books. Claire could have been happy here alone for hours. Cathy gestured to the furniture. "Make yourselves at home." She shrugged and smiled. "Hey, it was donated. I never say 'no.'"

Claire understood when she looked at the chairs. She studied Lena for a moment. "Maroon vinyl or orange flowers?"

Lena sat on the orange one. Claire knelt beside her and put a small rubber tourniquet around Lena's arm. Claire then swabbed the inside of her patient's elbow and made quick work of drawing a blood sample for a pregnancy test. "I'll drop it by the university lab on my way out. I'll call you with the results tomorrow."

Claire took a deep breath. Where should she start? She leaned back and tried to appear relaxed. "I've brought you some prenatal vitamins. I want you to take one a day."

Lena shook her head. "I'm not keepin' this baby."

"Give this some time, Lena. An abortion isn't something a clinic will want to do in the first few weeks of pregnancy anyway. Give it some time and think about what I said last night. And take the vitamins for your own health. They certainly won't hurt you." She held up her hands. "And they're free."

Lena nodded quietly.

"Will you talk to me, Lena?" She hesitated. "Sometimes it helps if you have someone . . . a friend, a mother . . . even a doctor to talk things out with."

Lena stared at the floor.

"Do you have anyone you can talk to? Anyone supporting you?"

She spoke quietly. "Billy Ray. That's all."

"Will you talk to me? It won't be easy, but I think it will relieve your sorrow if you share it with me."

Lena nodded. "I guess."

"I want you to tell me about Billy Ray. What happened yesterday before you called?"

"It was supposed to be a celebration," she began. "I'd fixed a special dinner." Lena paused and stared out the window.

"A celebration? An anniversary?"

Lena shook her head. "I wanted to tell him about the pregnancy. To surprise him with the news." She sniffed. "I wanted it to be so special. We were going to celebrate his not drinkin' for the last three weeks, so I used that as an excuse to make a nice dinner. Then after we ate, I told him he was going to be a father."

Claire waited without speaking.

"That's when he exploded. He accused me of cheatin' on him. I couldn't talk to him. He just went crazy."

"How did you stop him?"

She put her hand to her mouth and began to cry. Through her sobs, she continued. "I thought I was going to die. He'd knocked over the table. He knocked me down and held me by the hair. When he jerked me up, I stabbed him in the arm with a piece of broken glass."

"So he left you alone?"

She shook her head. "I think it just scared him. It gave me a chance to get away. When he grabbed his arm, I ran."

"Good for you."

"I grabbed a butcher knife. That's when he left." She smiled through her tears. "Maybe he was afraid."

You're my hero, Lena.

They sat quietly for a minute before Lena added, "It's the first time he hit me when he wasn't drinkin'."

"He was mad about the baby?"

"I guess."

"He didn't want kids?"

"We'd been trying for a while. I'd been off my pills for six months. Billy Ray hasn't always been a bad guy. He's just bad when he drinks, mostly. I thought if we'd have a baby, he'd settle down. Stay home more." She looked up. "He'd usually drink when he went out with friends."

"Why would he accuse you of cheating on him?"

"I don't know. I've always been faithful to Billy Ray. I know I'm not perfect, but I wasn't cheatin' on him or nothing like that. He's always been a jealous type, though. He never liked it if I talked to other guys. I think if I was cheating, he'd kill me and whoever I was with." She paused. "But I'd never do that." She looked at the floor. "I always planned to have a family with Billy Ray. I just figured he'd settle down if we had a family together."

Wishful thinking. "Did you ever fight back?"

Lena's gaze hardened. "Once."

"Will you tell me about it?"

"I remember it because it was the first time I thought I was really going to die. Billy Ray came home drunk after bowling with his friends. He hit me and held my face into the pillow. I couldn't breathe, but he let me up just enough to gasp for air." Lena's face flattened. "Then we had sex." She continued without emotion like she was reporting events that happened to someone else. "It was the day after I'd come in to see you. My ankle hurt so bad, I couldn't have run from him if I'd had the chance."

"He forced himself on you?"

She nodded and wiped her eyes. Her nose wrinkled like she smelled something unpleasant. "I was pretty torn up down there. I bled for a week even though I wasn't on my period." She hesitated before the memory seemed to flood to the surface. She lifted her top lip in a snarl to reveal a small chip in her front incisor. "That's when I decided I'd had enough. I decided to kill him. I lay awake most of the night planning how I'd do it. The next morning, when he was passed out on the couch, I put a shotgun to his head and pulled the trigger, but I'd forgotten to load the gun."

Claire put a hand over her mouth. "What happened?"

"I scared him to death. He begged for forgiveness like he always did." She shrugged. "But this time he stopped drinking. And I thought that meant that he wouldn't hit me anymore. But that time was weird."

"Why's that?"

"Sex for Billy Ray had always been his way of proving to me or to himself that we were okay together. It was his way of making up. He'd never used it to hurt me before."

"Rape isn't usually about sex. It's a power thing."

Claire let the comment hang for a moment, hoping it would jar Lena with some insight. "I want to ask you about one more thing. When you talked to Ms. Rivera, she wasn't sure about something. She had the idea that you were talking about two different men in your life."

Lena stared quietly at the floor, shaking her head. "I've never cheated on Billy Ray."

"I believe you."

"She thinks I'm crazy, doesn't she?"

"No, Lena." Claire hesitated. "Why would she think that?"

Lena stood up. "Look, maybe this wasn't such a good idea."

"Sharing your problems is a good idea. Sometimes it helps us see the reasons we do what we do, and keeps us from repeating our mistakes."

Lena paced slowly around the little library room. When she paused at the door, Claire was sure she was going to bolt.

"Lena, you're an intelligent woman. You've got so much going for you. You're young, attractive, and you've got your health. But more than that, the things you've told me show how much insight you already have." Claire threw up her hands. "You've been so open with me. That's a great start to winning over this problem and getting a life back. Why wouldn't you talk to the other women? Why wouldn't you talk to Cathy?"

The teenager stayed quiet.

"Why do you talk to me?"

Lena's hand went to her eye, where she touched a scar hidden in her eyebrow, and then she headed back to the door. As she moved, Claire noticed a slight limp, something she hadn't seen when they'd walked to the room. Lena pulled open the door and stepped into the hall. Before she disappeared, her eyes met Claire's. "You've seen what Billy Ray does. It's stupid to pretend with you."

Chapter Fourteen

ohn Cerelli was a patient man. But twelve nights, two tickbites, and more briar scratches than he could count had broken his will to return to Lena's place to risk life or limb from the monster dog or the gun-totin' Billy Ray. The engagement ring was gone forever, and John would have to face facts.

John pulled into the parking lot behind the clinic and lifted a cool sausage and mushroom pizza from the passenger seat. He popped the trunk and shoved aside the night-vision goggles and the metal detector with disgust, and hoisted a cardboard box of medical supplies into his arms. He closed the trunk with his elbow. On the top of the supplies, he balanced the pizza box.

He used his own key to the back door. "Claire?"

"In here."

He found Claire at her desk. He set the box of supplies on the floor and plopped the pizza on the desk on top of her patient charts.

"Hey!"

He met her stare. She broke away and hung her head. "John." She shook her head. "I'm sorry. I completely forgot."

"I noticed."

"Did you wait long?"

"Thirty minutes."

"You should have called."

"I tried. I got voice mail."

"Ugh. My phone's in the car." She closed the large medical textbook. "I'm sorry."

He shrugged. "I went by your place. When I didn't find you, I thought I'd look here."

"Good guess."

"Claire, it doesn't take a college degree to know where to find you. What's going on?"

She let his comments fall. "Work, John. Sick people. I'm a doctor."

"No one has to work twenty-four/seven."

"I'm seeing new stuff around here. It may be common to some people, but my internship was surgery, remember? I've got a little catching up to do."

"Why did you come home, Claire?"

She looked up and lifted the top of the pizza box. "You ate?"

John nodded. He couldn't quite resist holding up his hurt for her to admire. "Alone. At our favorite pizza place." He added one more twist of an emotional knife. "I asked Tony to put the cheese on the top of the pepperonis just like you like it."

"I said I was sorry, John." She dropped the lid. "I'll eat later."

"Answer the question."

She leaned back and glared at him.

He decided to rephrase it. "Did you come back for this? To work day and night?"

"These people need me."

"Remember why you came back, Claire."

"I don't need this."

He whispered under his breath. "You need it. You just don't see it."

"You're just angry because I stood you up, is that it?"

"It's not about our date. It's about what you're doing."

She sighed. "I'm working, John. I'm not sure I see the catastrophe here." She held up her hands. "What do you want me to say?"

"I want you to see why you're doing this to yourself."

"This is a demanding job. My patients need me."

"Give me a break. This isn't about your patients. It's about you. You keep yourself so busy so you won't have to face life, Claire. *Your* life. You just walk around pretending your life is normal."

"Oh, now you're my psychiatrist. Since when did you—"

"I'm no psychiatrist." He took a step toward her. "I'm just a man who loves you."

She looked away. "You have a funny way of showing it."

"Why did you come home, Claire? Tell me what you want."

162

Claire took a deep breath. "You know why I came home."

"You left a life you loved, Claire. Surgery. High risk. High glamour. You loved it. Tell me why you left." He sat on the corner of her desk. "I just don't want you to lose sight of what you wanted."

Claire appeared to be studying her hands. She had long, fluent fingers. After a minute, she spoke slowly, "I came home to recapture life. I wanted to connect with a father I'd lost. I wanted to find the faith that I'd lost." Her eyes met his. "And I wanted to find love again."

John stayed quiet and kept her gaze until she broke away.

"I knew my mom needed help. I had to come. It was the right thing. For once I wanted to do something that wasn't for me."

"Claire, you changed locations, but you're still running away from HD."

She stood up. "I just want a normal life! I want a meaningful job, a man, maybe a family. I don't want to think about HD."

"You can't just walk around pretending it doesn't exist. That's a fantasy world."

"How can I pretend it doesn't exist? Every time I go home, I see it. I can't escape it."

"Deal with it, Claire. Get your test results and get on with life. Then you'll know what you're up against."

"Is that what this is about? You can't live with the uncertainty. You want to know if I've got the HD gene so you will know if a relationship is worth pursuing."

"My desire to be with you has nothing to do with whether you will get HD."

"You can't say that. Look at Wally. I asked my mom straight out. Would she have chosen this man if she'd have known he'd get HD? No. That's an honest answer, John."

"If you had HD right now, I might feel differently. But you don't. We may have years together, Claire, without HD. Just being able to have you with me for a little while is enough."

"Say the word, Cerelli. Get on your knee."

John stepped forward and took her in his arms. She had been everything he dreamed of wanting. Strong. Smart. Beautiful. Full of energy and life, and best of all, a soulmate who shared his love for God. He nudged her gently until he felt her relax against him. He kissed her forehead gently and buried his face into her hair, breathing in her aroma. When she had been a medical student, it was her scent that always pushed him to the limit of control. She carried a delightful fragrance mix of her favorite shampoo, of freshly washed clothing, and the unique hint of a clinical antiseptic bouquet she absorbed at the hospital. For someone else, it may have been a turnoff. For him, because of all she meant, it was the essence of heaven. He kissed her again, snuggling his face against her neck. He took a deep breath and eased her back to place his mouth against hers. After a moment, he gently pushed her to arm's length and took her hands in his. "I'm not proposing, Claire."

"But you just said—"

"I just said you've got to get your head out of the sand. Stop pretending. Face the cards you've been dealt. Only then can you reconnect with your family, your father . . . with love . . . with me."

"But I don't have to know the future in order to face reality."

"No. But how can you know what to do, Claire? Are you heading back into surgery? You've said you won't if you're HD positive."

"I'm afraid."

"But knowing is better than fear of the unknown. What if you're negative? Then all your anxiety has been for nothing."

"I'm not afraid of being negative. I'm afraid of being positive." Her eyes met his. "I'm afraid you won't be around."

"The crux of the problem is what is in your mind, Claire, not what's in mine. I've told you what's in my heart."

"What do you want from me? Did you just come over here to tell me I'm not living in reality?"

"I came over here because we had a date, Claire, you know, time a guy and a girl spend together for—"

"I know what a date is, John. I just forgot."

"You just forgot about your father, your mother, your boyfriend, about making sense of a life at risk for HD. You can't hide in your work forever."

"Okay, Cerelli, I've been open. Answer the same question for me. Why did you come to Stoney Creek?"

"You know why I came."

"I want to hear it."

"I want you back in my life, Claire. That should be obvious."

"You love me?"

He sighed. "I love you."

"What keeps you from asking me to be your wife?"

"It's not time."

"You're afraid of the future. You're not ready for unconditional commitment."

He backed away to the door. "The trouble is not my fear of the future. It's yours." He paused. "You're the one who's not ready for the commitment."

He walked to the back hall toward the exit. *How can I make her understand what I feel? Why can't she believe in real love?* "Good night, Claire."

He heard her call his name as he let the door close behind him, but he just didn't have the energy to return.

By the time Claire quietly slipped in the front door of her house, she was wondering if John might be right about more than just Luigi's pizza. Perhaps it was time for her to take a surgeon's approach to her problems: gather the facts and face them head-on.

She met Della at the kitchen table, sorting laundry.

"You're still up."

"Where were you? I tried calling."

"I went to Brighton to see a patient at the women's shelter after work. Then I had some reading to do."

"Wally's got some sort of stomach flu."

Claire wrinkled her nose. "Vomiting?"

"Diarrhea. His butt is so sore from me cleaning him up that he throws a fit every time I try to change him."

"I'm sorry, Mom."

"Just changing a regular diaper on him is an adventure. The man can't hold still. The last time he got his hands in it. So I'm weaving and bobbing like Mohammad Ali trying not to get hit. Wally is cursing me and we're getting poop everywhere. It was on the sheets, the bed rails, under his fingernails. And get this. I finish cleaning everything up, changing the bed and everything, I'm sweating like a pig, so I go to wipe my forehead with my hand because I presume I feel beads of sweat, and I see it's not sweat at all. It was a little blob of Wally's diarrhea."

By this time, Claire was beginning to see the humor in the situation, especially with her mother's exasperation over the event. She tried to squelch a snicker. "What'd you do?"

"I stripped naked in the laundry room and took a thirty-minute shower. I could hear him screamin' in the bedroom for me, but at that point, I didn't even care. I had to preserve my sanity." She paused, as if searching for an affirmation that she'd done the right thing. "So I stayed in the bathroom and showered. I even put on my lipstick and that new eyeliner you bought me. Then, when I felt human again, I went back to see Wally."

Claire laughed and held her abdomen.

Della threw a bath towel at her daughter. "Easy for you to laugh. I'm going grocery shopping."

"It's after ten."

"I'll go to Carlisle to the Super Wal-Mart."

"Mom, that's a half-hour drive. You won't be home until midnight. I can go tomorrow."

"You don't get it. I want to go grocery shopping. It's a normal activity," she said, walking toward the door, pausing to check her face in the mirror by the door. She lifted her blond hair from her collar and sent a kiss to her reflection, before continuing to talk to herself. "You take all the time you need." She looked at Claire and tossed back her head and laughed. "It's a sad life when you look forward to spending time alone in Wal-Mart."

Claire just shook her head and watched her mother disappear through the door. She could hear her mother call back one last remark from the front lawn: "He's all yours!"

She fixed herself a cup of peppermint tea and thought about why she had returned to Stoney Creek. The house was quiet except for Wally noises, the soft bumping of his arms and legs against the bed rails, and what Della called his noises of frustration. Instead of saying, "I'm thirsty" or "I'm angry" or "I'm wet," he often just made grunting vocalizations or yelled, "Hey!" until someone figured out what he wanted.

She'd come home to reconnect with a father she'd left as a teenager, the father she'd grown to hate, the one she'd eventually grown up to forgive. Last year, she'd even sensed the quiet return of a daughter's love.

She listened to his noises. *How can I reconnect with him? I'm not even sure he knows I'm his daughter half the time.*

She walked down the short hall and into his room. "Hi, Daddy."

"Hey. Uh uh."

"Are you thirsty? Wet?" She thickened a glass of lemonade for him, but he took only one swallow, and kept up his agitated grunting.

She checked his diaper. That wasn't the problem.

She felt his forehead. "Pain? Are you hot?" She looked at a bowl of oatmeal which was largely untouched. "Do you feel like eating? Are you hungry? Does your stomach hurt?"

"Nnn. Nnn."

No.

Finally, she just turned off the lamp by his hospital bed and sat down in a padded kitchen chair that Della kept by the bed. She leaned forward and took his hand, straining against his involuntary jerking movements to keep his hand in hers.

His grunting stopped.

She released his hand.

"Nnn. Nnn. I–I–I–"

"It's okay, Daddy." She took his hand again, and as before, he quieted. *Daddy just wants to hold my hand.*

Softly, in the dimness of the room, she began to tell Wally of her pain. "I think John's afraid. He's holding back from me." She jerked forward, following Wally's movements. *I just want to know he loves me.*

"I hear him say he loves me, but ..." *He knows I might end up like you.* "He says I'm the one that's not ready for commitment, but I think he's the one protecting his heart." She sniffed.

She rested her head on her free hand, crying in the dark. "He may be right, Daddy. I don't want to think about the future. I say I've put it all in God's hands, and that I'll trust him to do what's best, but ..." *It still scares me to death to think I'll end up dancing just like you.*

"It's just not fair. It's just not fair." She wiped her tears with the back of her hand. "It's never far away. The cloud is always there, threatening me." She shook her head. "I can't just keep pretending I'm not at risk.

"I thought John was ready to ask me to be his wife. Oh, Daddy, I was so thrilled. I knew he had my ring. I just wanted to throw my arms around him and say 'yes' almost before he asked." She listened as Wally's grunting started up, then quieted again as she stroked the back of his hand.

"But I know he's waiting for my test results. He wants to know whether I'm free of HD, so he can decide." She shook her head. "So much for my dream of unconditional love, huh, Daddy?" She stood up and took his head in her hands, trying to hold it still so she could talk face to face. "They don't make 'em like Della anymore, Pops."

Wally grinned, mouth open and grunting.

Claire risked a quick kiss on his forehead. "Night, Daddy. I love you."

It struck her as she neared the door to leave. She did love him. In spite of their long separation, in spite of the HD, in spite of his inability to communicate it in return, she loved Wally. He was her father, and their blood link, the very thing that produced her life's dark cloud, was the very thing that produced her desire to love him.

He was her father. She loved him.

And for now, that was normal enough for Claire McCall.

Chapter Fifteen

‧◦◦◦⋙⋘◦◦◦‧

The following day, Claire tended to the business of a severe sunburn, an infant with colic, a well-baby check, two high school athletic physicals, and three blood-pressure checks. She reviewed Stephanie Blackwell's ultrasound and asked Lisa to tell her she didn't have cysts on the kidneys and to set up a referral to the transplant coordinator at Brighton University. As she set the ultrasound report aside, she found her spirit buoyed with joy. *Stephanie is not at risk for inheriting her father's illness. Perhaps the same is true for me!*

By midday, she was catching up on her dictation in her office, her door open. Sensing someone's presence in her peripheral vision, she looked over expecting to see her nurse.

Billy Ray Chisholm was holding his left elbow in his right hand. He wore faded blue jeans and a NASCAR T-shirt. "Hi, Doc."

Claire jerked her head upright, then slowly slid her chair away from the doorway. "What do you need, Mr. Chisholm? How did you get back here?"

"Walked right in the back door." He grinned. "I don't need much. I thought I'd just catch you between patients."

She glared at him and stood up. She didn't like him standing so much taller over her when she was in the chair. She moved to her left to put the large oak desk between them.

He nodded his head with plastic sincerity. "I need to find Lena."

"You know I can't help you with that," she said at a near shout, hoping to alert her staff of Billy Ray's presence. *Where is Cyrus when I need him?* "Why, Billy Ray? Why should I help you find her?"

The question seemed to set him off-balance. "Well, I—. She needs me. I need her, Doc. She's probably told you some bad stuff about me and well . . . some of it's true, Doc. I lose my temper when I drink. But

169

I'm workin' on that. I'm in AA now. I need to talk to her. Find out how she's doing."

"She's fine."

"So you've seen her, Doc?"

Claire took a deep breath. *Where is my staff?* "I can't give you details, you know that. A doctor-patient relationship is confidential." She shrugged, knowing she was way over Billy Ray's head. "Listen, Billy, I think it's nice you want to talk to her. But now is not the time. I recommend getting into counseling to work on your own problems before you see Lena again. Let's see some proof that you're ready."

"Lena's brought some of this on herself, you know. Our marriage needs some work, but it's not all me."

"No woman deserves to be struck. I don't care what she does." Claire bit her lower lip. She didn't want to argue with him.

"A woman is supposed to be faithful. When I found out she was cheatin' on me, well, I just didn't keep my head. It wasn't right."

"Lena says she's hasn't been running around on you. How do you know these things?"

"A man just knows." He looked down.

"But how do you—"

"I caught her boyfriend," he said in a low voice. "My dog ran him right up a tree."

Just then, Lucy, Lisa, Kelly, and Amy appeared behind Billy Ray. Lucy talked for the quartet. "Mr. Chisholm, if you want to see the doctor, you'll have to register out front."

"Oh, no. Doc McCall and I was just talkin' like friends, weren't we?" He quickly pulled up his left sleeve. "I did want to show you this gash in my arm. What'ya make of that?"

Claire could see from her comfortable distance that Billy Ray's arm was beet red and swollen, hot with infection. This was the last thing she wanted to see: a legitimate reason not to quickly rush him out of the office.

"We've got other patients waiting, Dr. McCall."

Claire nodded. "Just put him in the procedure room. And get me some Augmentin samples."

Lucy wasn't happy. But Claire didn't want to risk angering Billy Ray any more. She probed his wound without anesthesia, gently breaking into a pocket of creamy drainage. She dressed the wound, and gave him instructions and the pills. "Take these twice a day until they're gone. Then I'll need to see you back." She lifted her hand toward the door. "But make an appointment for next week."

She had him out the door before her staff could even locate an old record of previous clinic visits. When Claire finally saw it at her desk later that day, she huffed in disgust and dropped it in the out box without opening it. The day couldn't be long enough to spend precious minutes thinking about Billy Ray.

Lena leaned against the base of the large oak tree on the commons lawn at Brighton University. She opened the book in her hand slowly, admiring the ring on her hand. The book was a novel, the only fiction she could find amidst the shelves of self-help and Christian books at the center.

Decision time was coming. She had one job possibility, a kitchen assistant in the campus cafeteria. She would have to sell the ring if she didn't get a job soon. Cathy Rivera had emphasized how important it was to start being proactive in her life. She needed to set goals and make plans. But plans were hard to make when she didn't know what Billy Ray was up to. If three-adjective Eddie could be trusted to keep a secret, she could stay around. But the likelihood that Eddie was going to keep his trap shut was about as likely as snow in that eternal hot place. For now, she just wanted to lay low, wait a few days to see how things played out. If she found out Billy Ray was looking for her, she'd have to move on, and in that case, she'd certainly have to part with her beautiful ring. She sighed and tried to concentrate on her reading, but her attention continually turned to her ring and her mind to William Raymond.

He leaned over and she accepted his kiss on her cheek. "Hey, doll, I was just on my way to class. Will you be here when I'm done?"

"Of course."

The ring dazzled in the sunlight filtering through the leaves above. It was so special, this ring of promise. The promise of a bright future filled with the life she'd always dreamed of.

She lifted her hand, allowing it to stay nestled safely within his. He kissed her again. As they parted, their hands drifted slowly apart until at last only their fingertips touched and he was on his way to his medical school classes again.

Her hand was still in the air when a voice shocked her back to the present. "The time. I asked if you knew what time it was."

The handsome young man had a thick backpack and a two-day beard. He was thin, with round wire-rimmed glasses, a Beatle of another era.

Lena blushed and looked at her watch. "Four o'clock."

The man squinted in her direction for a moment before moving on. His eyes were intense, as if he could see right through to her mind. Her hand went instinctively to cover her ring, as if in doing so, she could also hide her soul.

"Thanks," he said. "I'm late for class."

"What class?" She was surprised she had the boldness to ask.

"Medical school," he said, as if it was no big deal. "Gross anatomy lab."

"Gross anatomy?" She wasn't sure what it was, but she twisted her face at the name.

"You know, cadaver dissection."

"Oh," she said, now even more embarrassed at her ignorance. She waved her hand, playing the dizzy blond. "Of course I knew that."

He smiled at her and kept walking.

And as he left, she held her hand up toward him. *Bye, William. I'll have dinner ready by seven.*

Chapter Sixteen

Somewhere after two A.M. the next morning, Brittany Lewis fell into fitful sleep. It was nice to be out of the hospital, but her first night at home was far from normal. The pain she had from her gallbladder surgery wasn't severe, unless she moved too fast or took a deep breath. It was better with the Percocet, but the drug left her feeling like a zombie: zoned out, sleepy, and thick-headed, as if she'd had too many beers at Chico's.

The thumping sound pushed her to semi-alertness, that stage between fully awake and dead-to-the-world asleep. In her Percocet-induced slumber, the thumping fit in with her dream world. Dr. Branum tapped his cowboy boots on the floor and ordered the other doctor to put her to sleep so he could get started.

The regular beep of her heart monitor skipped erratically, taking on the sound of a dull pounding.

Thump. Thump-thump. Her heart stopped. The doctor pounded on her chest to save her life.

Brittany opened her eyes. She was back in her little basement apartment alone. Someone was pounding on the front door. *Good grief! What time is it?* She rubbed her eyes and studied the clock. "Coming!" She flipped on the light in the bedroom and let it guide her toward the pounding.

Who could be here at this hour? Her first thought was that her on-again-off-again boyfriend Jason must have finally caught up with the news that she'd had surgery. It would be just like him to show up in the middle of the night to check on her. He had never had an abundance of what her mother called "social graces."

She crept slowly forward, holding her right side. The thumping had ceased since she yelled out, but now, it continued again, except as a sharper sound, with a familiar rhythm which called for her response. It was the childhood rhythm game that everyone seemed to know: *knock, knock-knock, knock, knock....* She sang out her response, "Knock, knock!" She tried to remember the stupid little phrase. *Shave and a haircut... two bits! Knock, knock-knock, knock-knock... knock, knock!*

She had only time to twist the lock on the doorknob to open when the door popped open, slamming into her forehead. It exploded forward with such force that she was knocked backward, dazed. She reached for her head and squinted toward the doorway, but he was already on her, throwing her to the floor.

She pulled to her hands and knees, attempting to crawl away, but she was slammed forward into the floor again. Her scream was immediately squelched by a hand over her mouth. She bit down on her attacker's finger. She heard him yell and felt his grip lessen. She managed to roll to her back. That's when she got her first glimpse of him in the dim light coming from her bedroom.

Who is he? He was wearing a surgical mask. Like the ones she'd seen only yesterday.

Claire awakened to the electronic chirp from her phone. She groaned. *Have I overslept?* She squinted at the darkness. *No, it's still dark.* She groped for her phone. *Who would be calling at this hour?* She studied the digital readout of the number on her phone without recognition. With a groan, she pressed the talk button. "Hello. Dr. McCall speaking."

The voice was female and youthful with palpable apprehension. "Oh, Dr. McCall," she began in a low, nearly whispered volume. "You've got to help me. Please help me," she cried.

Anxiety tightened a grip just below Claire's breast. "I ... uh ... sure. Who's calling?"

The syllables tumbled out in erratic sobs. "Brit–tan–y." She sniffed. "Lew–is."

"Brittany. I am here to help you," she responded with calmness she did not feel. "Try to settle down and tell me what has happened. Are you in pain from your surgery?"

"No—o," she sobbed. "A man—A man—tried to ki—ll me."

Claire couldn't believe her ears. *What? Here? In Stoney Creek?* "Brittany. Where are you?"

"Home." She sniffed. "He, he r—raped me."

"Have you called the police?"

"No. He's gone now. I'm alone."

"Who did this? Do you know him?"

"I don't know. He was wearing a mask."

"Can you come to my office?" Immediately, Claire realized the stupidity of her question. The patient was traumatized, and early post-op. "I'll come pick you up at your apartment. You will need an examination."

"Okay."

"Listen to me very carefully. Did this just happen?"

"A little while ago. Tonight," she sobbed.

"Okay. Don't clean up. Don't even wash your hands or change your clothes. I need you to promise me this. It will help the police to figure out who did this, okay?"

"I want to take a shower."

"Please don't. Let me collect the evidence first. Brittany, this is so important. I'll be there as soon as I can. Give me fifteen minutes. I can have the police meet us at my office. Will that be okay?"

Her voice was quiet. Resolved. "Yes."

Claire terminated the call and quickly dressed. She called Lucy Dellinger, her nurse, from her car.

"Hello."

"Lucy. This is Claire. I'm so sorry to wake you so early. I'm on my way to pick up Brittany Lewis. She was sexually assaulted tonight."

She could hear Lucy's audible sigh. Lucy was the only Sexual Assault Nurse Examiner for the county and was used to nighttime interruptions.

"Can you open up the SANE room for us? And call the police and tell them to meet us at the office."

"I'm on my way."

Claire shut off the phone and whispered a prayer for Brittany and for herself. This was not part of her training as a surgery intern, but she knew Lucy would guide her so the evidence would not be mishandled.

When she arrived at Brittany Lewis's apartment a few minutes later, Claire stood by her VW for a moment looking at the front of the house. A chill raised Claire's skin into a sea of goosebumps. It was over a block to the nearest streetlight, and at this predawn hour, the sidewalk leading around the house was dark with shadows. *Of all the times not to have a flashlight.* Images of a lurking predator hiding in the bushes flashed in her mind, freezing her feet to the road.

Oh, Father, keep me safe. Claire edged forward, forcing her paralyzed feet to move. A dog's sudden and menacing bark from across the street provided the stimulus she needed to move. Walking briskly, and then running, she drove herself forward along the sidewalk leading around the house. Beside each bush, Claire accelerated, imagining a rapist hidden behind the rustling branches.

At the back door, Claire knocked quickly, wanting to appear calm, but desperately wanting off the small concrete stoop and into the relative safety of Brittany's apartment. She took a deep breath and whispered to her soul, "Yea, though I walk in the valley of the shadow of death I will fear no evil . . ." *Answer the door, Brittany!*

She heard a timid voice from across the door. "Dr. McCall?"

She steadied her response. "Yes. Brittany, it's me, Dr. McCall."

She listened to the snap of a dead bolt. Claire resisted the urge to push her way in. She squinted into the dimness of the room, trying to make out the dark silhouette in front of her. "Brittany?"

Claire stepped forward as her patient's face came into view. She felt Brittany's hand on her arm. "Come in."

The door closed behind her. "Brittany!" she spoke at a low volume. "Why are you standing in the dark?"

"I was afraid he might see in."

Claire squeezed Brittany's hands and waited as her eyes adjusted to the dim light. Slowly the scene came into view. Brittany stood in the middle of her small den wearing nothing but an old University of Virgina T-shirt. On the front was a cavalier, with a long curving sword arcing toward the right, and disappearing in a maroon stain. Instinctively, Claire reached for the spot. "You're bleeding."

"It's my surgery wound," she said, gripping her upper abdomen. "I think it stopped now."

Claire put her arms on her shoulders and gently coaxed her into an embrace. For a moment, Brittany stiffened, then yielded, collapsing into her doctor's arms. There she began to sob, and Claire felt the young girl tremble. "Oh, Brittany," Claire responded. "You're safe now. He's not coming back. I'm here."

For the first time in her memory, Claire had a sense of being a mom. She squinted around the room. "Where are the clothes you were wearing . . . during the attack?"

"I was in this." She pointed to the bedroom, where pale light illuminated a doorway in a shallow hall. "My panties were torn. I threw them away."

"Do you have a zip-lock bag?"

She followed Brittany to the kitchen and bedroom, giving instructions and placing Brittany's underwear into the zip-lock bag for evidence. Then, she helped collect a pair of jeans and a sweatshirt for her patient to put on later in the office, and placed a blanket around her shoulders. "Let's get going."

On the way to the Stoney Creek Family Medical Center, Claire carefully explained what would happen to Brittany during the SANE examination. Her patient trembled and responded only with an uneasy silence and a nod of the head.

"Why didn't you call your mother?"

"She lives with her new husband over in Brighton . . . we're not close."

"You're so young to be on your own."

"I'm in school. Blue Ridge Community College. I want to transfer to Brighton University after two years. My apartment is cheap. Hopefully when I go to Brighton, I can live in a dorm with other girls."

Claire was thankful to have something other than the assault to talk about. She wanted Brittany to relax. Claire glanced at her as they drove through the small-town streets, which showed little signs that Stoney Creek was beginning to awaken. A paperboy undulated up the sidewalk, pushing his bicycle to cooperate under the weight of papers in a large handlebar basket. A poultry truck passed in the other direction, carrying the first load of birds toward the Tyson plant near Fisher's Retreat. A white chicken feather floated onto her windshield as they sped by.

When they arrived at the clinic a few minutes later, the lights were on and a member of the county sheriff's department was sitting in a marked brown car.

Claire reached for Brittany's arm before getting out. "Don't worry. He won't be in on the exam. He's just here to get your story and to take the evidence to deliver to the State Police forensics lab down in Roanoke."

Brittany nodded.

Claire introduced herself to the officer, a thin man of about thirty, who walked forward with quick steps, his shoes clipping along against the asphalt in regular snaps.

He held out his hand. "Randy Jensen, Warren County Deputy." He nodded his head in a rhythm which reminded Claire of a Parkinson's patient.

"This is Brittany Lewis. Why don't you follow us in? You may sit in our waiting area if you like. We have our equipment in our SANE room," she explained to the officer as she ushered Brittany into the office ahead of them. "All of our equipment was given to the clinic on a grant by the state after Lucy Dellinger received the SANE training and agreed to do the exams in this county."

Officer Jensen cleared his throat. "Unfortunately, I've been with Dr. Jenkins and Lucy before. But I suspect this is a first for you," he said, continuing to bob his forehead.

Claire wanted to club him, wondering if he could manage to show a little tact to inspire confidence in her tremulous patient. Instead, she glared at him for an instant before shaking her head. *Thanks a lot, pal.* She extended her hand toward the chairs in the waiting room, and allowed the door to swing shut behind her, leaving Randy in the front room.

Lucy met them in the hall. "Hi, Brittany. Come right this way."

She ushered them into the exam room. Lucy pointed to an area on the floor where she had unfolded a white paper. "Stand on this, Brittany, and take off all of your clothing. Leave them here on the sheet and then put on this gown." Lucy and Claire stepped out and pulled a curtain to give the patient privacy. When she indicated she was finished, Claire dropped the torn pair of panties from the zip-lock bag onto the sheet and watched as Lucy carefully folded the clothing items up in the paper sheet and sealed it, labeled it, and signed it across the seal. She placed the small package into a cardboard box on the counter. It was the size of a woman's boot box, and was labeled "PERK." Lucy looked at Claire. "This is the Physical Evidence Recovery Kit." To Brittany, she added, "I'm going to need you to lie down on this table. Have you had a pelvic examination before?"

Brittany nodded. "Once."

"I'm going to video the exam for evidence. Your face will not appear on the tape. Just lie down and put your heels in these stirrups. That's a girl," she gently coaxed. "Lift your butt," she said, sliding a second white paper sheet onto the exam table beneath the patient. Lucy initiated the video, which was mounted on a tripod over her left shoulder. "I need to do a combing first. This will allow us to collect anything from the attack which may have been left behind." Lucy combed through Brittany's pubic hair, teasing out loose hair and a few flakes of dried mucus. The paper towel was retrieved, folded, labeled, signed, and placed in the PERK box.

Brittany began to cry. "I'm on my period. I couldn't find my tampon string."

"That's okay," Lucy coached. "You're going to feel my fingers." She lubricated a pair of examining gloves and retrieved the tampon from the vaginal vault, and placed it in a sealed plastic evidence bag. Again, she meticuously followed protocol to preserve the evidence.

Lucy guided Brittany through the twenty-minute exam which included obtaining patient pubic and scalp hair samples, anal and vaginal swabs, and collections of material from the patient's inner thighs. Each specimen was labeled, sealed, and signed by Lucy and placed into the PERK box. Then she instructed Brittany to clean beneath her fingernails with a sharp plastic probe to remove any possible skin from her attacker she might have lodged there during the assault. This too was done over a special white paper which was then folded over the scrapings and placed in the box.

During the exam, Claire assumed the role of hand-holder and support, letting Lucy perform all the technical aspects. This was a first for Claire; Lucy had been in this situation dozens of times. While the nurse worked, Claire forced herself not to twist her expression in response to what she was saw. At the end, Lucy drew blood, explaining gently that it was just for baseline information and for precautions. Claire knew the blood would be screened for sexually transmitted disease screen and pregnancy. With all the evidence collected, Claire sealed the top of the box with a special tape and signed her name across its overlapping edge.

Once the exam was completed, Claire inspected and redressed Brittany's cholecystectomy incisions. "The bleeding has stopped. It looks like they will be fine."

Brittany was given her own clothing and allowed to dress alone. When she emerged from the exam room, she was ashen and quiet, but no longer trembling. Claire led her to the waiting area which was uninhabited except for Officer Jensen. "I need to hear your story," he began. "I know this is painful, but it is important for you to recall as many details as you can while the event is fresh."

Claire watched him nod his head and she tried to push the image of a bobble-head doll from her mind.

Brittany told a story punctuated with sobs. She detailed the attack, including the details of the rape, her fear of suffocating, and her first disoriented awakening after the trauma. As she spoke, Claire began to feel a vague sense of déjà vu, as if the description carried some sick familiarity for her. *Lena?*

Randy Jensen took meticulous notes, pausing to ask for clarifications, and apologizing repeatedly for the intrusive nature of his need to know. In spite of his irritating quirks, Claire came away impressed with his sensitivity.

"I need a physical description," Randy urged.

Brittany shook her head. "It was dark."

"Tall? Short?"

Brittany stood up and held her hand a bit above her head. "About this tall."

Officer Jensen responded, "Looks like about five ten or eleven." He scribbled on the pad in his lap and continued, "Heavy, fat, skinny?"

"Medium." Her hand went to her mouth. "He smelled of alcohol. He was wearing a mask."

"A mask? Really?" Jensen looked at Claire. "Most rapists do very little to disguise themselves." He tapped his pen on his notepad. "What kind of mask? Ski mask?"

"No. A medical mask of some sort. Like the ones my surgeon wore at the hospital."

Claire leaned forward. "A surgical mask?"

Brittany nodded.

Jensen's head bobbed. "Did he speak to you? Tell you to shut up, threaten you?"

"No."

"How did he leave you? Any clue of tenderness? Any search for reassurance?"

"No. I don't remember him leaving. I thought I was going to suffocate. All I can remember was needing to get air." She paused. "I must have passed out. When I woke up, he was gone."

"What happened next?"

"I called Dr. McCall. She told me what to do. I didn't do anything. I just waited for her to pick me up."

As Claire listened to the story, she was struck by her solidarity with Brittany. For a moment, her heart rose to her throat as she remembered the abuses of her own past, growing up with the unpredictable violence of her alcoholic father. And in that moment, she felt vulnerable. An unexpected horror had crept into Stoney Creek, threatening her idyllic country town. And in that moment, she longed for the safety of the familiar. She wanted to run to a place of refuge, to the comfort of John Cerelli's arms. The place where she had found solace and the desire for love.

She coerced herself to listen, to pay attention to the details of her patient's pain. But again, an ill-at-ease feeling knotted her stomach. The story was vaguely familiar, as if a memory called her from the corner of a large hall, just beyond her ability to hear.

She strained to pinpoint her anxiety, unable to make sense of the perception. But one idea persisted. She needed to return to Brighton. She needed to talk to Lena Chisholm.

Billy Ray awoke to a pounding in his head. He felt terrible. He began to stretch when his arms struck the steering wheel in front of him. That was his first clue that he wasn't sleeping in his bed. *What's going on?* He opened his eyes, careful to squint away the sun glaring from the hood of his truck. He looked around and groaned. A fifth of cheap whiskey lay on the seat beside him, evidence of the night's activity. His legs were stiff, frozen in their cramped position beneath the brake pedal. He tried with limited success to extend his knees. Then, another sensation awakened. First his head demanded attention. Then his legs. Now his bladder seemed to pound in a rhythm with his head, a sick duet calling for relief.

He drained a swallow from the bottom of the bottle and tossed it to the floor, then stumbled out his door to look around. He was outside of town, halfway up Briary Branch Road, pulled off on a logging trail. *How'd I get here?*

Billy struggled into the trees, with each step awakening stiff muscles in his legs. *I must not have moved all night. How'd I get so sore?*

He faced away from the road to relieve himself and found his zipper was already down.

John Cerelli sat in the corner booth at Fisher's Cafe sipping a double chocolate malt with whipped cream and Ghirardelli white chocolate shavings. He tapped on the palm pilot in his hand and frowned. When he asked his father for a loan, Tony first smiled, then chuckled, then laughed like he always did when he watched improv comedy, holding his ample stomach and letting his breath out in a rhythmic spray. "I'd like to help. Really I would. Say, Johnny, tell me again about Claire's ring." He raised his voice and did his best baso-profundo opera imitation, *"Lascialo in libertá. Dagli il volo!"*

John sighed and slid his computer back in his pocket. Good things were worth waiting for.

A knock on the table lifted his eyes to Abby McAllister. "Is this becoming a habit?" She smiled. "What's this, twice in a month we get to see the famous Italian entrepreneur?"

"Right."

She sat down across from him.

"Light day?"

"It'll pick up soon. Always does after the noon whistle at Tysons." She leaned forward with her eyes intent on his face. "So?"

Her intensity was too much. He looked away. "So what?"

"I haven't seen Claire. She's dissin' the cafe since she started at the clinic. So I have to ask. Did she like the ring? When's the big day?"

He lifted his hands. "Whoa, Nellie! What are you talking about?"

"Come on, Cerelli, I saw the ring box the last time you were in." She straightened. "By the way you talked, I thought . . . well, I thought you were about to . . ."

"Pop the question."

"Exactly."

"No." He shook his head.

"What's the holdup, John?" She leaned forward again and grasped his arm with her hand and lowered her voice. "I listen to a whole lot of stuff in this little cafe. Plenty of guys will be standing at her door if you step aside." She squeezed his arm before leaning back again. "Don't mess this up."

"Well, I—"

"John, she's a gem. And I've seen you two together. She starts a sentence and you complete it. You start a question and she answers it before you're halfway done. You guys are already communicating like an old married couple."

"Thanks. I think."

They sat quietly for a moment as John pondered Abby's accuracy. Claire McCall was under his skin. In his mind. In his heart.

Abby lifted a rebellious strand of curly dark hair and placed it behind her ear. "So what's holdin' you back?"

He wasn't sure how much to share. Abby was wise beyond her years, and had a wealth of personal experience living with a severely disabled husband, but he wasn't sure he wanted to open up to the ear of the Apple Valley. He folded his hands. "It's complicated."

"It's the curse, isn't it?"

"Don't call it that. It's not a curse. It's a genetic illness. Claire hates that word."

Abby shrugged. "Well, maybe it's not a curse per se, but it is a result of the curse."

"The Fall? Adam's sin?"

She nodded.

"I just don't like people thinking that it's a direct result of some stupid old story about a man making moonshine, being cursed by Eleazar Potts, or some-such unbalanced itinerant preacher."

"Okay," she said with a defensive whine. "I'm sorry I used that word. But Huntington's disease is why you haven't given her the ring. Am I right?"

He nodded slowly. "In a way." He stopped for a moment before going on. "Huntington's disease is a horrible suffering. But it doesn't mean God is cursing anyone. And it isn't a punishment."

Now Abby held up her hands. "Hey, don't misread me. I haven't said any of those things. The Christian life is full of suffering. What was it Dietrich Bonhoeffer said? An invitation to Christ is an invitation to come and die?"

The phrase was too familiar. "That's what you said about marriage."

"So I made my own application. It's called parallel thinking, John. Marriage is supposed to be a mirror of our relationship to Christ. We're his bride."

"I know the metaphor, Abby."

"What do you think? Just because I'm waitressing a small cafe, doesn't mean I don't read." She stopped and put her hand to her mouth, as if to mechanically lower her passion volume. "I'm sorry, John. I'm not supposed to preach. It's just that there hasn't been a day since Nathan's accident that I haven't suffered along with him. Day after day, he's bound to that wheelchair." She shook her head. "And over and over, I've gone to the cross seeking answers. And to the theologians who help us make sense of our pain." She hesitated. "I'd always dreamed of going to school like Claire." She shook her head and stared off through the lettering on the front window of the cafe. "That all changed when Nathan was shot."

"A commitment to Christ doesn't give us an exemption from pain."

"I hate to break up this heart-to-heart, but I've got a cafe to run."

Abby's face reddened as she looked over to see Ralph Knitter, the proprietor and soda jock par excellence.

Mr. Knitter jabbed John's shoulder. "You're supposed to bring your dates here, not pick up the help," he chuckled. "Where's Claire? She's been too scarce."

John lifted his hands. "The life of a doctor. Sometimes I think I'll have to marry the woman just to see her."

Abby stood up. "Good idea."

Mr. Knitter touched her shoulder. "The counter needs coffee refills."

"Sure," she said, scurrying away.

The owner leaned down to John. "I love Claire like a daughter. Don't wait forever, John."

Why is this suddenly everyone's business? Stoney Creek needs to get a life other than mine. "Uh, sure." He lifted his malt to change the subject. "I'm going to have to work out an extra two hours because of you."

He walked away, wiping his hands on his apron. "Glad to be of help."

John laid five dollars on the table, thinking of what Abby told him the last time. *"The advice is free, but the malts are three bucks apiece."*

⁕⁓§§§⁓⁕

The girl's dark eyes brimmed with tears as she tried hard to hold still. "You're hurting me."

Claire paused from her job of removing the fine row of sutures she'd put in the week before to close a nasty laceration on Cindy's scalp. "I'm sorry, honey. Just two more."

Cindy's mother stroked her daughter's forehead and moved away to give Claire closer access to her work.

"Why does it have to hurt?"

Claire looked at Cindy's mom. "Tough question."

"She's thirteen going on twenty-one."

"Ow!"

Claire squinted. "Sorry. This one seems to be buried a little."

Cindy gritted her teeth. "I wasn't talking about philosophy or whatever. I just wanted to know why it hurts."

"Hmm. The wound edge is a little swollen, making the stitches harder to cut without pulling on them a little." She stopped and snipped the last suture. "There. All done."

"About time."

Her mother gasped. "Cindy!"

"It's okay," Claire responded. "Most of us get cranky when we have to face pain." She smiled at the young woman. "I do."

She handed Cindy's charge sheet to her mom. "Just show them this at the front window." With that, she checked her watch and walked out.

Five-fifteen P.M. The waiting room was miraculously empty. She quickly dictated her last note, initialed and dated the lab data in her in-box, and noted that Lena Chisholm's pregnancy test was indeed positive.

She lifted her stack of unopened mail. John was to meet her at six to take her to Brighton to talk to Lena. It had been a long day and twenty-seven patients since she'd started her day with the SANE examination. She sifted through the mail, tossing out everything that wasn't first class. She didn't have time for junk mail. Within the stack, one letter caught her attention. It was a thank-you note from Mr. Sugimoto, expressing his gratitude for her treatment of his "problem." He was too refined even to write the word *hemorrhoid*. She smiled at the memory of the gentleman from Tokyo and reminded herself again to ask her uncle Leon about the possible buyout of the shoe factory. Here she was in the same town and she didn't know anything more about the running of the family business than she did when she was in Boston. And Della was no help. Every time Claire asked her mother about the shoe factory business, she just started talking about how well Uncle Leon had treated their family. She reassured Claire that Uncle Leon always acted with the family's interests at heart. Claire shook her head. Secrecy from the public was one thing, but she was suspicious that Leon was holding out on everyone, Della and Elizabeth included. She looked at her watch. Her days were too full to worry about everything. She pushed ahead with her deskwork and hoped Della's blind trust was well founded.

Just before signing her last note, she heard the electronic ring of her cell phone. *Maybe it's John.* "Hello. Dr. McCall."

The voice on the other end was thick and slurred, slow and masculine. "Doctor McCall."

She waited, already suspicious that it was Billy Ray.

"I need to find Lena. I know she's in Brighton. Eddie told me so."

"Billy Ray, my office is closed. If you have a clinical concern, call me during office hours!"

His words fell out in a tumble. "Oh, Doc, I'm sorry about the time. Listen, Doc, it's about Lena. She's lying about me, Doc. I never hit her when I'm not drinkin'. You got to believe me and help me find her."

Claire wanted to hang up. She'd call her phone service and ask how to have his calls blocked.

Billy Ray went on. "Eddie saw her at the university. She admitted she had a boyfriend." He paused. "It ain't right. But maybe I drove her to it. I gotta get her back, Doc."

"I'll be glad to pass along your concern. Now if you don't mind only calling when—"

Billy Ray sounded as if he may cry. "Who's her boyfriend, Doc? A man shouldn't be messing with another man's wife. It ain't right."

She raised her voice. The last thing she wanted to do was talk to a crying drunk. "Mr. Chisholm, I have no idea about what you're talking about. I am going to hang up now."

"Doc, you know what I'm talkin' 'bout. You were with him when she ran away."

"Good night, Mr. Chisholm!"

She terminated the call and pondered turning off her phone. After a moment, she decided to keep it on, in case Brittany would need to call. Fortunately, Billy Ray didn't call again, and Claire dispatched with her work and headed outside to wait for John.

John was punctual, and for once, she was ready for him, needing only the image of John in his red Mustang with the top down to relax her a notch. She needed this drive over to Brighton to regroup. The day had been stressful, and it wasn't over yet. An outing with John Cerelli was just what she needed to unwind.

She walked toward the car holding her little black medical bag. She wanted to check Lena's blood pressure in addition to satisfying her own curiosity about something her patient had said. Claire just couldn't shake the uneasy feeling that Billy Ray may be involved in Brittany's rape, and she wanted to ask Lena a few additional questions. "Open the trunk, Cerelli. I don't want my bag out in the wind."

"Hello to you, too."

He hopped out and walked around to where she stood behind the car. He gave her a quick kiss and held out his hand. "I'll get it."

She handed him the bag and waited. John seemed to hesitate before sliding his key in to unlock the trunk. He looked at her. "I said, I'll get it."

She shrugged and walked around and sat down. "Whatever."

Behind her, John made quick work of opening and slamming his trunk lid. "Hey," he said, tossing a small container of surgical masks onto the backseat. "These must have fallen out of a box of supplies I picked up for you."

The sight of the masks unsettled her. She inspected the box, turning it over and over in her hands. The top seal was intact, apparently unopened.

"Are you okay? Do you want me to take it inside?"

She studied him for a moment before tossing it onto the backseat again. "No, let's get going. I need some mountain air after a day like today."

John nodded, and soon they were on their way. The straight road out of Stoney Creek began a gradual undulation before sharply snaking up the side of North Mountain. "Do you want to talk about it?"

"What?"

"You're quiet. Share the weight with me."

She sighed. "I saw a lot of pitiful things when I was on the trauma service in Boston, John. And nothing broke my heart like seeing children who were hurt." She stared through the windshield. "Until this morning."

John stayed silent. He had always been a good listener. She glanced at him. His face showed no hint of anxiety.

"I don't feel like hashing through the gory details."

He nodded and didn't push. In a few minutes he probed again. "I saw Abby at the cafe again this morning. Mr. Knitter said he wants to see you."

"Probably just looking for free medical advice."

"Claire, they like you. You're their hero. You know it."

"Is that supposed to make me proud? That a bunch of country red-necks look up to me?"

"Stop it, Claire. It's not like that. As far as Abby is concerned, you're the one living the dream. She wanted to go to school, like you did, but she needs to work to help care for her husband."

"Why are you telling me this? You want me to feel sorry that I might put you through the same thing some day? Is this to give me a guilt trip?"

"No!" He glared at her. "How can you say that? I was merely trying to say that there are some smart people around that hold *you* in high esteem. It was supposed to be a compliment."

"It sounded like a reminder that HD may ruin your life some day, just like a quad for a husband has ruined Abby's."

"Don't project your guilt on me. I was trying to compliment you."

She huffed. *Some compliment. It just reminds me of "the cloud."* She tried to return her attention to the forested mountainside and reminded herself that she'd been looking forward to a ride with the top down to relax, not think about her problems. After a few minutes, she spoke again. "John, I'm sorry. I shouldn't have snapped."

He lifted her hand from her lap and pressed it to his lips. "Forget it."

She leaned over, laying her head against his shoulder.

"I know just what you need," he said, pressing a button on the dash board. In a moment, a clear tenor voice filled the air around them.

"Great. Of all the men who want me, I had to choose the Italian renaissance one."

She felt John's chest expand. "Hey. Even a Stoney Creek boy can appreciate baseball *and* opera."

"You're no Stoney Creek boy."

He laughed. "Oh, yeah? I fit right in down at the cafe. What sets me apart from a Stoney Creek boy?"

"They don't like baseball."

He turned up the music. "Good answer."

She shook her head and listened. She certainly hadn't been raised on classical music like this. Life growing up with Wally and Della was nothing like the supportive and refined upbringing John experienced with Tony and Christine Cerelli. But since John liked it, she did her best to give it a fair shake. It didn't quite lift her soul like it did John's, but she did enjoy it more than she'd admit.

After they pulled to a stop in front of the Brighton women's shelter, John bolted from the car and had her medical bag in hand and the trunk closed again before Claire unbuckled her seat belt.

In a hurry, John? She let it pass and accepted the bag from his hand. "Meet me back here in an hour?"

"Sure. I'll pick up dinner." He wasn't looking at her. His gaze was already beyond her, lifted above her head. She'd seen that look in his eyes before. Intensity. Longing. She followed his gaze to a window on the second floor. Lena Chisholm leaned forward with her face against the glass.

She waved at Lena and forced herself to smile to hide her irritation. "Anything but pizza. I had that for lunch."

189

Lena Chisholm took the small leatherbound Bible from Claire's hand. "I appreciate all you've done, but . . ." She looked away. "I know what you want."

Claire didn't understand. "I—"

"But I can't keep this baby."

"This isn't about the baby, Lena. Your child is important to me, but so are you. I just wanted to make sure you had a Bible. We left in such a hurry, I thought that, well, you might need it." Inside, Claire cringed. She wanted to be able to reach out to her patients in a natural way, sharing her hope in God's grace as a solution, but she felt like an unstable toddler.

Lena looked away and placed the book at her side. "Okay."

Claire shifted in her seat, wanting to say something encouraging, but not sure how to penetrate Lena's shell. "It's helped me."

Lena looked up.

"The Bible, I mean. Things haven't always been a breeze in my life, Lena. I couldn't make it without my faith."

Lena nodded quietly.

They sat together for an awkward moment as Claire pondered what to say, and wondered how to bring up her suspicions about Brittany's rape. "Lena," she began slowly. "Once when I asked you about fighting back, you told me about Billy Ray forcing you to . . ." She paused. ". . . have sex with him. Did he, well . . . do anything, well, you know, use a disguise or anything?"

Lena turned around and blushed. "You're not married, are you?"

Claire shook her head.

"You want to know what it's like, is that it?" Lena couldn't suppress an immature giggle. "I've read a lot of novels that tell about love. Billy Ray was never into romance. I don't think you should ask me for advice." Her eyes met Claire's. "John is your boyfriend, huh? He's hot. I'll bet he's romantic."

This wasn't going where Claire intended. She shrugged. "I guess."

Suddenly Lena looked away. "There was one time . . ." She trailed off.

"What?"

"Billy Ray wore a mask once. The time he almost killed me."

"A mask? What kind of mask?"

"You know, a mask like a doctor wears." She lifted her hands up over her mouth to illustrate. "Billy Ray said he always wanted to be a doctor. He joked with me about wanting to 'play doctor.' I think the mask was just his way of pretending to be something he wasn't. He was drunk. It was a game."

The information hit Claire in the gut. Billy Ray had used a surgical mask just like Brittany's attacker. Her mind began to race. Billy Ray had become increasingly violent. Now, since his wife was gone, was he looking for other targets?

Claire tried to focus. How much could she reveal and not be betraying a patient confidence? She couldn't share the details of Brittany's assault. *But I'd better tell the police about my thoughts about Billy Ray.*

"Lena, maybe it's best if you stay out of sight for a while. Billy Ray knows you're in Brighton."

"What! How'd he find out?"

"He called me this afternoon, Lena. He mentioned some guy named Eddie—"

Lena slapped her hand on the back of an orange chair. "I told him not to say anything! I should have known."

"Have you been able to find work?"

"I applied for a job at the university cafeteria. I haven't heard back yet."

Claire blew her breath out through pursed lips. "I know he wants to see you. He told me that much."

"You didn't tell him where I was, did you?"

"Of course not, Lena. And the shelter won't give any information out about you on the phone. This is a safe place."

"I can't just stay inside all the time."

"If you get a job, just keep your eyes open for his truck. I doubt he'll ever find you. Besides, why would he come after you?"

"If Billy Ray's got it in his mind that I've done him wrong, he might."

"He told me that Eddie told him that you have a new boyfriend." She hesitated, then continued. "He said you admitted it to Eddie."

"I just said that to make him jealous. I don't have a boyfriend. Eddie's a jerk. He shouldn't have told Billy Ray where I was."

Claire finished by taking Lena's blood pressure and asking her about her vitamins. Lena acted irritated and restated the futility of caring for a baby she wanted to abort. Claire nodded and was pleased that Lena was finally calling it a baby rather than a pregnancy.

As she left, Claire mused about what would make Lena lie. She was obviously lying to someone, either Eddie or herself. Why would Lena lie and tell Eddie she had a boyfriend when she knew that would infuriate her violent husband? That made no sense. On the other hand, if she was telling the truth to Eddie, then what she was telling Claire must be false. But why would Lena lie to Claire about having a boyfriend?

Unless she was involved with a man she didn't want me to know about.

Her mind flashed back to the conversation she'd had with Billy Ray. She had been in such a fog, waking up so abruptly in the middle of the night. *Didn't he say something about me being with Lena and her boyfriend when they ran away?* The thought struck her. *That's crazy! Does he think Lena and John . . . ?* She shook her head. *That's ridiculous.*

Claire walked down the steps from the porch, seeing John's Mustang approaching. She was about to say something to John about the whole thing when she saw the pizza box on the seat beside him.

"Sausage and mushroom," he said with a smile. "Your favorite."

I told you anything but pizza. Where was your concentration, John? "I'm not hungry."

"Are you okay?"

"Fine."

"Could you drive then? This smell is driving me crazy."

~⁂~

After John dropped her back off at the Stoney Creek Family Medical Center, Claire went in and retrieved a small business card from the top drawer of her desk. She dialed the number for the county sheriff's department and thought about Randy Jensen.

"Sheriff's department."

"May I speak to Deputy Jensen please."

"Hold on, ma'am. I'll see if he's still in."

A few moments later, he answered. Claire could imagine that he nodded his head to emphasize his words. "Deputy Jensen."

She identified herself and told of her suspicions about Billy Ray.

He sounded like he knew of him. "Billy Ray Chisholm?"

"You know him?"

"I went to high school with him."

Great. An old school bud. She was trying to decide whether that was good or bad information, when he continued. "He beat his first wife, too."

"Doesn't surprise me."

"I warned him not to go after Lena."

"You did? How'd you know she was gone?"

"Billy Ray told me. He was half-drunk, called to tell me his wife had been kidnapped." He laughed. "We knew better."

"The man is violent. We had to get Lena out of there."

"I understand. I told him clearly that we wouldn't look too kindly on hearing that he was stalking her."

"What did he say?"

"The routine answer, I suppose, that he knew his rights and he had a right to see his wife and that unless there was a restraining order against him, he could look for her." He chuckled. "I think he'll think twice before he does, though." He paused. "I don't suppose you'd know what day this alleged attack took place on Lena Chisholm, would you?"

"Hmmm. Lena told me something . . . yes, could you hold on a minute? If I pull her chart, I can pinpoint it for you. She said it was the night following the day after I saw her here in the office for a bad sprained ankle and a cut on her eyebrow. She reported that she'd fallen down the stairs. I remember because she told me she hurt so bad she couldn't have gotten away from him if she'd tried. Hold on." She put down the phone and went to a long chart rack. She sorted through the "C's." There were too many "Chisholms" in the Apple Valley. In a minute, she found the record and returned to her conversation with the officer. "Okay, I've got it."

She repeated the date a few times to be sure he heard.

"So what makes you think Billy Ray Chisholm is Brittany Lewis's attacker?"

"Three things." *Didn't I tell you this already?* She held up a finger, knowing he couldn't see. "One, his wife said he used a similar mask when he forced her to have relations with him. Two, he came straight into my office yesterday and could have seen Brittany's chart on my desk. He would have known she would have a hard time fighting back if she'd just had surgery. And three, it just follows that now that Lena's gone, Billy Ray will have to turn somewhere else to prove his manhood."

She listened as the deputy tapped his pen against the phone. "I'll check him out. My gut says you're wrong. But I'll check him out." He made clicking sounds with his cheek and seemed to be musing to himself. "Ol' Billy Ray, I can't believe it."

"Deputy Jensen, I do hope you will take this seriously. Billy Ray is a sick man. He could—"

"Dr. McCall, I said I will check him out."

She took a deep breath. She wasn't reassured. "Okay. Thank you. Can you call me if you find out anything?"

More tapping. "Sure."

He ended the call without saying good-bye. Claire headed home with her body and mind near exhaustion. It had been a long day since her rude awakening at 3:15 A.M. Thoughts of the day's events assaulted her. Brittany's rape, the patients she'd seen, the letter from Mr. Sugimoto, the trip to Brighton to see Lena, and John's distracted behavior all came to her in a collage of images.

Ten minutes later, she found her mother asleep on the couch. She nudged her, then helped her to her feet. The house was in disarray. Claire knew better than to ask. It must have been another day fighting to change diarrhea diapers. They supported each other down the hall, both in balance leaning on the other.

Plodding forward into her room, Claire collapsed on her old bed and yielded to the solace of sleep. Driven by exhaustion and unaffected by routine Wally background noise, she slept until her mother shook her shoulder at seven the next morning.

Chapter Seventeen

laire forced open her eyes. Slowly things came into focus. "It's my day off."

Her mother wiggled Claire's shoulder again. "Your father is burnin' up. He won't talk."

Claire groaned and rolled over, pushing herself from the comfort of her mattress. "What's been going on?"

"Same stuff. Diarrhea all day yesterday. Some vomiting."

Claire ran her fingers through her blond bangs. "You should have called me."

"I called the office yesterday. Lucy told me what you were going through."

Claire nodded. "A day to remember." She plodded to her father's room and began her assessment. Wally was her patient. She was in doctor-mode and the adrenaline started to pump from the first moment she saw him.

"Daddy. Daddy! Wally!" She touched his head. He was warm. Too warm. Her hands stilled his roving head to study his eyes, which were glassed over and looking beyond her. His mucus membranes were dry, his scalp moist with sweat. His lungs were clear, his abdomen soft, his diaper stained with yellow runny stool. She looked at Della. "He's dehydrated. Has he been drinking anything?"

"Not much. Lucy suggested Gatorade." She frowned. "I can't blame him for not wanting it. Have you ever tasted thickened Gatorade?"

"He'll need an IV. We've got to get him up to Carlisle to the hospital."

Della shook her head. "I've had this conversation with him over and over. He doesn't want to go to the hospital anymore. He doesn't want special treatment."

"Mom, this isn't special treatment. He probably just has the stomach flu. He'll be over it in a day or two. He just needs some fluid to help him pull through."

"Wally said he didn't want to go to the hospital for treatment if the only reason he was going was because he couldn't swallow. He doesn't want artificial feeding."

"This isn't feedings, Mom. It isn't a feeding tube or anything. He just needs a little IV fluid to keep him hydrated."

Della sighed. "I don't know. Can you do it here?"

Claire weighed her options. Getting and maintaining an IV in Wally would be difficult in a hospital. It would need constant watching to prevent him from pulling it out as he flailed his arms around. She did have the day off, although this wasn't exactly in her plans. She had hoped to spend a little time with John. She held up her hands. "We can try. We have to do something. He could go into renal failure if he doesn't get some fluid. Has he been urinating?"

"I think," Della hesitated. "It's a little hard to tell with his stool being loose like it is."

She checked her watch. "Lucy should be in by 7:30. I'll call and see if she can bring by some supplies."

Della agreed and tried in vain to get Wally to drink.

A few minutes later, mother and daughter sat down over a cup of coffee at the kitchen table. They talked about the weather, the Atlanta Braves, and the upcoming fire-engine parade at the Fishers Retreat Lawn Party. Anything but the obvious: Huntington's disease in its final stages, and how it changed even the intestinal flu into a life-threatening situation.

As Claire drained the last of the French vanilla creamer into her cup, Della leaned forward. "How are things with John?"

Claire shrugged. "Who knows?"

Her mother answered only with a look of curiosity.

"There are days when I'm sure he's the one." She hesitated. "And others when I wonder if I really know him at all. Some days he is the most caring, nuturing, praying man ..."

"But?"

"Maybe it's nothing, but my intuition says something isn't right."

Della shook her head. "John's good with Wally."

"I know. But something is up with him lately. I can't explain it exactly. He's distracted. Yet sometimes he seems so open with me."

"Wally was never vulnerable with me. It's as if his Navy days taught him how to be self-sufficient and he was afraid to show me he needed me after that."

"John isn't like that. But sometimes, I think he's hiding something from me." She took a sip from her cup. "I think down inside he's as afraid of this HD thing as I am."

"Wouldn't it be normal to be afraid?"

Claire nodded, picking up the phone to call Lucy. When her nurse answered, Claire slipped naturally into medical-resident slang to explain her father's situation. "Wally's chipped out."

"Gastrointeritis?"

"I think so. But he's not taking any fluids. I need some IV supplies."

"For home?" Lucy sounded incredulous.

Claire wanted to sound positive. "That's the plan."

She heard Lucy sigh.

"I'll take care of him. All I need is the supplies. D–5 lactated ringers. Bring me at least four liters and a half-dozen angiocaths. He'll be a hard stick."

They said good-bye and Claire set the phone down. So much for a day off.

Randy Jensen frowned and tossed the empty donut box in the trash. Getting his fellow officers to clean up after taking the last pastry was a hopeless cause. He lifted a pizza box and was about to toss it, when he realized it was too heavy. He opened the lid and lifted out a slice of cheese pizza. He smelled it, then decided to nuke it in the microwave to kill anything that could have grown since the night shift concluded. Pizza and coffee wasn't exactly the breakfast of champions, but in the absence of his normal chocolate donut, it would have to do.

Randy looked back over his police logs. Early in the morning after the alleged attack on Lena, Billy Ray had called the sheriff's department to complain about a trespasser. Randy himself had been out on patrol and had pulled John Cerelli because he matched the description of the red Mustang Billy Ray reported seeing fleeing from his property. Randy had let him go with a warning. He massaged his chin. Was it mere coincidence that John Cerelli was snooping around the Chisholm property the morning after an assault on Lena? Things didn't add up. Maybe he should talk to this Cerelli.

He shoved the front of the pizza slice into his mouth and didn't bite down until both edges touched the corners of his mouth. He tore it away, the pizza triangle half gone in one bite. He chewed the grease-slicked cheese as he pondered what he knew. He couldn't shake his detective instincts. Things weren't adding up. It was time to go visit Billy Ray.

He found him forty-five minutes later at a metal fabricator's shop in Carlisle. They talked while standing in the summer sun outside a double-high garage door to the shop. Billy Ray wiped the sweat from his forehead with a dingy white hand towel. His face was dirty, almost black, except for a raccoonish mask where his goggles had been. Other than the workers inside the shop, they were alone. A metallic, almost acrid smell was thick, causing Randy to back away from the entrance.

"You mind telling me what this is all about?"

"I need to ask a few questions. That's all." Jensen tipped back the brim of his hat. "What were you doing last night, Billy Ray?"

He shuffled his feet. "Nothing special. Hangin' out with Eddie."

"What time did you get in?"

He shrugged. "I don't remember."

"Where'd you go?"

"I don't know. Around."

Jensen shook his head. "I think you're going to have to do better than that. Do I need to talk to Eddie? Or won't he remember either?"

"What's this about? If Lena's complaining about me, I haven't even been—"

"This isn't about Lena. Maybe you should come on down to the department and explain exactly where you were last night."

"We didn't do anything."

"Can you verify your location early this morning?"

Billy Ray shielded his eyes to the morning sun. "Eddie and me were just cruising around."

"How about between two and three o'clock?"

Billy Ray smiled. "I was sleeping. In my bed at home."

"Listen, Billy, a young woman was raped in Stoney Creek in the early hours of the morning."

"So why are you asking me? You can't believe that I—"

"We have at least one person that thinks you may have been involved, so you'd better refresh your memory a little. 'I don't remember' isn't going to cut it."

"Look, Eddie and me were just out. We had a few beers. That's it."

"Why can't you remember where you were?"

Billy Ray picked at some black debris beneath his thumbnail. "Listen, we went to Brighton, okay?" He held up his hand. "But I didn't see Lena. We just went to a bar."

"What was the name? Will someone there remember you? What time did you leave?"

"Buffalo Wild Wings. It's on North Boulevard. We left at midnight."

Deputy Jensen made notes and grunted. "Who was your waitress?"

"Blond girl. Maybe twenty, twenty-two. She has a little space between her teeth that makes her whistle when she says, 'Something for you, gentlemen?'" The memory brought a grin to Billy Ray's face.

"And then what?"

"We came home."

Jensen paged through his notepad. "Remember when you called us about a month ago? You reported a man for trespassing, someone Old Jeb had treed."

Billy Ray huffed. "What are you gettin' at?"

"Do you remember what you did the night before?"

"Friday night? I bowl on Fridays. You know that. You still roll with the Steamers?"

"When I can."

"Are you going to the Bud invitational in Brighton?"

Jensen shook his head. He wasn't there to talk about bowling. "What happened to Lena that night? Were you drinking, Billy Ray? Did you come home, maybe feel like having a little fun with Lena? What happened? Did she refuse you, make you mad?"

Billy Ray dropped his eyes to the asphalt. "What did she tell you?"

"I haven't talked to Lena. But the word I have is that she was roughed up pretty bad, and you forced yourself on her."

"I don't remember."

"You don't remember?"

He sighed. "Look. You won't believe me. She showed me the next day what I'd . . ." His voice trailed off.

For a moment Randy thought Billy Ray was going to start crying right there in the parking lot.

"I passed out on the couch. Honest."

For a moment a hissing sound and the sound of metal banging against metal halted their conversation. "You mean you had a blackout? From drinking too much?"

"When I woke up the next morning, I had no idea how I got there. Eddie said he dropped me off. That's all I know."

"And what last night? Another blackout?"

"No. I was at home. I slept until the next morning."

The officer wasn't sure what to make of the report. He'd have to check out the waitress at the bar where Billy drank, and see if she remembered Billy Ray. He could also talk to Eddie to see if he had any helpful recall. If they left the bar at midnight, Billy Ray could still have easily been in Stoney Creek to commit the attack by two or three.

Billy wiped his forehead with the towel where large beads of water glistened in the morning sun. The excuse of a blackout was almost too lame to be believable.

Jensen pointed to Billy's left arm. "What's under the bandage?"

"I got a cut. It's infected so I leave it covered." He lifted his hands up in surrender. "I'm serious. I went to the doctor for it. That new one over in Stoney Creek. You can ask her."

She did mention you were in the office. He studied Billy Ray for a moment. The deputy had known Billy Ray most of his life. He'd worked for the same employer for fifteen years, bowled every Friday night for the last ten, and hunted bear every fall since he was in the seventh grade. Billy Ray had been in and out of AA for the past decade and had been arrested for beating his first wife.

Redneck was not a term the deputy liked, having bristled when his attorney brother used the term to describe Randy. But *redneck* did seem an adequate way to describe Billy Ray. But sexual predator? *Could alcohol-related blackouts be responsible for a dark side of this man?*

"I'll be in touch. Do yourself a favor. Stay off the bottle. And stay away from Lena."

With that, the deputy nodded his head and returned to his police cruiser. It was time to find John Cerelli.

John Cerelli enjoyed the flexibility that his job as a regional sales representative gave him to live where he wanted, but the move to Stoney Creek had lengthened the number of hours he spent on the road to reach a few of his clients. His employer developed software for electronic record-keeping for medical and surgical practices. The success of the company had allowed John to take over a smaller area, now consisting mainly of northern and western Virginia, and thanks to the internet, much of his interaction with established clients could be handled from his apartment near Stoney Creek. But today, an orthopedic surgery practice in Alexandria was having problems, and no amount of online interaction could calm the savage beast like a face-to-face company rep. Old-fashioned service-with-a-smile just couldn't be sent through a T–1 connection.

John couldn't resist a chance to put the top down and avoid the interstate. He would head over North Mountain to Brighton, then catch I–64 toward Richmond after he'd had his fix of tight curves and mountain air.

He tossed his sport coat onto the backseat and loosened his tie before settling in behind the wheel. He hoped Claire would meet him in Fisher's Retreat for breakfast at the cafe since he wouldn't be able to see her later as planned. He dialed her number on his cell phone. "Hey, Claire."

"Oh, John. I'm glad you called. We're not going to be able to go out today. I need to stay with Wally."

"Want to meet for breakfast? I'm on my way toward Fisher's Retreat. We could meet at the cafe."

"Why don't you just come here? I'll make pancakes."

"I can't. I have to go to Alexandria on business."

"John, I need you here. Wally is sick. He's so dehydrated, he is nearly unresponsive. It took Lucy and Della both to hold him down so I could put an IV in to give him fluids."

"You're doing that at home?"

"I had to." Frustration laced her voice. "He won't go to the hospital." She sighed into the phone. "Do you have to go?"

"Emily called me this morning. The doctors in one of the orthopedic practices are giving her a fit. Their whole electronic medical system is down."

Claire stayed quiet. The silence was ice.

"Look, it's not like I want to go. I have to. It's my territory. I'm responsible."

"This is my only day off this week. I wanted to see you."

"Claire, I wanted that too."

"When will you be back?"

"It depends on how long it takes in Alexandria. I have two other clients in Richmond that I need to see. It could be tomorrow afternoon."

He listened to the silence. He wasn't giving her the answers she wanted.

"I'll call you tonight."

A pause. "Fine." A sarcastic remark that John heard as "You're letting me down."

He wasn't sure how to respond. He was in a bind, and Claire wasn't giving him an inch. "Look, I'll try to get back early tomorrow. If I can watch Wally for a while in the afternoon, maybe Della can watch him tomorrow night and we can go out."

"Fine." There was noise in the background. "I've got to run."

John shook his head. "Love you." He looked at the phone. Claire had hung up.

He banged the steering wheel with his hand. Claire wasn't being fair. It wasn't like she didn't put her work in front of spending time with him.

He drove on to Fisher's Retreat, stopping at the cafe for breakfast alone. The air was eighty degrees and damp with a promise of rain. He abandoned his business look, extracting his tie from his white button-down shirt and tossing it into the backseat. There would be time for that later.

The corner booth, *their* booth, was full of locals discussing the upcoming lawn party. There were two open seats at the counter, but he didn't feel like talking to Ralph, and sitting there was an open invitation for an earful of Knitter philosophy served up fresh with the coffee.

He selected the only available booth for privacy, and was handed a breakfast menu by a girl who appeared to be in high school. Her smile was almost enough to lift him from his present funk. She held up a container of coffee and lifted her eyebrows in a silent question.

He responded in kind, turning over the mug which was already on the table. Since he had her eye, he continued their silent communication, pointing to his selection on the laminated menu. She nodded and made a note on a little pad. She was strawberry blond, just like Claire, and her face freckled with the sun. When she smiled, small dimples appeared and her eyes danced with a noiseless giggle. She lifted her eyebrows again, and tilted her head to the side. She paused for a moment, then touched her mouth with the end of her pencil. The eraser indented her soft lower lip to reveal an even row of white teeth. She was addicted to Crest or the daughter of an orthodontist. Her lips parted as she concentrated and pointed to a small picture of a glass of orange juice on the menu. *Anything else?*

He tried to supress a smile. He could see that she enjoyed this game, too. He squinted and paused. *Why not? Orange juice will be fine.* He nodded quickly.

She scribbled waitress-shorthand. Theirs was the communication of an old married couple, able to speak volumes in a glance.

He dismissed her with a wink, which she returned. She pivoted and hurriedly clipped away. He watched as her hand went to her mouth and her laughter escaped.

Within moments, John sensed only the invisible company of self-pity joining him in the booth for four. He glanced around the room. There was a married couple here, a table of white-haired men sharing the morning paper there, and a dusty work crew of men in sweaty shirts and shorts devouring large plates of Ralph's pancakes. John slipped out to his Mustang for his briefcase. He wasn't planning to work, but setting out a few papers and opening the case on the table seemed to justify his occupation of the booth.

His perfect young waitress refilled his coffee once, then brought him a cheese omelette instead of the French toast he thought he'd ordered. He widened his eyes in surprise, then watched as she carefully placed his orange juice on the table. This was no time for disputing his order. She was pleased. The game of quiet was on, and he didn't have the heart to argue with her. Besides, he was too proud to admit that he hadn't communicated perfectly with his young enchantress.

He nodded his approval. He would have eaten raw oats and carrot juice if she'd have brought it.

⚬⚬⚬

Outside, Randy Jensen spotted the red Mustang convertible and pulled his cruiser to the curb in front of Fisher's Cafe. He ran the license plates for confirmation. Indeed, John Cerelli had been found.

Randy sauntered by the front of the cafe, squinting into the restaurant, before walking on to where the Mustang was parked. Randy wasn't sure, but it looked like a model from the late seventies or early eighties. The interior was immaculate, and the paint waxed to a high sheen. A blue and gold silk tie was draped over the back of the driver's seat and a navy blazer was slightly crumpled in the backseat.

The deputy squinted at a box partially covered by the coat. *What is this?*

He glanced over his shoulder before quickly lifting it from the back of the car. *Surgical masks!*

He dropped the masks into the back of the car. He made a small note on a pad, taking down the manufacturer's name from the side of the box.

He wondered just what occupation this Cerelli was in. He wasn't a doctor, he was pretty sure of that. But just what were masks of this type doing in his car?

A man with dark curly hair, a white shirt, and carrying a maroon briefcase approached. Randy recognized him as John Cerelli, the man he'd stopped on Briary Branch Road. He stepped between the man and his car.

John looked up. "Excuse me," he said, dropping his briefcase into the backseat.

"Mr. Cerelli?" He held out his hand. "Officer Jensen, county deputy."

John looked surprised that his name was known. He took the officer's palm in a firm handshake. "What can I do for you?"

"Early yesterday morning a young woman in Stoney Creek was assaulted."

John looked at him questioningly.

"I'm wondering if you can account for your whereabouts during that time."

The man's jaw dropped. "Wh–why are you asking me?" His head jutted forward. "I was at home in my apartment. Asleep." He looked incredulous.

"I'm just doing a routine investigation."

John Cerelli's color faded. His mouth slowly closed. "But why ask me? Certainly you don't think that—"

Randy pointed at the box in the backseat. "What are you doing with those?"

"They don't belong to me. I was delivering them to Dr. McCall's office." He shrugged. "I make a lot of trips to Brighton, and I pick up medical supplies for her on occasion."

"So why is this box here? On your way to make a delivery, are you?"

He shook his head. "No, sir. It must have fallen out of a larger box of supplies. I just saw it yesterday in the trunk and threw them up here so I would remember to give them to Claire, uh, Dr. McCall."

"What sort of work do you do, Mr. Cerelli?"

"I'm a representative for a software firm. I assist medical practices with computerized patient recordkeeping."

Randy Jensen noted his response and paced around the car. "Remember a few weeks back when we had a little chat about trespassing on Billy Ray Chisholm's property?"

"Sure."

"Correct me if I'm wrong, Mr. Cerelli, but I seem to recall you saying you did not personally know the Chisholms, and that you were concerned that something had flown out of your car as you passed by the night before."

The man stayed quiet. The memory obviously disturbed him. He nodded his head as he looked at the pavement.

"Maybe you need to give me a little more information about just what you were doing at the Chisholms."

John shuffled his feet. "Where are you going with this? Why are you asking me this?"

"I'm just trying to put some facts together, Mr. Cerelli."

"Am I in some sort of trouble here?"

"Not that I know of. But maybe you'd like to think about answering my questions so I can put my mind to rest." He paused, and tapped his fingers on the shiny red hood. "Just what were you looking for at the Chisholms?"

The man sighed. A sign of aggravation? Frustration? "A ring."

"A ring?"

"An engagement ring. A diamond."

"You said you were looking for something that had flown from your car. I thought you meant a car part."

"That's what you assumed. The ring is what flew from my car." He halted and lifted his eyes from the ground. "Why do you need to know this?"

"Ms. Chisholm was raped, Mr. Cerelli. On the very night you say you lost something in front of her house." He walked around toward Mr. Cerelli. Closing the distance between them was likely to make a guilty subject uncomfortable. "It just seemed like such a coincidence that you were around on that night, I thought I'd ask what you were doing."

The man held up his hands. "I don't like this at all. You are implying that I may have been involved in these rapes?" He got into his car. "And I don't like it. Now unless I'm under arrest, I don't think I'm obligated to stay and finish this conversation."

Randy backed up a step as Cerelli started the Mustang and began to pull away. He shook his head and thought about the lame excuse Cerelli had told him. *He was looking for an engagement ring?*

He scratched himself a one-word summary of his interview. "Evasive."

Chapter Eighteen

fter three liters of intravenous fluid, Wally finally urinated in his diaper. After four, he started responding to questions again. By seven o'clock in the evening, he was able to take some thickened liquids, and Claire fed him a protein-enhanced strawberry smoothie.

"You scared me, Daddy," she said, wiping his chin with a towel. "The only way you made it was with the IV."

His eyes were wide open, jerking around the room with his head. It gave him a wild look, like someone who wasn't connected with reality. But the untamed look did not reflect his understanding. "I kn–know," he said.

It was the waxing and waning of his intellect that puzzled Claire the most. Wally went days without communicating in a meaningful way, only to speak and respond to questions appropriately again after a lapse. She wasn't sure whether it was his varied moods that made him more cooperative on some days than others, or simply that the progression of his Huntington's disease seemed to stutter-step. Regardless, she was glad he was responding again, knowing that he had dodged a potentially fatal problem had Claire not been able to give him intravenous hydration.

Speaking with Wally had been predominantly a one-sided conversation for months. Della did the best with him, interpreting his slurs and grunts like a second language. And although Claire tried to speak with her father about his wishes to avoid hospitalizations and possible life-support measures, she was never confident that her father really understood. For this, Claire relied on her mother, to whom Wally had made his wishes clear when he was a bit more coherent.

Claire sighed with both relief and anxiety; there was relief in her father's recovery, and anxiety in being both her father's doctor and his daughter. She set the empty glass on the dresser and plopped into a chair beside his bed.

"We can't keep doing this."

Claire looked up to see her mother in the doorway. "I know." She re-angled the chair to talk to her mother. "I never thought I'd hear you say it."

"I've never had three days in a row like I've just had."

"He's better. He answered a question."

Her mother's chin quivered and she put her hand to her mouth. "I almost let him die, Claire. I didn't realize he was so sick."

Claire shook her head. "Don't kick yourself. People like this can walk a fine line. One hour they're okay. The next, they're over the edge."

Della approached her husband's bed. She grasped and held tightly to his moving hand. "I'm sorry, honey. I can't do this again."

Wally grunted.

"Leon won't be happy. He has always been such an advocate of in-home care."

"He's not the one living this—" Claire stopped herself before she said something in front of her father that he might resent.

"Try to rest, Wally. Your fever has broken. You need to rest," Della said.

Claire followed her mother down the hallway which was again lined with family photographs, as it had been up until the time that Wally's stumbling made keeping things on the wall impossible. The dishes sat unwashed in the sink, the cereal boxes which provided their supper still on the table with the cardboard flaps open. "I keep meaning to ask, did you ever question Uncle Leon about selling McCall Shoes?"

Della looked up. "No." She hesitated. "I can't believe he would ever do that."

Claire put her hands on her hips and sighed. "Mom, I told you about a patient who said he was in town to discuss a buyout. He says his company has been in communication with Leon for months."

"That makes no sense, unless he's finally just giving up. McCall Shoes is having a hard time keeping up with some of the competition. He's already bought Elizabeth out to save her the misery of watching the ship sink on her watch."

"That snake!"

"Claire! Without your uncle we wouldn't have meat on the table."

She flicked the top of a bran cereal box. "This isn't meat. And that man wouldn't do anything unless his own wallet is being padded."

"Claire!" Her mother's mouth dropped open.

"I don't trust him."

"You've had a hard day."

"Grandma is out of McCall Shoes?"

"Yep. She sold all her stock to Leon."

"Why didn't you tell me?"

"Why should you be upset? It was no secret. You've been so busy, it just didn't come up, that's all."

"Grandma McCall has been Wally's advocate from the beginning. Even when Grandpa was alive, she was the one who kept him from writing Wally out of the will. And it's no secret that Leon was only too happy to learn that Wally wasn't blood McCall."

"But he's changed. He's been helping us out financially, and now that McCall Shoes hit rough waters, he's coming through to assure Grandma will be okay in retirement."

Claire shook her head. "Did you ever ask Uncle Leon about a potential buyout of the company? I thought he was on the verge of making a pile of money."

"I talked to him, honey. He said it's all very speculative at this stage. He is exploring every option to try to keep the company afloat."

Claire didn't feel like arguing. Della was right. Claire's day had been rough. And Uncle Leon *had* been helping with the grocery bills. But the nagging feeling remained. Claire yawned and stretched her hands toward the ceiling. "I'm going to cash it in early."

"I'll check Wally at midnight if you'll do it at four."

Claire plodded down the hall. "Deal."

She undressed and prepared for sleep, lying down on the old bed and thinking about the day. Della was nearing the end of her rope. Claire needed to make some inquiries about nursing-home care for Wally. It would be a sad day, but a necessary one if they were going to preserve their sanity.

Chapter Nineteen

eople should carry Rolaids on the first day of any new job. Lena Chisholm didn't exactly care for the heat of the kitchen, but she liked the opportunity to see university students coming through the cafeteria line, and she enjoyed keeping the salad bar stocked, if for no other reason, it was cooler in the dining hall than in the kitchen. But she'd sliced the carrots she was supposed to shred, forgot to put out the cherry tomatoes, and dropped a gallon of blue-cheese dressing on the center of the kitchen tile.

She was busy for her entire eight-hour shift, a good thing for Lena, who had a tendency to think of William Raymond when her mind was idle.

But he was one of the reasons she'd taken the job in the first place. She could have sold her ring and had enough to live on for a month, maybe two if she found a cheap apartment and pinched every penny. But selling the ring seemed to be an emotional letdown, like she was giving up a dream. She knew it wasn't really her engagement ring, but wearing it made it easier to pretend that her life wasn't as dull and frightening as it really was.

She frowned at her new ID badge. If she'd known she would have her picture taken, she would have put on some lipstick. As it was, her lips were pale, and her cheeks needed more sun. She swiped the badge through the time clock and exited the back of the cafeteria. The air was damp, with the threat of a summer thunderstorm in the wind. She lifted her eyes toward the darkened western sky and shivered. It had been a rough day. She wanted to stroll in the evening sunshine and relax, not run back to the women's shelter to escape the rain. The last thing she wanted was to spend another evening trapped with other women in crisis.

She patted the front pocket of her slacks before sliding out the ring she'd kept nestled there. She slid the ring onto her finger and tried a fantasy to lift her spirits. She imagined heading home to meet her husband after his day of med-school classes. The ring sparkled even with the clouded sky and just wearing it made it a little easier to believe her life was happy. Let it rain. She could snuggle with William Raymond in the lobby of the student center.

A thunderclap startled Lena into reality. She squinted at the darkening horizon and fought the sudden urge to cry. Her fantasies couldn't even offer adequate respite from the mess her life had become. She was a pregnant, married teenager separated from an alcoholic, abusive husband, trapped in a town she didn't know, with a menial job and no car. Her own father had abused her. Her sister had warned her and walked away. Her mother had remarried and moved on. She was alone with only a diamond to give her any hope of a future life. She looked down at the ring. Billy Ray had promised her a ring once. And she was just glassy-eyed enough to believe he really would get her one. She cut across a parking lot and crossed the grassy commons area on a diagonal, picking up her pace just as large raindrops began to fall from the sky. The leaves on the maple trees bordering the sidewalk sang a noisy chorus with the wind.

Rain pelted the back of her hand which she raised to shield her face. She lowered her head, fixed on the sidewalk in front of her, and rushed toward the portico of the student center. Just when she reached the announcement area, a man imposed himself directly in her path. She froze as she recognized the work boots stained from the metal shop. She lifted her eyes and gasped.

"Hi, Lena."

She tried to step backwards as Billy Ray clamped his fingers around her arm. Her jaw dropped without sound.

"I've been lookin' for you." With his breath came the familiar stench of his addiction, the lubricant which removed whatever inhibition a real man has to prevent him from striking a woman.

"Billy Ray, I had to leave. I was afraid."

"After all I gave to you," he began.

She trembled as she felt his grip tighten.

"You turn around and treat me like this." His eyes were on the ring. "Where'd you get that?" His face was red with rage, his eyes steel.

Lena glanced right and left, searching the empty sidewalks, but the rain which fell steadily now had driven sensible humans inside for cover. She curled her hand into a fist, anticipating his next move.

He slid his left hand to her wrist and yanked her fingers toward his face for a better look.

"Billy Ray! I found it! It's not from another man!"

He raised his right hand to strike. "You lyin'—"

Her shrill scream interrupted his sentence and apparently his intention.

His face was twisted in a scowl as he looked around and lowered his hand. Even Billy Ray didn't want to hit a woman in public.

Her eyes followed his to a group of students who had just exited the library across the commons. They were tiny from this distance, standing on the broad covered porch. She let out a second cry, a high piercing note familiar to parents of ten-year-old girls at noisy pajama parties.

He glanced toward the library again as she twisted her rainslicked arm from his grip. She backed up a step and filled her lungs for another scream.

With his hushed voice pleading, he hissed, "Lena, don't!"

She caught a glimpse of something she'd seen in Billy a few times before. Once in the fleeting moment after she'd driven a glass shard into his arm, and another just after she'd shoved his shotgun under his chin. She recognized it now with a flash of clarity. His upper lip was pulled taut, an attempt to keep it from quivering. "You coward," she said, her voice thick with disgust.

She backed another step, matching his forward movement. His hands were out, palms up, a surrender posture she would never trust again. He took another step, and she did the same, the duo locked in an untouching dance on the brick sidewalk.

"You're bringin' shame on yourself, Lena. Shame on me. And shame on you."

"Me? You're the jerk."

He shook his head and halted his forward progression. "What'd you tell the cops, Lena?"

"Nothing."

He cursed.

"I haven't told them anything."

He shook his head. "Randy came 'round this morning at work. I know you've been talking to him."

She held up her hands and took another step away. "I haven't, Billy. I swear." Her back touched the outdoor announcement board, which sat in the middle of the brick-paved area in front of the student center. Trapped, she contemplated screaming again.

"I'm not stupid, Lena. You've been playin' a game behind my back for a long time, haven't you? You think you can run around on me, then squeal to the cops that I've been hurting you?"

"I don't know what you're talking a—"

"Shut up!" His index finger was in her face, as he stepped closer. She needed to do something fast to evade his grasp a second time.

She screamed again only to have it cut short as he clamped his left hand over her mouth, shoving her head against the glass covering the bulletin board. She could taste blood as her lips pushed into her front teeth. His body penned her in, as his right hand searched and found her left fingers. She closed her fist to prevent him from pulling off the ring.

"Rachel cheated on me." His eyes, glassed over by alcohol, locked on hers.

She felt tears spill onto her cheeks as he pinched her fingers together against her diamond ring. She couldn't scream. She could barely breathe as her silent crying filled her nose with snot. She desperately wanted to blow her nose so she could inhale with freedom.

Billy Ray continued, "And now you." He yanked the ring from her rain-slicked fingers.

She quickened her breathing, hungry for more air than she could get through her nose. She watched with fear as he lifted the ring for a better look, shifting his body weight off of her for a second, but still keeping his left hand pushed against her mouth. "Money? Is that what your new boyfriend has that I don't?"

She needed more air. *Now.* Instinctively, she exhaled with all her might, spraying tear-thinned mucus over Billy Ray's hand and arm. He recoiled, giving her the fraction of a second she needed. She brought her right knee up between his legs, impacting him with a fury driven by her pain, her need for air, and her rage at his taking her ring.

He groaned and leaned over, dropping the diamond on the patio. Lena scrambled after the ring as it bounced and rolled toward the edge of the brick pavement and the grass beyond. She slipped on the wet sidewalk, sprawling onto her chest and abdomen beside a concrete bench. But she never lost her focus on the shiny little ring. Her hand closed around it as Billy Ray stumbled forward and grasped at her ankle.

She screamed as she pulled her foot away from him, leaving her shoe in his hand. She rolled, stood up, screamed again, and sprinted through the rain, waving her arms at the group that still stood on the portico in front of the library.

She looked back only once to realize that Billy Ray hadn't given chase. When she neared the students, their horrified silent looks greeted and disturbed her. She pointed toward the student center. "A man tried to attack me," she gasped.

She followed their gaze to the empty walkways in front of the student center. Billy Ray had vanished.

Hadn't they seen him?

A man wearing a backwards baseball cap and a black T-shirt lifted a cell phone to his ring-studded ear. "I'll call campus police."

"No," she responded, suddenly self-conscious. She wiped her nose with the back of her hand only to see a blood stain on her hand. "It was my husband." She pointed to the library door. "I'll call from inside."

She jogged toward the door in search of a place to hide.

She didn't stop to rest until she was in the basement women's rest room, locked in the third stall. She sat down on the commode and released her emotions in a flood of tears. It was there she unfolded her hand to look at her ring. He hadn't won. She still had the ring. He may have found her. But she could move on.

She stood and shoved the ring deep in her pocket before preparing to answer a distressing call from her bladder. She sat back down and let herself relax, allowing the panic she'd felt only moments before to melt into relief. She wondered if there was a back door to the library, if Billy Ray would be waiting for her when she left, and if she could outlast him by waiting until the library closed at eleven. She took a deep breath. None of that really mattered right now. She was safe for the moment, and her diamond was nestled in her pocket. It was then she dropped her eyes to focus on the underwear she'd slipped to her knees only moments before. And for the second time in a minute, her emotions swung on a pendulum. One moment she felt relief, and now, at the sight of the bright stain on her panties, anxiety gripped her heart again.

She was bleeding!

The next morning Wally's color was back to his normal sunless pale and he drank most of a thickened nutritional shake without choking. Claire helped give him a quick sponge bath and headed for the clinic, promising her mom that she'd try to get home early and reminding her that John intended to come by in the afternoon to help.

She arrived in time to sip coffee from a mug emblazoned with the words "A chance to cut . . . a chance to cure" while signing off on office notes and incoming labs and X rays she'd ordered. By seven-fifty, a small light appeared on the wall by her desk, indicating Lucy had her first patient in room A.

Tracy McGinnis sat fully clothed on the exam table, her hands in her lap but her fingers never still. Her face was etched with worry beyond her years and she glanced frequently at her husband, who sat in a chair beside her with arms folded across his chest.

Claire listened as Tracy tearfully confessed her thoughts of harming her infant daughter. Every time she began meal preparations that involved sharp utensils, dark impulses to stab her precious little Heather crept in, filling Tracy with guilt. The idea repulsed her, horrified her, and eventually paralyzed her from picking up anything but a soup spoon to eat with. Anxiety overwhelmed her, and the thoughts of harming her daughter became stronger the more she tried to avoid it. It was only when she started refusing to go into the kitchen altogether that her desperate husband brought her in.

After taking additional history, Claire recognized the classic symptoms of obsessive compulsive disease and recommended referral to a psychiatrist. The couple, as expected, refused. Just coming to the local physician was threatening enough. A Stoney Creek native was not likely to consent to visiting a psychiatrist.

"Just tell her she has to go into the kitchen again. I'm a horrible cook myself, and I'm gonna starve," her husband whined.

"I'd like to prescribe a medication. This condition is very common, more common than sugar," she added, using the country vernacular for diabetes mellitus.

"She's just got wrong ideas in her head, Doc."

The patient put her head in her hands. "I've been praying hard. It's an attack from the devil."

Claire sighed. She didn't have time to fight the small-town stigma that surrounded the treatment of mental illness. It didn't matter if Claire knew it was from a chemical imbalance. She reassured her new patient, encouraged her to fight back against the illness and not to give in to its demands. "If you let it," she explained, "it will start with your kitchen and not touching sharp utensils. If you don't fight, it may try eventually to keep you from using any utensil to eat or allow you to touch your baby at all."

"You think I'm crazy." She twisted her fingers into a knot. "I just need more faith."

"You're not crazy. You have a disease. It's called OCD, obsessive compulsive disorder. It is a real physical problem, a chemical imbalance. It's very common."

Claire wrote her patient a prescription for a medication to help with her fight and scheduled her for a follow-up visit in two weeks. Before she left the room, Claire asked for permission to pray for her patient, and concluded her visit by a request for God to hold Tracy in his arms of peace, and to help her separate her real love for her daughter from the unwanted obsessions of her disease which didn't represent her true intentions.

Tracy's eyes were red as she reached to hug Claire with choke-hold enthusiasm.

"Here," Claire gasped, reaching for her pen. She handed Tracy a piece of paper on which she'd written *Brain Lock*. "Get this book. I think it will be a godsend."

In room B, Ada Broome had diverticulitis. In room C, Todd Alty needed a high school football physical. As Claire emptied the rooms, Lucy filled them.

In room A, Blaire Shifflett had strep throat; in B, old Joel Thomason had a flare-up of shingles; in room C, thirteen-year-old Evan Jacobs refused to show Claire the splinter in his backside until his mother left the room. And back in A, Sam Harris needed his ankle wrapped for a bad sprain.

It was noon before Claire saw the note from Lucy on her desk. It was attached to Lena Chisholm's chart. "Lena called. She's spotting, with abdominal cramps. Counseled to go to E.R. in Brighton. Patient refused. She wants to see you."

Claire lifted her rebellious blond bangs from her forehead. She'd cut her hair to be manageable during surgery, and was letting it grow out again since coming back to Stoney Creek. Now, it was in an unmanageable middle stage, too long, and too short. She wanted patients to trust her judgment, but she also wanted them to lean on others when it was outside her expertise. Lena needed an obstetrician. Maybe she could persuade her to see one of her old professors at the medical school in Brighton.

She dialed the number on the bottom of Lucy's note and waited while Cathy Rivera brought Lena to the phone.

"Hello."

"Lena, this is Dr. McCall. Lucy told me you had some spotting?"

"Yes. It started yesterday."

"Yesterday? Why didn't you call?"

"It's a long story. I was kind of tied up until the library closed."

Claire let it go. "Are you having pain? Cramps?"

"Some."

"You need to get some help. You could be having a miscarriage."

"I know," she said without expression. "Maybe it's an answer to prayer."

Claire shook her head. Lena needed a lesson in theology that Claire didn't have time to teach. "Do you know your blood type?"

"No."

"Did you ever give blood? Have a blood donor card?"

"I'm not bleeding that much. I don't need blood, Dr. McCall."

"I know that. But if you are having a miscarriage, the baby's blood and your blood have a chance of mixing together. If your blood type is Rh negative and your baby is Rh positive, you will make antibodies that could attack the blood of any future child you carry."

"Antibodies?"

Claire knew she was losing her. "Listen, it's important for you to get your blood drawn so we can figure out what type you are. If you are Rh negative, you'll need to get a shot."

"I don't have a car."

"Cathy Rivera can take you to the outpatient lab at the university hospital. I can call ahead and ask them to do the test."

"I guess."

"Let me know if things get worse. Can you put Cathy back on?"

Claire gave Cathy the instructions and put down the phone. Then she scrawled a handwritten entry into the chart documenting Lena's complaints and her intervention. When she lifted her head, her nurse was standing to her left, leaning over the desk. She didn't look happy. She opened her fingers and allowed the paper in her hand to float to the desktop. It was the day's appointments. "Mabel Henderson is on the phone. Her foot is worse and she's having chills."

Claire studied the schedule. There wasn't an opening all afternoon. "We have to see her. Just tell her to come over and we'll work her in."

Lucy shook her head. "You're an hour and a half behind. We've already added two walk-ins with the flu. If you tell Mabel to come in, she'll spend two hours sitting in that waiting room with her foot down. It will swell like a balloon before you see her."

Claire sighed. She knew her nurse was right. "But if she sits in the waiting room with her smelly foot for two hours, maybe the odor will smoke some of the other patients away and lighten the load for the afternoon."

Lucy snickered. "It won't work," she said, walking her fingers over the schedule, naming each patient's diagnosis. "Sinusitis, flu, flu, follow-up nose-bleed, Daisy Biller. She's ninety-four. I don't think any of these patients can smell."

"Mabel really needs to go up to Carlisle to see a surgeon."

"You know she won't do that. At least not until she's on death's door."

Claire nodded. "Tell her I'll stop by her house on my way home."

"You don't have to do that."

"Who else will make Mabel do what's right?"

The nurse took Claire by the hand. "When Dr. Jenkins quit, I thought we'd never find a young doctor with the same compassion. Everyone we talked to seemed more concerned about big salary and short hours." Her eyes locked on Claire's. Lucy's eyes were suddenly moist. This woman could be strong one minute, and melting the next. "I was wrong."

Claire felt her own throat tighten. What else could she do for patients? Going the second mile was instinct to her. "Thanks."

"I'll tell her you'll be by." When she reached the doorway, she paused. "Oh. I got a call from Stephanie Blackwell's mother. Her husband is getting a kidney transplant this afternoon."

"Stephanie's a match?"

Lucy nodded.

"Boy, they didn't waste any time."

"Nope."

Lucy disappeared down the hall leaving Claire alone with her thoughts. Polycystic kidney disease, OCD, the flu, first trimester bleeding, diabetic foot infections, splinters, earaches, football physicals, gallstones, kidney stones, hypertension, backaches, headaches, and shingles. The mundane and the life-threatening side by side in a list as varied as her patients themselves. She was just as likely to see someone with an imagined illness as she was a myocardial infarction. The list of things she needed to know about as a general practicioner was staggering, and the dilemma was in sorting out the common from the serious. Momentarily, she dropped her head in her hands to pray. Frontline medicine wasn't for the faint of heart. She needed to know something about everything, and right now, she felt a bit overwhelmed. She whispered a prayer for wisdom and for thanks, then picked up her stethoscope in anticipation of the afternoon load.

John finished business in Richmond by ten, and put the top down for a summer's morning drive back to Stoney Creek. He took the Gordonsville exit off I–64 and cut over to Route 33 to take the scenic route over the Blue Ridge mountains. Summer rhododendron and honeysuckle were in bloom. The sky was clear, and the temperature had cooled to the high seventies. This was heaven on earth to John on any other day. But today, his thoughts were fixed on another matter. The beautiful mountain scenery passed without appreciation. He gripped the steering wheel with white knuckles as he thought about his encounter with the county deputy the day before.

Perhaps he should just confess the whole mess to Claire and be over with it. He wrinkled his forehead, squinting into the afternoon sun. That didn't seem to be a good idea. If he told her about the deputy, he'd end up having to tell her about the night out at Lena's place and then the ring, and then he'd have to tell her everything, and that would never do.

But things had a way of snowballing on him. One problem seemed to be leading to another, and that one to another. Claire couldn't or wouldn't follow through with her genetic testing, so John's engagement plans crashed, and he let his remorse and impulsive behavior get the best of him when he tossed the ring out of his car. Now, it seemed, the law was suspicious of him, and that's what scared him even more.

He'd moved to Stoney Creek to be near Claire, anticipating a short engagement and a happy life together. But nothing seemed to be working the way he planned. Claire worked constantly, not as much as during her internship, but enough to occupy her so that even when he did spend time with her away from her office, he could tell she was mulling over decisions she'd made.

By four, he pulled in to Wally and Della's place, hoping to see Claire's blue VW. It was wishful thinking. Fridays were the worst for overrunning the closing time at the office. Every mother in the Apple Valley seemed to think about the horror of facing the weekend with a fussy child at four P.M., and in they'd come to Claire's clinic, hoping to be worked in at the last minute. He sat and talked with Della for an hour, before he finally insisted that she let him watch Wally while she did errands in Carlisle.

It scared him how much he enjoyed talking with Della. With her, there was no pressure to make the relationship work. She was confident, pretty, and had a great sense of humor. Of course, Claire was all of those things as well, but his relationship with Claire had seemed like such a strain lately that relating to Della was a relief.

He walked down the hall to pour out his heart to the Wall-man. One good thing about Wally was you could trust him never to tell a secret. Wally hardly ever said anything. "Hi, Wally."

Wally's head and limbs flailed. "John."

"Della went to Carlisle. Need anything? Something to drink?"

John mixed thick-it into a glass of juice and let Wally drink. Then John sat in the chair and talked about Claire. "It's frustrating, Wally. She's so fixated on her risk of HD that she can't enjoy today. She's running away, sticking her head in the sand. She enjoys being busy so she can't have time to deal with thinking about the future. And until she comes to grips with that, I'm not sure we can have a future together."

John leaned forward and clasped his hands together. "It's like she's made HD an idol." He thought for a moment. "She thinks HD will have the ability to control her life and she's afraid of what that might mean."

Wally grunted and flung his legs across the sheets. His eyes were open but glassed over. He wasn't with John, but that didn't stop John from working out his thoughts aloud. He stood up and started to pace around the little room, wildly gesticulating with his hands like a true Italian.

"I read something about fear once, how it's a lot like faith except with a different object of focus. With faith, your confidence is in God, acknowledging that he has ultimate control of your situation. With fear, you've put something else on the throne of your life, giving the control that's supposed to be God's over to something else. If you fear man, you are placing him in the position that only God is to be in. You're fearing that man has the ultimate control over your situation. Whatever you fear has taken a position that God is supposed to have, and in a way it's become an idol in your life. It's idolatry. And for Claire, that's HD." He slammed his fist in his hand. Maybe he'd missed his calling. He had the passion to lead a crusade.

"Cl–Cl–Claire!" Wally's eyes were wild but fixed on the doorway behind John. It always amazed John how Wally could keep his eyes on one place even though his head was in motion.

"Are you quite finished?" He recognized the feminine voice instantly. Busted!

He whirled around. "Claire!"

She offered a saccharine smile. "In the flesh."

He winced. "How long have you been standing there?"

"Too long," she said, turning on her heels. She walked away muttering, "I'm so glad you have me all figured out."

He followed her down the hall. "Claire, it's not like that. I was just venting my feelings to Wally."

Claire backed away as John advanced, his arms open for a hug. "Wait a minute, Cerelli. Give me a chance to process what you said."

He stopped and watched as Claire folded her hands across her chest and quietly repeated what she'd heard John say. With each new phrase, she nodded her head from side to side. "What you fear has in effect taken the place God is supposed to have in your life. Trust means you believe God is in control. Fear means you are not trusting that God has ultimate control of your future. What you fear has taken God's place." She nodded and plopped down on the couch. "You're right. My fear of HD is idolatry."

John felt his jaw slacken. "You agree?"

"Sure." She shrugged. "Is that supposed to be a special revelation?"

"Well, no, it's—" He halted. "I just didn't think you'd admit it."

"If you're going to define idolatry that way, I guess it's true. But it doesn't have anything to do with my decision not to get my test results." She caught his eyes and held them with hers. "I'm just making a decision that I can trust without knowing the future."

He raised his eyebrows. "You don't think you're just avoiding the result because of fear?"

She took a deep breath and looked away. She never looked him in the eye when she wasn't sure. "No."

My ever-confident Claire, not always right, but never in doubt. He let it drop. He didn't believe it, but it wasn't worth pushing her. "Hungry?"

"Starved. I worked through lunch to catch back up." She looked back toward the kitchen. "Where's Mom?"

He sat beside her. "Carlisle. She needed to shop."

She touched his dark curls and smiled. "So we're alone."

His pulse quickened as Claire pushed her face into his neck and ran her hand into his hair. Goosebumps rose on his arms as he felt her breath in his ear.

"I thought you said you were hungry."

She teased his earlobe, pinching it in her lips. "I am."

His resolve began to melt. He turned to meet her mouth with his and cradled her head in his arms. Their kisses were soft, her mouth open and receptive. They were quickly heading down a path they had decided was off limits because of their past together.

After a passionate kiss, Claire put her hand on his forehead.

He felt her hand pressing with more firmness until his neck yielded and he allowed his face to be pushed away.

"Easy, Cerelli."

"You're killing me."

"I'm kissing you."

"You know what I mean."

She captured his eyes, unflinching. "I know." Her eyes closed and she shifted to her side on the couch, her head resting on his lap.

"What are you doing?" He stroked her cheek. "You're just going to rev my engines and then slam the brakes?"

She opened one eye, then closed it when she saw him watching her. "I'm tired. I just want to rest for a moment. Then we can find something for dinner."

He sighed. He knew he needed to be a strong leader, but sometimes he didn't want to be. Sometimes all he wanted was to wisk Claire off to a romantic rendezvous and fulfill all his pent-up fantasies. But he knew she was right to put on the brakes. There would be a time for their passion's expression ... if only he could make Claire believe that he really loved her, that he would commit to loving her regardless of what their future held. And until she faced her future head-on, he knew she wouldn't be ready to trust the love he had in his heart for her.

If she sensed his unspoken frustration, she didn't show it. Instead, she began to vent about her own pressures. "When I was at the university, I let the arrogance of the ivory tower convince me that the LMD was a second-class citizen."

"LMD?"

"Local medical doctor. My attendings would throw around the term like they were a bunch of rejects that couldn't handle the rigors of university medical practice."

"You've changed your mind?"

"John, I'm an LMD now. I see it completely differently. The LMD is where the rubber meets the road, where practicality needs to mix with proven science. Where cost concerns meet high technology."

"Not as easy as you thought?"

"Having to know something about everything can be overwhelming."

"Can't you just refer the problems you don't understand to a specialist?"

"I wish it was that easy. Even if I wanted to send away a problem I didn't understand, people in Stoney Creek are reluctant to go."

Claire reached over to the top of the coffee table in front of the couch where Della had placed the day's mail. John watched her face as she flipped through the letters. She frowned. "I hadn't thought about my school loans when I came back to Stoney Creek. They were all deferred as long as I was in training. Now that I'm working, my payback has started." She ripped open the top of a business letter and sighed. "Look at this. Even if I pay back a thousand dollars a month, it's going to take me forever to pay this back."

John lifted the statement from her hand and looked at the principal remaining on her loan. It was a few dollars shy of one hundred twenty thousand. Marrying Claire wasn't exactly a ticket to a life of riches and ease.

"I might not be able to practice long enough to pay this back."

He refolded the statement and shoved it back in the envelope. "Things will work out. You could always accelerate your payments. Plenty of people in Stoney Creek live off half your income. You could pay this off in a few years."

"Not if my dad needs full-time nursing care. Even with my grandma's help, funds are bound to get tight."

He shook his head.

"It's not fair, John. If I could have only known about HD before I made my career choices—"

"Oh, like you would have run off to be tested while you were still in college?"

Her expression steeled. "Yes." She hesitated. "Better to find out whether you have the HD gene before you spend half your life training to do something you may only be able to do for a few years."

He didn't really feel like arguing through this again. Why couldn't they just cuddle on the couch like normal couples?

When he didn't respond, she continued. "It's almost like God kept HD hidden away from me, set me up to make choices I would have never made if only I'd known."

"You mean to tell me you wouldn't have gone into medicine if you'd known your father had Huntington's disease?"

"I didn't say that. But I would have been tested. If I'm carrying the gene, I'd be a fool to go into medicine."

"But you love this stuff! I've seen your eyes light up when you tell me about the things you treat, the people you've helped. So what if you only have a few years at it?"

She closed her eyes, apparently to squeeze back the tears. He touched her forehead and stroked her blond bangs. She used to seem like such a rock, confident and steady, always focused on her goals. Now, she vacillated, confident and excited about life one moment, on the verge of tears the next. "So go get your test results, Claire. Find out so you can know for sure. Then we can plan our future together. If you'd have gotten tested before starting your education, why not now?"

"The stakes are higher now," she said, her voice weakening. Her eyelids were tightly pinched, but he could see the tears pooling in the corner of her eyes. "You wouldn't love me if you knew I'd be like Daddy."

The accusation stung. It infuriated him to hear her lack of trust. He strained to keep his volume in a normal range. "That's not fair. You don't know that—"

She sat up, pulling her head from his embrace. "And you can't predict your reaction to something so horrible," she interrupted.

They stared at each other a moment, locked in silent hurt and accusation. John broke away and shook his head. This is what loving Claire McCall had become. Hold-onto-your-seat fast. Mind-numbing. Intimate one minute, confrontational the next. Intensity with a capital "I."

The electronic chirp of her cell phone sounded. One ring. Two.

Claire glanced toward her purse on the kitchen counter.

"Let it ring."

"It might be a patient."

"Your voice mail will answer."

"They might not leave a message."

John rolled his eyes as she walked over and picked up her phone.

"Dr. McCall speaking." John watched as her expression initially hardened, then changed again, her eyes widening with fear. "Billy Ray? . . . What? . . . Where are you? . . . She passed out? . . . Slow down, Mr. Chisholm, I don't understand."

Claire held the phone back from her ear. John could hear a man's voice cursing Claire.

John crept forward to hear. He leaned his head in to share the phone with Claire. He could hear Billy Ray Chisholm's loud voice. "She's in surgery now. The doctor told me you should have ordered an ultrasound test."

"Mr. Chisholm, I—"

"She almost bled to death because of you! Some doctor you are! You're gonna pay for this!"

"Mr. Chisholm? Mr. Chisholm?" Claire looked at John. "He hung up."

"What's going on, Claire?"

Her face blanched as she stumbled backwards and sat in a kitchen chair. "Lena Chisholm called the office this morning. She was having some spotting of blood. I thought she must be having a miscarriage." Claire's hand went to her mouth. "I didn't even think of an ectopic pregnancy."

He was confused. "What?"

"She had a pregnancy in her fallopian tube, John. I missed it."

"Why did they call Billy Ray?"

Claire shook her head. "Who knows?" She stood back up. "I've got to go to Brighton. I need to straighten this out."

"What can you do?"

"I'm not sure. But I need to make sure they protect Lena from Billy Ray." Claire picked up her purse and started for the door.

"Claire, you can't go without me."

"Then come on."

"We can't leave Wally alone."

Her hands flew up in frustration. "Ahh!"

Chapter Twenty

{F}or the next hour while they waited for Della's return, Claire nibbled on a BLT sandwich with little enthusiasm. In between bites, she made phone calls and pieced together what must have happened to Lena.

From one of the girls at the shelter, she learned that Lena had come back from her lab test, then promptly complained of severe stomach pains and sought refuge in the bathroom where she passed out and struck her head on the commode. "I'm sure it's an ectopic pregnancy," the woman answering Claire's call responded. "My sister had one and acted the same way." *Great,* Claire thought. *Someone without any medical training picked up on her diagnosis right away. And I was so consumed with esoterica that I missed the diagnosis staring me in the face!*

She wanted to talk to Cathy Rivera, but she was reportedly over at the hospital waiting for word on Lena.

Next Claire had called Dr. Jenkins. If anyone would know what the standard workup for first-trimester bleeding was, it was him. Their conversation did little to comfort her. "What did I do for first-trimester bleeding? In recent years we relied a lot on transvaginal ultrasound for anyone who is having any pain. If a patient has a rising beta-HcG in between one and two thousand, and no visible pregnancy in the uterus, you can be virtually positive she has a pregnancy in a tube. Then you'd better act fast to give methotrexate to end the pregancy before it can rupture a tube." He paused. "Oh, and you need to check the blood type of the mother. If she's Rh negative, give a dose of Rhogam just in case the baby's Rh positive."

"At least I checked her blood type. She was positive, so I thought I was off the hook."

"You can always call me from the office if you're not sure about a situation."

The problem was, I wasn't "unsure." I just wasn't thinking about ectopic.

"Don't kick yourself, Claire. How many cases of first-trimester bleeding did you see in your surgical internship?"

Claire shrugged. "None, I guess."

"And I've seen hundreds. How would you have known?"

But I'm supposed to know.

Claire doubted a malpractice jury would give her a break just because she hadn't seen a patient with the problem since medical school. Her failure to make the diagnosis may have had serious deleterious consequences for Lena. The whole thing was like a bad dream, and it freshened the memories of a lawsuit she faced during her internship. Images flitted through her mind . . . an adorable girl riding her purple bicycle on her birthday . . . a drunk driver . . . a scared little girl who had died under Claire's watch during a CT scan.

When Della returned, Claire's story tumbled out in a rush. Groceries were put away, and Claire and John were on their way to Brighton within minutes. They took John's convertible, but the wind in her hair and the mountain scenery did little to soothe her racing heart.

She felt the back of John's hand brush against her cheek. "Remember who's in control. We don't have to worry about this."

"You didn't miss a diagnosis."

He dropped his hand to her knee. "I hate to see you do this, honey. You have no idea if the outcome would have been different if you'd have sent her straight for an ultrasound."

He was right, but it was easier for the compulsive physician to take responsibility.

She stayed quiet. John went on, trying to comfort her. "Lena would never sue you. You know that. She knows you are trying to help. Don't let Billy Ray's stupid threats get to you. He can't sue you without her."

"He can if she's dead."

John raised his voice. "She's not going to die, Claire."

She nodded her head without speaking. She knew John couldn't see her, but she didn't care.

"You're letting your imagination get the best of you."

"I know."

She watched as his hand slowly drifted from her knee to the controls of his CD player. "Oh, no, you don't, Cerelli. No opera. Not now."

He started singing, bellowing his best baritone imitation opera.

"Spare me," she groaned. "That's not singing."

"I can sing."

She pulled his hand away from his control. "Sing to me then, Cerelli. But no opera."

She studied him for a moment. He appeared to be thinking, suddenly very serious. After a minute, he nodded, as if he had located the perfect thought. Slowly, he began to sing, his volume just enough to be heard above the engine noise.

"O, Claire, voglio stare con te per sempre. O, Claire, mi sono innamorato di te. Mi sposerai?"

His voice was full. He glanced her way each time he mentioned her name, each time lingering a little longer before he turned his eyes back toward the road. The melody of his voice lifted her soul, each time swelling as he sang her name, and falling silent at the end of each phrase, his words wisked away by the passing wind. She had no idea what he was saying, only that his eyes were moist, and his lips quivering silently when his words were done.

"What does it mean?"

She leaned over and laid her head on his shoulder.

He shook his head.

"Don't do this to me. I want to know. It's so pretty, John."

"I can't tell you."

"You don't know."

"It's Italian."

"I know that. Tell me what it means."

"I can't." She pinched his side. He pulled away. "Not yet."

She slapped his arm and sat up straight in her seat. "You're not fair." She shook her head and decided to try a different tactic to get the information from him. "It's probably the words to a commercial for spaghetti."

"It isn't." A smile flashed across his face.

"It's an Italian ad for a car, isn't it?" She poked his shoulder with her index finger. "You were getting choked up about Italian pizza, weren't you? Admit it."

"It's romantic."

"You don't know enough Italian to be romantic."

"I know enough."

"Why did you sing it if you weren't going to interpret? You just want to torture me."

"You stopped thinking about Billy Ray, didn't you?"

She took a deep breath. He was right. He had taken her mind off Billy Ray. She stuck her tongue out at him and made a raspberry. "Who cares? I don't need to know what it means. I just know it made me feel special. In fact," she said resolutely, "I don't want to know what it means. It would spoil it." She began to imitate him. "Oh, Claire, our pasta is the best," she sang. "Our pasta is the best in the world. Enjoy it every night on your table." She copied his melody.

John began to laugh. Soon he was wiping tears from the corners of his eyes. "Oooh weee!" he shouted.

"Getting misty on me, Cerelli? I knew I shouldn't have fallen for an Italian."

"You're crazy." He finally stopped laughing at her and wiped his face one last time with his shirtsleeve. "I just got the wind in my eyes is all."

She hit him again and leaned back in her seat. After a minute, she laid her head against his shoulder.

In twenty minutes, they pulled into the Brighton University Hospital parking lot. Claire walked beside John and looked at the hospital building in front of her. It was a strange moment for her. She'd spent endless hours in this very hospital during her four medical school years. She belonged here then. She was a Brighton student, recognized by the nursing staff and the attendings. Now, just a little over a year since she'd left, she tried to shake off the feeling that she didn't belong. She'd become one of "them," the outside referring physicians that relied on the university to bail them out when things got too hot or complicated.

They quickened their pace across the lot and entered through an automatic revolving door. As she entered the lobby, she took in the familiar scent that immediately brought her back to her medical school experience. She looked around, wondering if she'd see anyone she knew. She checked to see that her blouse was tucked into her slacks and took a deep breath. *Will anyone recognize me with my short hair?*

She pulled John's arm to her side, and walked forward with an air of confidence she didn't feel. Chairs were linked to line small carpeted areas around tables of outdated magazines. Potted ferns and an aquarium intended to make the atmosphere more homey reminded Claire of an airport. Patients and families filled the chairs and men and women in white coats shuffled past without acknowledgment. She recognized the chief of medicine, and lifted her face as he walked by. His eyes caught hers for a moment of question, but no recognition lit as he paused and unclipped a pager from his belt.

Ahead, two uniformed officers were talking to a man who faced away from Claire and John. As they approached, the man glanced at them, and suddenly whirled around to face them, his expression twisted with anger. Claire let out a squeal as she recognized Billy Ray Chisholm.

Billy Ray advanced toward them quickly, pulling away from an officer behind him. Claire thought he was going to strike her so she raised her hand to protect her face. Instead, he shoved John by the shoulder. "I should have known you'd be around. You're asking for trouble."

John stepped back. "What?"

Immediately Billy Ray was flanked by the officers, one on each of his arms. "Let's not have any trouble here, Billy."

Billy Ray twisted his right arm free and pointed at John's face, cursing. "You—"

"Enough!" The officers pulled Billy Ray back.

"A man doesn't sleep with another man's wife and get away with it!"

Claire looked at John's face. What did she see there? Fear? Confusion?

"Easy, Billy," an officer said. "Let's go!"

Billy Ray's shoes were barely touching the ground as the two officers escorted him toward the front of the hospital. Billy Ray shouted over his shoulder. "And you'll be hearing from my lawyer, Dr. McCall. You almost let Lena die!" When he said "doctor," he puckered his mouth and sneered.

Claire slowly unclenched her closed fist from the front of her blouse. "What was that all about?"

"I have no idea."

"He seems to think you've been having an affair with Lena. Why would he think that?" John looked scared. Or guilty. Claire wasn't sure which.

John raised his voice. "I don't know. The man's crazy."

Claire watched John's eyes flash with anger, his cheeks already reddening, his head shaking back and forth. What was he thinking? What was going on? She cleared her throat to inquire, then looked at him for a second longer before deciding to let it drop. Maybe it was just the outrageousness of Billy's accusation. It wasn't like John to cover up.

They walked past a large fish tank. She looked back toward the front of the hospital. Billy Ray and the officers had disappeared. "Let's ask the admitting office what room Lena's in," she said, pointing at a door in the back of the lobby.

When they arrived in her room a few minutes later, they found the bed empty and Cathy Rivera sitting in a chair by the window. "Claire," she said, standing to her feet. She opened her arms for a hug. "So good to see you."

Cathy shook John's hand. "Hi."

Cathy pointed to the bed. "Have a seat. The surgeon just came by. Lena's in the recovery room. She's doing fine."

Relief struck Claire. She smiled and hugged John.

John squeezed her shoulders. "I knew she'd be okay."

Cathy sat back down in her chair. "You just missed the other excitement." She paused and folded her arms across her chest. "Billy Ray was here."

"We know. That's how we heard Lena was here," Claire explained. "Billy Ray called me."

"Oh, my. I just thought the women at the shelter must have called."

Claire shook her head. "What I want to know is, how did Billy ever find out?"

"One of the interns called him. The squad that picked her up didn't know she was from a shelter for abused women." Cathy held up her hands. "It's the first time I wished we had a sign out front." She forced a chuckle. "I was furious with the poor doctor who had called. He had no idea who I was, but I'm sure he won't forget me."

Claire traded smiles with John. "So what happened with Billy Ray? We saw him downstairs with two police officers."

"He demanded to know where his wife was and they told him to wait in her room. When I saw him, I called the police. He tried to convince them that he could stay because Lena hadn't gotten a restraining order against him. But I got the doctor to request him to be removed out of concern for his patient's safety."

"The doctor—"

She smiled. "The same intern that had called Billy Ray. When he saw me coming up to him again, I think he was ready to do anything to make me happy."

Claire clapped her hands together. "Good for you!"

Cathy held her hands. "I look out for my girls." She paused. "So after some discussion, Billy Ray saw the wisdom of leaving voluntarily." She held up two fingers. "With the assistance of a few friends."

A knock at the open door caught their attention. "Dr. McCall?"

Stephanie Blackwell was standing in a hospital gown hanging onto an IV pole. She smiled. "I thought I saw you go by my room."

"Stephanie? You look great! My nurse told me you were having surgery today. And you're already walking the halls?"

She nodded. "The surgeon was great. He took my kidney out lapar-o ..."

"Laparoscopically."

Stephanie nodded. "That's it." She held her left side. "Besides the four Band-Aids, I just have this little incision where he took my kidney out."

Claire looked at Cathy and John and made introductions. "Stephanie is one of my patients back in Stoney Creek. She just donated a kidney to her father." She paused. "How's he doing?"

"I just visited him down in the ICU. He's doing great. He's already making urine." She smiled again. "If everything goes well, I'll be discharged tomorrow. Thanks for helping to set this up."

"I didn't do anything."

"You talked to me. You ordered my test to find out I wasn't a carrier of polycystic kidney disease, didn't you? You made my referral to the transplant team."

Claire really didn't feel like she deserved any credit. "You did all the work, kid. You get the credit for this one, not me."

John's eyes widened. "You just had surgery, and now you're walking?"

Stephanie nodded. "I'm a little slow."

Claire gave her young patient a thumbs-up and watched her turn to leave. Then, she whacked John's knee when she saw him staring at the back of Stephanie's gaping gown.

"What? I was just amazed she was up and walking," he protested.

Claire wanted to smack him again, but restrained herself in front of the others. Instead, she leaned forward and whispered, "Right!"

When John dropped Claire off at midnight, they found Della leaning over a four-page application for the Pleasant View Nursing Home. She looked up and yawned. "How's your patient?"

"She's okay." Claire opened the refrigerator and pulled out a jug of milk. "I think she was glad to see us."

"What about her husband? Did he cause any trouble?"

"A little. But he left the hospital before she got out of surgery."

John smiled. "The police helped him make up his mind to go."

"I see." Della pushed aside the application as John set a cookie jar on the table in front of her. It was a ceramic snowman, one of the few things from Claire's childhood that Wally hadn't managed to break. "Do you think Dr. V would fill out this physical exam portion of this application?"

"If he won't, I will," Claire offered.

Della sighed. "Duh. I wasn't even thinking that my own daughter might be able to do it." She lifted a chocolate-chip cookie from the jar. "I might as well just stick this right to my hips," she said, licking her lips. Claire watched as she caught John's eye. "Anything a McCall woman eats after ten o'clock goes straight to her hips, you know." She nodded at Claire. "You'd better watch this one."

"Mom!" Claire pinched her own thigh. "I watch what I eat. I just didn't feel like eating much supper, that's all."

John laughed. "You talked to the social worker about the nursing home?"

Della nodded. "They may have an opening as early as next week." She looked at Claire. "Can you get him a chest X ray? It's a requirement for admission."

"Sure. John and I can take him up to my clinic tomorrow."

"Tomorrow's Saturday."

"I work there, remember? He can get an X ray on the weekend."

"You can't strap Wally in a regular car."

"Hmm. We can get G and W ambulance service to do it. Blake Henderson owes me a favor anyway."

Della rested her head on her left hand and stared at the table. "The administrator thinks it would be best if Wally had a feeding tube."

"We've been over this, Mom. Dad has made it clear. He won't have it."

"I know. I told her that. I told her I could come by once a day and help feed him."

"You don't have to do that, Mom."

"He's still my husband," she said, shaking her head. "I can't believe I'm even considering putting him in a home."

John reached over and squeezed Della's arm. "I can't believe you've kept him at home this long."

Claire watched as a tear escaped onto her mother's cheek. "It's really okay, Mother. You can still visit him. Every day if you want. Your relationship with Daddy will be better if you don't have to take care of him every minute."

"My relationship with Wally is fine."

John shook his head. "You're amazing, Della. How do you love a man like Wally?"

Claire was incensed at the question. "John!"

"I'm not saying he's not lovable, Claire. I just want to know how she does it."

"You don't look at him like I do," Della said, wiping a tear with the palm of her hand. "When I see Wally, I try to see the man that HD has left behind. I don't focus on his illness." She picked up another cookie. "I've had a lot of good times with him, too."

John pushed back his chair, nodding his head. The highest pressure produces diamonds. And the pressure in Della's life was no different. Her attitude was a gem mined from the life of adversity. "I'm going to sleep on that thought." He leaned over and kissed Della on the forehead. "Thanks."

He walked toward the door.

"Hey," Claire called out to his back. "Where's mine?"

John turned and blew her a kiss, before singing a phrase in Italian, *"O, Claire, mi sono innamorato di te. Mi sposerai?"*

Chapter Twenty-One

S aturday night came with overcast skies that obscured the light of the moon and a damp wind that prophesied rain. It was pitch black by nine P.M., which was okay by Stephanie Blackwell, who was spending her first night out of the hospital alone. She hadn't slept well in the hospital the night before, so she hoped to turn in early tonight to make up for lost sleep. She chased her fiancé, Mark, out of the house by eight, promising to call him if she had any trouble. He had wanted to stay, but he tended to be a Nervous Nelly, and his constant questioning about her every little need was getting on her last nerve.

By nine-thirty, her incision in her left lower abdomen was beginning to ache, so she took two Percocet tablets and a glass of wine and opened a romance. By ten, even the heartache of love lost and the hint of future love ignited couldn't keep her eyelids from drooping. She set down the novel after swirling the remaining red liquid. She drained the glass and grabbed each arm of the chair for assistance in standing. Her head was swiming delightfully. The dull ache in her side was still there, but at a tolerable level, and with her head buzzing, who cared?

She flipped off the porchlight and plodded into her bedroom, not bothering to brush her teeth. She was too tired. She slipped off her robe, letting it fall to the floor. Underneath, she wore only undies and an old T-shirt. She lowered herself onto the bed and gently curled up on her right side. In less than a minute, she slept.

Thump. Thump-thump, thump, thump. Vague perceptions of pounding aroused her after midnight. Her first thought was of thunder. She rolled over only to be reminded of her recent surgery. She looked toward the sheer curtains and the window beyond, listening to the pounding and wondering why the thunder wasn't accompanied by lightning flashes. *It must be too far away.*

The pounding continued, now more crisp and rhythmic. Through a painkiller haze, she slowly recognized the sound as someone knocking on her front door. *Knock, knock-knock, knock, knock—knock knock!*

Her house was two hundred feet back from Route 2, nestled in a little grove of trees. It was halfway between Stoney Creek and Fisher's Retreat, a perfect acre to start a family out of the reach of nosey neighbors. She dragged herself from the bed, standing on her feet a moment to allow her head to quit spinning. She should have known Mark would be worried about her. He'd probably called and when she didn't answer the phone, came to investigate.

Knock, knock-knock, knock, knock—knock knock.

She smacked her lips and frowned at the sour aftertaste of Percocet and Bordeaux.

"I'm coming. Give me a second."

She paused at the front entrance, steadying her hand against the door, her head swimming again. The knocking resumed, this time sharp and stronger, palpable with her hand against the oak door.

She recognized the pattern of the schoolyard rhythm. *Knock, knock-knock, knock, knock.*

Mark, you are so goofy. She smiled and answered with two knocks of her own. *Knock! Knock!*

She flipped the deadbeat. "I told you I'd be okay. I—"

The door flew inward with explosive force, striking her hand as it blew by, barely missing her right hip. She stumbled backward, squinting at the doorway. "Mark?"

She saw someone spring like a cat from just outside the door, a man with a clinical mask like the ones she'd seen in the hospital. Sheer terror arrived before the impact of the man who drove her backwards to the carpeted floor. And sheer terror would awaken her when he was gone.

Summer Sunday mornings meant casual dress and the "relaxed" starting time of 10:00 at Community Chapel. It had been weeks since Claire attended with John, since Wally-duty and John's job travels interfered. Claire was up early helping Della with feeding and dressing her father.

Then, after a leisurely second cup of coffee sipped over her open Bible, she dressed, and read about office orthopedics until she heard the low growl of John's Mustang.

She met him at the door where John lifted her off her feet in a passionate embrace. "Whoa, cowboy," she gasped.

"Morning, beautiful."

She pushed him away. When he frowned, she pecked his cheek with a quick kiss before she picked up her purse and a slim leather Bible. "Let's go."

"The air is cooler this morning. Want to walk up Cedar Knob?"

"It's been too long since we've been together at church."

"Let's have our own service. I'll pick up some subs. We'll have a picnic."

"I want to hear Pastor Phil. Besides, I'm not dressed for the mountains."

John shrugged and brushed past her.

"Come on."

"I just want to say 'hi' to the Wall." He disappeared into the hall, just as Della appeared giggling and saying something about an Italian stallion. She was holding Claire's cell phone at arm's length. "Here," she said. "Answer this crazy thing."

Claire sighed as the electronic song ended with a push of her index finger on a green button. "Hello, Dr. McCall."

"Good morning, Doctor. It's Lucy." Her voice was quick, all business. Claire knew with one sentence that this phone call wasn't to chat about Monday's office schedule. Her office nurse wouldn't interrupt a Sunday morning for anything less than an emergency.

Claire's voice tightened, anticipating a wrench in her plans to attend church. "What's up?"

"Deputy Jensen just called. I'm on for SANE duty. There's been another rape. I thought you should attend."

Claire winced. Lucy had been doing sexual assault exams for years without her. Claire did need to learn the techniques, but this Sunday morning was meant for church. "I was just walking out the door. I—"

"I think the victim would do better with you present."

"Lucy, I—"

"She's our patient."

Claire set down her Bible and plugged her free ear. John and Wally were laughing loudly in the bedroom. "Our patient?"

241

"Stephanie Blackwell."

Claire shook her head. "She's in the hospital."

"She was released yesterday." Lucy paused. "I'll be at the office in ten minutes."

Claire sighed. "I'll meet you there."

John reentered, smiling. "Okay, church-lady. Let's go." He halted in the middle of the room. "What's wrong?"

She was frozen with the phone at her ear. She slowly lowered her hand. "Stephanie Blackwell was raped."

John lifted his hand to his forehead. "No. When?"

"Sometime last night. This is too weird. A second rape within a few weeks, and they were both my patients." She looked at John. "I need to go to my office."

"Should I come along? Will you be okay?"

"I'll be fine." She kissed his cheek good-bye. "I'll see you after church?"

"Sure."

Claire bounded down the sidewalk toward her car, her thoughts ahead on the exam she would perform. As she drove, she pondered an odd similarity in the rape cases she'd encountered. Both were young single girls living alone, vulnerable because of recent surgery. Her mind fixated on the man she'd suspected of attacking Brittany Lewis: Billy Ray. He'd been around her office the day before Brittany's attack, and two days ago, he was in the hospital in Brighton to see Lena ... right down the hall from Stephanie Blackwell.

When she pulled into the office parking lot, she saw Lucy's Subaru wagon next to a county sheriff patrol car. Inside, she found Stephanie Blackwell sitting in the waiting room wrapped in a brown wool blanket pulled up under her chin. A young man sat next to her, staring at the floor. Officer Jensen stood when Claire entered.

Claire extended her hand. "Hello."

He nodded, then pointed his head toward Stephanie. "She'll be glad to see you."

Claire went to her patient, who sat unspeaking with her eyes straight ahead. "Stephanie," she said gently. "I'm so sorry this happened."

The patient looked up. An irregular laceration extended from her left eyebrow across the bridge of her nose.

The man next to Stephanie stood and held his hand out to Claire. "I'm Mark, Stephanie's fiancé."

Claire shook his hand and nodded.

"We'll need to do an examination, Stephanie. It's important to get as much evidence about the attack as we can while it's still fresh. Then I'll look more closely at your forehead."

"Let's get this over with," Stephanie muttered.

"Fair enough." She put her arm around Stephanie's shoulder and guided her down the hall, leaving Deputy Jensen and Mark alone.

Lucy guided Claire through the evidence collection, sealing, initialing, and placing each item in the PERK box. After they finished, Lucy drew Stephanie's blood while Claire examined the cut on the patient's forehead. "I can sew you up here, or I can send you up to Carlisle to see a plastic surgeon if you'd rather. I know a Dr. Reid up there. He does nice work."

"You do it. I want to go home."

Claire didn't want to push, but she knew if Stephanie ended up with an ugly scar, she'd think about the rape every time she looked in the mirror. "The laceration will leave a scar. The plastic surgeon may be able to do a neater job. I—"

"Please, Dr. McCall. I don't want to go anywhere else."

Claire consented. She set up a sterile laceration tray and spent the next forty-five minutes placing a fine row of 6–0 nylon sutures in Stephanie's face.

When the wound was dressed, Stephanie limped from the office holding tightly to her boyfriend's arm. Claire turned from the door to see that Deputy Jensen waited for her, holding a small plastic bag up for her inspection. "Ever seen anything like this?"

She turned the bag over, inspecting what appeared to be a white strip of paper about a quarter inch wide and six inches in length.

"Don't open it," he coached. "I picked it up from the floor at Stephanie's house."

She shrugged. "What is it?"

"I think it's the string from one of those surgical masks."

"What? Did she say her attacker wore a mask?"

He nodded. "Just like Brittany Lewis."

Her hand went to her mouth. "It's Billy Ray Chisholm. I saw him the night before last at Brighton University Hospital. He went to find his wife. She was on the same floor as Stephanie. He could have seen her, known she was an easy target."

Randy Jensen raised his hand to slow Claire's pressured speech. "Easy, Dr. McCall. Let us do the detective work." He lowered his arm to support a notebook in his other hand and lifted his eyebrows while scribbling something on the yellow paper. "May I see a mask from your office supplies?"

Claire held her tongue. If Officer Jensen needed to feel in control, it wouldn't do any good to press him to look at the obvious. She shook her head while she walked back down the hall to an exam room. *Some men are so insecure they can't stand an intelligent woman one-upping them. Ego!* She retrieved a mask from a cabinet. She handed it to Randy, who held it up against the strand in the bag. It appeared to be a perfect match.

"These girls were both from your practice. They were unable to fight back because of recent surgery." He tapped a pen against his thigh. "I need to have a list of all your employees, everyone who could have seen a patient record. I need to know everyone on staff, their spouses, and their children."

Claire looked up to see Lucy standing at the door to the exam room. "Help me out, Lucy. You know everyone's family."

Lucy listed everyone. She was amazing.

"Who has keys to the office?"

Claire numbered three employees, holding up a finger for each as she named them. "Me, Lucy, and Lisa. That's all."

"Anyone making deliveries, medical supplies, that sort of thing?"

"Not unless we're here."

Randy flipped a few pages on his little notepad. "What about a guy named Cerelli? John Cerelli?"

"John?" Claire couldn't hide her surprise.

She watched as Jensen lifted his eyebrows again. "Does your office use his software? Would he have access to your patient records?"

"We are too small a practice to use E-Patient." She halted. "Why are you asking about John Cerelli?"

"You know him, I take it?"

244

"I know him," she responded, nodding her head. She straightened her shoulders, and squinted her eyes at the deputy. "But why are you—"

"I'll be asking the questions, Doctor. Does this man have access to your office?"

Claire felt her stomach churn. She had given John a key a few weeks back so he could bring in some supplies. She shrugged. "He's got a key, but—" Her voice trailed off. *What's this all about?*

"You seem to have left him off your list of people with keys."

"Well, I was thinking of employees. He's not on staff here or anything like that."

"Just what is your relationship with him?"

"You don't think he's involved with these rapes? That's ridiculous. He's practically a saint. He's—"

"What is he doing with a key to the office? This would give him access to patient records, who is getting surgery, stuff like that, wouldn't it?"

"Well, sure, but—"

"Why don't you tell me who he is?" He paused, hands folded across his broad chest. "Or perhaps you don't know him as well as you think."

Her hand went to her mouth until she thought about how people with things to hide often speak through their hand. She forced her hand back to her side and tried to keep her voice steady. *This is crazy!* She cleared her throat. "John is my boyfriend."

<hr/>

That afternoon, under a cloudless sky, but sheltered by a thick canopy of evergreen, Claire and John hiked the two and a half miles up to Cedar Knob. The climb was steady, not overly taxing, but just enough to keep the chatting to a minimum. As they walked, Claire watched the back of the man she loved, the man she thought she knew. The deputy had divulged one piece of information about his interest in John Cerelli, that he had seen a package of surgical masks in John's car. Claire had defended John, stating the obvious: that they were only a pack that had fallen from a larger box of medical supplies that John had picked up for her office. Claire thought back to snatches of other conversations where Billy Ray seemed to be implying that John was involved with Lena. When she questioned John in the hospital the night they'd gone to visit Lena, John seemed annoyed . . . or was he just a little bit afraid of a man as crazy as Billy Ray?

When they reached the top, the duo edged forward and sat on a rocky outcropping with their legs dangling over a view of the Apple Valley. After catching her breath and downing most of a bottle of water, Claire decided to air out her concerns. "Why would Deputy Jensen ask me about you?"

John didn't look at her, but she watched a barely perceptible jerk of his head. He kept his eyes on the magnificent view in front of them. "He asked about me?"

"John, if you count Lena Chisholm, three women have been raped. They were all my patients. The deputy wanted to know who had access to my records, who had keys to my office. I told him, but I forgot I'd given a key to you."

Now John's head turned, his eyes narrowed with concern. "I don't like where this is going. You don't think I had anything to do with those women—"

"Whoa, Cerelli. I didn't say that. But I only thought about you after the deputy brought up your name." She paused and watched as John smirked. "He said he saw the masks in your car."

"So what?"

"John, the masks that were worn by the rapist were like the ones I stock in my office."

"Claire! You know why I had those masks!"

"I know!" she responded, raising her voice above the wind. "I told Deputy Jensen."

John shook his head and huffed, then seemed to be searching Claire's eyes. She had to break away.

"Look at me," he said. When she kept her eyes on the horizon, he touched her chin with his hand. "Claire, look at me!"

She felt anxiety rising within her. She yielded to the coaxing of his hand, looked at his troubled face. "What?"

"You think I had something to do with the rapes?"

It seemed preposterous, totally out of character for John, but a nagging doubt remained like a grain of sand under a sandal strap. She couldn't voice her concern. "Of course not," she reassured herself. "That's ridiculous." She tried to make light of it, turn it into a game. It was a lighthearted stab at covering the turmoil bubbling in her soul. She pointed a finger in his face and raised her voice, imitating a crime-show prosecuting attorney. "Where were you at midnight Saturday night?" She forced a laugh, but it came out sounding more diabolical than jovial.

"Cut it out, Claire. You worry me."

Maybe you worry me. "Can't you take a joke?"

"It isn't funny."

"You didn't answer my question. Why would the deputy ask me about you?"

John's eyes narrowed. "How should I know?"

"There has to be a reason."

He looked out toward the horizon. "He was looking at my car the other day when I was at Fisher's Cafe. He saw the masks in my Mustang and asked me about them."

"So why didn't you tell me?"

"I just did."

"But first you said, 'How should I know?'"

"Maybe I don't like this conversation. You don't have any reason not to trust me."

"I never said I didn't trust you."

"So why are we having this conversation? Why do you feel the need to ask me where I was on Saturday night?"

"I was joking."

He mumbled, "Some joke."

"I only wanted to know why the deputy would bring up your name. I didn't say I didn't trust you." She reached over and laid her hand on the back of John's. He didn't open his hand to receive hers. "But maybe you should be careful. Officer Jensen seemed concerned."

"He's an idiot."

Claire let his comment fall. It wasn't like John to speak like that. But he didn't seem to be in the mood to discuss his feelings.

She watched as John picked up a smooth fragment of rock and rubbed it between his fingers for a moment before heaving it into the abyss. "I'll bet it's some hospital orderly or something."

"What?"

"The rapist. If he's attacking women who have had surgery, he must be around the hospital to know they are weak from their procedures."

"Doesn't work. Stephanie Blackwell was operated on at Brighton University. Brittany Lewis had surgery in Carlisle."

"Hmmm. Who else would know? Are there any surgeons who work in both hospitals?"

"You seem to be forgetting about Billy Ray. He could have seen Brittany Lewis's office records the day he came to my office."

"But what about Stephanie?"

"John, you were there. Stephanie was up walking in the hall the other night when we went to the hospital to see Lena." She paused, as the realization of what she was saying dawned on her brain's frontal lobes. *John was there. And he certainly was interested in looking at pretty little Stephanie in her immodest gown.* A low-level dread returned to her gut. She looked away from John and tried to discount her thoughts. "Remember who else was there."

He nodded his head slowly. "Billy Ray." He threw another stone over the dropoff. "He's one weird dude."

"I wouldn't exactly describe him as weird."

"So what's your diagnosis, Doctor?"

"Sarcasm isn't your best quality."

John pulled his hand from under hers and stood up. His face reddened and he took a step back from the cliff's edge before he started gesticulating with Italian fervor. "Do you mind telling me what your agenda is here? You question me like I'm a rape suspect. You don't agree with anything I say. If I say 'up,' you say 'down.' What's the deal?"

Claire felt her own defensiveness rise. She wanted to scream back. Instead, she attempted to steady her voice. "I'd like to ask you the same question."

"That's it, isn't it? You always want to be the one in control. You want to ask the questions, not answer someone else's!"

She huffed and clenched her fists. She and John had experienced lover's spats before, but it was rare that she saw him show more than a casual amount of anger. "I'm just asking questions, John. Curiosity is a normal characteristic of the intelligent mind."

"It feels more like an inquisition."

"You're not being fair."

"And maybe you're not being understanding."

She pointed at him. "And you're being defensive. What are you hiding?"

He held his hands out to his side, palms forward. "What man wouldn't be a little defensive when his girl suggests he might be a sexual predator?"

Claire looked in the direction of the trail, hearing voices approaching through the trees. Their timing was impeccable. She lowered her voice, desperately wanting to keep a cap on her fury. Growing up with a violent drunk had taught her a lot about screaming. She knew she was capable of outblasting even the most exuberant Italian, but this certainly wasn't the time or the place. "You've got this all wrong, Cerelli," she seethed. "But maybe the way you've reacted should make me suspicious!"

She turned and started down the path, leaving John standing on the boulders behind her. She smiled sweetly at a family of four, a father carrying a toddler on his shoulders and a mother walking behind a young boy who looked at Claire with pleading eyes. "How much farther?" he moaned.

"Just around the corner."

The boy, appearing about kindergarten age, cried out, "At last! Uggh! I'm dyin'."

She walked on as she heard the mother's quiet remark. "That's the new town doctor."

There was no place to hide for the doctor of a small town.

A minute later, she heard heavy footfalls on the path behind her. "Claire, wait up. I'm sorry."

She didn't feel like making up. What she'd seen wasn't the John Cerelli she loved. The idea that he could be something so different than she understood frightened her. She felt her voice tighten, as if a candy was lodged in her throat. "John, what's wrong?"

She felt his hand brush hers. She kept walking down the path and pulled her hand away.

"Look, I didn't tell you about Jensen asking me about the masks 'cause I didn't want you to worry. The whole thing made me angry." He seemed to hesitate. "I thought you had enough on your mind without me adding to your stress."

"Well, maybe I don't want you protecting me. Maybe a good relationship means we share our problems with each other."

Claire kept up her pace, with long strides aided by gravity. John was nearly jogging to keep pace at her elbow. "Claire, that's why I came to be with you."

She offered a saccharine smile. "Why would you want to be with a control freak?"

He sighed and touched her arm. "Slow down."

She sped up and pulled her arm away.

"I never called you a control freak! I just said you like to be in control." He huffed. "It's a human thing, everybody wants it."

"John, you're softening what you said."

"I was angry."

"Are angry," she corrected, keeping her pace at a clip just beyond a comfortable walk.

"I want to be with you, Claire. You should know that."

She glanced at him from the corner of her eye. She mustered up a confident voice. "I want to be with you, too." *At least I think so.*

"Claire, slow down."

She stopped in her tracks, coming to an abrupt halt, as John's momentum carried him a few steps beyond. She lifted her hands to her hips and stared him down. He looked at her, his brown eyes open and pleading, framed perfectly in a head of dark curls. Sweat glistened on his face and darkened the collarless Brighton University T-shirt he wore. Fear and love tugged at opposite ends of her soul.

"Can we stop and talk this out?"

She took a deep breath. "I stopped."

John sighed and stepped to the side of the trail to sit on a large rock. After a full minute of listening only to the sounds of the forest around them, he spoke. "You're afraid, is that it?"

"Women are being raped. My patients, John." She leaned against a tree. "Of course I'm afraid."

"Are you afraid of me?"

She didn't want to look at him. He'd always been able to read her, to see through whatever front she displayed. It had been that way with John ever since their undergraduate days at Brighton. And it was that way last year in Boston when John gave her an engagement ring and she responded with enthusiasm on her lips but ambivalence in her heart. John had read her then and he could do it now. She lowered her head and scraped her Nike running shoe against the edge of a stone. "I don't know." She shook her head, then added quietly, "I guess the circumstances have me freaked out a little."

His voice dripped with sarcasm. "A little?" He threw up his hands. "I'm not like *Brett,*" he added.

"This isn't about him."

"Is that why you're questioning me? You were taken in by Brett. He was so slick, wasn't he?" John expanded his chest with a big breath, pushing his shoulders back. His voice was caustic, cutting with jealousy. "A real man. A surgeon. Smart. Caring."

Claire nodded, remembering the resident with a lifeguard body, a friendly smile, and the heart of a deceiver.

"What a fraud!"

"I really don't want to think about him."

"But he's still affecting you, interfering with the way you interact with others . . . with me!"

"This is crazy."

"Is it? Then why do you find it so hard to trust me? Where do these little doubts come from?"

She didn't have an answer. His questions made sense, but his insistence that she trust him made her all the more uneasy.

John shook his head. "What can I do?" He put his hands on her shoulders, squaring her to look in her eyes.

He seemed sincere. He was from a family she knew and loved, nothing like the outward-perfect, inside-broken family of Brett Daniels. So what made her hold back? She was at a loss for words. She couldn't share her fear with John. Instead, she shrugged and rocked forward on her tiptoes to plant a kiss on his cheek. "There aren't always answers for why a woman feels a certain way."

She sidestepped John and slipped from his grasp. "Let's go."

She heard him sigh behind her. They walked on without speaking, the tension between them growing as she tried to analyze John's hypothesis about her. Maybe he was right. Maybe it was normal for her to be suspicious after the bad experience she'd had in Boston. But as they descended the trail, images of the past flitted through her mind like pieces of a puzzle. The masks in John's car. The way he looked at Lena. Billy Ray's accusation. John's defensiveness. John's access to her medical records.

For the next forty-five minutes, the silence hung between them like a heavy drape. Claire spoke twice during the return to the small gravel parking lot, both times to fellow hikers they met on the trail. Pleasantries are expected with strangers, but not with close companions where volumes can be communicated without vocalization.

She slowed where the trail crossed a shallow stream, allowed John to pass, and watched as he stepped from rock to rock, meticulously, sure-footed, testing any landing spot with partial weight before committing. There, revealed in his movements, she saw a metaphor of John's life. Testing, being sure, committing his all, then repeating the process again. Claire, ever the visionary, was often on to the third or fourth project while John was hammering down the first one.

Maybe this is why he hasn't proposed. He needs to test the water before jumping in. He needs to know the future before committing to it. She wavered, one minute wishing their future together would be cemented, the next, entertaining a silent doubt that maybe John wasn't the man of God she'd always thought he was.

At the car, John paused by the trunk of his Mustang. Claire stopped, hoping for a cold drink from the cooler John had locked in the trunk since his top was down. He motioned toward the passenger seat. "I'll get you a drink."

She didn't move.

John hesitated. "What do you want? Diet Pepsi? Water?"

She leaned over and grabbed her ankles, stretching her hamstrings with her knees straight. "Water," she replied, straightening up.

He set his hand on the roof of the trunk. "Have a seat. I'll get it for you."

"What is it, Cerelli? What are you hiding? Open the trunk."

He shrugged with nonchalance, but she detected a reddening hue above his collar. He opened the trunk and quickly lifted the lid to the cooler and grabbed two drinks. Claire stared into the trunk and lifted what appeared to be an odd pair of binoculars.

"What's this?"

"Night-vision goggles."

She squinted at John.

"These things are really cool. In situations of minimal light, just strap these babies on and it really seems to brighten everything."

An uneasiness touched her. Since when was her renaissance boyfriend into outdoor survival gear? She eyed him pensively and tried not to look bothered. "Oh," she responded. "Sweet." She laid the goggles back into the trunk and took a bottled water from his hand, suddenly unable to look in his eyes.

She wasn't sure how to file this new information. John was clearly uncomfortable, perhaps sensing her suspicion. She listened to the memory tape of her conversation with Officer Jensen she'd had earlier in the day. *Or perhaps you don't know him as well as you think.* She shook her head. Her fears were ridiculous.

She pressed back into the seat and stared straight ahead as John began the journey back toward Stoney Creek. She didn't feel like making small talk and found herself in the rare position of hoping John might flip on an Italian opera, anything to take her mind away from the dark obsessions she entertained.

She glanced at him discreetly as he drove. John's eyes squinted at the road as he silently tapped at his forehead, a sure sign he was concerned about something. As they neared the outskirts of the town, she spoke in a quiet tone. "Are you at all afraid for me, John? I mean, with a number of rapes in our community and all . . . do you worry . . . well, you know . . . have you given it any thought?"

He glanced over at her, then apparently into his rearview mirror before turning his eyes to the road again. "No. I guess I hadn't really been thinking about it."

That's what I was afraid of.

He shrugged. "You don't really fit the profile. He's attacking pretty women who live alone and are disabled in some way. That's not you."

"Which one?" She punched his arm.

"Ow!" He laughed, apparently relieved that she could still be jovial. "Duh!"

She twisted his rearview mirror around and looked at her reflection. "You think I'm pretty."

He was silent, shaking his head.

She flipped the mirror back toward him in disgust. John wasn't exactly making her more comfortable. *I know I'm pretty.*

And I'm not disabled . . . yet.

John stayed quiet until he pulled to a stop in front of the McCall house. "Look, Claire," he started, clearing his throat.

She waited a moment as he twisted his expression as if he tasted something sour. Suddenly, she felt her own stomach tighten in response to his manner. "What's the matter?"

He took a deep breath. "I'm thinking of going to Brighton."

She waited for more. Going to Brighton wasn't exactly big news. "So?"

"To live. To be closer to my work."

She felt the blood drain from her face. "But . . ." She halted. "Your work? You came here to be with me. If you—"

"This just isn't working like I'd expected."

She shook her head. "Your boss isn't upset. You're still covering your clients okay, and you—"

"You know what I mean, Claire."

She knew. In her heart, she knew his statement about being closer to his work was only a cover for the real reason he was leaving. Their relationship had stalled, without apparent hope for progression. John had tested the water, jumped in, and waited. Waited for Claire to jump in.

She hadn't responded. Their relationship hadn't progressed as planned. His test hadn't worked out, so it was time to move on. "This isn't about your work." She looked away. "You're walking away from us." She snapped her long, delicate fingers. "Just like that, huh? You're outta here."

She listened as he slowly exhaled. She knew he would try to control his response. He didn't like her accusing him of making a loud, Italian reaction. He kept quiet, thinking.

"But what did you just tell me on the mountain?" Her voice thickened. "You said you wanted to be with me."

"I wasn't lying, Claire. But wanting to be with you and understanding the reality that this isn't working are true, true, and unrelated."

"Unrelated? If you want to be with me, you try to make this work."

"Maybe I just need some time away."

"What is this, John? Are you breaking up with me? Pulling away again?"

A gasp escaped his throat. She watched as his hand went to his mouth before he continued, his voice on the edge of control. "Me? You know I did not pull away before. I asked for my ring back long after you—" He halted. "Listen, I don't want to rehash the past, but you have to see I'm only responding to your lack of willingness to give yourself to me."

"You're blaming this on me?"

"I'm not blaming you. I'm asking you to understand. I pulled out of our relationship when I thought another man had taken my place. I came back here because I thought I could win your trust." He paused. "Apparently, I was wrong."

She turned and studied his eyes. She didn't want him to go. She longed to reach for him and beg him to stay. But she knew he could sense the war within her. She wanted to trust him, but couldn't find the voice to reassure him of her confidence in his love.

His eyes were open, pleading for her to reject his statement, waiting for the argument she wanted to make but couldn't seem to find amidst a sea of suspicion.

Instead of arguing the point, she clenched her jaw. "Go ahead, John. You've given it a test. You've tried living around me." She feigned nonchalance and shrugged. "It didn't work. Now try living without me again."

"Claire, I—"

She opened the door and climbed out, not bothering to turn again to face him. When Della met her on the porch, she just pushed past her without speaking. Behind her, she heard the Mustang's engine rev and the spray of gravel as John accelerated down the driveway.

Away.

And out of Claire's life again.

⁂

That evening, John returned to his apartment with a heavy heart. He'd spent a great deal of energy pursuing Claire McCall, but every time he thought a lasting commitment was within reach, she seemed to pull back, not always physically, but emotionally, with John's heart on a yo-yo string.

He tossed a stack of unopened junk mail on the kitchen table. He was tired of the ride. He had hoped that telling Claire that he was thinking about moving back to Brighton would cause her to tell him to stay. He sighed. So much for that little idea.

Brighton was only an hour away, and he might even see more of Claire after his move because it would force her to actually schedule time to see him, instead of just assuming it would happen, which never seemed to work.

He opened the refrigerator and stared at a lonely milk carton and a box of leftover pizza. He cautiously sniffed the milk and shrugged, setting it on the table beside a box of natural oat flakes, a cereal he'd bought out of guilt, and the only one remaining since he'd snarfed the last of the sugar cereal that morning for breakfast.

He sat and sampled the heart-healthy mix. It was a choice that would make Claire smile. After one bite, he added two tablespoons of brown sugar; after another, he added two more, until each flake was coated with a sweet, granular texture. He shook his head, satisfied with the improvement. He chewed mechanically, listening to the crunch of the cereal and thinking about Claire. The move to Stoney Creek was, by first intention, a temporary situation, a testing of the water on the way to a lifetime swim with the woman he loved. And contrary to his liking, John was starting to realize the answer to the test may not be yes.

A blinking red light on his phone caught his eye. It was probably Claire. She was famous for sending him little messages during their get-togethers, knowing he'd hear them later. Sometimes it was her way of saying something personal, a compliment she wanted him to hear, but not in front of a group. Once, on one of their first dates, they hadn't been alone all evening, mixing with a group at a Campus Crusade meeting at Brighton University. So, knowing she wouldn't have a chance to bend his ear alone, she'd retreated to the ladies' room and pulled out her cell phone in the seclusion of a bathroom stall. She told him how much she'd admired the comments he'd made during the meeting and how much she'd enjoyed his company. Then, she'd wished him pleasant dreams. After hearing the message, he'd spent half the night up thinking about her. So much for dreams.

He hesitated as he reached for the replay button. He wasn't sure he wanted to hear her voice, especially a message she'd sent before he'd driven away from her in frustration. That first phone message had set up a playful pattern for them, each one finding opportunities to encourage the other, sending secrets or other messages that would be fun to listen to later. Once John had secretly unfolded his cell phone and dialed her number as he pretended to be searching for his jacket in the car, while Claire dutifully waited in front of her dormitory. After listening to her message, he hurried up the sidewalk and took her in his arms. He recited a corny little poem he'd made up, told her he loved her, and planted a kiss behind her ear to make her giggle. All the while, he held up the phone behind her head to record his romantic good-bye. She never knew he'd done it until she got inside a few minutes later. That one had reaped consequences good and bad. Good because he let her play the same trick on him, and it forced her to write him a silly love poem. Bad because she was forever distracted looking for a phone in his hands when he wanted to steal a goodnight kiss.

He pressed the "replay" button. He was right. It was Claire, but she must have called right after he left. "John, it's Claire." She sniffed. "I know what you're doing. It's just like you to make an impulsive decision like this." Her voice cracked. "But maybe we can blame that on your Italian heritage, huh?" She hesitated. "I know you were just trying one more tactic to see if I'd respond in the right way, to see if I'd confess my undying trust." She began to cry. "It's my fault, John. I think it's not that I can't trust that you could love me. Maybe I can't believe anyone would want me unless they know I won't end up like my father."

He didn't care that tears began to fill his eyes. He was alone with no one to impress with bravado. "Don't say that, Claire," he whispered.

He could hear Claire sigh into the phone. A deep-cleansing breath, she would call it. "Don't give up on me." Click.

He pressed the button to replay the message and choked out a little prayer. "Thanks, Father. It looks like maybe it was the right decision after all."

Chapter Twenty-Two

he next morning, Randy Jensen sorted through the files involving the assaults of Stephanie Blackwell and Brittany Lewis. Similarities abounded with drastic implications for his jurisdiction. This was more than a random act. He was dealing with a serial rapist, and one thing was clear. He needed more help. His chief of police, Manny Morton, recommended an FBI consultant, Vance Fitzgerald, from the regional office in Roanoke, Virginia. Vance, an FBI lifer, had a dozen years of profiling experience, a nose for details, and an intolerance for peripheral detractions.

By ten A.M., Randy was seated across the desk from the balding agent in his meticulous, spartan office. There were no pictures to clutter Vance's desk, and a six-inch pile of folders was stacked as neatly as if it sat within an unseen box. Vance frowned as he waited for a page to load on the computer screen in front of him. "Dang computer," he mumbled. "Uncle Sam's been promising a budget increase so we can upgrade, but I think I could walk downstairs to get what I want faster than old Nelly here."

"Nelly?"

Vance chuckled. "Every computer I've ever owned, I've called Nelly." He wiped the top of his head with a handkerchief. "It was the name of my first wife. She frustrated the life out of me. Lost my hair within two years of marrying that woman."

Randy let the comment pass. He'd been in the office only ten minutes and had heard the names of three different women, all of which he referred to as a numbered wife. *Old Vance might have a good reputation as a profiler, but he doesn't seem to be able to pick a suitable mate for himself.*

Vance looked over the materials as Randy gave the *Reader's Digest* version of the cases. Then Vance sat back and paged through the materials in silence, pausing periodically to pound his chubby fingers on the keyboard in front of him and mumble something about Nelly. After twenty minutes, he looked up at Randy, who sat picking the dirt from beneath his thumbnail. "I'll need a bit more time. I'd like to interview this girl," he said, circling Lena Chisholm's name on a yellow legal pad beside his computer. "What do you think of the doctor's suspicions about Lena's husband?"

"The doctor is following a red herring," he replied, trying his best to sound confident in front of this veteran. "Her logic isn't clean."

"Clean?" Vance blotted his glistening forehead again. "Have you interviewed Lena?"

"I've talked to Billy Ray. He doesn't take me as a sexual predator. He's a beer enthusiast with a bent toward violence with the women he marries, but only when he's under the influence."

Vance shifted in his seat. "Red herring."

"Excuse me?"

"I'm just using the logic term you threw at me. I asked you a direct question, 'Have you interviewed Lena Chisholm?' and you gave me peripheral information that dances off the trail." He folded his arms across his chest and sighed. "The direct answer, I presume, is 'no.'"

Randy didn't need a lesson in fallacies. He recognized his answer as a justification. He felt his defensiveness rising. "No," he responded, shifting in his seat. "No, I haven't talked to her."

The FBI agent nodded silently, apparently pleased with his read of the situation. His silence was a stabbing judgment finding a mark in Randy's gut. He tapped the side of the monitor and mumbled again, "I'd put a magnifying glass on this boyfriend of Dr. McCall's."

Randy wanted to say that the agent was only pointing out the obvious, but found himself nodding and writing a note. Superiors liked that.

Vance closed the folder of information Randy had brought in and slid it across his desk toward Randy. "Start with Lena Chisholm. I'll do some looking around. I'll see if I can find a similar MO for rapists from our database." He nodded.

Randy cleared his throat. The brief consultation was over, just like that?

After a moment, Vance must have sensed the detective's discomfort. "I'll be in touch. If I can free up some time, I'll be up myself, maybe interview a few of the players."

Players? This isn't Hollywood. Randy needed an antacid. He stood up and held out his hand. "I'll let Chief Morton know to expect your call."

Vance didn't stand to shake his hand. He kept his seat and offered a perfunctory wave before turning his attention back to Nelly. Randy turned to go. The initial consultation wasn't what he'd expected. He walked to the door of the office, not pausing to say thanks.

When he stepped into the summer humidity, he checked his watch. He still had plenty of time. Perhaps with a few phone calls he could figure out how to find Lena Chisholm to set up an interview.

He unfolded a cell phone. The only thing more annoying than an arrogant consultant was an arrogant consultant who was right.

Claire McCall, M.D., slogged mechanically through the morning patient list, barely able to concentrate, supporting her heavy eyelids by refusing to sit down and guzzling extra-strength coffee. She'd finally slept at three A.M., having mentally rehashed and examined her relationship with John Cerelli from top to bottom without insight. She was left with a bubbling turmoil of emotion. Love pulled against fear, desire against rationality, heart against head. Now she found herself fighting back a yawn, her eyes watering from the effort. She was used to operating on an empty tank. The surgery internship had done nothing if it hadn't prepared her to run on fumes. She coped with the news that John was contemplating leaving town in typical Claire fashion: immersion in her work. If she loaded her mind with her patients' problems and concerns, she wouldn't obsess over her lost love, her risk of Huntington's disease, or the Stoney Creek rapist.

Claire reached forward and took the hand of the elderly female patient sitting on the exam table in front of her. For the previous ten minutes, Olivia Rodriguez had spilled her story of losing her mother to cancer the same week as she had found a lump in her own breast. Claire knew she was a believer in Christ. She'd seen her at Community Chapel with her husband, Roy, on numerous occasions. "Would it be okay if I shared a Bible passage with you?"

"Of course."

Claire opened a pocket New Testament to Romans 8 and pointed to a verse she had underlined in red. "See what it says here? 'Who shall separate us from the love of Christ? Shall tribulation, or distress, or persecution, or famine, or nakedness, or danger, or sword?'" She continued to the end of the chapter, then looked up. "See, nothing, not even our health problems, can separate us from his love. If anything, they force us to cling even tighter to the one who loves us best."

Her patient nodded.

"May I pray for you?"

Olivia bit her lower lip and bowed her head.

Claire prayed for wisdom, understanding, and strength for her patient as she faced this new potential challenge to her health. Claire prayed that Olivia would face the future knowing God's grace was sufficient, that she would be confident that his arms of love were wrapped tightly around her.

When she looked up, Olivia was beaming. "Thank you, Dr. McCall. I know my future is in his hands." She paused and squeezed Claire's hand with a grip that belied her seventy-five years. "I can tell you believe what you prayed. I'm glad you've come back to us, Dr. McCall."

Claire nodded, feeling the first twinge of an accusation from her conscience. *You fraud!* She paused and set her eyes on the chart in her lap. *I do believe my prayer for Olivia. But why can't I seem to walk in the same light for myself?*

Just as she was helping her patient down from the exam table, her nurse notified her of a phone call. Claire nodded. "Could you see to it that Mrs. Rodriguez gets an appointment with Dr. Branum for a breast biopsy?"

She went to the hall and picked up the phone. "Dr. McCall."

"Dr. McCall, I'm sorry to have to call during your work time."

She recognized the voice of Deputy Jensen. "It's okay. I was actually curious about your work. Any leads in the case?"

"I'm workin' on it. That's why I called. I'd like to talk to Lena Chisholm. Can you help me find her?"

Claire bit her lower lip. "Uh . . ." She stopped and thought about patient confidentiality. "I'm not sure."

"Listen, Dr. McCall, you're the one who raised concerns about her husband. If I'm going to make a serious effort at finding the truth, I'm going to need to follow every possible lead I can. Help me out here."

Claire had promised Lena that her whereabouts would remain confidential. She chewed the inside of her cheek. Suddenly, a compromise popped into consciousness. Lena wasn't at the shelter. She was in the university hospital. She could pass on that information without breaking a promise to Lena. "You'll find her in Brighton University Hospital."

Jensen huffed. "Of course. I remember now. You told me Billy Ray went to see her there."

"She had emergency surgery." Claire looked at the floor. *Because I missed the diagnosis staring me in the face.*

"Is she able to talk?"

"I think so."

"Thanks, Dr. McCall. Thanks."

She heard the phone click. Jensen wasn't much for pleasantries like "good-bye."

Claire rolled her eyes and set the phone in its cradle, then picked up the record of the day's appointments.

"Oh, no, you don't," Lucy chided, snatching the list from her hands. "You know it's bad to start counting how many patients are left."

"How did you know I was counting?"

"I just know. Now go to A to see if Jane Altmeyer has pneumonia."

Claire sighed. "I want to visit Lena Chisholm. Want to go with me to Brighton after work?"

Lucy laughed. "Not a chance. My grandson has a baseball game."

"Right."

"Where's Cerelli? You shouldn't be asking your old nurse to travel with you when you've got that man at your beck and call."

Claire stayed quiet and nodded. *Not anymore.* "Ms. Altmeyer's back?"

The nurse smiled. "Sheesh. Just mention that man's name and you forget what I've told you?"

Claire feigned a smile and headed to room A so she could think of something besides "that man."

Della knew this day would come. And she knew she'd feel terrible when it did. Wally needed more than she could provide, didn't he? Claire wasn't home as much as Della expected, and even if she was around every evening, Wally was just too much for them. He needed care twenty-four/seven. Wasn't that justification enough?

So why couldn't she feel relief when she saw the van from G and W ambulance service pulling up their gravel lane? Della sighed and let the curtain fall back into place. Standing at the window when the staff arrived to transport Wally to Pleasant View Nursing Home would only make her look anxious to be rid of him. She turned and straightened the already meticulous room, adjusting a family photograph by a millimeter and trying not to listen to her own conscience reciting a vow she'd made more than thirty years ago ... *in sickness and in health, 'til death do us part.*

Once the decision had been made, things progressed at a speed that left Della feeling like she'd better tighten life's seat belt. There were curves ahead, and whoever was in control seemed to be accelerating. For Della, the only comfort she took in the speed was that it didn't give her more time for regret. An application was filed, Claire had arranged a weekend chest X ray, and an opening was expected within a month or two, not a day or two. But two days it was, and the only clue Della had that the nursing home might call was the obituary in the morning's paper. Old Paul Hollingsworth had passed unexpectedly. The vacancy was Wally's if Della wanted it.

Della paced and reassured herself again. Things had worked out so easily and efficiently, it had to be the Lord's will, didn't it? Everyone at the nursing home thought Doris Stevens would be next to go. She'd been too weak to get out of bed for days. Either God wanted Paul back home or wasn't ready for Doris, or he just wanted a place for Wally in the nursing home bad enough to ... Della shook her head and chided herself for even trying to figure it out. The Lord's ways were the Lord's ways. Period. And the way was open for Wally to get the care he needed. So why was her stomach knotted with regret instead of relief?

She hadn't even called Claire about the opening. Claire had enough on her mind as it was. She could just find out about her father's move when she came home from the clinic. And so Della had called Margo, her oldest daughter, instead, asking if Kyle, Margo's husband, could bring by his pickup for Wally's hospital bed. Pleasant View was okay with Wally using the same bed he used at his own home as long as it met their specifications. Della knew it was okay, and insisted that his bed be taken with him on the first day. She wanted everything to be as familiar as it could be for Wally. Change wasn't easy for a Huntington's patient, so she planned to do anything she could to ease the transition.

She took a deep breath and opened the front door. Two men were unloading a stretcher from the back of the van.

"Morning, Mrs. McCall," a young man called out.

She recognized him as Blake Henderson. She bent down and set the catch on the screen door to hold it open, then retreated back down the hall to Wally's room. Wally knew this day was coming. She'd told him about it after his last battle with the intestinal flu, again on the weekend when they took him for an X ray, and that morning after the Pleasant View administrator called. She wasn't sure if he understood. His reaction was a silent stare, a "Wall Response," as she called it. When he didn't like something, he'd just clam up, sometimes not speaking for days. She wondered how long the silence would last when he understood he was outside his own home. She looked at him and sighed, trying not to cry, but unable to keep her breath from coming in with erratic jerks as the sobs refused her will.

She steadied her voice. He needed her to be calm. "The men from the ambulance service are here, Wall. You'll remember Blake. He's the talkative young man who took you for your chest X ray at Claire's clinic just the other day.

"I'm not leaving you," she spoke softly. "We've been through tough times. This is just another phase. I'm still your wife." She lowered the bed railing and took his right hand, cupping it in both of hers. She needed to speak the words, hoping he'd understand, but all the while knowing that the one heart she was reassuring was her own. "I love you, Wally. I just can't care for you the way you need me to now. I'll still be over to visit." She heard the men in the hall, the rumble of the stretcher wheels on the floor. She glanced over her shoulder to see them trying to manipulate the stretcher in the door.

Blake spoke to his older associate. "It won't make the turn into his room. I tried it on Saturday. Just leave it in the hall and we'll have to carry him to it."

Della turned her attention to her husband. She dropped his hand and gripped his forehead instead. She timed the lowering of her head perfectly.

She paused as his arms moved right and his head danced left, then quickly lowered her face to his and planted a kiss on his lips. Wally responded with a suction that pulled her lower lip into his mouth and stretched it to the point of pain as she made a hasty retreat and tore her lips away. "Wow!" she gasped.

Wally grinned. "Della."

It was the first on-the-lips kiss they'd shared in months. And it was the first time in as many months that she'd heard him say her name.

She backed away, unembarrassed by her display of affection in front of the ambulance crew. "I'll see you later today in your new room," she promised. "Kyle will help me bring over your bed."

Wally grunted.

Blake cradled Wally like a child, easily hoisting him into his arms with one arm behind Wally's shoulders and another behind his knees. Della winced at the sight. Her husband had lost so much weight that his body offered little challenge to a strapping young EMT like Blake.

They strapped Wally down to the gurney and began the journey to the van, pausing once on the front sidewalk to cinch the straps an inch tighter against Wally's roving arms and legs.

Della stood on the front steps and waved feebly at the van, imagining Wally's confusion or agitation at his predicament. She lowered herself to sit on the steps as the van pulled onto the highway.

Except for Wally's time in the Navy, Della had shared the same residence with him for the better part of four decades. A chapter was closing on their relationship. Her eyes welled with tears. This time there was no holding back the sobs.

Della pressed her face into her hands and wept.

Chapter Twenty-Three

laire plodded across the small parking lot behind the clinic with one goal in mind. Make a short visit to Lena Chisholm and then head home to crash early. Lena should be up for a visit from a familiar face. Besides, it certainly wouldn't hurt to do some serious hand-holding, since she felt responsible for missing the diagnosis of Lena's ectopic pregnancy.

She started the Bug and shifted into reverse when she heard the screech of tire rubber. She stepped on the brakes and looked in the rearview mirror to see a large red pickup stopped inches from her bumper, blocking her exit.

Her heart quickened. *Billy Ray Chisholm!* Should she run for the office? She unbuckled her seat belt and reached for the door handle. This was crazy. He'd catch her halfway to the back door, and she couldn't very well drive forward over the concrete parking bumper.

She frantically reached for the locks, then looked back to see Billy Ray climbing out of his truck. He walked slowly toward her car and leaned close to the window.

"We need to talk," he said. "Open your window."

Claire left the car running. "I can hear you just fine." She glanced at the empty parking lot. So much for being the last one out of the office. That practice would have to change.

"I need some information."

"Is this about Lena? You know I can't talk to you about her."

"This isn't about me trying to find her, if that's what you're talkin' about. I could just go up to that hospital in Brighton if I wanted to find her now."

Claire imagined Billy Ray plotting to get even with his wife. She shook her head. "I can't tell you where she lives. You know that."

Billy Ray leaned both hands against the metal lip above the driver's seat window and begin rocking the little Volkswagen side to side, not violently, but just enough to send a chilling signal of his power. "I'm not asking you that." He seemed to hesitate and looked away. "I need to know about a medical condition."

She watched as he steeled his gaze toward his left and clenched his jaw. What did she see there. Fear?

"Stop rocking my car." *My cell phone! I can call the police!* She slipped her hand into her purse, closing it around her phone. When she pulled it out, the car stopped rocking.

"What are you doing?"

"I'm going to call the police."

He threw up his hands, his eyes wide. "Hey, we're just having a conversation here. I'm not doing anything."

"You're blocking me in."

"I'll move if you'll talk to me."

"Move your vehicle and maybe we'll talk."

Billy Ray huffed and stepped back, his eyes now on the ground. "Okay."

He walked around, jumped in his truck, and slowly backed it into the space beside her. She wondered if she could outrun him. Maybe she could race into the streets beeping her horn and attract some attention. She looked toward the street. There wasn't a car in sight.

In a moment, Billy Ray was back at her window. His expression had softened, and for a moment he laid aside the bravado image. "Are you afraid of me?"

Claire wasn't sure how to answer. "Should I be?"

"No."

"You threatened me when I saw you at the hospital in Brighton."

He spit on the blacktop. "I'd been drinking." He paused. "I'm different when I drink. Look, Doc, I'm sorry about the things I said. I'm not planning to sue you."

She wasn't about to grace him with a "thank you." "Is this the information you wanted? To find out if I was afraid of you?"

He shook his head. "Have you ever heard of someone doing something really bad when they were drinking?"

"Of course. People do stupid things all the time when they drink alcohol." She wanted to leave. "This isn't exactly breaking news."

He leaned toward her window to hear. "But what I mean to ask is can they do stuff they don't know about and have no memory of it afterwards?"

"Alcoholics have blackouts."

"But could they do bad things . . . things they wouldn't normally do and not remember it?"

It felt creepy talking with Billy Ray this way. He was practically shouting to get her to hear. She slipped her hand into her purse again and closed her fingers around a small tube of pepper spray. She used to carry it when she jogged in Boston. Then she dared to lower the window a few inches.

In response, Billy Ray lifted his head away from the car.

"I don't know, Billy. Why are you asking me these things?"

He shrugged. "You're the only doc I know. And Deputy Jensen has been snooping around my workplace, asking me questions again." He shuffled his feet. "From what I can gather from the questions he's askin', you'd think he was trying to pin a crime on me."

"What kind of crime?"

"Don't play games with me, Doc. You know all about the rapes."

"Do you?" Her boldness surprised her. Maybe she could trap him into revealing something he oughtn't know.

"Only what I glean from the deputy."

Right. You think you can suck me into your little delusion that you cannot commit crimes you have no memory of? "I've got a novel idea for you, Mr. Chisholm. Why don't you stop drinking if you're worried about your behavior?"

He nodded slowly. Was it agreement or just what Billy Ray did when he was thinking? "I've stopped, Doc. I'm going to do it this time."

Right! "Get some help."

He twisted his lips around as if he was considering the idea. "I've got another idea. Something else I think a doc could help me out with, something that will prove I'm innocent and point at the guilty party."

Claire waited without responding.

"Lena says I raped her, huh?"

"You were drunk. You saw what you did."

"Lena also claims she hasn't been fooling around on me. And the deputy seems to think that Lena was treated the same way as these other girls."

Claire nodded slowly. *I think I gave the deputy that lead.* "So?"

"So get the doctors to examine the baby that was in her. It will prove it wasn't mine."

The baby. Claire loosened her grip on the pepper spray. She was surprised that Billy had come up with this. "So the baby's father is . . . ?" She waited for him to complete the sentence.

"The rapist," he said.

Claire shook her head. She'd missed a step somewhere.

"Last night I started thinkin' that maybe I'd misjudged Lena, thinkin' she was running around on me. Maybe she told the truth. Maybe she was raped."

"Lena says she was raped by *you.*"

"I caught the guy hiding in a tree in my yard. Old Jeb ran him up a tree . . . that man you were with at the hospital."

"What?" Claire's heart quickened. She knew she'd entertained secret doubts about John Cerelli, but it sounded outrageous coming from Billy Ray Chisholm. "You have no idea what you're saying."

He shook his head and shrugged. "Have the doctors check out the baby. Then you'll find out I'm telling the truth."

Claire took a deep breath. This was crazy.

Or was it?

She looked at Billy Ray, who held up his hand in a gesture of "right this way." He seemed to be done talking and was allowing her to leave. Was he just playing with her head? Or was he manipulating her into believing a lie to cover for his crimes?

She drove away, her head swimming. She checked the rearview mirror to see Billy Ray leaning over the hood of his truck, his face in his hands. Was this the posture of frustration? Or guilt? Or an act until she was out of sight?

She accelerated to the town limit of Stoney Creek, glancing at her mirrors frequently, paranoid of Billy Ray's red truck.

By the time she passed Fisher's Retreat, her heart, but not her VW bug, had slowed to an allowable speed.

An hour later, Claire exited the elevator at Brighton University Hospital and took a slow, deep breath. She stood still until a wave of nausea passed. She'd noticed a vague cramping in her stomach soon after leaving her office. She thought she was just upset by Billy Ray Chisholm. Later, she thought the winding mountain road might be responsible. Now, as she scanned the hallway for the nearest public rest room, she was beginning to wonder whether she'd finally caught the flu that had been streaming through her office in the people of Stoney Creek. She found the bathroom she needed and splashed water on her face, then looked up and sighed. She was pale and suddenly aware of her exhaustion. She whispered a prayer, a generic request. "Help me, God. Help."

A minute later and feeling a little better, she pushed open the door to Lena's hospital room, knocking as the door moved. "Lena? It's Claire McCall."

Lena looked over from behind her tray table, which held an assortment of clear liquids and a stack of unopened dimestore romances. A vase of pink roses sat on the bedside table. Inwardly, Claire recoiled at the thought of Lena spending hours reading the soap opera equivalents. Above her head a TV blared country music videos. "Hi," Lena said, reaching for the volume control.

"Hi," Claire responded, sitting in a chair beside the bed. She looked at the empty bed beside her. "Lucky you. No roommate tonight."

Lena nodded.

"How do you feel?"

"Sore. And tired. This stuff makes me sleepy," she said, pointing to the patient-controlled analgesia device on her IV pole.

Claire squinted at the IV bag to read the label. "Morphine. No wonder you're sleepy."

"I wondered if you would come by."

Claire stayed quiet.

"Deputy Jensen was here." Lena paused. "I think Billy Ray's in big trouble." She knotted the sheet to her chest. "The nurses say he came to see me."

Claire nodded.

"Ms. Rivera convinced security to make him leave before I got out of surgery."

"I know."

"He sent flowers." She looked at the vase of roses.

"He's a dangerous man."

"You don't know him like I do."

"Don't do this, Lena. Think about how he treated you." Claire took a deep breath and exhaled her frustration slowly. She couldn't believe she was having this conversation.

"I know he treated me bad. But mostly when he was drinking."

"Not only when he was drinking. What about the day we picked you up? He wasn't drinking that day. He could have killed you."

"I'm tired of the shelter." Lena continued to roll the sheet around her hands, knotting it over her patient gown. "I'm going to lose my new job because I'm missing work."

"Are you thinking of going back to him?"

Lena stared at the tray of clear liquids in front of her without reply. Red jello, chicken bouillon, cranberry juice, and coffee provided the sum total of the tasty fare.

"Please don't do this, Lena. He may be more dangerous than you realize. What if Deputy Jensen is right? What if Billy Ray has started taking out his rage on other women?"

Lena shook her head. "Billy Ray has some other ideas."

Claire sighed. "How has he gotten to you? He sent you a letter?"

Lena's non-response was answer enough.

Claire hadn't anticipated this. She sat without talking for a minute, watching as Lena's eyes drifted back to the music video where she stared at colorful images of love lost and found. Clair saw a man and woman in conflict, a woman in a seductive nightgown looking longingly from a rain-streaked window, a man in a western bar, a woman with a guitar singing of the power of love, the man in a pickup truck on a lonely road, the view of the house with a light in the window . . . and then reunion, the couple falling into each other's arms, the man's hat falling to the floor as he lowered the woman onto a bed.

Claire closed her eyes to pray. How could she compete with the empty tripe that provided Lena a constant diet of false messages?

Perhaps she could convince Lena to make a short-term commitment that would buy her some time to get some sense in her head. "Lena, I know the shelter isn't a perfect solution. It's going to be hard making it on your own. But just promise me you'll stay for a little longer. At least until you've had a chance to recover from your surgery and put this in a little perspective. Maybe you should set some requirements for Billy Ray. Give him the idea that you'll only come home if he can fulfill certain requirements. Tell him he needs to be in AA and get into counseling for his anger. He can write to you by sending letters to me at my office, which I'll forward to you. If he agrees to those things, tell him you'll need to meet with a counselor together for a while before you move back. But please, don't talk to him on the phone. And by all means, don't go back to him yet."

Lena wrinkled her nose. "I'll need some cash."

"Give a budget of your needs to Cathy Rivera. Since you're not able to work, donors will help cover your needs."

Lena nodded. "You must think I'm crazy or something."

"Not at all," Claire said, reaching forward with her palm open to receive Lena's hand. "I think you're normal. Lots of women in your position feel exactly the same way. But you're tough. You've proven that. Don't sell yourself short, young lady."

Lena took her eyes from the TV screen, unwound her hands, and placed her left hand in Claire's.

Claire shared a moment of eye contact before her attention was turned to the ring she felt on Lena's hand. She leaned forward and gently pulled on Lena's hand. She was wearing a beautiful diamond solitaire! "Where'd this come from? I don't remember seeing such a beautiful ring on you before . . . Did Billy Ray—"

Lena pulled her hand away, blushing. "No, I—" She shook her head, and looked away and hesitated. She shrugged. "I don't wear it often. It makes me feel special."

"Billy Ray sent this to you?" Claire shook her head, imagining that Billy Ray must have resources beyond his apparent means. Was he making a plea to get her back? A letter, flowers . . . and a diamond ring? "He's trying to buy you back, Lena. Don't fall for this."

"It's not from Billy Ray, Dr. McCall."

"What?"

"For a while, I thought it might be, that maybe he was going to surprise me or something."

"I'm not following you. You have a ring but you don't know who it's from?"

"I found it." She held the ring out to admire it. "Well, actually, Old Jeb found it and brought it to me." Lena looked over, her eyes suddenly moist. "Have you ever wanted something so much that you were willing to pretend it was true?"

"I–I think lots of people do, Lena."

"When I wear the ring, I pretend I have a happy life, a rich husband who loves me and gives me what I want." She closed her eyes. "It's stupid, I know."

"It's not stupid, Lena. Dreams are important."

Lena sniffed and nodded. "I kept the ring thinkin' I could cash it in if things get really tight. I took it to a pawn shop . . ." Her voice cracked. "But then I just couldn't part with it. Anyway, the ring was like some sort of miracle . . . a message maybe . . . a sign that things were going to work out. I almost believed God sent it to me so I'd be brave enough to run away." She hung her head. "That sounds stupid."

"It is pretty." Claire took her fingers and lifted the ring to her face to admire it again. As she did, a hint of familiarity surfaced, and she felt another wave of stomach upset. She took a deep breath. "Can I see it?"

Lena pulled it off, and Claire took the ring in her hand and rolled it around. *Could it be?* She would know this ring anywhere. She'd spent hours looking at it, memorizing every lovely detail. She turned the ring to look at the inscription, a simple blend of her and John's last initials. *M.C. McCall Cerelli.* This was Claire's ring!

As she stared at the ring, Lena gushed. "Isn't it weird? It has my initials in it! That's why I'd hoped Billy Ray had secretly gotten it for me."

"Lena, it says, 'M.C.'"

She shrugged. "My real name is Melinda Chisholm."

"Oh." Claire looked down, her heart racing. "When did you find this ring?"

Lena thought for a moment. "Old Jeb brought it to me. He must have dug it up around the place, 'cause he hasn't been out huntin' since last fall."

"When was this?"

"I remember just where I was. I was just recovering from . . . well, Billy Ray'd been drinking and had roughed me up pretty bad. That's when he . . ."

Claire spoke gently. "He raped you, is that what you were going to say?"

Lena nodded. "Anyway, Billy Ray was treating me real sweet." She managed a little smile. "Maybe because he'd woken up with a shotgun barrel in his face." Lena slipped the ring back on. "Anyway, he went to AA and propped me up on the porch swing with a pillow under my ankle and that's when Old Jeb carried up the felt box." She frowned. "It was disgusting, covered with dog slobber."

"Do you know the date?" She pulled out a little calendar from her purse and opened it for Lena.

Lena looked puzzled. "I remember calling around to find an AA meeting that Billy Ray could attend on a Saturday. That's right, it was a Saturday. And it was right after I first saw you in the clinic in Stoney Creek, 'cause I was limping pretty bad from a swollen ankle."

"So you found the ring on a Saturday. And the night before was when you were assaulted."

"Yes." She squinted toward Claire. "Why does it matter?"

Claire couldn't explain her concern. "I'll explain it later." She stood up. "Listen, Lena, I'm glad you're doing well. Remember your promise to me."

Lena looked away. "I never promised."

"Lena, please. Don't go back to him without talking to me. At least promise me that." She paused. "I care about you."

Lena nodded. "Okay."

Claire needed to leave. She was having abdominal cramps. If for no other reason, the ring she'd just seen was enough to give her indigestion. At the door, she turned back. "Please don't pawn off the ring, Lena. It's too beautiful for that. I'll buy it from you if you get real desperate."

Lena held out the ring to admire it once more and smiled. "I knew this ring was good luck," she said.

Claire shook her head as she left. *Good luck for you, maybe.*

On her way out, Claire walked past the operating rooms and down the hall to the surgical pathology lab. There, she was pleased to see a medical school friend, Eddie McCullough, who had stayed at Brighton University for a pathology residency. Eddie's back was to her, bending over a microscope, but she could recognize his hair pattern easily. Prematurely bald, and with the remaining hair around the sides buzz-cut with the same number-two razor guard as his dirty-blond goatee.

"What's the world coming to? A path resident in the hospital after six?"

He turned from the microscope and lowered the wire-rim glasses from the top of his head. "Well, well," he said, grinning. "I should have known."

"Hey, Eddie."

He opened his arms and walked toward her. "Claire McCall!"

She stuck out her hand. "Oh, no, you don't. I don't hug men wearing plastic aprons."

He laughed and pointed to a stool under a high counter filled with tissue stains and microscope slides. "Have a seat. What brings you back?"

"You didn't answer my question."

He thought for a moment. "What's the world coming to? Dr. Blythe is doing some sort of head and neck commando operation. He must have sent me a thousand frozen sections to do." He halted and turned to a young woman standing in the doorway. She was wide-eyed and wearing a pair of scrubs. "Tell Dr. Blythe the pharyngeal margin is free of cancer . . . finally!"

The woman, wearing a medical student ID, nodded. "Thanks," she said before scurrying from the room again.

Eddie rolled his eyes. "There's another crazy medical student who wants to be a surgeon."

"Careful, Eddie."

He smiled again. "What's up?"

"How much trouble would it be to get some DNA studies on an ectopic pregancy?"

"Come again?"

"A girl, a patient of mine, came in yesterday with an ectopic pregnancy. Her husband insists the baby isn't his." She halted. "The story is complicated. But the baby might be important evidence in a rape case."

"The girl was raped?"

"And got pregnant, but it was an ectopic pregancy. She was operated on here yesterday when her fallopian tube ruptured."

"Listen, Claire, you know I can't take this and do anything outside of official channels. The forensic lab can do all of that stuff, but first the law will have to make a request for the specimen after getting approval by a magistrate that agrees that the baby is important evidence of a crime." He shook his head. "I'd get skinned alive if I just took the specimen to forensics myself. The chain of evidence the law follows would be broken. I'd screw up the case."

Claire listened and nodded. "I thought that's what you'd say."

"Why do you need to know?"

She looked at Eddie and held her tongue. *Because my boyfriend is a suspect in the case.* She shrugged. "I just want to know."

He pushed his glasses up on his nose. "Are you feeling okay? You're pale."

She shrugged. She rubbed her abdomen. "I'm an LMD now. I think one of my pediatric patients must have brought some flu bug in the office." She sighed. "But I'm always pale, Eddie. I spend my life inside the clinic."

"It's summertime, Claire. You need to get out more."

"Fine advice from someone who spends his evenings staring into a microscope."

"I'm a resident. I'm supposed to be pale."

Claire nodded and started for the door. "Thanks, Eddie."

"Hey, Claire," he called from behind her. "Why don't you ask this girl's husband why he's so sure it's not his child? I'll bet the guy's had a vasectomy or something. That's the usual way a guy can be so sure his pregnant wife has been foolin' around on him."

Why didn't I think of that? She smiled. "Thanks."

Claire pulled over twice on the way back to Stoney Creek to empty her stomach on the roadside as the mountain curves and indigestion joined forces to create a very bad situation. She stopped at her clinic and raided the sample cabinet for Cipro in case she started with diarrhea and Protonix for her acid stomach. She took one of each and walked to the file room to search for Billy Ray Chisholm's record.

With the record in hand, she sat at her desk and opened it for inspection. The first page documented her involvement in caring for a laceration in his arm. She didn't have to go much further to find what she was looking for. Billy Ray hadn't been to the doctor too many times. On the pages to follow, Claire read about Mr. and Mrs. William Raymond Chisholm's workup for infertility. Apparently, his wife, Rachel, had every conceivable test, including a laparoscopy under general anesthesia, before Billy would submit a semen sample. She pulled out a lab slip, a sperm count from a semen specimen. "No sperm seen." Underneath, Dr. Jenkins had written, "Azoospermia."

That liar! He knew about this when he married Lena. She wanted children and he never told her he was unable to father children.

So . . . Billy Ray was telling me the truth!

Claire stood up, as a pain shot through her stomach again. It was dull, but aggravating. She held her abdomen. It felt better not to move around.

She walked slowly to her VW bug and drove home with her memory working overtime, trying to piece together the new information she'd gathered.

I saw Lena in the office for the first time the evening before D day.

John had the ring in his pocket when he went with me the next day to get the results of my Huntington's gene test.

And, accordiing to Lena, Billy Ray raped her Friday night, woke up to face a shotgun Saturday morning, and promised to change. He goes to AA and Old Jeb brings Lena the ring John had in his pocket.

Wasn't that the day that John's father called the house looking for John? Tony told of the phone message John had left, how John had said he'd really blown it and that he was in a jam. What was that about? A confession? Claire shook her head. *Impossible!*

Then Lena is pregnant, but denies ever being with anyone except Billy Ray. And he is incapable of fathering a child.

The implications made her sick. "No," she spoke aloud. "This is too crazy!"

She pulled in the lane to her house to see Della loading a suitcase into the trunk of her car. Della slammed the trunk and put her hands on her hips.

Claire climbed from the VW slowly, trying not to upset her volatile stomach.

"Where have you been?"

"I went to Brighton to visit Lena after work. I was concerned about her."

"A phone call would be nice."

Claire winced. She had meant to call from the car, but her escapade in the parking lot with Billy Ray had so occupied her that she forgot. "I'm sorry, Mom. I meant to."

"Your father went to Pleasant View Home today."

"Mom, why didn't you call?"

"I knew you were busy. And I thought I'd tell you myself tonight at supper." She pointed to the house. "I left it on the stove for you."

"I'm not hungry," she mumbled. "What's with the suitcase? Taking some stuff over for Wally?"

"This is my stuff. I'm the one leaving now."

"What?"

Della motioned to the door. "I'll explain. I was hoping you'd get home sooner so we'd have a chance to talk. As it is, I'm going to be driving in the dark."

Claire came in and sat slowly on the old couch. As she did, she thought about her menstrual cycle. *I just finished. This shouldn't be ovulatory pain.* She looked at her mother. "So give me the short version."

"John came over this morning."

Claire didn't understand and she was losing patience. "So John came over. So . . ."

"My leaving has nothing to do with John. But he came to say good-bye to Wally. He told me about last night." She stared at Claire. "Too bad I have to get it from him."

"Mom, I'm sorry. I was planning to tell you, but I didn't feel like hashing it out yesterday. Besides, I didn't know he was really going to leave, like now. What did he say?"

"Only that he needed a little time away from Stoney Creek. I think he needs some time to sort through his feelings."

"Did he say that?"

"Not exactly that. He said he needed to go to northern Virginia and Richmond for a few days, then see how he felt. It sounded like he wanted to talk to his father for some advice, then make a final decision." She lifted an index finger and pointed it at Claire. "You'd better be careful. You don't want to drive this one off. I think he needs to see that you really trust him to be around through thick and thin."

"Did he say that?"

"Not exactly." She offered a smile. "But close enough."

"Fair enough. Now where are you going?"

"Hawaii."

"Hawaii!" Claire allowed her jaw to hang open. "Just like that? Put Wally in a home and it's off on vacation?"

"It's not just like that. It's a gift from your uncle Leon. I notified him of Wally's move this morning. And then he dropped by with this printed flight itinerary. I leave from Dulles at 6:00 A.M."

"But what about Dad? He needs you to help him adjust."

"I explained it to Wally. I promised him that you'd visit every day." She flinched. "You will do that, won't you? I couldn't stand the thought of Wally thinking we just dumped him in that place. He'll feel abandoned. He'll—"

"Easy, Mom. Of course I'll visit every day. I'll remind him where you are. He may not like it, but I think he'll understand."

Della sighed. "Oh, I knew you'd do it. I told Leon I couldn't leave Wally, but he claimed Wally wouldn't know the difference."

"He doesn't know Wally like we do."

"That's what I told Leon. But he insisted that I take a break. He'd already talked it over with the staff at Pleasant View. Evidently they feel the adjustment may actually be easier for him if I stay away a few days." She held up a piece of paper. "I'm only going to be gone a week. Leon has a time-share for me to use." She frowned. "You don't think I should go?"

"No, I . . . well, it's just so sudden . . . and so unlike Uncle Leon to be so generous."

"What about Wally? Do you think he'll be okay?"

"What does it matter what I say? You're already packed."

"Claire!"

Claire moaned. "He'll be okay. I'll go see him every day."

"Would you? That makes me feel better."

Claire could sense her mom's reluctance. "Mom. I said I'll go every day. I promise."

"Okay," she said slowly. "I think I can do this." Della stood up. "Times a-wastin'. I've got a two-hour drive tonight. I'm stayin' at the Hampton Inn tonight so I can just shuttle over to the airport in the morning."

"Wonderful. I'll bet that was arranged by Uncle Leon too."

Della waved. "How'd you guess?" She turned to leave.

"Mom?"

Della stopped and looked back.

"If anyone deserves this, it's you. When's the last time you spent a week on vacation by yourself?"

She shook her head. "Never, child." She nodded. "I guess it is time. Maybe I'll go crazy without Wally to talk to."

"Have fun."

Her mother walked away, leaving Claire sitting on the couch. Her mind was weary. She wanted to call Randy Jensen, but she wanted a quick nap. She curled up on the couch and pulled a worn afghan from the back of the couch over her shoulders. In two minutes, she surrendered to exhaustion and slept.

Chapter Twenty-Four

⚜

{C}laire awoke with a start to the piercing scream of the smoke alarm. *Fire!* She sat up, the smell of burning milk assaulting her nostrils. The air was thick with smoke and the room dark. *What time is it? The sun has gone down.* She lowered herself to the floor on her hands and knees. Then, more alert, she stood up and rushed to the kitchen, coughing and waving her hands at the smoke. Her eyes burned. She opened the back door, then attacked the source of the problem, a smoking saucepan.

Claire carried it out and dropped it in the backyard. She peered into the bottom of the pan, but the smoke was a thick plume and she couldn't see anything in the dim moonlight except a black char of something her mother left for her dinner.

She wasn't hungry anyway. She walked back into the house where the smoke alarm continued to shriek. She opened the front door for cross ventilation and silenced the alarm on the kitchen ceiling by standing on a wooden chair to reach the silence button. That's when she felt another stab of pain in her abdomen. "Ugh," she groaned.

She retrieved a Diet Pepsi from the refrigerator and sat at the kitchen table. The wall clock read ten-thirty. She didn't feel like eating. She sniffed. The smell seemed to be making the nausea return. She should have checked the office for some Phenergan. She sipped the Pepsi and walked to her bedroom, where she undressed and lay on the bed.

In a few minutes, she got up and shut the doors to the house before walking back down the dark hallway. That's when it first struck her. The house was quiet. There was no Wally noise, no whistling of his legs on his sheets or the thumping of his arms or legs against the rails.

Claire crawled into bed, fighting another wave of nausea. There, she shed tears for her father and for the disaster her own life had become. Then, quietly in the darkness, she began to pray.

"Help Daddy to adjust to his new home . . ."

Claire was up at two and four leaning over the toilet with dry heaves, an action her twin Clay had always described as "hugging the porcelain Buick." She slept until seven, rising slowly so as not to jar her abdomen. She edged her feet along the floor doing her own version of what OB/GYN residents call the PID shuffle. She'd never had pelvic inflammatory disease, but she thought she'd walk like this if she ever did.

The pain was constant now, centered in her lower abdomen. Her throat was parched, but she didn't want to drink for fear of more rounds with the Buick. She walked up the hall while cupping her hand to her mouth to see if her breath was as stinky as most of her patients she evaluated for belly pain. It was a futile test. No one with halitosis ever knows they have it.

She phoned Lucy and told her she wouldn't make it in. Lucy insisted on coming by. Claire didn't dissuade her. She needed another clinician to confirm her suspicions.

Twenty minutes later she lay on the couch while Lucy palpated Claire's abdomen. "Your mom sure picked a good time to be gone," Lucy commented.

"Ouch."

Lucy moved her hand to the right lower quadrant.

"Ow!" Claire moaned. "You're on it now."

"You need a surgeon."

"Appendicitis, huh?"

"That's my bet. When did you get sick?"

"I didn't feel so good leaving the office yesterday, but it was more just in the middle, a feeling of cramps or indigestion." Claire shook her head. "I've been kind of stressed out lately."

"Kind of?"

"Okay," she said. "Don't make me laugh. It hurts too much." Claire paused. "I thought it might just be the stress or the flu we've been seeing."

"Denial isn't just a river in Egypt."

"Hey, symptoms aren't exactly classic for anything until the pain localizes."

Lucy conceded. "Let me pack you a bag. You're going to be gone for a few days."

Claire started to get up, but met a forceful protest from her nurse.

"I'll get it. Stay put."

Claire sighed. "My gym bag is on the floor. Pack my sweats or something without a heavy waistband. If we're right, I don't want to have to squeeze into my jeans after surgery."

Lucy disappeared back down the hall, but kept talking. "I'll tell Lisa to reschedule the office for the rest of the week. Do you mind if I see a few folks for suture removal?"

"Of course not. Give flu shots. Do blood pressure checks. Draw blood for the patients on Coumadin scheduled for PT checks."

"I'll take care of it. Have you called John?"

"He's out of town. I'll call him later."

"Should I do it?"

Claire didn't want to explain. "I'll do it. I want to call him," she said, emphasizing the "I'll" and "I."

A few minutes later, Lucy came back with the gym bag. "I presumed the only toothbrush in the bathroom was yours."

Claire nodded. "Let's go," she said, rising up to a position bent at the waist. "Now I know why all my appendicitis patients walk this way. It's murder to stand up straight."

The ride to the hospital in Carlisle was fine for Claire once they were beyond their pot-holed gravel lane. Until she felt every bump, she hadn't noticed just how badly her parents' driveway had deteriorated. As they drove, Lucy insisted on calling ahead to Dr. Branum. He would meet them in the ER. Lucy also promised to call Claire's sister Margo and agreed not to try and call Della. The last thing Claire wanted was to mess up her mother's first vacation in years. It was only an appendectomy. Nothing bad was going to happen. Let her mom enjoy herself without worrying about her baby girl.

Once they were checked in, things moved rapidly. Dr. Branum gave his assent to Lucy's diagnosis and told Claire never to let her nurse retire. An IV was started, antibiotics given, a consent signed, and Claire was whisked into surgery in front of Dr. Branum's elective patient schedule for the day.

Perfect. While everyone is fresh. And an experienced surgeon without a medical student to hold the laparoscopic camera and make everyone ill as he weaves around trying to find the surgeon's instruments. She thought of her first experience "running the camera" on a laparoscopic case. As the team focused on the video screen, Claire had tried in vain to hold the camera steady, but the surgeon moved so fast that occasionally she would drift back and forth in an effort to find him. She remembered the snide comments. *"Anyone else getting motion sickness? Where's the Scopalamine patches when I need them?"*

In a minute, Claire was lying on a stretcher outside an OR. She looked up to see a female in scrub attire. The only deviation from standard dress was her hat, a homemade one sewn out of cloth covered with lighthouses. "I'm Dr. Guererro. I'll be putting you to sleep." She smiled and put her hand on Claire's shoulder.

Claire answered a dozen questions about her past medical history, and then, anticipating the questions she'd heard in Boston during her internship, she added, "And I last ate or drank last night at ten-thirty, a few sips of Diet Pepsi. And I don't have any caps or false teeth for you to worry about during intubation."

The anesthesiologist's eyes narrowed. "Are you one of our floor nurses?"

She shook her head. She didn't need to vocalize a response as Dr. Branum intervened.

"Dr. McCall runs a clinic in Stoney Creek. Just like you, she's one of the new breed of women breaking into sub-specialty medical fields that have been dominated by men. She finished her surgical internship in Boston in June and took off for a year to help care for her father, who has latter-stage Huntington's."

Dr. Guererro shook her head. "I'm sorry. I can't believe I assumed— me of all people, uh, well, you know, everybody always calls me nurse and I hate it. Especially men, they always think I'm here just to take their temperature or something."

Claire touched her female comrade's hand. "Forget it." Then she smiled and looked at Dr. Branum and continued, "Men!"

Dr. Guererro began to push the stretcher forward into the OR. "Arrogant men."

Dr. Branum cleared his throat. "Careful, ladies," he grumbled.

"I'm giving you some Versed."

She remembered being positioned on a cool, padded table . . . a rubber mask over her mouth . . . the taste of garlic . . . the face of a man with a mask . . . a flash of fear . . .

⁓ §§§ ⁓

A man with medium build and curly hair with a surgical mask. Pain in her lower abdomen. "Stop. Somebody help me!"

Fight for air. Fight for air. Get this tube out of my throat. A strong grip on her wrist. The rapist. I'm being choked!

"He's here. Why doesn't somebody help me!"

Blackness. Am I blind? Something over my eyes. Night vision. I need John's goggles. John? Are you here to help me?

The rapist is here! Sharp pain in her lower abdomen right above . . . Get your hands off me. "Help!"

Claire fought to awake from the post-anesthetic fog.

"Let me get that tube out of your throat."

A female voice. "You're okay, honey. Settle down. You're in the recovery room."

Another female. "Look at her. She's terrified."

"Hold her wrist! She's going to pull out her IV. Dr. Guererro!"

"Here, that should hold her."

Bright lights. A touch on my forehead. I'm drooling. Someone is cleaning up my chin.

Claire heard a female voice. "Little Joe, look at your arm!"

"I know. She did it! She had a death grip on me. I'm glad she keeps her nails short."

"Oooh. Look at that. You can feel the indentations."

"She's a fighter."

What is going on? Where am I?

A man with a surgical mask. The rapist!

"Lie down, Claire. You're okay!"

Someone help me. He's forcing me down!

"Joe, give me a hand over here."

Help me! Help me!

"Whoa, honey. Easy! You just had surgery."

That's when he attacks! The rapist!

Hands are cupping my face. He's going to suffocate me! The hands are tightening their grip.

"Claire! Open your eyes, honey. You're in the recovery room. Try to relax!"

The recovery room?

"Claire! Look at me. You're okay! Take a deep breath!"

Claire opened her eyes. Bright images were blurred.

"Here. Let me wipe your eyes. It's just some protective salve."

I had surgery.

"Try to relax, honey."

Claire pinched her eyelids shut again.

I had surgery. Relax? Yeah, right!

Chapter Twenty-Five

Billy Ray pulled his truck up behind the clinic building and stopped. He wanted to see Dr. McCall. If everything went according to his plan, she could be counted on to shift some of the mounting suspicions about him in a different direction. At this point, things were getting too hot for him. Something needed to change, and he wanted to know if Dr. McCall had acted like he'd asked.

He looked around the near-empty lot. This wasn't typical for a weekday. *What's going on? Maybe Dr. McCall ran away like a scared little girl.*

The lot was empty except for a pickup truck with a trailer holding a lawn tractor. He looked toward the clinic building where a man knelt in the mulch, pulling weeds. *The jerk I met the first time Dr. McCall treated Lena.*

The man stood up. "Can I help you?"

"I just came by to talk to Dr. McCall."

"The clinic's closed. Try back next week."

"The doc take a vacation or something?"

Billy Ray watched as the man sized him from top to bottom. "Something like that."

"Maybe I'll try her at home."

"She's in the hospital."

"Hospital? I just saw her yesterday."

The man shrugged. "Emergency surgery. She had appendicitis. Don't that beat all? The doctor gets sick. Nobody thinks about that."

"Hmm."

"She'll be home in a day or two." The man knelt again to continue his work.

Billy Ray turned. *Now ain't that an interesting twist. The doctor becomes the patient. She'll be hurtin' for a while. She'll get a little taste of what her patients experience.*

He walked back to his truck, humming a country song and wondering if the cops were smart enough to figure it all out by themselves.

That afternoon, Claire was asleep in a private room when her first visitor came. She opened her eyes to a touch on her shoulder. "Hey, little sis."

"Hey, Margo." Claire looked at the baby in her arms. "Hi, Kristin."

Margo lifted the baby's hand. "Say hi to Aunt Claire."

The baby pulled back the corner of her mouth. A smile? Claire knew better. It was probably just gas.

"How are you feeling?"

"A lot better than I did last night. I'm just tired."

"Lucy called me this morning. You could have called me, you know. I'd have picked you up."

"I know. But you have the girls."

Margo didn't argue. She sat down, cradling little Kristin in her arms. "You know, if you'd get your own place, I'd come to see you more."

Claire didn't want to get into it. She didn't think she'd ever see eye to eye with Margo about Wally. Margo held tightly to her stubborn belief that Wally was responsible for most of her problems in life, including her own decision to marry young, and her husband's decision to run off with a college coed when he heard that Margo was in line for Huntington's disease. That, of course, didn't last, and Kyle crawled back to his family after Margo tested negative for the HD gene.

Claire sighed. "Dad's in Pleasant View now, so it's not an issue."

"True. Mom told me." She sat quietly combing Kristin's fine hair with her hand for a moment before adding, "She told me about John." She looked up. "Claire, I'm sorry."

"Don't be. I'm beginning to think it's for the best myself." She pushed the electronic control to raise the head of her bed. Once she was in the seated position, she continued. "I guess you've heard about the rapes."

"I've read the papers. Why?"

Claire slowly reiterated the facts as she understood them, the similarity of the cases, the masks, the phone conversation with Tony, John's father, the night-vision goggles, the ring that must have fallen from John's pocket outside Lena's house, and her latest findings about Billy Ray's infertility and her conversation with John on the mountain and his angry response.

Margo sat with her jaw slackened. "You actually accused him of being a rapist? Are you out of your mind? What were you thinking? What if you were right? He could have killed you!"

"Margo, slow down! I didn't exactly accuse him of being a rapist. I just asked him why the deputy would ask about him, that's all." She looked down. "I never really believed it. I just had a nagging question in my gut and I had to ask."

"It was stupid, Claire. If you have a gut check about something, it's called intuition. You put your life in jeopardy because of your compulsion to ask."

Claire looked at her sister. Leave it to a flesh-and-blood sibling to be blunt. She nodded. "It was stupid, I guess." She hesitated. "But all of this seems so out of character for John. I've known him for years. He—"

"Claire, think about it, would you? You give the man a hint about your doubts and he suddenly thinks he needs some space in your relationship."

"He just told Mom he needed to get away from Stoney Creek for a while."

"Duh! Of course he needs to get away. What would you do if you were guilty and someone was starting to ask questions?"

Claire looked up. She didn't want to believe it. "Leave town," she said quietly before shaking her head. "There has to be some other explanation."

Her sister huffed. "Do I need to remind you of your track record with men? You're not exactly a stellar judge of a man's character. Who was that psychopath you dated who scrawled threats on your door in Boston and killed our brother?"

"He didn't exactly kill Clay. It was an accident."

"You're hopeless." Margo stood up. "Have you told the detective about this stuff?"

"All but the stuff I learned yesterday about Billy Ray's infertility and my engagement ring."

"Claire!"

"I just found out last night, Margo. I was going to call him, but I needed emergency surgery! Give me a break!"

Margo backed down. "I'm sorry." She took a step forward. "I'm just worried about you."

Claire nodded. She understood. Margo always called it as she saw it. Claire didn't always agree with her, but she knew she could count on Margo to say exactly what was on her mind.

"Does Della know you're here?"

"I didn't want to bother her. Besides, she was flying today. I didn't know how to reach her."

"You'd better tell her. Moms likes to know these things."

"It's the first vacation she's had in years. I don't want to ruin it by making her worry about me."

"She gave me a number for her time-share. I think I'd better at least tell her what happened and that everything is okay. I'll tell her not to worry."

"She'll worry about Wally. I promised I'd visit him every day. She's counting on it."

"Wally will be fine. Do you think the man can actually remember from day to day who visits?"

Claire felt her dander rising. And most folks in Stoney Creek knew it wasn't a pretty sight to see a country woman with her dander up. She took a deep breath and controlled her response. "Yes, Wally does know it." *As if you care.* Claire didn't want to argue. "If Mom knows I'm not following through to visit Daddy, it will ruin her vacation."

"And if I don't tell her that her baby girl is in the hospital, she'll be mad at me!"

There was a sharp knock at the door. She turned to see a familiar face, a petite Japanese man, Mr. Sugimoto, who was carrying a large bouquet of flowers.

"Mr. Sugimoto! What a surprise! How did you know I was here?"

"I called your office to talk to you this morning. Lucy told me where I could find you."

Claire held her hand up to her sister. "Mr. Sugimoto, this is my sister, Margo. Margo, this gentleman is working on some business with Uncle Leon."

Margo shook his hand and raised her eyebrows. She looked at Claire. "You amaze me. You're always in the middle of everything."

"I'm not."

Margo shook her head and addressed Mr. Sugimoto. "Don't let her fool you. If she becomes a surgeon, she'll be the first one *not* to think that the world revolves around her."

"I've got to run, sis."

"I hope I'm not interrupting anything."

"Not at all," Margo said. "I had already stood to leave." She looked back at Claire. "Any idea when they'll let you out of here?"

"Probably tonight. Dr. Branum hopes to get me out in under twenty-four hours."

"So much for compassion."

Claire didn't want to admit that she'd begged Dr. Branum to get her out as soon as possible. Because of her at-risk status for HD, she'd been unable to get a reasonably priced medical insurance policy, so she was officially uninsured since leaving the Layfayette Surgery Residency. Besides, she'd made a promise to Della she intended to keep.

Margo leaned over and whispered her good-bye. "Just don't let this news get out. You're just as much a target for this rapist as your patients were now. And for pity sakes, just to be safe, don't call John Cerelli to tell him you had surgery."

Thanks for the vote of confidence, sis. Claire nodded her assent.

"And call the deputy!" she whispered. Then, standing and extending her hand, Margo added, "Mr. Sugimoto, so nice to meet you."

Mr. Sugimoto bowed slightly. "My pleasure."

Claire watched her sister wag her index finger at her once more in a silent warning before slipping away. Then she turned her attention to her unexpected guest. "Mr. Sugimoto, what a pleasant surprise. The flowers are wonderful!"

The noise of clinking silverware and the muffled talk of business discussed above and below the table provided the atmosphere Leon McCall enjoyed. Cellular phones chirped, deals were discussed, and waitresses with short skirts offered fine Cuban cigars to the patrons. The music was classical. He was okay with that, but preferred something with a little more contemporary appeal; at least that was the image he tried to leave with the pretty young things who took his order.

He touched the top of his balding head and looked at Alfred Pittington. "Harvard, my boy, did I ever tell you bald men have more testosterone?"

His attorney rolled his eyes. "I told you that. Remember?"

"Just look at her." Leon was nearly drooling. "If she knew how much I was worth she'd be falling all over me."

Alfred straightened his tie and glanced at the young waitress. "You're a fool. She's young enough to be your daughter."

"Love knows no age limit."

"Neither does foolishness or the love of money."

"Careful, Harvard. I can hire new attorneys."

"I know too much about you, Leon." He pushed his chair away from the remains of a double-martini, four-course lunch. "How'd your wife ever put up with you for thirty years?"

"My soon-to-be ex-wife."

"Whatever."

"My father didn't believe in divorce."

"Ahh. And your father was in control of McCall Shoes."

Leon took a deep breath. "Let's grab a cigar on the veranda. Sugimoto isn't due for another two hours."

"I thought you were worried about Wally's family getting wind of this, trying to interfere." He made a slurping noise as he sucked at a piece of filet mignon in between his front teeth. "But you haven't even mentioned them."

"Providence is caring for Leon McCall, Harvard. Wally went into a nursing home, so I sent Della on a vacation to Hawaii. Claire's too busy to know or care. Margo has essentially nothing to do with the McCalls, and Elizabeth is summering at Martha's Vineyard." He smiled. "That just leaves little ol' Leon at home by himself to run things as best as he can."

"Poor little Leon." Pittington smiled and sampled the space between his front teeth with his tongue. Evidently pleased that he'd extracted the filet, he continued. "They have a special place in hell for people like you, Leon."

"Don't tell me you believe in hell."

He chuckled. "No. You know that."

"If there is, you'll be right beside me."

"Knowing you, you'll try to fool the devil into buying McCall Shoes for all the demons."

"I'll let you work the contract, my boy." Leon stood up and patted his belly. "I've got to stop celebrating this deal."

"Especially before the contract is signed."

"Sugimoto is already here. This is a formality." He laid a twenty-dollar tip on the table. "I'll bet the gorgeous redhead fights to serve me the next time. Let's get a smoke."

Randy Jensen set down the phone and shook his head before opening the lid to a pizza box sitting on his desk.

His superior, Police Chief Manny Morton, came in sniffing the air. "Ah, I thought I smelled pepperoni."

"You can identify a pepperoni from a thousand yards, can't you, Chief?" He motioned to the box. "Have a slice. I'll never eat it all."

"Thanks. Who was on the phone?"

"Dr. McCall." He sighed. "She's giving me her latest theories on the rape cases."

"New leads?"

"She looked up Billy Ray Chisholm's chart. The guy is azoospermic."

"What?"

"That's what I said. She said it's a rare cause of male infertility. He doesn't have any sperm in his semen."

"Shoots blanks, huh?" Manny shoved the tip of the pizza into his mouth.

"We need to take a close look at the forensic evidence the SANE nurse provided. If any of the samples contained actual sperm, it would appear we can take old Billy off our suspect list."

Manny chewed slowly. "I thought you told me Billy's wife was in the hospital with some problems with a pregnancy. That would mean—"

"Exactly," Jensen interrupted. "Lovely little Lena has a boyfriend other than Billy Ray."

"Hmm." The chief wiped his chin.

"But Claire is questioning another theory that Billy Ray himself is promoting. Billy Ray thinks that maybe Lena is telling the truth, and that she hasn't been fooling around, that her pregnancy wasn't from an affair, but from a rape."

"She didn't report any rape."

"Not to us, but evidently, Dr. McCall says that Lena told her about it. She said Billy Ray was wearing a surgical mask and attacked her."

"I see." The chief started eyeing a second piece of pizza.

Jensen waved his hand toward the box. "Go ahead."

The chief helped himself. "My take? The girl is lying."

"Exactly. She's been running around on her husband."

"But she must not have known about her husband's azoo-whatever."

"Azoospermia."

"Or she would have known her denial of an affair would never have been believed."

"But why would she make up the story about Billy Ray attacking her?"

Manny pulled a slice of pizza away from his mouth, trailing a cheese tail like a comet. He snapped the cheese with his other hand and responded. "Maybe she didn't make it up. Maybe Billy Ray is still our rapist. The only lie we know Lena has told is the fact that she hasn't been running around on Billy Ray."

"I'd like to confront her with the lie. Tell her about Billy Ray's little problem."

"Careful," the chief warned. "I wouldn't do that. You could get Dr. McCall into some trouble. I'd doubt she released that medical information about Billy Ray with his permission." He pushed the pizza box toward Jensen, a sign that Manny was done mooching. "Besides, what difference does it make to us now? We know she hasn't been on the up and up. For now that may be enough."

"Dr. McCall also said Lena was wearing a diamond ring that Lena told the doc Billy Ray's dog brought her."

"What?"

"She claims the dog carried up an old felt ring box, and get this, Dr. McCall says it is the exact ring owned by John Cerelli, her former fiancé. Dr. McCall said the inscription proves it is the ring she used to wear, the same ring she gave back to John Cerelli."

"So what's the doc implying?"

Jensen shook his head. "She is hesitant to implicate Cerelli, but she knows he had the ring in his pocket right before the night Lena claims that Billy Ray attacked her."

"She thinks John Cerelli is the rapist?"

The deputy raised his hands, palms up. "She won't come right out and say it, but she wanted me to know just in case it is important to the investigation."

"You want to know what I think?"

"Sure."

Manny pointed his finger at Jensen. "Lena is lying again. John Cerelli and Lena must be catchin' a little action together on the side. He gives her the ring, and Lena has to make up some cockamamie story to cover for John." He laughed. "A dog brought the ring to her! That's too crazy."

"I talked to Cerelli outside Fisher's Cafe one day. He told me a ring flew out of his car when he was passing Lena's place."

"That makes little sense. How likely is it that a ring would just fly out of his car?"

Jensen shuffled through a file on his desk. "Well, that's what he said. When I questioned him about it, he got real defensive and asked me why I wanted to know."

"He's hiding something. No doubt."

"Maybe we should get forensics to look at Lena's baby."

"So what if we can prove it's John Cerelli's child? That evidence gets us nowhere in this case. It only proves something which isn't a crime in this state. Adultery."

Randy Jensen started pacing around his small office. He held up one finger. "Lies." He held up a second finger. "Defensiveness." He nodded. "I'd better keep a close eye on Cerelli. Things aren't adding up."

Della was already beginning to understand America's love affair with Hawaii. She lifted the flower lei to her face again and inhaled the delightful fragrance. She'd been on the ground for only a few minutes when the stress from a thousand nights with Wally began to melt from her like snow on a warm spring day. She walked up a stone path bordered by flowers of such brilliant color she wanted to stop and photograph each one. Under a broad front porch, she accepted a tropical punch from a hostess, and was ushered to a desk where she could register.

"I'm Della McCall."

The young woman smiled. "McCall? Yes, we're expecting you. You have a phone message waiting."

"A message for me?" Thoughts of disaster at the Pleasant View Nursing Home accompanied a lump in her throat.

"You may receive it at our courtesy phone on the lobby wall by entering your suite number, or wait to use the phone in your room."

Wally won't cooperate without me. Or he's choked. They didn't thicken his liquids like Dr. V instructed.

"Ma'am?"

"Oh, I'll take it here."

The woman handed her a small folder. "Here are your suite keys. Just enter the room number after pressing the button marked 'messages.'" She smiled. "Would you like to leave your room charges on the credit card which secured the reservation?"

"Credit card?"

"Yes, let's see. Mr. Leon McCall. Your husband?"

"No. I mean yes. Oh, I mean no, he's not my husband, and yes, leave the bill on his card." Della shuffled off toward the phone on the wall. She pressed the message button and followed the instructions. After a moment, she heard Margo's voice.

"Mom, this is Margo. I hope you had a wonderful flight. I just wanted to let you know about Claire. She came down with appendicitis and had an appendectomy this morning, probably just after you'd left Dulles. Anyway, she's fine. Wally's fine. There is absolutely no reason to come home. Enjoy your vacation. I just wanted you to know. I knew you would want to know. Bye."

Della walked back outside where a bellman assisted her to her room. She tipped him with five dollars. Tipping generously was easy since Leon had paid for everything else.

She looked at herself in the full-length mirror and shook her head. *"Wally's fine. There is absolutely no reason to come home."* As if Margo

would ever check on Wally. If Claire's in the hospital, no one will be check-
ing in on him.

She started to pace. *What to do?* It was near insanity to turn around and fly back to Virginia, but what joy could there be here, if she knew Wally was alone?

She sat on the side of her king-sized bed and pulled out a small book from her purse. Then she carefully dialed the number she had written there. She got voice-mail.

"John. This is Della. I wanted to be sure you heard about Claire. She had surgery this morning for appendicitis." She hesitated. "Look, I shouldn't pry, but I know how you two have struggled lately. I can't pretend to know what's in my daughter's mind, but maybe it's because she's made some bad decisions to trust in the past that makes it so hard for her to trust now. I know you wanted some time away from her to think, but, well, I'm sure a visit from you and a little help might just convince her that you are ready to love her through thick and thin."

Next, she made a series of calls, finding out first the number to the hospital in Carlisle, then calling to be connected to Claire's room.

⚬⚬⚬

Claire lifted the chirping phone from its cradle in the bed railing. "Mom? How'd you find me?" *Margo, I'm going to kill you.*

"Your sister left a message. How are you?"

"Mom, I'm fine. I'm going to be released today."

"Today? You just had surgery! What kind of—"

"Mom, I had appendicitis. But it wasn't ruptured. And Dr. Branum used a laparoscope, so I just have a few Band-Aids on my stomach."

"I'm coming home. I can catch a return flight and be there by tomorrow evening."

"Don't be insane! I'm fine!"

"But Wally will—"

"I'm going by to see him as soon as I'm discharged. Don't ruin your vacation. Stay and enjoy yourself."

Silence hung between them for a moment before Della's voice returned. It was soft and pleading, like a child. "Are you sure? I knew this wasn't a good idea. I should have never let Leon talk me into such foolishness."

"Mom, stop it. I'm not going to be working tomorrow. I can even spend the day with Daddy. Stay put."

She heard her mother sigh. "You're a godsend, Claire."

Claire smiled. "Just bring me a pound of Kona. It's the best java in the world."

She listened as Della began to sniff.

"Don't cry, Mom, it's only coffee."

Della lobbed. That was a term she had coined herself during one of a multitude of frustrating moments with Wally when she didn't know whether to laugh or cry. She would start to cry when somehow she found the strength to find humor in the craziness of it all . . . so she would begin a sob that gushed and ended in a laugh, in effect, combining the two into a laugh-sob or just "lob." "You, my dear doctor-daughter, are too much!"

"Good-bye, Mom. I love you."

After another wet sniff, Della responded, "You too. Bye."

Claire had done all the right things to qualify for early discharge. She'd walked. She'd urinated. And she'd tolerated a full liquid diet without nausea. So, even though she hadn't officially been discharged, she didn't feel it was too much of a stretch of truth to make a promise to her mother that she was leaving soon. What she didn't anticipate was her surgeon's reluctance.

When Dr. Branum came in a few minutes later, Claire tried to look her best. "I'm ready to go, Doc."

He offered a Texas-sized smile. "I'm all for early discharges, Claire, but it's not a crime to spend a night in the hospital."

"I know. But it's, well . . ."

"I know. No insurance. Listen, don't worry about the hospital bills. You send this hospital enough business that I think I can twist an arm or two to give you a deal."

"It's not just the money."

"Image? You don't need to prove anything to anyone. We know you're tough. I can get you out early in the morning and you'll still be out in less than twenty-four hours. I thought that's what we talked about."

"But I'm getting along fine. I've walked and I'm eating this cruel and unusual nourishment they call a full-liquid diet." She paused and flashed her sweetest smile before resorting to pouting. "I want to sleep in my own bed."

"Look," he started, the smile having melted from his face, "I'll not stand in your way. There's really no medical reason for you not to go, except . . ." He pushed a chair closer to the bed and sat down.

"Except," she prompted.

"I'm sure you know the 'except.'" His face was deadpan serious. "Our surgical staff was briefed by the FBI this morning. All women who are post-surgery are to be warned about the rapes that have been going around Stoney Creek."

"The FBI? Really?"

He nodded.

"I'll take precautions." She leaned forward. "Listen, if it's of any help, I've been very involved with this case. The women involved were all my patients. As far as I know, that piece of information hasn't gone public."

He shook his head. "All I've read in the local papers is that the assaults involved women who were recovering from recent surgery. And of course I knew Brittany Lewis because you sent her to me for her cholecystectomy."

"Believe me, I won't take any chances. I'll be sure the police are watching, too."

Dr. Branum stood up. "Okay, I give. At least stick around until after supper. I wouldn't want you to miss out on the vanilla pudding." His smile returned. "I'll fill out the paperwork to set you free." He shook her hand gently before turning to leave. "I'll leave a prescription on your chart for some pain medicine. Call my office in the morning. I'd like to see you in my office in two weeks."

With that, he was gone, and Claire picked up the phone to call Lucy. Hopefully, she would be willing to pick her up and take her by Pleasant View Home on the way back to Stoney Creek.

Leon McCall pushed the stack of contracts across the walnut boardroom table. "I think you'll find that Har—uh, Mr. Pittington has prepared the papers to your specifications." He smiled broadly and stood up, motioning with his hand for Mr. Sugimoto to follow.

He walked to the far wall and opened a curtain, revealing a row of windows looking out over the plant. "I knew you would be looking to increase productivity, and so we've already added the machinery for the expansion. As you can see, it's ninety percent complete."

"You should not have proceeded without contacting us."

Leon gushed. "I know. But we copied the specifications of your plant in Tokyo. And although the new line came to us at considerable personal expense—"

"One point two million dollars," Pittington interrupted, clearing his throat.

"It's all money we will recoup within the first year of production." Leon walked back to the table. "Harvard, where are the projections I showed you?" Then, turning to Mr. Sugimoto, he continued. "Let me show you my figures. I'm sure you'll agree."

"Slow down, Mr. McCall. We have not even signed a contract for buyout, and already you are wanting to show me earnings projections."

Leon cast a glance toward Harvard and tried to swallow the lump in his throat. "Okay, um, sure, I'm sure there will be time for this later."

Mr. Sugimoto came over and stood over the stack of contracts.

"Have a seat, please. And here," Leon said, sliding a wrapped gift box across the table. "I've bought you a new pen for the formalities."

Leon sat and pushed a button on the intercom. "Til? Could you bring us some coffee?"

Mr. Sugimoto did not sit down. Instead he started shaking his head slowly, looking at the contract in front of him. "I am very sorry to say this, Mr. McCall, but we have decided to withdraw our offer."

Chapter Twenty-Six

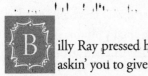

{B} illy Ray pressed his ear closer to the pay phone to hear. "I'm not askin' you to give me medical information. I'm a friend, that's all. I want to visit her, you know? Can't you just tell me her room number?"

The female sighed. "Hold on."

He waited, tapping his fingers against the phone.

"I'm sorry, sir, we have no one by the name of McCall in the hospital." The female voice was pleasant. Billy Ray wondered if she was as pretty as she sounded.

"Was she there? She's supposed to be there."

"Sir, she may have been here in the past. I'm not privileged to give you that information."

She must have been discharged!

"Okay, thank you," he said, before hanging up.

He checked his watch and walked toward his truck. "Now don't that beat all."

He wasn't expecting her to be discharged so soon. Now he would have to alter his evening plans. He had thought about going over to Brighton to sneak into Lena's hospital room, but knowing Dr. McCall was going to be home would change all that.

He slapped his hand on the seat beside him and cursed. He wasn't ready for an all-nighter. It wasn't close enough to the weekend for that.

But the cops were inept in Stoney Creek. If he could count on one thing, he was sure he could bet on that.

He started the truck and slammed it in reverse. Maybe he could grab a quick nap before it got too late.

He squealed his tires as he pulled onto the highway, making a mental list of the supplies he would need.

He looked around at his empty gun rack. *I may need my shotgun for this.*

Claire talked to Wally like he understood every word. She helped him drink some thickened lemonade and promised to buy him some new socks. She told him about her surgery, about how weird it was being the patient, and how she had talked to Della, whom she had to convince to stay in Hawaii. She talked about the weather, about baseball and the Atlanta Braves. In fact, she managed to hit the high points of all of his favorite subjects except one: his friend, John Cerelli. That was one place she didn't want to go.

She thought Wally had been in Hawaii when he was in the Navy, but she wasn't sure, so she asked him, but her father didn't say one word during her entire visit. Eventually, she just gave up and left with Lucy, giving him a promise she'd come back the next day to see him.

When they arrived, it was almost ten, and Claire had to convince Lucy to go home so she could get some sleep. Lucy had protested, to be sure, and waited until Claire got through to the Stoney Creek Police dispatch and received a call back from Randy Jensen, who promised to keep her house under tight watch.

Claire set the phone down on the nightstand beside her bed. "He'll be watching."

Lucy forced a smile. "That makes me feel better."

"I'll be okay. Think about it, Lucy. No one even expects me to be home so early."

"I guess so." She shrugged. "I'm not sure Lee could sleep without me anyway. We haven't slept apart in thirty-three years, you know."

"Wow."

"I'm going to check the locks again. You have your mace?"

"Yes, ma'am." She responded with the tone of an irritated teen talking to her mother.

"You call me first thing in the morning, hear?"

In a minute, Lucy reappeared in Claire's bedroom. "Everything's tight. I even checked the window. Don't even think of answering the door."

"Yes, ma'am."

"Follow me to the door, so you can lock me out."

Claire obeyed, then did a slow walk through the house herself, missing the sounds of her father and feeling alone. Her stomach muscles ached. She was exhausted. But she knew her preparations for the night weren't yet complete. In her mother's room, she pulled open the filing cabinet which doubled as Della's nightstand. There, behind the files of the bottom drawer, she found what she was looking for. She picked up the Colt pistol and weighed it in her hand. It was another gift from Uncle Leon, something he thought every woman without a man to protect her ought to learn to use.

Claire often questioned her uncle's motives. Everything for Leon came down to money. If it made him more, he was all for whatever was under consideration. So when he gave Della the pistol, Claire couldn't think of a way it could possibly work in favor of Leon's pocketbook. A possible connection was made by John, one afternoon that he'd taken Claire out back to practice firing a few rounds. "He probably wants Della to put Wally out of his misery one day. That way he can have his cut of Wally's inheritance."

She knew John spoke in jest, but scolded him anyway. She wanted to forget it, but the thought returned to nag her like a fever blister, an ugly inconvenience that pops up after a stress. She'd bury the thought for a month or two again, and then up it would surface, especially on the days she saw her mother cry.

She popped out the clip and loaded in a few shells. It was only .22 caliber, not suitable for a real gunfight, but all Uncle Leon thought Della could handle, and it could certainly do the job if you held the gun tightly against someone's temple. Claire shook her head to dispel the horrid thought. She cocked the pistol, loading a bullet into the chamber, and smiled.

Just let the Stoney Creek rapist try to pull a fast one on me. She did a second, slow circle through the house, turning on every light except the one in her bedroom. Once she was there, she lowered herself to the bed, noting that standing wasn't too bad, and lying down wasn't too bad. It was making the transition that provided her the biggest pain.

She set the pistol on her nightstand and her pepper spray beneath her pillow, then switched the two and closed her hand around the grip of the pistol beneath her head. *No, I might fire this thing if I start dreaming.* Sleeping with a gun beneath her pillow seemed like overkill. She again switched the pepper spray with the pistol, placing it within reach on her nightstand.

Her eyes stayed open until midnight, her mind alert to every creak of the old house. But at midnight, a gentle rain began to fall, and the rhythm of the raindrops soon soothed her troubled soul into slumber.

⁓§§§⁓

Billy Ray pulled off the highway a hundred yards beyond and across from the McCall lane. There, the trees had been cut away for power lines and he had a relatively sheltered vantage point to watch.

There were lights on in the house, and only one car in the driveway: Claire's.

From the point of the power lines, the road made a slight turn, making the McCall house even easier for Billy to see from his truck, and making his truck a little less obvious to folks traveling from town. In fact, in the last hour, he was sure he'd seen a county sheriff pass through twice, both times slowing to a crawl in front of the house, with the attention away from Billy Ray and right on the little McCall ranch-style home.

He reached behind him and lifted a twelve-gauge shotgun from the rack in his back window. He chambered a shell and put the safety on before setting the gun on the seat beside him.

Perfect. Now all I have to do is wait.

⁓§§§⁓

John Cerelli pulled off Interstate 64 and parked under an overpass to put the top up on his Mustang. Rain wasn't in his plans and was slowing his progress during his unexpected return to Stoney Creek.

He'd finally listened to his voice-mail at ten P.M., after dining with a new potential client. He left in haste, canceled his hotel reservations, and grabbed a liter bottle of Mountain Dew for the drive.

He called ahead to the hospital in Carlisle, to find, to his amazement, that Claire was no longer registered as a patient.

Home alone. Post-op.

He finished with the last fastener and jumped back into the driver's seat, before speeding back onto the interstate.

Opportunities like this don't present themselves every day.

Claire slept fitfully, used to sleeping on her side or stomach, but was forced to lie on her back because of her incisions. When she slept, she dreamed. Distressing images intertwined with twinges of pain from her surgical sites to create a morbid hallucination. She was being raped. A man with a surgical mask was beginning to operate before the anesthetic had taken effect.

She awoke and groaned, turned to one side and back again, and drifted into a dreamlike place between sleep and consciousness. John Cerelli, Margo, Dr. Branum, Mr. Sugimoto, Uncle Leon, Lucy, and Billy Ray all gathered to look at her appendix floating in a jar.

She heard only one sound before she felt the full weight of her attacker, a heavy footfall on the floor beside her bed. She screamed as her senses were jarred into full alert. This was no dream!

The room was dark. Her attacker had either closed the door to the hall or turned off the lights. His hands were on her neck and shoulders, pushing her back, then flipping her over so that her face was buried in her pillow.

Deputy Jensen slowed as he neared the McCall house again, noting this time the absence of lights. He looked at his watch and wished for the passage of time. Night patrol around Stoney Creek could be dreadfully slow. He patted his pocket and reached for a cigar, something he indulged himself in only during his night shifts.

He slowed further and lowered his window. "Blasted rain," he muttered. That's when he saw a reflection of his headlights off of a vehicle parked in the woods beyond the McCall lane. It was a red truck. He decided to pass slowly and turned around to come in from the other side where he would have a better angle to see the license plate.

The shoulder where he stopped was soft, so he couldn't get all the way off the road. His element of surprise would be lost, but he couldn't risk not being seen by an approaching vehicle. He turned on his flashing blue lights and stopped the car with two wheels still on the highway. He spotlighted the truck license plate, but didn't need that for an ID. He knew this vehicle by heart. It was Billy Ray Chisholm's pride and joy.

Randy Jensen mumbled to himself about Billy Ray's foolishness and slipped from his vehicle, one hand on a strong flashlight and another on his firearm.

Throbbing pain erupted from the back of Claire's neck where her attacker held her face against her pillow. She locked her ankles together and prayed. He shoved her forward again, harder this time, until her eyes smashed against an object on the other side of her pillow. Color burst into her vision as her eye flattened.

The pepper spray! She pulled her hand forward under her pillow and closed her fist around the small canister. She needed air, but she knew she'd dare not breathe in if she was able to just get off a shot of the spray.

Seconds seemed like forever. She felt her lungs would burst. Finally, she had the moment she needed. As her attacker shifted his weight off of her neck, she wiggled her right hand up beside her ear. Hoping she had the spray pointed in the right direction, she clinched her eyes even tighter and began to spray.

Her attacker screamed.

The weight lessened and she rolled to her right, ignoring the pain in her abdomen. She gripped the pillow over her mouth and nose with her left hand, willing herself not to breathe. With the pepper spray pointed at her attacker's face, she sprayed a second stream, as she slid to the floor and took her first gasp of air from under the bed.

The man was howling now, his hands rubbing his eyes.

Claire strained to see in the dim light. He was wearing a mask. She quickly slid against the wall and crawled to her feet. The spray had slowed her attacker, but he was not fleeing, perhaps because of the mask. He stumbled forward, reaching for Claire. His arms were making wide circles.

Can he see me?

She held her breath and huddled against the wall next to the night-stand.

The man took another step and turned his head as if to listen. When he edged closer again, she leaped up and leveled the spray at his face.

He fell backwards, tripping across the corner of the bed. Claire felt the top of the nightstand for the pistol, but closed her hand around a glass lamp. She tore the shade away and stood to her feet. She had the advantage now. Her attacker was writhing on the floor, his breath coming with distinct wheezing noises between retching coughs. She was not sure if he could see, but she knew the room and crawled across the bed with the lamp in hand, ripping the cord from the socket. When she reached the wall by the door, she flipped on the overhead light.

Now, with her attacker in full view, she brought the lamp crashing onto his forehead.

His hands were on his eyes, so he didn't have a chance to prepare. Silence followed the shattering of glass. Claire moved quickly while the man lay motionless on the floor. She found the pistol on the table and her cell phone on the floor by the wall.

She trained the pistol on her attacker and moved slowly into a crouching position. Blood streamed from his forehead. His hair was brown and curly, and his build muscular just like John's and Billy Ray's, but the smell was definitely Billy Ray. She reached for the mask and ripped it from his face. As the mask pulled free, his head snapped forward and thudded back against the floor. *Cyrus?*

She quickly dialed 9–1–1.

"Nine one one emergency."

Cyrus lifted his hand and began to moan.

Claire asked for help and gave her address.

Her maintenance man opened his eyes and coughed, then struggled to sit up to wipe away the blood running into his eyes.

"I need help now."

Cyrus moaned. "You shouldn't have done that, Dr. McCall."

"Stay put! I'll shoot you," she screamed.

The 911 operator spoke again. "Calm down, ma'am. The police will be right there."

"Hurry!"

She locked eyes with Cyrus, who shook his head and moved forward, cursing her.

"Don't move!"

The 911 operator spoke again. "Please be calm. The police have been notified."

Claire steadied her grip on the pistol.

Cyrus grinned and stood to his feet.

She screamed into the phone. "Get me an ambulance. A man's been shot!"

She tossed aside the phone, held the pistol with two hands, and slowly depressed the trigger.

Chapter Twenty-Seven

ohn Cerelli turned up the music to overcome the sound of the rain pounding his windshield. He had ten miles to go. Ten miles that seemed like an eternity.

He envisioned their reunion, a chance for him to pamper her through her recovery, a chance to prove he could be counted on to be there when she needed it.

He only wished she would have called, but he supposed he understood. He had been the one to initiate this new distance between them. He squinted through the streaked windshield as a new sense of foreboding mounted. Claire was alone. Post-op and alone. *God, keep her in your hands. Protect her from evil.*

Lightning streaked across the sky in front of him, illuminating the forest bordering the road. His windshield wipers thumped a rhythm just ahead of the tempo of the opera. He began to sing along and pressed the accelerator closer to the floor.

"L'amore ci guiderá." Love will guide us.

"Senza di te, il mio cuore non canterá mai piú." Without you, my heart will never sing again.

Randy Jensen tipped his hat forward so the rain ran off onto the ground and pointed the light into the truck's cab.

Billy Ray squinted.

"Whatcha doin' in there, Billy Ray?"

Billy held up his hands to cover his face. "Turn that thing off, would ya? I'm just sittin' here. What's it look like?"

"With a shotgun in your lap?" Jensen shone his light across the front of the cab. "You're not getting ready to spot a deer, are ya, Billy Ray?"

Billy Ray yawned. "I'm just watching, okay? I'm not hunting."

"What are you watching?" Jensen stepped back. "Get out of the truck!"

Billy Ray reached for the door handle.

"Put the gun aside!"

The deputy watched Billy set his shotgun in the passenger seat, then turned and looked at the McCall house. "You watching for anything special? Turn around and put your hands on the truck!"

"I'm here watchin' Dr. McCall's place. She just had surgery. She could be the next target."

Jensen didn't understand. "You want me to believe you are waiting here to protect her?"

Billy Ray spat on the ground. "I'm here to find the man you want."

Jensen scoffed. "You're nuts if you think I'm buyin' this."

"I'm here to protect me, Randy. You guys think I would be out here if my reputation weren't on the line? I'm here because you guys are on the wrong track."

A sharp pop pulled their attention toward the McCall house. Jensen's first thought was thunder, which had been occurring sporadically through the night. But this wasn't thunder. It was quicker, a sharp report characteristic of gunfire.

Billy Ray knew it right away. He pulled his hands away from the truck and held them up as if to ask, "Is this okay?"

Jensen started running toward the house, scrambling across the wet pavement toward the gravel lane.

Billy Ray started behind him and then turned back to pick up his shotgun before jogging behind the deputy.

⁂

Inside, Cyrus fell to the floor, gripping the top of his left leg. "You shot me! You shot me in the leg!"

"I wasn't aiming for your leg."

"I'm bleeding." He stumbled backwards, teetering for a second, as Claire wondered if he would stand or fall.

"I told you to stay put." She raised the gun again, this time pointing for his chest.

A red stain rapidly expanded away from his left groin. When he hit the floor, blood erupted in a pulsatile fountain, spraying into the air.

"Your femoral artery has been severed."

"I'll kill you."

Claire kept the gun trained on her attacker. "You'll be unconscious in two minutes."

Alarm picked up the tenor of his voice. "Help me," he said, grasping at a bedsheet hanging from the bed. Desperately, he wadded the sheet against his upper leg. Blood sprayed through his fingers. "I can't see it! I'm bleeding!"

Slowly, she knelt, the gun trained on the man's chest. With her other hand, she reached forward and shoved her hand over his to push tightly over the artery. "You will bleed to death in a minute or two unless this is done correctly!" Her eyes bore in on his.

He reached for her neck, but Claire was too quick. She pulled back, releasing his hand as a red geyser sprayed from his leg. His eyes widened with the terror that comes just before impending death.

She shoved the wadded sheet back over the artery. She spoke with a firm, but quiet demeanor. "If you touch me again, I'll let you bleed to death."

She looked toward the doorway. Someone was pounding. Pounding hard. "Police! Open up."

Cyrus pleaded. "Don't leave me."

Claire screamed. "We're in the bedroom. I can't come!"

The front door exploded in. Deputy Randy Jensen came in with his weapon drawn. Behind him was Billy Ray.

"We need an ambulance. He's got a femoral artery injury."

Jensen lowered his gun. "What's going on here?"

Claire looked up from where she knelt over Cyrus, her rapist, who now, in a sudden twist, had become her patient. "He attacked me. He's bleeding. I can't take my hand from his femoral region here or he'll exsanguinate." She winced at her own pain in her lower abdomen. "Just keep his hands off me."

"You!" Billy Ray stepped forward, leveling his shotgun at Cyrus's head. "You work for her!"

Jensen grabbed Billy's arm. "Careful." He grabbed a radio from his belt. "He's not going anywhere."

Billy Ray cursed, but yielded to the officer and lowered his weapon. "That jerk told me she was in the hospital."

"Let's get an ambulance," Jensen said, raising the radio to his mouth.

"Listen," Claire said, tilting her head. "Sirens!"

Cyrus twisted in agony. "She shot me! She's got a gun!"

"Shut up," Jensen ordered. "Hold still." Claire watched as the deputy's eyes scanned the room and moved to grab a blanket from the bed. He leaned over and pulled it around Claire's shoulders.

Claire moaned. With her concentration on surviving, and then on Cyrus's life-threatening situation, she hadn't even paused to think about her clothes—or lack of them. Fortunately, she was still wearing a baggy sweatshirt, and her resistance had kept him from removing her underwear. The blanket would cover the rest for now.

"Hey," Cyrus yelled. "Cover me!"

"Shut up," Jensen shouted. "Billy Ray, help the doc. Hold pressure on the bleeding."

Billy Ray's eyes were wide as he obeyed and knelt at Claire's side.

"Here," she said, guiding his hands to the right spot, before easing her own hand back and checking for blood running around the wadded sheet. "Don't rock to the side or you'll lose control."

"No! Stay with me, Doc!"

Jensen kept his weapon trained on Cyrus's chest and laid one hand under Claire's arm to help her up. "Put on some pants," he said quietly.

She stood, gripping the blanket around her waist.

"Don't clean up. You'll need a SANE exam."

She nodded slowly and listened as the sirens grew in volume.

"He works for you?"

"Cyrus Hensley." She shook her head. "He's my maintenance man."

John Cerelli sped on, nearing Claire's place, daring to push his speed to the limits of safety on the wet road. His pulse quickened as questions of Claire's safety surfaced again. He argued with himself, reminding himself that Claire would be prepared. She had never been a woman to proceed into situations without a sense of control.

He raised his voice again, and sang with the Italian baritone, singing phrases that rolled from his tongue with natural grace.

But a flashing light in his rearview mirror and the scream of a siren squelched his song and tightened a knot in his throat. He glanced instinctively at his speedometer. He really wasn't going that much over the limit. John slowed and began to pull over, but the car behind responded only by accelerating past. It was a state-patrol car followed closely behind by an ambulance.

John pulled back into the road, his pulse rate quickening again. He edged his speed higher, but the flashing lights disappeared beyond the crest of a hill. Once he arrived at the top of the hill, he could hear the distant, rhythmic warble of the sirens, but the flashing lights had vanished.

Anxiety tightened his chest. *Claire!*

With a mile to go, John rubbed at the moisture on the inside of his windshield and muttered about his faulty defroster. Then, he began a prayer, this time out loud with the opera still blaring. "Keep Claire in your hands."

He shifted the wipers to high again and approached the final turn before the lane to the McCall house.

John prepared to brake and again wiped at the windshield with his hand. That's when he saw the flashing lights of a police car parked beside, *no, partially on the road!* He cut to the left to avoid sideswiping the vehicle and began a skid when he added the brakes.

The Mustang missed the car by inches, skidded into the oncoming lane, then back, spinning a one-eighty off the highway on the right, then flipped as it careened onto the road's soft shoulder.

John held his breath, bracing for impact. The trees were upside down, the ground a dark ceiling which fell with smothering force. *I'm going to hit those tr—*

Claire sat huddled in a blanket and watched the paramedics hoist Cyrus Hensley into the back of the emergency van. She stood from her position on the front steps of the house when she heard the noise. "What was that?"

Jensen shook his head. "More thunder."

She tilted her head. "That's not thunder." She paused. "Listen!"

Jensen hesitated as he walked toward the ambulance. "Aw, someone's playing a radio or something."

A paramedic slammed the back double doors of his vehicle. "Let's roll."

Claire sensed trouble. "Shut up!" she yelled.

Her scream met curious stares of the emergency personnel.

"That's not a radio," she said, beginning to hobble toward the road, ignoring the light rain. "That's opera!"

Jensen started after her, calling out, "Dr. McCall!"

She heard a muffled question about her bizarre behavior, someone saying something about the trauma she'd undergone. She halted in her tracks and screamed at the paramedics. "Pull to the end of the lane. There's a car in the ditch!"

Claire half walked, half limped, holding her abdomen with her eyes focused on the roadside just beyond Jensen's vehicle. "John!"

She saw the Mustang just before Deputy Jensen began to bark orders at the paramedic crew. The red car was upside down, its roof collapsed except for a corner where the passenger door rested against a large pine. Italian opera blared. The engine was off, but steam hissed from beneath the crumpled hood.

She dropped to the ground beside the driver's door, ignoring her own pain. "John! John!"

There was no response.

She scrambled to the other side where the car body was elevated by the tree. "John?" She dropped to her stomach, trying to see into the front seat. The window was smashed, the ragtop nearly ripped away. "I need light!"

A paramedic knelt at her side. "What've you got?"

"The driver's trapped."

"We'll call for another vehicle."

"You'll take this man first!"

"The other patient could exsanguinate!"

316

"This one's unconscious!"

"This guy might already be dead. It could take an hour to extract him! Our patient could lose his leg!"

"Then take them both!" she screamed. She began to squeeze forward under the Mustang. With as much control as she could manage, she spoke again to the paramedic. "Have one person stay with Mr. Hensley, and you and your driver get over here with your tools. *Now!*"

She turned her attention to John. She felt along the seat until she found his hand. A light came on as Randy Jensen crawled in beside her. The beam illuminated the grim situation. John was buckled in, but the steering column was collapsed onto his left leg. Blood streamed from his forehead. There was blood coming from his right ear, but he was breathing, gurgling as blood and saliva filled his airway.

It took only ten minutes to extract him, another five to establish an IV and slide in an endotracheal tube to assist his breathing. John never responded.

Claire looked at the sky. "We need a helicopter."

The young male paramedic shook his head. "The university chopper has been grounded all night."

She steeled her gaze on the young man, anticipating another hurdle. "Take 'em to Brighton."

"Carlisle's closer. Protocol mandates—"

"Forget the protocol! There is no neurosurgeon in Carlisle! This patient needs a neurosurgeon!"

The paramedic was about to protest again when Jensen stepped forward. "Protocol allows the transport decision to be made by the ranking medical professional in the field."

"I'm the chief on the crew tonight."

Randy raised his voice. "And this is *Doctor* McCall. Now get rolling."

The paramedic shook his head and helped load John Cerelli into the van beside Cyrus Hensley, but his comments to his partner weren't lost on Claire. "I swear, I thought she was a nurse. I knew she was pushy, but I didn't know who she was."

Claire gave one more set of instructions before the ambulance crew pulled away. "Call for a neuro-trauma alert when you're ten minutes out. I want everything done by the book on this one."

The driver, a woman who appeared about Claire's age, nodded. "I'll see to it."

As the van pulled away, Claire felt her knees weaken. After a moment, she slumped to the roadside and began to cry.

Randy Jensen put his arm around her shoulder. "Let's get you to the house."

She shook her head. "Take me to Brighton," she sobbed. "But first turn off that music."

⤜∰⤏

In spite of her objections, Claire relented to a SANE exam. She knew the importance of every step in gathering the evidence needed to ensure her attacker would not go unpunished.

Even though there had been no penetration there was still important documentation to make. Lucy was gentle, as always, photographing every abrasion, collecting hair samples and clothing with precision and organization. In a touch of irony, Lucy was the one who cried through the exam, with Claire providing the reassurances to continue.

"I should have stayed with you," the gray-haired nurse remarked for the fifth time as they walked toward the clinic waiting room.

Randy Jensen stood. "I doubt it would have made much difference."

Lucy sniffed. "I could have stayed up. I'd have heard him come in."

Randy shook his head. "I just heard from some of our men at the scene. It looked like he'd been in the house for hours. What time did you get home?"

Claire shrugged. "Must have been close to ten."

"He was already in the house."

"But we looked around."

"He was hiding in a back bedroom closet. He had a pillow, some magazines. The boys even found a bottle of whiskey." The deputy nodded. "He probably entered the house earlier in the day, not even caring if you'd come home that day. He knew you'd be home eventually, and when you did, he hid in the closet."

The thought of Cyrus hiding in the closet gave Claire a chill. "I'm not staying there alone again." She looked at Lucy. "I want to call my mother. Then can you take me to Brighton?"

Lucy offered a weak smile. "The sun's just beginning to rise here. What time is it in Hawaii?"

Claire shrugged. "I'm sure Mom's internal clock isn't reset anyway."

"Call your mom. Then I'll take you home. Rest for a few hours. Then I'll take you."

"I'll never sleep. Not in that house. And not without knowing what's happening to John."

Lucy sighed. "I guess you're right." She put her arm around Claire's shoulders. "But let's go home and pack a bag for you. Then we'll get you a hotel room next to the hospital so you have someplace to crash."

She could live with that plan. "Thanks, Lucy."

Randy Jensen promised to keep her updated, and promised to arrange a police guard for Cyrus Hensley.

Claire walked numbly back down the hallway and sat at her desk. She called Margo first, waking her from sleep and asking for the number to reach Della. Claire recited the events of the morning beginning with her attack and ending with John Cerelli's accident. Perhaps it was her sister's sleepy response, or the emotional distance in their relationship, but Claire felt as if she were talking about horrible events that had happened to someone else. It wasn't until she had her mom on the phone a few minutes later that the emotional cap came unplugged.

"Mom!" She started to sob.

"Claire?"

She sniffed. "It's me, Mom. The rapist attacked me and I shot him with your pistol and John was coming to help me when he crashed the Mustang in front of our house." She gasped for air before launching ahead again. "John's in the university hospital. He's unconscious. I entubated him for the paramedic team before they took ... him ... a-way." Her voice cracked and halted.

"Oh, Claire, I'm so sorry."

"Mom, I'm not even sure he's still alive. Lucy is here and she's going to take me up to Brighton."

"Claire, listen to me. As dark as this seems, God is still in control. He still loves you and holds you in his hand." She paused. "Claire? Are you there?"

She sniffed. "I'm here, Mom."

Della began to pray. She asked for peace and strength for Claire and for guidance for John's doctors. She asked for healing and for comfort, knowing God knew best, and loved them more than they understood.

Claire whispered, "Amen."

"I'll be home as soon as I can arrange a flight."

"But, Mom—"

"No arguments! I'm your mother. And I know best!"

The phone went dead. Della couldn't be dissuaded from her plan to come home.

And for that, Claire was very thankful.

Chapter Twenty-Eight

y ten A.M., Claire was standing in the Brighton University neurosurgical ICU at the bedside of John Cerelli. She stroked his hand and watched the rise and fall of his chest as the mechanical ventilator provided him oxygen. He hardly looked like the John she loved. A strip of hair was shaved in an irregular diagonal across his scalp, revealing an even row of surgical clips where a complex laceration had been repaired. A breathing tube exited his mouth, a central venous line exited his neck, and a tube which drained stomach fluid exited his right nostril. A thick white gauze taped beneath his nose reminded her of a cheap Santa Claus mustache used in an elementary school Christmas play. His eyes were closed with the head of his bed elevated to thirty degrees, a nice position for reading or to assist with venous drainage from a swollen brain.

Wires connected to his chest provided information about his cardiac rhythms, and a tube in his bladder monitored his urine output. Inflatable devices surrounded his calves and intermittently were pumped tight to squeeze blood through the calf veins to prevent clots from forming.

His heart rate was fast, over one hundred twenty, probably from dehydration rather than pain.

Ryan Hannah, M.D., stood across the bed from Claire and nodded slowly. Claire rotated on neurosurgery as a medical student under Dr. Hannah, and as the chairman of surgery, he had tried to convince her to stay at Brighton for her surgical training. At the time, Claire had designs on a more prestigious position in Boston and declined his offer. Having a familiar face and one whom she trusted implicitly gave Claire reassurance. He folded his hands and gave her the update. "His CT scan is mostly okay."

"Mostly okay?"

Dr. Hannah motioned for her to follow him to a computer monitor on the counter at the nurse's station. After entering John's medical record number, the neurosurgeon called up the images of the CT scan. "Look here, Claire." He pointed to several areas on the scan. "He has a basilar skull fracture and a contrecoup injury to his frontal lobes. You can see evidence of contusion here and here."

"Is that impressive?"

"Not really."

"Frontal lobe injury means personality changes?"

"You remember well. But realize that many injuries to this area are silent or temporary."

"Or permanent."

"True, but don't let your knowledge of what might be rob you of hope. We know very little at this point, Claire."

"Will he be okay?"

Dr. Hannah took her hand. "You know I can't answer that. The CT scan can appear normal and the patient can have diffuse brain damage from axonal injury."

Claire nodded knowingly. She'd spent enough time with head-injury patients during her internship to have seen it before.

Back at John's bedside, Hannah continued. "He's leaking spinal fluid from his nose." He pointed to the cloth mustache. "That's what the bandage is for: collecting cerebral spinal fluid. We'll keep his head elevated, keep him on antibiotics, and the leak will most likely seal on its own."

"Was he responsive when he came in?"

"He responded to pain and he was a bit combative." He shrugged. "It is not unusual."

"How long will you leave him on the ventilator?"

"Only a day or two. He got hard to manage, thrashing about, so we've sedated him to help him tolerate the ventilator and protect him from dangerous rises in his intracerebral pressures."

"The nurse mentioned a femur fracture."

He spoke softly. "Right. The orthopods want to rod his left femur but we wanted to complete his neuro workup first. It looks like his foot is okay. It's a typical mid-shaft fracture, easy to fix for the bone docs, but by the time we okayed him for surgery, they were busy with another." Dr.

Hannah put his hands on his hips. "That's the way it is around here. They'll get to him in an hour or two."

She nodded and slipped the sheet back to uncover John's feet, laying her hand on the top of his left foot near the ankle. He still had a strong pulse in spite of the break.

"When will you know about his brain?" She bit her lower lip, already knowing the answer, but asking hopefully just the same.

"Not until it's safe to take him off the ventilator." He shifted his feet. "Hard to say. I'm guessing a day or two."

A nurse walked to the bedside. "OR estimates they'll be calling for him in two hours. It's time for my hourly assessment. Could you wait in the waiting room again?"

Claire scribbled a name and number on a piece of paper. "Here's where I'll be staying." She pointed at the number. "It's the Holiday Inn down the block. Call me if there are any changes, and as soon as he's going to surgery. I want to be here when he goes in."

The nurse nodded. "Of course."

Claire turned to leave and limped to the doors of the ICU with her hand holding her stomach. Each hour beyond her attack seemed to bring more pain. It was either pain which she had ignored in the intensity of the fight or the kind of pain which is always worse the second day.

As the doors closed behind her, she heard the nurse's voice. "She must have been in the accident too."

Claire limped to the Holiday Inn trying to remember the last time she'd eaten anything solid. She rubbed her stomach. *I ate lunch at the office the day before my appendectomy. No wonder I'm exhausted.*

When was the last time I had a good night's rest? She shook her head. The days and nights were a blur, and it took too much energy and effort to remember.

Once in her room, she slipped off her shoes and closed the drapes. Then she lowered herself to the bed. She turned off the bedside lamp and stared at the ceiling. In spite of her exhaustion, every noise in the hall brought her to alertness and quickened her heart. Images of her attacker interrupted every attempt she made to surrender to sleep. She turned the light back on and doublechecked the locks. After lying down again, she closed her eyes, but every time she did, Cyrus was there.

After twenty minutes, she searched the hotel room, looking carefully in the bathroom behind the curtain, even dropping to her knees to check beneath the bed.

The phone rang at one P.M. They were preparing John for transport to surgery. If she wanted to see him before he left, she'd better hurry.

She looked at the woman staring back at her in the bathroom mirror. "You need makeup," she muttered. Applying lipstick during the walk to the ICU would have to do.

Claire arrived in the ICU ten minutes later, where all John's IV lines and monitoring apparatus had been arranged for transport. She knew all about the spaghetti tangle the lines could get in during a move to and from the OR. It was always the ICU nurse's nightmare to untangle the mess after transport to and from OR or X ray. "Any changes?"

The nurse shook her head. "We've kept him sedated. We'll let him wake up after surgery and see how he is."

Claire nodded and kissed John's cheek. Tears stung her eyes. "I love you," she whispered.

An orthopedic resident clapped his hands together. "Let's roll."

Claire backed up to let them move him out. Just to move a patient like John took a coordinated team. A respiratory therapist ventilated him with a manual bag, a nurse jealously guarded the IVs and watched the cardiac monitor, and a surgical intern and an orderly walked at the head and foot of the bed to push it along.

She stood staring at the spot where the stretcher had disappeared, feeling suddenly very alone. She walked into the hall where she shared hugs with John's parents, Tony and Christine.

Tony held her shoulders and looked into her face. "How are you holding up?"

She bit her lip. "Okay," she offered.

Christine slipped her arm around Claire's waist. "You shouldn't need to stay at a hotel. You belong with us."

"I know I'm welcome, but I need to be near John."

They waited in the ICU waiting room, flipping through outdated magazines. Images of her brother Clay in the ICU, the dreadful waiting as he declined in spite of the efforts of his physicians, added to the ache in the pit of her stomach. In a few minutes they were joined by Phil Carlson, pastor of Community Chapel, the same man who had performed Clay's funeral only a few months ago. He was flanked by Lucy and Margo.

She stood to be enveloped in a bear hug by the gentle man.

"They've just taken him to surgery to fix a fractured femur. They still don't know about his brain."

The trio nodded soberly.

Pastor Phil held up his hands, palms open. "Time to pray."

Claire listened in a daze, hardly able to believe what was happening.

After the prayer, Lucy put her arm around her. "Can you eat? Let's get something in the cafeteria."

"I want to wait for John."

Phil nodded his head toward the hall. "You have time. Besides, you need to stay strong for John."

Stay strong for John. She conceded. "Let's go."

By five P.M., John was back from surgery, and Claire began an evening vigil at his bedside. The sedative medication and all narcotics were withheld. Nothing was to be given after anesthesia. It was time to let him wake up and see how alert he could be off medications.

Claire expected John to do something by an hour, even if it were an attempt for him to breathe on his own above the set ventilator rate. But instead, one hour became two, two became three, and by nine P.M., John hadn't so much as twitched. As the hours rolled on, attention around John intensified and Claire's anxiety rose. "Why isn't he waking up?"

"Maybe the anesthetic is just hanging around longer than usual," the nurse offered.

A new head CT revealed no evidence of change. There was no interval bleeding and no new signs of swelling. The anesthesiology resident and attending stopped by and questioned John's parents about family history of reactions to anesthesia. They had both undergone elective surgery without any anesthetic problems.

Ryan Hannah, the neurosurgery chairman, scratched his head after a careful examination. "His pupils are still pinpoint. So I think he'll come around. He must be sensitive to the narcotics."

Claire liked everything he said except the "I think." She wanted assurances that John would be okay, that he would return to being the same man she knew and loved. But at this point, no one would or could give her that reassurance.

"We can get an EEG tomorrow," Dr. Hannah suggested.

To see if he's brain dead. Claire nodded soberly.

By midnight, Tony gently insisted that Claire get some rest. The nurses promised to call her at the hotel if John made any turn for the worse.

It was only a block, but Tony and Christine drove, and Claire cried. In their presence, she had always been treated, and felt like, a daughter.

"Will you be okay?" Christine asked.

She nodded her silent response.

After a hug, she retreated to her room.

John's life was balanced on a razor-sharp edge. Claire hadn't had a complete night's sleep for three days. She was numb. She undressed and looked at the three Band-Aids on her abdomen. On the day after surgery, she had barely given her own post-operative state a second thought.

She looked at a Gideon-placed Bible on the nightstand. "You've gotten me through tough times before," she whispered. "Through Clay's death, through the discovery of Huntington's disease in Daddy, through Brett's betrayal, and through giving John up once before . . ." Her voice cracked.

She thought back to her last conversation with John and dropped her eyes to the floor and slumped on the edge of the bed.

"I came back here because I thought I could win your trust. Apparently, I was wrong."

"Go ahead, John. You've given it a test. You've tried living around me. It didn't work. Now try living without me again."

She fell sideways onto the bed and curled up, hugging one of the large pillows. Weeping, she prayed, "Please God, give me another chance."

Chapter Twenty-Nine

laire slept fitfully with the lights on, waking frequently from imagined dangers lurking in the hotel closets. She watched the eerie green glowing numbers of the clock change from twelve to one to two and three before her mind allowed her body more than one hour of uninterrupted sleep. The following morning, Claire awoke with the first rays of sunlight streaming through the thin curtain liner, feeling more exhausted than renewed. She hadn't been called all night. She hoped that was good news. She showered and was preparing to leave when the phone rang.

It was Christine, John's mother. "John's nurse just called. He's waking up. He's been moving his arms and legs. She thinks they'll get the tube out of his throat this morning."

Why didn't the nurse call me? "That's great." Claire took a deep breath. "I'm on my way to see him now."

"We can pick you up."

"I want to walk. I'm feeling fine."

Ten minutes later, Claire purchased a tall cup of coffee from a street vendor in front of the hospital. Five minutes after that, she was at John's bedside.

She squeezed his hand.

He opened his eyes. Recognition flashed. His eyes got bigger. He stared at Claire and wiggled his head, working his tongue along the endotracheal tube and the tape that held it in place.

"Easy, John," she coached, as her voice began to thicken. "It's a tube in your windpipe to help you breathe. You had a car accident." She sniffed. *He knows me!*

He shook his head again, this time a bit more enthusiastically.

A nurse came up behind Claire. "When he woke up," she said, pointing to the wrist and ankle restraints, "he really woke up."

"He's fighting the tube. He should be taken off the ventilator."

"We'll have to wait for the neurosurgery team to round."

Claire held her tongue. The nurse should be able to call a doc to get an order to remove the tube. "Why wasn't I told about his improvement?"

The nurse squinted. "You're his wife?"

"His girlfriend."

"Oh, we have a policy of only calling blood relatives with information. Mr. Cerelli's parents were given the updates."

She looked at her watch, then looked up to see Ryan Hannah and his entourage of residents and students come through the double doors. Claire stood aside as Dr. Hannah quizzed the team on everything from expected outcomes from closed head injuries to ventilator management. After they moved on to the next patient beyond John, an intern held back to pull out John's endotracheal tube.

"Cough," he instructed as he slipped out the tube.

John looked at Claire. "Where am I?"

"Brighton. At the University Hospital."

"What happened?"

"You had a car accident. You rolled your Mustang in front of my house."

"My Mustang? How is it?"

"Totaled, John, but you're okay."

A four-letter word slipped from his lips. "I loved that car!" Tears welled in his eyes, before he cursed again.

She frowned. "It can be replaced. At least you're okay." She looked up to see Tony and Christine. "John, your parents are here."

"My car!"

Christine cradled her son's face. "Oh, John, we thought we'd lost you." Christine started crying.

John tugged against the wrist restraints. "Untie my hands, would you?"

Christine put her hands to her mouth and looked at Claire. "Do you think we should?"

"I'm sure it's okay. They just wanted to keep him from pulling out the tube. Now that it's out, I'm sure it doesn't matter."

"Take the restraints home, Claire. I can tie you to the bed and—"

"John!" Claire gasped.

He shrugged his shoulders. "What?"

Claire felt her cheeks redden and exchanged glances with Christine. Then she undid the wrist restraints.

John pulled away the gauze from under his nose, then touched his scalp. "What happened to my hair?" Tears began to well in his eyes again.

"You were in a car accident, John. You have a skull fracture and a concussion. Your scalp was badly cut. They had to shave part of your hair to repair the laceration."

He explored his head with his fingers. "I want a mirror."

Tony smiled. "Believe me, son. You *don't* want a mirror."

John dropped another curse word as casually as an overworked sailor.

This time it was Tony and Claire who traded concerned glances. As the hour passed, John burped loudly, passed gas, cursed, and scratched private places without regard to those around.

By the afternoon, when Pastor Phil and his wife, Debbie, were visiting, John chose the middle of a prayer of thanksgiving to use the urinal, and did so in front of the pastor's wife without asking to be excused. When they finished praying, John asked Debbie to set the still-warm container on the bedside table because he couldn't reach.

Claire was mortified and quickly covered John up again with a sheet and took the urinal herself. Clearly this was John. He had the same appearance, the same voice, the same sense of humor, but whatever proper inhibitions he had garnered in his upbringing had vanished with the blow to his head.

By noon, John had been unreasonable to the nurses, commented to Claire about the young nurse's anatomy, and picked his nose quite successfully right in front of her.

When she protested, John just didn't get it. He acted as if everyone did those things. Claire tested his memory and it seemed intact, right up until his trip back to Stoney Creek. At that point, he became concerned. "You had surgery, didn't you?"

She nodded and waited for him to express some concern, but it never came.

When she joined Tony and Christine in the ICU waiting area a few minutes later, John's mother was in tears. Claire had little comfort to offer.

She sat in the chair beside Christine and cried tears of her own. It was as if someone had stolen the John they knew and substituted a Beavis and Butthead version.

Ryan Hannah met with them in the afternoon. "John has lost some of his social inhibitions," he began. "But this is very common following frontal lobe contusions."

Claire folded her hands together. "This will go away . . . right?"

"Most do."

She hated the way he left room for John to be a permanent social misfit.

"He may normalize over a few days to weeks or . . ." The neurosurgeon shrugged. "Rare cases have been known to have trouble adjusting back into normal society without significant problems."

"He doesn't act like he's doing anything abnormal."

"Exactly," explained Dr. Hannah. "For now, he's lost the ability to understand that certain things are socially unacceptable."

Christine wiped her eyes. "He was always so polite."

Dr. Hannah nodded. "He still is, Ms. Cerelli. He's the same man, but he's suffering from a frontal brain contusion."

Tony Cerelli touched Claire's shoulder. "I know this seems horrible, but remember only yesterday, we didn't even know if he would survive. If he survived, we had no reassurance that he wouldn't be a total vegetable."

Dr. Hannah agreed. "This is good news, really. I'd much rather be discussing these minor personality problems than whether John might never walk, talk, or swallow again." He hung his head. "Some weeks it seems that's all I do."

Tony shook the neurosurgeon's hand. "It's just the first day. He'll get better."

Claire watched with moist eyes. It was just like Tony to be encouraging the surgeon. *Tony, the eternal optimist.*

Dr. Hannah excused himself and Tony sat beside Claire. "Why don't you slip back to your hotel room? We'll watch John. You need your rest."

She shook her head. "I can't sleep alone in that room." Her eyes brimmed with tears.

Christine flanked Claire on the other side. "We've been so concerned about John, we haven't even talked about you. Did you sleep last night?"

"Very little." Claire dropped her head in her hands. "Every time I close my eyes, I see . . ."

"The attack? Do you want to talk about it?"

She shook her head and just started to cry. She fell into Christine's embrace and sobbed with all the emotions she'd been holding in as her attention had been focused on John.

Christine rocked her like a child, holding her head to her chest and brushing her tears away. Claire cried for the disgrace she felt as a victim, for the hatred she felt toward Cyrus, for the fear that held her captive. She cried for her father whom she'd let down and for John and the loss of his dignity.

When she straightened again to blow her nose, she saw Della, her eyes red and her hand held to her lips. "Is John . . . ?"

Tony stepped up and greeted Della with a hug. "He's fine. He's had his bell rung pretty good."

"Then why . . . ?" Della's eyes fell upon Claire.

Tony smiled. "It's been a rough couple days. But God will see us all through," he said, looking at Claire. He lifted Christine by the hand. "Why don't you and Della take Claire back to our place and put her to bed for a few hours? I will stay here with John and join you around dinner-time. Then Claire can come back and visit with John again tonight."

It was a good plan. Claire needed rest. The Cerellis were a godsend.

Claire took a week off from the clinic after her appendectomy, a week she spent in Brighton attending to John. She encouraged him through his physical therapy sessions, washed his hair, reminded him of old times they spent together in Brighton, and in general saw more and more of the old John shining through. After two days, he didn't remember the urinal incident and seemed embarrassed when Claire recounted the event. After a week, other than subtleties, Claire was convinced John was on the right path. The horrible fright that John would be a social misfit for life was finally receding.

For Claire, Christine, and Tony, the first week following John's accident was a roller-coaster ride of rising dread, sudden fear, and exhilaration at the realization of recovery. She knew the neurosurgery carnival ride to be unpredictable. She had ridden it only once before, when she and her family kept a vigil at the bedside of her twin. But she had observed the process dozens of times while caring for brain-injured patients during her surgical internship in Boston. For days, families agonize over little or no recovery in their loved ones. Fears and expectations build as imaginations take over and worst-case-scenario outcomes are anticipated. Then, for some, the days of rising dread are dissipated in the realization of a sudden improvement. For others, the recovery comes in awkward lurches, without rhythm. For still others, the first week following brain injury is a steep slide ending in brain-death. For days, Claire felt she wore a blindfold, riding the roller coaster in complete darkness, the next rise, fall, or turn completely hidden from view.

For Claire and John, it was a dual recovery, she from her appendectomy and rape attempt, and he from his accident. It was a time to vent and to heal. Day after day, without agenda or hurried schedule, their time became a marathon of memories about their past together. It seemed no subject from the past was off limits. Only a formal discussion of their future, and Claire's gene status, did they deftly avoid. That was an iceberg looming large and threatening, yet silent and shielded by the fog. The other thing she refused to bring up was the diamond ring she'd seen on Lena. That was one subject she wanted John to bring up on his own.

Two weeks after she returned to work, Claire sat at the kitchen table with a medicine text open in front of her. She pushed the heavy book away when Della entered.

"I've been talking to Ginny at the genetics clinic."

Della nodded and waited for more. "And?"

"I want to get my test results." Claire paused. "I've made an appointment."

Della sat across from Claire. "What makes you think you're ready this time?"

Claire took a deep breath. "I want to know so I can prepare for the future."

"John finally convinced you, huh?"

"He hasn't said anything about it. I think he's trying a new tactic of silence."

"Silence?"

Claire shrugged. "I know how he feels. I guess he doesn't think it will help to keep bugging me."

"Do you really think you know his heart? Do you know what John wants for the future?"

"When John first moved to Stoney Creek, I was convinced he knew we were a match." Claire closed the textbook. "But now I think he was just doing what seemed natural to him. He was giving it a trial to see if it would work. I think he wanted to be close to Wally, to see if he could handle a life like you've had."

"He's great with Wally."

"I know. I see that. He's patient, so patient with him, but it's different if you're married. You can't walk away like he does now."

"So you think he's decided he can't handle it if you test positive?"

"He's had ample opportunity to ask me to marry. It's obvious he's holding back for a reason."

"So what's changed? Why do you want to be tested now?"

"Always before, I was looking for a commitment from John first, worried that if I was positive, I'd lose him."

"What's changed?"

"When John was ill, lying in the hospital on a ventilator, recovering from his accident, my focus changed. Suddenly I seemed to understand what you and Abby have been talking about. Marriage isn't about what I can get from John, it's about dying to myself and giving myself away. For the first time, I wanted to know if I was going to be able to take care of John. I was suddenly looking at a situation where I didn't know if he might need some form of continuous care . . . and I wondered whether I would be able to provide it."

"So, how does getting your test results play into this?"

"If I test negative, I know I can give myself to John." She smiled. "If he'll have me, of course.

"If I test positive for the Huntington's gene, I won't ask John to make the choice to leave. I think I'll encourage John to move on. He needs to find a life beyond me. I think he knows he couldn't handle a life like that. I don't want to saddle him with caring for me." She gave her mother's hand a squeeze. "I see what Wally put you through. I can't do that to John."

Della nodded. "Life with Wally has not been all bad."

"But it's not a life you'd have chosen."

"If I'd been given a chance to choose, which we're not. God reveals some things to us in his timing for our good. We would never choose hardship, but it is the trials that bring the sweetest character."

"I want you to go with me."

"What about John?"

"Ginny wants me to have someone for support. I don't want John there to find out right away. I want to find out first, then help him to move on if I'm positive before he finds out."

"You think he'll be willing to move on after all you've been through?"

Claire nodded resolutely. "I think John's mature enough to know he couldn't make it if I'm HD positive. I'll make him go. I think I love him enough to make sure he doesn't have to take care of me."

Della shrugged. "I'll be with you if you want. When's the new D day?"

"Friday afternoon."

Della stood and smiled. "You've finally figured it out."

"What?"

Her mother disappeared into the hallway, but called out her answer. "A successful marriage is about dying to your own wants."

Chapter Thirty

For Claire, D day number two began with a short run, in which she refused to count trucks or cars. Today was not to be a day tainted by superstitious obsessions. Today, she decided, come good news or bad, would be a day of trust.

After preparing to leave, she sat on the couch and opened her Bible to reread a passage she'd shared with her own patients so many times the book practically fell open to the exact page.

"Who shall separate us from the love of Christ? . . . I am sure that neither death nor life, nor angels nor rulers, nor powers, nor height nor depth, nor anything else in all creation, will be able to separate us from the love of God in Christ Jesus our Lord."

"Talking to yourself?"

Claire looked up at the sound of Della's voice. "I'm hoping that reading it, speaking it, and hearing it all at the same time might help it sink in."

Della smiled. "Ready?"

Claire gently closed the leather cover of her Bible. "Let's roll."

Claire sat quietly beside Della across the desk from Ginny, who smiled broadly.

"What do you think?" The genetics counselor made an exaggerated grin.

"You got your braces off!" Claire leaned forward.

"Tuesday. Now I just have to wear a retainer."

"You look great."

"I look older!" she said. "There's nothing like braces to make you look young." She laughed, lifting up her gray-streaked braid. "I really felt young sitting in my orthodontist's waiting room."

Della smiled. "I'll bet."

The trio fell silent, knowing the light conversation was just a compulsory warmup. Claire looked around the room. Everything was just as she remembered it. The African motif, the carved animals, the old oak desk without clutter . . . everything. It felt strangely as if she'd never left Ginny's office, that the horrible events of the preceding weeks hadn't occurred. The only difference was that now Della, instead of John, sat to her left, and there wasn't a diamond ring about to be placed upon her finger.

Ginny looked up. "How's John?"

"Better. He's walking with a cane."

"Well," she said, lifting a folder from the desk, "this is what we're here for." She made eye contact with Claire. "I don't need to remind you that we're available to work through any issues you encounter, whether your test is positive or negative."

Claire closed her eyes, feeling a rush of insecurity. Did she really want to know the future? Could she handle knowing?

She opened her eyes and nodded at Ginny. She could do this, she told herself. *Nothing can separate me from the love of God.*

Ginny handed her a piece of paper. Claire carefully unfolded it. She'd rehearsed this moment in her mind a thousand times, reacting to good news, reacting to bad.

She made eye contact with her mom, who nodded her encouragement. Claire looked at the sheet, her eyes falling on the word written in the right-hand column across from the wording, "Huntington's disease gene assay."

Positive.

She handed the paper to her mom, who, unlike Claire, could not hold her tears. Claire would not let herself weep. She knew there would be enough tears in her future. After all the anticipation, she felt exactly numb. She knew if she was negative, she would cry from relief, for the ability to finally let go a fear that had tightened her gut for months. With the news that she was positive, she felt no surge of bad news, only the affirmation of the cloud that she'd walked under for so long.

Claire stood and looked at Ginny. "We'll talk." Then, she reached out to Della, who sat sobbing softly. "It'll be okay, Mom. Let's go."

She didn't want to fall into her mother's arms. She hugged her lightly before separating and holding the door. Claire wanted only to be alone, perhaps to pray and consider what this news meant to her life.

She would not give up. She'd decided that months ago. She would meet this challenge the way she'd met earlier ones. Headfirst, without hesitation. She would continue to work; after all, she was the same competent physician she was before she knew her gene status.

But one thing would have to change, and that would be the most painful. She loved John Cerelli too much to behave differently. She had to make him go away.

Claire drove home with Della curled into the seat beside her, silent except for an occasional gasp that comes when you're finishing up a good cry. Claire mused about her career, glad to have some objective problem she needed to solve. Even if the decision of what to do with her life was totally wrapped up in her gene status, at least formulating a plan of action kept her from obsessing about withering away in a nursing home, dancing like Wally.

She'd had months to think about it. Today was not to be a day of sudden decisions. Today was merely meeting a fork in the myriad of decision trees that hinged on her Huntington's disease gene status: If positive, go left; if negative, go right. She'd decided weeks ago that a positive meant leaving her career in surgery. Her patients would be at risk; she'd be uninsurable by any knowing malpractice carrier; and the years of training were too long to give her a reasonable expectation of practice life before she faced a forced retirement. So, as she weaved up the snake of a road over North Mountain, she resolutely stated her first D day decision: "I'm not going back into surgery."

Della nodded her head and sniffed. "Y—you love surgery."

"But I have also grown to love these people in Stoney Creek. I understand them. I can help them."

"I know you can."

Claire held her hand out at arm's length, steering with her left hand on the wheel. She stared at her hand for a moment. There was no movement, no drift. Not a single tremor or twitch. She had complete control. "I'll need some additional training in family medicine if I want to stay at the clinic."

"Keep your hands on the wheel."

Claire sighed and obeyed.

"I want to apply for a family medicine residency. With credit for my internship training at Lafayette, I should be able to finish in two years."

"You shouldn't make rash decisions today. How can you talk this way so soon after . . ." Her voice faded before continuing with a sob. ". . . finding out your results?"

"This isn't a rash decision. I've been thinking about this for months."

Della steadied her voice. "The folks in Stoney Creek can't afford to be without a doctor if you leave."

"I want to set up a meeting between Dr. Jenkins and Dr. Marsh, the head of family medicine at Brighton University. The Stoney Creek clinic would be a perfect site for resident training. If the university would provide attending coverage, our clinic could be run by residents." She nodded. "I could even keep working there on some rotations and then once I've completed my training, I could supervise the residents myself until . . ."

"Jimmy isn't likely to look kindly to a tight relationship with the university. He's always had an attitude about 'the Ivory Tower.'"

"He'll have to get over it if he wants to sell his practice. He's been looking for a long time for someone to take over. No one is biting. Everyone wants to practice where the money is best."

"I suppose if anyone can make him think seriously about this plan of yours, it's you. He adores you. Always has."

"I know."

Claire downshifted the Volkswagon as the grade steepened, forcing the engine to rev higher and work a little harder. She listened to the whine of the little powerplant until Della placed her hand over Claire's as it rested on the gearshift. Her mother spoke in a winsome tone. "Unraveling the mystery of the Stoney Creek curse has been hard on Dr. Jenkins."

Claire waited for her mother to explain.

"Until you forced everything into the open, I think Jimmy always believed you were his daughter." She huffed. "At least he wanted to believe it."

"What makes—"

"He came to all your high school games, Claire. He always cheered the loudest when you succeeded and he bragged the most when you went off to Brighton for medical school." She patted Claire's hand. "I think you burst his little fantasy that he had fathered the most beautiful woman in Stoney Creek."

Suddenly Claire found her own eyes tearing. "That's silly."

"Not really."

They passed the summit and started the winding descent toward Fisher's Retreat. "Today, I wish he would have been right."

Della shook her head. "It took Wally McCall's genes to make you who you are. Every strength. Every weakness."

When they finally slowed to turn into the lane leading up to their home, a second car pulled in right behind them. "Mom, look. It's Grandma Elizabeth."

"She's in Martha's Vineyard."

Claire shook her head. "Don't tell her about my test. I'll tell her when I'm ready."

"Of course." The car stopped and the duo got out with gaping mouths.

They watched as Elizabeth pulled in. Claire squealed. "Grandma, what are you doing here?"

Elizabeth lowered her window and shook her head in apparent disgust. "Doesn't anyone in my dysfunctional family talk to each other?"

Claire and Della exchanged glances.

Elizabeth snorted. "Your aunt Gracie called me last night. Your uncle Leon is dead."

Chapter Thirty-One

randma Elizabeth tilted her head to the side as she sat at Della's kitchen table. "Where's Wally?"

"Pleasant View."

Elizabeth nodded. "Good."

Claire poured her grandmother a glass of sweetened iced tea. "What happened to Uncle Leon?"

"Gracie found him in his study, slumped over an account ledger for the business."

Claire winced. "Suicide?"

"The medical examiner is looking into it. Gracie thought he'd been drinking, maybe taking some sleeping pills. There wasn't an empty bottle lying around or anything, so it's going to be a mystery until we get the lab results back from the medical examiner."

"I guess you know he sold the business."

Elizabeth shook her head. "Gracie told me the deal went sour at the last minute."

"It did? But Mr. Sugimoto said—" Claire put her hand to her mouth.

Elizabeth's eye's narrowed. "You know Mr. Sugimoto? Did you know about this deal?"

"I heard about the possible sale from Mr. Sugimoto, but when I first asked Mom if she knew anything about it, you'd already sold your stock to Uncle Leon."

Elizabeth sighed. "Leon had to know about this deal before he bought me out." She shook her head. "Your grandfather would roll over in his grave if he knew."

"When did the deal fall through?"

"Just a few days ago. Evidently the Japanese buyer got cold feet at the last minute."

Claire looked away and held her thoughts to herself. *Mr. Sugimoto asked me so many questions about the family business. I told him that Uncle Leon had just bought out Grandma Elizabeth's stock. I wonder if seeing the way Uncle Leon treated his family made Mr. Sugimoto nervous about doing business with him.*

Della reached for Elizabeth's hand. "I'm so sorry."

"Don't be sorry for me," Elizabeth responded. "I learned a long time ago that parents can rarely take full credit for their children's successes."

Claire winked at Della and whispered, "Sorry, Mom."

Elizabeth continued, "Likewise, parents can't take full blame for their children's failures."

"Has anyone made any funeral arrangements?"

"Gracie is doing that. There is a memorial at Community Chapel on Sunday afternoon. The graveside service for the family will be at two. The memorial is at four."

Claire's cell phone began an electronic song, "Take Me Out to the Ballgame."

She stood and retrieved it from her purse, and walked into the front room. "Hello."

It was John. "Hey, babe. I called your office. I didn't know you were off."

"Yeah. Um. Mom and I had some stuff to do. We needed some time together."

John was quiet for a moment. "Will you be coming over to Brighton? We could grab dinner out, maybe catch a movie. The old downtown theatre is showing a French film."

"I don't know, John. I just found out my uncle Leon died. Maybe I should stay around here for the family."

Elizabeth called out from the kitchen. "Don't stay here for my sake. Go see that man of yours."

Claire focused her attention back to the phone to hear John. "Your uncle Leon? What happened?"

"No one knows. Maybe he just had a sudden MI or a stroke or something. His wife found him slumped at his desk."

"I'm sorry, Claire."

She lowered her voice. "It's not like we were close."

"What will happen to McCall Shoes?"

"I'm not sure." She paused. "Listen, John, I was planning to come up to Brighton this weekend, but, with everything that's going on here, I think I'd better stick around."

"I'll come over for the funeral. When is it?"

"Sunday, but stay in Brighton, John. You hardly knew my uncle."

"But I want to be there for you. To be with your family."

"You're not up to driving. People will understand if you don't show."

"But I—"

"I'll be tied up with everyone asking about Uncle Leon. I'll come up to see you on Monday evening."

John pouted. "I can tell when I'm not wanted."

Oh, you're wanted. I just need to make a break from you. You need to get used to being without me.

She didn't know how to respond. "Funny. I'll see you Monday." She made a noisy kiss into the phone and pressed a red button to terminate the call.

She looked back into the kitchen to see her grandma with her head in her hands. Claire moaned. Her life seemed to flow from crisis to crisis. She closed her eyes and reminded herself of the verse she'd started her day with. "Nothing can separate me from the love of God," she whispered. She had to believe it. *Our pain has to have a purpose.* A loving God wouldn't have it otherwise.

Wally McCall hadn't been seen in public for months. He hadn't even been in a chair for six weeks, but when he heard that his brother Leon was going to be memorialized, he insisted on attending. Della claimed it was revenge on the brother who'd always despised him. Margo refused to go if her father was going, so Della invited her not to attend. He was Wally's only brother. If he wanted to go to the funeral, she was going to get him there. Period.

It took an ambulance crew to get him to the service and a generous supply of six-inch velcro straps to secure Wally to the chair. Della pushed him up the aisle herself, parking him in the center aisle next to Claire.

343

Claire watched him from the corner of her eye as Pastor Phil Carlson pulled out all the stops in an attempt to say something nice about the uncle Claire always called Moneybags.

"Leon worked hard to bring jobs and recovery to this valley. His dedication to the people of Stoney Creek will certainly be missed."

Wally twitched and heaved his body forward against the velcro strap.

Claire winced and glanced over her shoulder to the standing-room-only crowd. Benches were filled with employees from the McCall Shoe factory. Obligation rather than love filled the sanctuary.

Wally pitched his head right and left and slipped an inch lower in the wheelchair.

"I first met Leon the first week I came to town. He introduced himself and measured my foot himself, right back there in the pastor's study. A week later, and about every year since then, I've gotten a brand new pair of McCall dress shoes." He paused. "Sized nine, double E, brown leather wingtips, if anyone is interested," he added with a wink. A murmur of polite laughter rippled across the solemn crowd.

Wally slipped another inch. Claire wondered what to do. If he kept going, he could be choked against the top velcro chest strap. Fortunately, it seemed he had lodged against a second strap which was snug against his lower abdomen. Claire winced and hoped the velcro would hold. Pulling her father up in front of all these people would be a giant flail.

"Leon has left a legacy which has helped . . ."

Wally let out a garbled scream as his abdominal strap popped free, sending him into a free-slide toward the floor. His chin lodged in the chest strap as he let out a garbled, "Ahhh!"

Claire and Della scrambled to their feet. Wally's eyes were bulging as his weight pulled the strap tight against his neck. He sputtered as Claire grabbed her father beneath the armpits. "Grab behind his knees," Claire whispered. The sanctuary, including Pastor Phil, fell silent. Wally's foot lurched forward striking Della in the knee and sending a gasp from the audience. With a quick coordinated effort, the duo managed to get a strap around Wally's waist. Then, without pausing, Claire unlocked the wheels and began slowly wheeling her father up the center aisle, occasionally making eye contact with someone she recognized, nodding her head seriously as if nothing had happened at all.

As they entered the foyer, Claire heard a small snicker escape from Della. They exchanged smiles and covered their mouths. Claire sped to the exit, pushing Wally faster so she could get outside before she exploded. Della knew what was coming, and dashed ahead to hold the door. Once the door was shut, Claire dared to look at her mother's reddening face. Della doubled over, holding her stomach, laughter spilling out in an irreverent eruption shared by mother and daughter.

Claire blotted her eyes of the tears of laughter that threatened her mascara. It could have been a sober embarrassment. But for some reason, the event just struck them in a funny way, and provided the needed release from a stressful service.

When Della finally gained a semblance of control, she looked at Wally, who sat with a blank stare on his face. "You did it, Wally. You made quite a scene at Leon's funeral, didn't you? You got the old son of a gun back for the way he treated you."

Wally grinned.

Claire watched. "You did that on purpose, didn't you, Daddy?"

The thought made Claire laugh harder. Della cried. "Oooh-wee!"

Just then, someone with a black dress slipped through the door. The woman glanced with disdain, then cupped her hand around a cigarette she held to her lips. After a few moments, the woman was joined by a man in a black suit which appeared a size too large, the shoulders extending too far from his upper arms like pads for a football game, making his head look small and out of place. He called to the woman, "Couldn't you wait?"

"He's your client, not mine." She pulled hard on the cigarette and blew smoke toward the little man's face.

He frowned before looking over to see Claire and her parents and lifted his head in recognition. He placed his hand over his upper lip and squinted, before clearing his throat and stepping toward them. He addressed only Claire and held out his hand. "Doctor McCall," he said, smiling broadly. "I'm Alfred Pittington. I worked with your Uncle Leon."

"I know you," Claire responded. She took his hand for a second before replacing it on Wally's shoulder. "These are my parents. Wally is Leon's brother. Della is my mother."

Alfred nodded briefly at Wally, then took Della's hand, holding it for a moment as he spoke. "You have my deepest sympathy in what must be a difficult time in your family."

Claire wondered if he spoke of Leon's passing or about Wally's condition. She watched as Alfred turned his attention back to Claire. "May we speak privately for a moment?"

She shrugged and took a few steps to the side, following Alfred into the parking lot to stand behind a large silver Mercedes.

Alfred cleared his throat. Sweat beaded the top of his balding head, reflecting the light of the afternoon sun. "Your uncle thought an awful lot of you. He spoke of you often. Your accomplishments are an example to so many in this town."

Claire felt her defenses rise. Butter should be used for pancakes or Della's biscuits, not for greasing the wheels of business. She nodded without speaking.

The attorney continued. "I'm sure you know of your uncle's recent business proposal for McCall Shoes." He cleared his throat again. "Mr. Sugimoto indicated as much."

"I know only that he was planning to sell the family business. And recently I heard that the deal fell through. That's all." She shrugged.

"You've treated Mr. Sugimoto."

"Is that a question? You understand doctor-patient confidentiality."

His lips tightened. "Is that a question?"

"A statement."

"I see." He shuffled his feet, moving a cigarette butt to the side with his glossy black shoes. "The plant will close, Claire." He paused.

"What is that to me?"

"I think you care about this town."

Claire didn't see a connection. She waited for Alfred to make it for her.

"I need you to talk to Mr. Sugimoto. Come to the negotiation table with us, for the benefit of the town. Mr. Sugimoto seems to respect you." He looked down. "Something, I'm afraid, that he did not have for your uncle."

"You are concerned about this town? Or your own wallet?"

Mr. Pittington kept his face to the ground, allowing Claire a chance to inspect a hairy brown mole on the top of his scalp. He lifted his eyes. "A little of both."

346

"You were helping negotiate the deal with Mr. Sugimoto?"

He nodded.

"And what about my uncle's buyout of Grandma Elizabeth? I suppose you spearheaded that as well?"

His jaw clenched. "I was obligated to give advice on all of his business deals."

"What can I do?" She shook her head. "I'm a physician. Not a businessperson."

"Convince Mr. Sugimoto to give our company another look."

Claire took a step back. Alfred Pittington was an oily fish. Everyone in Stoney Creek knew that.

"It will save hundreds of jobs for this town. You know if the shoe plant closes, our town will dry up."

"The poultry industry is hiring."

"McCall Shoes helped define Stoney Creek. It set us apart."

She knew that much to be true. She didn't want the company to go under. "What makes you so sure Mr. Sugimoto will listen to me?"

"He mentioned you several times. He expressed regret to what his decision might mean to you. I think he had plans for supporting a local program to help those affected by . . ." He strained to look across the parking lot to where Wally was sitting in his wheelchair. "You know . . . Huntington's."

"Mr. Sugimoto seems to carry an air of decency and respect with him." She wanted to add, "which this business desperately needs," but held her tongue.

"Would you talk to him?" He hesitated. "Do you care about Stoney Creek or not?"

She followed his gaze to her father. Wally's head was in motion, a plane in a constant holding-circle pattern above an airport that never closed.

Claire looked back at the lawyer and felt her grit rise. "I'll agree to help only under very special circumstances. And you'd have to agree to my stipulations."

His eyes met hers, held, then broke away. "Such as?"

"My grandmother must be reinstated to the board, at least until after any transition. All of the stock which Leon bought from her must be sold back to her at its present value."

"The company is on the verge of chapter eleven."

"So her buy-in will be cheap." Claire smiled. "And you will remove yourself from the case. I will select an attorney to represent my grandmother and McCall Shoes to walk the company through a buyout."

"But I've given the best part of my career to—"

"I've heard all about your career, Mr. Pittington. But anyone who would sit by and help my uncle cheat his own mother is not going to work this deal."

He scoffed. "That's ridiculous!"

She looked away at her father again before poising Alfred's question back to him. "Do *you* care about Stoney Creek or not?"

"Of course, I—"

"Then do the right thing. Bring my grandmother back in. And I'll talk to Mr. Sugimoto."

She pivoted to leave. She wasn't going to negotiate. She had to walk away. As a McCall, for the sake of the company bearing her name, she couldn't see another way.

"Come on, Mom," she called. "Let's get Daddy back inside."

Chapter Thirty-Two

arly Sunday morning, Claire opened her eyes to the first rays of the sun painting the sky a palate of red and orange over North Mountain. *D day plus two.* She took a deep breath, sampling the summer air through her open window. She was the same Claire she'd always been. D day hadn't changed anything. Or had it?

She stretched her arms over her head as the realization dawned. The cloud was gone. The anxiety over an uncertain future had been replaced by a promise. *Nothing can separate me from the love of God.*

But an issue remained. John Cerelli. He had been the gift of grace Claire needed to see her through tough years at Brighton University. He had not faltered in spite of Claire's unfaithfulness to their relationship in Boston. She knew, beyond all doubts, that she loved him. Nearly losing him, facing the possibility of a life caring for John in a physically disabled state, had cemented her understanding that what they had together ran much deeper than casual commitment. She loved him. *Loved* him. And because of that, she knew the next step would be the most difficult. She could not take John into a forever-relationship, knowing the pathway would be marked by eventual suffering, dotted with the potholes of agony dealt by a cruel, unrelenting enemy, the enemy she called HD.

But something else had changed in Claire, even before D day. While assisting John through rehab, she'd had a true paradigm shift in her thinking. Before, when she went with John to get her gene test results, her heart's desire had been focused on whether John's love would be unconditional through the fire of HD. The rise and fall of her happiness swelled up or down with the tide of what she thought John was bringing to their relationship. Could John be trusted to love for better or for worse, in sickness and in health?

She stood and glanced at her reflection in the mirror. The woman looking back was wiser than the one who'd left Boston. This woman, this physician, was beginning to see that a long-term love commitment begins with a focus on the other. True love meant being concerned for John first. She smiled. It was not the smile of giddy happiness, but a smile born of maturity, a wisdom birthed from the understanding that God's love would carry her through even the most difficult life decisions. Her love for John Cerelli had blossomed to the point where she wanted to protect the one she loved from pain.

The cloud was gone. But a promise of God's love remained. Nothing that came her way could change that. She loved John. And because of that, she needed to set him free.

She dressed and made small talk with her mom over a cup of coffee with French vanilla creamer. They had jumped from crisis to crisis so quickly that they'd never debriefed together after learning Claire's HD status. But she didn't feel like talking it out with her mother. In many ways, she felt the news was a bigger blow to Della than to her. After all, many spouses who buried mates stricken with HD also buried their children after watching them suffer a similar fate.

Claire set down her mug. "I'm staying home this morning."

"Tired?"

She shook her head. "I just want to be alone."

Della nodded. "I'm going. I'm making up for lost time. I missed so many Sundays watchin' Wally that half the congregation thinks I'm a visitor." She paused. "Pastor Phil is teaching through Galatians. I'm in need of another dose of grace."

"I'm sure it will be great." She sighed. "But I need time to process some things on my own before I just answer 'fine' to a hundred inquiries of 'How are you?'"

"Shall we meet for lunch?"

"I need to go to Brighton."

Della's brow wrinkled. "What will you tell John?"

Claire looked down and swirled the creamy liquid in the bottom of her mug. She spoke in a monotone. "What I have to tell him."

"You love him."

Claire tried to keep her lip from quivering. "I love—" Her voice halted. "That's not the issue. Of course I love him."

"Nothing has changed, Claire. The man loves you, too. Knowing your gene status won't change anything."

Claire stayed quiet and shook her head. She didn't really believe what her mother said. As much as she wanted to believe that John would still want her, a nagging doubt remained. If John wanted to marry her regardless of her HD status, he would have given her the ring before she went to get her HD test.

"It doesn't really matter what he wants. If I really love him . . ." She paused. "I can't put him through a life like you had."

"You are nothing like your father, Claire. Life with you would be different."

"I'm destined to a life of progressive mental decline, personality changes, and a loss of control of my voluntary muscles."

"You sound like a doctor."

"I am a doctor, Mom."

"Doctors don't know everything. You have no absolute knowledge of the future."

Claire held up her hands. "You're right. All I have are best guesses, based on science."

"Don't throw love away just because you know you carry the HD gene. God brought you and John together for a reason."

"He won't want me."

Della pointed and raised her voice. "You don't know that!"

She shrugged and stood up. "It's moot. I'm going to be sure he moves on with his life."

Claire started down the hall to her room, with Della calling out behind her. "Don't do this, Claire. Don't make yourself a martyr. Huntington's is threat enough on its own. Why heap more misery on your life by turning away love?"

Claire whirled around to scream her response, then softened when she saw the tears in her mother's eyes. She lowered her voice in midsentence. "Loving John means I'll protect him from pain."

Della followed Claire into the hall, then pushed past her toward the opening to her room. "Within the contrast of pain, love finds its tenderest expression."

Claire let the words hang without response. From the context of the life Della had lived, there was little Claire could add. Instead, she nodded and entered the solitude of her little room.

⁓⸎⸎⸍

That afternoon, Claire found John Cerelli absorbed in a thriller, seated in the screened-in gazebo behind his parents' home. His left leg was out on the bench beside him, propped on two pillows. He held a quart-sized plastic container with a bendable straw exiting the cap. Overhead, a ceiling fan stirred the languid summer air.

Claire studied his image for a moment before revealing her arrival. John appeared the picture of contentment. She took a deep breath. *D day plus two. The shelling begins anew.* "Knock, knock," she called.

His face brightened. Even the perils of the protagonist couldn't compete with Claire for John's attention. "Hey, babe."

She slipped in and sat across from him, avoiding their usual kiss. Her heart ached. "Hi."

He squinted and laid the book aside. "What's up, Claire?"

She hadn't yet decided upon an opening line. She wanted to avoid tears, but already she felt a waterfall of Niagara force threatening to break. Her eyes began to mist. She sniffed and turned away. She reached for his cane and bounced the rubber stopper up and down on the wooden floor. "How's rehab?"

He leaned forward. He wasn't going to fall for a small-talk entry. "Claire, what's on your mind? You didn't want me at your uncle's funeral service. You call to say you want to get together, but you refuse to come to Sunday dinner with my family, and you don't want to go to the mall so I can get some walking in." His eyes were intense.

When she looked his way, his gaze was unflinching. She took another deep breath. "I just wanted to talk to you alone. We need some time together." She hesitated. "I didn't want to be in a crowd. Not even with your folks."

He leaned back. "So let's talk." He set down his drink and folded his arms across his chest.

She bounced the cane a few more times and wished he'd keep talking. He didn't.

"Look, John. I've been thinking about us. Our future."

He kept his eyes on her face, forcing her to be the one to break away.

"I think your decision to move back here is the right one. I've loved having you around Stoney Creek, but my medical practice is so demanding, I . . ." She halted.

"What? You don't have time for me? For us?"

"John, I'm not good for you. We've had great times together. I'm so thankful for all of that."

John shook his head and looked down, his shoulders sagging.

"But—"

"But," he muttered.

She raised her voice, determined to get through her speech. "But I can't be the wife you need. My calling, my vocation now and for the foreseeable future, is medicine. You need to find someone else."

"I need someone else?"

She nodded.

"Do you love me?"

She shut her eyes, pinching her lids tight as if to hold out the question she didn't want him to ask. When she opened them again, John was staring at her, just as she feared. "That doesn't matter, John. I may have strong feelings for you, but that doesn't change my ability to be a good wife."

"I made the decision to come back to Brighton because we needed to sort things out. I gave you space because you were having trouble trusting me. The day I finalized my decision was when we took our last hike." He paused, wagging his head as if he couldn't quite believe what he was about to say. "You thought I could be the rapist."

The accusation stung because of its accuracy. Claire knew he was right. She had begun to doubt his character. She didn't know how to explain. "I'm sorry. I was stupid." She wiped a tear from the corner of her eyes. "I was so stupid, John."

He stayed quiet.

She continued. "Maybe it will make this easier. It forced you to leave. The distance will make moving on without me even easier."

"You didn't answer my question."

Their eyes met again, his pleading, hers tearful. "Do you love me?"

He was making this difficult. Her silence answered his question.

"What changed, Claire? In the weeks following my move to Stoney Creek, you didn't hesitate to say it."

She couldn't meet his gaze.

"Claire, look at me. I love you. What will it take for you to believe in me?"

"You don't know me. I can't be the wife you need."

He straightened. "What's going on? Before, you seemed to doubt me. Now, you doubt yourself?"

"Your accident changed me. I stopped wondering if you could love me if I ended up dancing like Daddy." She halted as a sob escaped her lips. "I started to wonder if I could take care of you."

"And you doubt? Claire, you barely left my side while I was in the hospital. Every day your presence, your love was all I looked forward to." His voice was pleading. "Don't deny me now." He exhaled sharply as he dropped his head in his hands. "What's changed?"

"I got my genetics test back." She hesitated. "I'm positive for the HD gene."

He looked up, his eyes moist. He nodded slowly as if he understood.

John slowly lifted his left leg from the pillows and planted his feet together on the wooden floor so he faced Claire. He then pushed the pillows from the bench so that they bridged the space between them. John winced as he slipped forward to kneel on the pillows. He reached for her hand.

Claire thought he must be about to pray. Instead, he took her hand in his and began to cry. "Claire," he said through his tears. "I know you love me. You may not say it in words, but you've done nothing but show me love for weeks since my accident." He paused. "I want you to be my wife. Will you marry me?"

She felt her jaw slacken. He hadn't understood. "John, a positive test isn't a good result. A positive test means I'm carrying the Huntington's disease gene."

He nodded his head. "I understand." He repeated his question. "Will you marry me?"

She began to sob. This was not going like she'd planned. She wanted to let John go, to give him the freedom she thought he wanted. "I don't understand."

"What's to understand? I love you. I want you to be my wife."

"But I just told you—"

"You told me you are carrying the HD gene. I know all about it. And it doesn't change my desire one bit. I love you now. I've loved you for years. Knowing your genetic makeup doesn't change the love that God has placed in my heart for you."

"But—" She stopped and wiped her eyes with her free hand. "But why didn't you ask me before? Why now, after getting the results?"

"Because if we married and then later found out you were carrying the HD gene, it would have left open a crack for doubt in your mind. You would always wonder if I would have followed through and married you if I would have known."

"But, I—"

"Don't you see, Claire? I've been waiting for this moment, so I could ask for your hand. Now you will always know that my love for you has nothing to do with whether you will end up dancing like Wally."

Tears trickled across her cheeks, falling onto their hands, now tightly clasped in a knot of four. "But what if my test had been negative? Then, if you asked for my hand, I would not have believed that you could have wanted me if . . ." She sniffed. "If I was HD positive."

"I thought about that. But I've written my intentions on a card that I've dated and sealed, long before we went to get your test results. That way, I thought I could convince you if you doubted."

Everything in her wanted to swim in the love he was offering. But a second emotion pulled opposite to her desire. An agony rose from within her and caused her to lift her head and pull her hands from his gentle grasp. "I do love you. It is a torment for me to do what I know I must. I came here to say good-bye. Love will not allow me to take you down the path my mother has suffered."

John shook his head and drew her hands to his mouth, kissing them gently. "Don't say this." His eyes were brimming with tears as he pleaded. "I knew you would react this way, and that's why I love you." He hesitated before continuing, his voice just above a whisper. "I've rehearsed this moment a thousand times, knowing you would set me free."

Claire nodded. *Go on!*

"From the moment we met, the only suffering my soul has known is that of being without you. If you deny me this, my anguish will be so great, that no other pain could cast a shadow upon it. Caring for you, loving you, even through the suffering of HD, is a calling I will embrace with all my heart, if only you give me the chance."

Claire could not speak. Weeping, first for sorrow, and then for joy, seemed all she could do.

"You are young, Claire. You may have twenty years before you dance." He halted, watching for her response.

She quietly wept, making no attempts to stem the flow of her tears.

"But I would endure hell if it meant I could have your love for a day."

She sniffed and wiped her eyes with her palms, before whispering his name. "John." She hesitated, searching his face. "That was quite a speech."

He smiled and confessed, "I must have practiced it a thousand times."

She lowered her face to his. She paused to let her lips slide across his moistened cheek, tasting the salt of his tears before pressing her mouth to his.

He broke their embrace and whispered into her open mouth. She could feel the warmth of his breath. "Is this 'yes'?" he asked.

"Yes," she whispered, letting her breath mingle with his. She stayed that way a few moments longer, breathing in as he exhaled, exhaling as he took a breath. With only millimeters separating them, they shared an intimate exchange. She inhaled his aroma again, then kissed him softly as he gasped.

"I'm going to die if I stay in this position any longer."

She giggled. "You are hopeless, Cerelli. You're spoiling my romantic moment."

"I have a broken femur." He held up his hand. "Help me up."

She stood and grabbed his arm. Before she pulled, she stopped. "I'll help you if you agree to answer some of my questions."

"Anything," he grunted. "I haven't tried kneeling since before my accident. I think I'm stuck."

She assisted him back onto the gazebo bench, laughing at his predicament and wiping fresh tears from her cheeks. She carefully replaced and fluffed his pillows to allow him to prop up his leg. "There," she said, squaring her body to his and sitting next to him.

John took a sip of his drink. "Ahh."

"Now tell me a few things, John Cerelli," she began, pointing a slender finger at his chest. "If this is a true marriage proposal, where's my ring?"

John's face twisted as if he tasted sour candy. "Uhh. It's not like I was expecting to propose just now. I don't exactly carry it around with me."

Claire knew where her ring was. What she didn't know, but what she desperately wanted to know, was why. She thought for a moment while biting her lower lip. "Why don't we just go inside and get it? Then we can tell your parents the good news."

"I can't."

She stared at him, waiting for him to elaborate. He inhaled to start several times, but halted as if the words couldn't escape his lips. "I—" He shook his head. "I—"

Claire interrupted by cutting to the core of the mystery. "How did Lena Chisholm end up with my ring?"

The plastic container slid from his hand, landing with a thud on the wooden floor. "Lena has the ring?" He shook his head. "Man, oh, man."

Claire studied him. His surprise was evident. She repeated her question. "How'd she get it?"

He took a deep breath and winced. "I was hoping I'd never have to tell you this story. It's embarrassing."

"Start confessing, story-boy. That ring has our initials in it. I know you took it along to the genetics clinic that day." She let a smile escape. "I'll confess, too. I found the ring in your car. I thought you took it along to give it to me at the clinic. I thought you were going to propose right before I got my test results. I had a romantic notion that you were going to drop to your knees just as I unfolded the paper."

John's head began to bob. "I was going to give you the ring in the clinic . . . *after* you got the results."

Understanding began to dawn. "Oh." She shook her head. "So how did Lena get the ring?"

"Ugh," he said. "I guess I have to tell you, huh?"

She nodded.

"How do you know Lena has it?"

"I saw it on her finger, John. She was wearing it when I visited her in the hospital."

"She must have found it."

"She said her dog brought it to her."

"The monster dog," he mumbled.

She stared at him for a moment while he contemplated what he was going to say. "Well?"

"Remember D day?"

She nodded.

"I was pretty bummed when I left your office."

"You were bummed? I thought I was going to get a ring. I was the one who was bummed."

"Okay, so we were both bummed." He laughed. "I dropped you off and went to drown my sorrows in a malt at Fisher's Cafe. That evening when I stopped to pick you up, I brought you roses."

She smiled at the memory. "You did, didn't you?"

"We talked about getting the HD test. I wanted you to get the test, so I could ask for your hand . . ."

She finished his sentence, ". . . and I wanted you to ask for my hand so I could get the test results knowing it didn't matter to you."

"You were upset. You had a ton of paperwork to do. Do you remember what you told me?"

She shook her head.

"You told me you didn't want to be rescued. You just wanted me to understand, not fix anything." He paused. "Anyway, you said if I wanted to rescue someone, that I should rescue Lena from her drunken husband." He shrugged. "So that night, I went driving to clear my head. I had my music, the wind in my hair. I just drove and thought. Sometimes I sang along."

"Sometimes? Cerelli, get to the point."

"At one point, I saw Briary Branch Road. So I followed it to Lena's place. I didn't have anything else to do. So I thought I'd actually gather a little information for you."

"What, did the ring fall out of your pocket when you walked across her yard?"

"I wish it were that simple."

The surgeon in Claire wanted the facts without the fluff. Just the vital signs, not the social history. "John, you're killing me. How'd she get the ring?"

"I'm getting to that. I don't exactly know how the ring ended up in her hands."

She took a deep breath and waited.

"I crept up to her house, but after seeing the size of Billy Ray's truck, and hearing a big dog, I suddenly felt very stupid. I wasn't sure what I was doing. I had no plan, only a vague idea that I was there to keep Lena safe if her husband got out of hand. In the dark, my imagination ran wild. I imagined Billy Ray as some sort of gorilla, his barking dog as some monster." He smiled sheepishly. "So I tore back and jumped into my car, and landed squarely on the little felt ring box. I sat there for a moment listening to the music, feeling angry, a little sorry for myself, I guess. I had built the night up in my mind to the point that I'd imagined it to be a night of celebration. Instead, all I had was a smashed ring box and my dashed expectations."

"John, the ring. What happened to the ring?"

"That's when the music took over."

Claire dropped her head and pinched the bridge of her nose. She wasn't sure she wanted to hear this after all. Now she winced. "The music took over?"

John began to sing. *"L'amore é svanito. Il mio cuore non canterá mai piú. Non tenere stretto l'amore. Se lo lasci libero, tornerá da te. L'amata mia é andata via. Lascia libero l'amore. Cosí prenderá le ali e tornerá. Lascialo in libertá. Dagli il volo."*

She listened to the clear baritone as it hung and disappeared in the moist summer air. John had missed his calling. He shouldn't be representing medical office software. He should be singing. Claire found her own throat tightening as he carried each note with remarkable poise. "It's beautiful, John. It really is." She paused. "But what's it mean?"

"The song became a picture of what was happening to me. As I listened, then sang along, my mind melded with the music. I sang as I closed my fingers around the mangled little ring box."

"John," she said, almost pleading, "tell me what the words mean."

John sang each line, pausing to repeat the phrases in English. *"L'amore é svanito.* Love is gone. *Il mio cuore non canterá mai piú.* My heart will never sing again. *Non tenere stretto l'amore.* Don't hold tight to love. *Se lo lasci libero, tornerá da te.* It will return if you only set it free. *L'amata mia é andata via.* My lover is gone. *Lascia libero l'amore.* Let love go. *Cosí prenderá le ali e tornerá.* Give it wings so it will return. *Lascialo in libertá.* Give it freedom. *Dagli il volo.* Give it flight."

Claire began to shake her head. "You didn't." Her hand went to her mouth.

"I did. As I drove by the front of Lena's property, I launched the box into the air, into the night."

She giggled. "I'm engaged to marry a hopelessly emotional Italian."

"I went back the next morning, as soon as the sun was up and I'd come to my senses. But Billy Ray's dog ran me up a tree. Billy Ray came out with a big shotgun and called off his dog." He chuckled. "I thought I was a dead man."

The pieces began to fall together. Billy Ray assumed Lena was having an affair with John because he knew if his wife was pregnant, and he was incapable of fathering a child, the man he caught in his yard was the likely culprit. "Ahh."

"I went back night after night, using those stupid night-vision goggles and a metal detector, but I never found the ring."

"Because Billy Ray's dog found it. He carried it up to the house, where Lena retrieved it."

"She still has it?"

Claire nodded.

John shifted in his seat. "Well, let's go get your ring!"

She put her hand on his arm. "John, we can't. She's strapped. The ring is all she has. I couldn't take it from her."

"Okay." His voice was soft. "I never expected to get it back anyway." He looked toward the house. "My father said he'd float me a family loan. I can get another one."

"Don't, John. I don't care about the ring. If we have each other, I don't need an engagement ring. Let's shop for a pair of wedding rings instead." She took his hand. "Something that will show everyone that I'm yours."

"And I'm yours," he responded, coaxing her head to rest upon his chest.

She listened to his racing heart before speaking softly. "John, what were the other Italian phrases you kept calling out to me?"

"*O, Claire, voglio stare con te per sempre.* Oh, Claire, I want to be with you forever."

He halted, thinking. "*O, Claire, mi sono innamorato di te. Mi sposerai?*"

"What's it mean?"

"Oh, Claire, I'm in love with you. Will you be my wife?"

"Yes," she whispered, "for the rest of my life."

Christian
Medical
Association
Resources

Medically reliable ... biblically sound. That's the rock-solid promise of this dynamic new series offered by Zondervan and the Christian Medical Association. Because when your health is at stake, you can't settle for anything less than the whole truth.

Finally, people of faith can draw from both the knowledge of science and the wisdom of God's Word in addressing health care and medical ethics issues. This series allows you to benefit from cutting-edge knowledge of experienced, trusted, and respected medical scientists and practitioners. Now you can gain their insights into the vital interconnection of health and spirituality—a critical unity largely overlooked by secular science.

While integrating your faith and health can actually improve your physical well-being and even extend your life, it can also help you make health care decisions consistent with your beliefs. A sound biblical analysis of emerging treatments and technologies is essential to protecting yourself from seemingly harmless—yet spiritually, ethically, or medically unsound—options.

Founded in 1931, the Christian Medical Association helps thousands of doctors minister to their patients by imitating the Great Physician, Jesus Christ. Christian Medical Association members provide a Christian voice on medical ethics to policy makers and the media ... minister to needy patients on medical missions around the world ... evangelize and disciple students on more than 90 percent of the nation's medical school campuses ... and provide educational and inspirational resources to the church.

To learn more about Christian Medical Association ministries and resources on health care and ethical issues, browse the Web site at www.christianmedicalassociation.org or call Christian Medical Association Life & Health Resources toll free at 888-231-2637.

"Dear friend, I pray that you may enjoy good health and that all may go well with you, even as your soul is getting along well" (3 John 2 NIV).

You can't dance this dance unless it's in your blood.
Claire McCall is praying it's not in hers.

Could I Have This Dance?

Harry Kraus, M.D.

Claire McCall is used to fighting back against the odds. Hard work, aptitude, and sheer determination have helped her rise from adverse circumstances to an internship in one of the nation's most competitive surgical residencies. But talent and tenacity mean nothing in the face of the discovery that is about to rock her world.

It's called the "Stoney Creek Curse" by folks in the small mountain town where Claire grew up. Behind the superstition lies a reality that could destroy her career. But getting to the truth is far from easy in a community with secrets to hide. As a web of relationships becomes increasingly tangled, two things become apparent. One is that more than one person doesn't want Claire to probe too deeply into the "Stoney Creek Curse." The other is that someone has reasons other than the curse for wanting Claire out of the picture permanently.

Somewhere in the course of pursuing her career as a surgeon, Claire lost touch with the God who called her to it. Now she realizes how desperately she needs him. But can she reclaim a faith strong enough to see her through this deadly dance of circumstances?

Softcover: 0-310-24089-1

Pick up a copy today at your favorite bookstore!

ZONDERVAN™

GRAND RAPIDS, MICHIGAN 49530 USA

WWW.ZONDERVAN.COM

We want to hear from you. Please send your comments about this book to us in care of zreview@zondervan.com. Thank you.

GRAND RAPIDS, MICHIGAN 49530 USA

WWW.ZONDERVAN.COM